The Cockney Girl

The
Cockney
Girl

Gilda
O'NEILL

CANELO

First published in the United Kingdom in 1992 by Headline Book
Publishing

This edition published in the United Kingdom in 2019 by

Canelo Digital Publishing Limited
57 Shepherds Lane
Beaconsfield, Bucks HP9 2DU
United Kingdom

A CIP catalogue record for this book is available from the British Library.

Print ISBN 978 1 78863 561 5
Ebook ISBN 978 1 78863 457 1

Look for more great books at www.canelo.co

Printed and bound in Great Britain by Clays Ltd, Elcograf S.p.A.

For John, with all my love

Chapter 1

Two-Bob Deposit

'Mornin', Rose. Still got the cleanest step in Burton Street?'

The kneeling woman turned round from her labours, scrubbing brush still in hand. 'Yer know me, Jack. Clean 'ome and clean livin'.' She rubbed her nose with the back of her suds-covered hand. 'Got anythin' for us today?'

'As a matter of fact, I 'ave.' Jack reached into his sack and, like a conjuror producing a rabbit from a hat, held out an envelope. 'A letter.'

'Give it 'ere, then.'

Rose stood up to take it from him. But first she tucked a few stray auburn hairs back under her makeshift turban, and wiped her hands on the coarse sacking apron that covered her faded brown skirt. Appearances were important to Rose. She didn't have much, but she liked to keep herself respectable, that didn't cost anything.

'Jess. Jessie. Yer there?' she called into the house. 'Come and read me this letter.'

'Good gel yer got there, Rose.'

'An' too clever for the likes of you, eh, Jack?'

'All right, Rose, we can all dream.' As he spoke, Jack studied the toes of his boots.

'That's yer trouble, me lad, all yer do is dream. Yer wanna put yerself forward a bit more. Speak up for yerself.'

''Ello, Jacko. Let's see what yer've got for us, then.' It was Jessie. As she stepped out from the house's gloomy passageway, her hair gleamed red and golden in the bright summer sunshine.

'It's a letter, gorgeous,' Jack said cockily. 'What do yer think the postman's gonna bring yer, a pound of sausages?'

As soon as the words had left his mouth, Jack could have kicked himself. Why did he do it? It was like someone else took over when Jessie was around. No matter how hard he tried, every time he saw her he acted like a great daft kid. He either stood there all tongue-tied and said nothing, or tried to sound clever and lively and just wound up making a right chump of himself. Why couldn't he act like an ordinary, sensible bloke? Then Jess could see him for what he really was, Jack Barnes, a grown man who loved her, not Jacko, the snotty-nosed boy she had been to school with.

Jessie blushed, feeling silly. Lost for a reply, she couldn't imagine what he thought of her. She wished she knew how to talk to boys. It was stupid, she had three brothers and always knew what to say to them. And she used to know what to say to Jacko.

Jack squirmed as he saw Rose flash a warning look of disapproval at her daughter. He'd done it again – good and proper this time.

'OK, gel, don't play up,' Rose scolded her daughter. ''E never meant nothin'. Now come on, read us this letter. I've not got all day, an' nor 'ave you.'

Glad of the distraction, Jess carefully peeled open the flap of the envelope. Letters were a rarity in Poplar, and certainly not something to be rushed. She slipped out the paper from inside and unfolded it.

'Right, 'ere goes.'

She glanced at Jack through her lashes. He was watching her.

Rose nodded at Jack, acknowledging her clever daughter. '"Ere goes,' she repeated. She was proud of Jess, proud that she was one of the new breed of East End girls, the ones who didn't only have the chance of getting a decent education, but who had the opportunity to take it. It was a bit different in Rose's day. But she didn't mind at all, she was really proud of her girl's achievements, and glad that Jess had had a better start in life than hers.

'Dear Mrs Fairleigh,' Jess began.

'"Ang on, Jess, do it proper,' Rose complained. 'We don't get letters every day, gel. When was it sent? Where from, an' that?'

Jessie looked at her mother and smiled. She was always the same, making the best of life even though they had hardly anything. Rose would never get less than the full measure.

'Right,' said Jess, 'I'll start again. 'Ere goes.' She coughed theatrically and pronounced each word carefully, trying to make sure she sounded all the aitches in the right places. 'It's from Worlington Hall, Tilnhurst.'

Rose couldn't resist interrupting again, 'Oh, Jack, it's come. Our letter's come.' She grabbed Jess by the shoulders, then clapped her hands.

'All right, Mum, leave off. Do yer want me to read, or don't yer?' She looked up shyly at Jack, and was glad to see that he was smiling too – at her.

'Waited for weeks, I 'ave.' Rose was beaming, wanting to hear more. 'Well? What yer 'angin' about for? Go on, Jess. Read it to us, gel.'

Jess was as pleased as Rose, too happy to be cross, so she continued reading. 'Tilnhurst, Kent. July the thirtieth,

3

nineteen-thirteen. Dear Mrs Fairleigh. This is to inform you that you have been selected for casual employment at Worlington Hall Farm for the hop-picking season. You begin work on Monday, September the 6th, at seven o'clock. As usual, accommodation will be provided in the hoppers' huts. There is one minor change this year: all pickers will be asked for two shillings' deposit on the return of the key and padlock to their huts.'

Jess still wasn't allowed to finish.

'Do what? Two bob? Deposit? 'Oo the 'ell does that Worlington think 'e is? I'll give 'im deposit. We ain't goin', that's what. I'd rather stay at 'ome. I'd rather… Aw, I don't know.'

Unable to find the right words to express her anger, Rose fussed distractedly with her scarf, looked up and down the narrow street for inspiration, and then threw the scrubbing brush down hard into the pail. Dirty water splashed up over Jack and Jess but they didn't say anything, they didn't dare. Rose was furious, and they knew it. They kept silent, watching her, and waiting until she spoke.

'I tell yer what I'd rather do,' she said, nodding furiously, 'I'd rather go to Fanshawe's, that's what. Fanshawe's.'

'Mum!' Jess couldn't believe she'd heard right. 'Fanshawe's?'

'Yeh, Fanshawe's. What's it to yer?'

'Yer always said yer'd rather stay at 'ome than go to another farm. An' yer'd never stay at 'ome at 'opping time.'

'Well, I've changed me mind. All right?'

'But, Mum, yer can't.'

Jess threw her hands up in desperation and the letter fluttered to the ground; Jess was too upset to notice, but Jack quickly retrieved it.

'Don't tell me "can't",' fumed Rose.

'But it's only a couple o' bob, Mum.'

Rose spoke slowly and quietly, but with fierce determination. 'Not once in all them years we've been goin' to Worlington's farm 'ave we ever done nothin' for 'im to treat us like this. Nothin'. An' that's the truth. An' everyone knows it.'

'Not like some of 'em round 'ere, eh?' said the postman, gesturing along the street with a nod.

'An' there's no need for that sort of talk, Jack Barnes,' snapped Rose. 'Yer know I won't 'ave gossip.'

'But 'e is right, Mum,' said Jess. 'Some of 'em round 'ere take right liberties, yer know they do. Nick anythin' what ain't bolted down.' She spoke quickly, before Rose could object. 'Yer know 'ow some of 'em mess up the 'op 'uts. Pinch all the apples. Get drunk, shoutin' an' 'ollerin'. 'E's doin' it cos of them. To warn 'em to be 'ave proper.'

'I don't care about no one else. It's us I'm worried about.' Rose lifted her chin. 'It's the good name of the Fairleighs what concerns me.'

'Come on, Mum, Worlington don't mean us. It's the others. Yer know it is. 'E's gotta do it cos of them.'

Eager to please her, Jack agreed. 'Jessie's right, Rose. Yer know 'ow some of 'em round 'ere carry on. Right old tarts.' He winked. 'Mentionin' no names, of course.'

'I've told yer, Jack. That's none of our business. An' I don't 'old with talk like that.'

'Sorry, Rose.'

'Mum?' Jess pleaded.

'I really ain't 'appy with the 'ole idea. I ain't never 'eard nothin' like it in all the years our family's been 'opping. An' that's some years.'

'Listen, Mum. 'Ow about if I save the money? Tanner a week. Then it won't be like yer payin' nothin', will it?' Jess looked at Jack for support.

'She's got a point there, Rose,' he said.

'Yeh. Yer wait an' see. I'll 'ave it ready, honest.'

'I dunno,' said Rose, her voice less angry.

Jess could sense her mother coming round to the idea, so she carried on with her pleas. 'There's four weeks till we go. So there's plenty of time. Go on, Mum, say we can go. It can't be the first year I've stayed at 'ome durin' 'opping. Go on, Mum. Please.'

'It'd be the first year any of us lot would've stayed at 'ome,' said Rose. 'Yer old gran went when she was carryin' me. Nearly born down 'opping, I was. An' you, Jess. Yer was kind of thought of down there. Good times we've 'ad in Kent.'

Rose was reminiscing now, softening under Jess's persuasion and the happy memories of days and nights spent in the beautiful Kent countryside.

'Yer right. I wouldn't wanna miss it, an' I could definitely do with a break from this filthy 'ole.'

Rose folded her arms and studied the half-scrubbed step, running her toe backwards and forwards acrossworn surface. Giving it a decisive kick with her buttoned-up boot she turned to face Jess. 'Yer sure yer can save the money, gel?'

'Course I can. Yer know me when I set me mind on somethin'.'

'I know that all right. Determined, like yer dad.'

'Stubborn like you, yer mean,' laughed Jess.

'But it still don't mean I'm 'appy with this deposit lark,' said Rose tersely.

'I'll tell yer what,' said Jess quickly, not wanting Rose to start changing her mind. 'I'll tell Winnie and Lil I can't go down the Mission for the next few weeks. They won't mind.' Jess was speaking quicker and quicker. 'I'll save me entrance money, and the other thrupence I spend on buns and sarsaparilla an' that. Then I'll soon 'ave it. Yer just see if I don't.'

Jack's face dropped. The thrupenny hop at the Mission was the highlight of his week. He went to the little hut every Saturday night to listen to the gramophone and to see his mates, but most of all he went for the chance of dancing with Jess. He would have gladly paid the three pennies admission just to watch her joking and chatting with the other girls. Not one of them could hold a candle to Jess. He pictured her standing there in the hut, her gleaming auburn hair tied back with a bit of ribbon, her face bright with laughter. He sighed with disappointment. She wasn't going to the Mission and she'd be down hopping for weeks. It was hard being in love.

'Four weeks missin' the 'op and then we can go 'opping.' Jess laughed at the joke she'd made, and was relieved to see Rose do the same. It would be all right, they would be going to Kent after all.

'Don't get too carried away, gel. Yer won't 'ave nothin' and we won't be going nowhere if yer don't get yerself off to work. Now move yerself. You too, Jack Barnes, or yer'll have Clara after yer, and none of us likes yer mum once she gets going.'

Despite his disappointment about the dance, Jack had to chuckle at the thought of his mum getting angry. Clara was only a little woman but a real terror if she was crossed. Many a Saturday night she could be seen striding down Burton Street towards The Star, her arms swinging across her body from the elbows, sleeves rolled up ready, her face determined. She would pull Cyril, Jack's long-suffering dad, out of the public bar and drag him back home for his tea, all to the accompaniment of his mates' cheers and jeers.

'Yer right, Rose. I might be silly but I ain't daft.'

'I ain't so sure sometimes,' said Rose shaking her head. He was a good boy, but slow with girls. She really wanted to see him settled. She had a proper soft spot for Jack, having had him practically living in Number 8 when he was a youngster. She used to take him in, treat him just as though he was one of her own, whenever Clara decided to go off on one of her unexpected, and usually unannounced, trips back to her family in Ireland. Jack would wander along from Number 42, no shoes on his feet as usual, and hang round till Rose told him to come inside. He'd eat his fill of whatever Rose had going on the stove, then bunk in with Rose's three boys, happy as a sandboy. His dad, Cyril, was never happier either than when Clara was away. With Jack safely tucked up in Number 8, he could spend as much time in The Star as he liked, with no Clara to ruck him or show him up.

'Go on, off with yer,' Rose said, the gentle expression in her eyes contradicting the sternness in her voice.

'See yer later then, gels,' he said and hoisted his sack on to his shoulder.

'Yeh. See yer, Jacko,' said Jess softly.

'Yeh. See yer,' said Rose, delighted to see her daughter's sudden shyness.

Jack walked off in the direction of the East India Dock Road, whistling the tune that had been playing when Jess had first danced with him. He didn't suppose it meant anything to her, but it was special to him all right. He even called it 'our song', but only to himself of course. And he could always hope. Perhaps one day Jess would feel the same about him as he did about her.

–

Jessie Fairleigh went back in the house to get her things ready for work, leaving Rose to finish her cleaning out the front. Her mum was right as usual, if she didn't get a move on there'd be trouble. Jobs weren't two a penny in Poplar, even for bright girls like her.

After the brilliance of the morning sunshine, the inside of Number 8 Burton Street seemed dingier than ever. In the gloom, Jess had to be careful not to trip on the frayed hall runner as she carried the washbasin down from her parents' room to the little back kitchen. She always slept in with her mum when her dad was away. She loved sleeping in the big brass bed that Granny Fairleigh had given her son when he had married Rose.

Bill Fairleigh had been in the merchant navy since before his daughter was born, and whenever he was on a trip it meant that Jess didn't have to sleep in the front parlour. The bed in there was awful, not much more than a big child's cot really, and far too small for her now. Sharing the big bed with her mum was the only good thing about her dad being away, though. What Jess didn't like about his trips was her poor mum missing him, and her having to cope with the boys all by herself. Rose had enough on her plate just managing to make ends meet without putting up with Sammy and Charlie and their nonsense. Young Ted was getting just as bad, and he was barely fifteen. Rose had said it herself: now the three boys were growing up they could be a real handful for her, especially their Charlie.

Jess often wondered how Rose did it. Feeding them all; doing the laundry in the old boiler in the yard; fighting the continued battle with dirt to keep their little terraced house decent and free from bugs; and all that was without the scrubbing jobs she did in the City and up West. Jess really missed her dad as well, all his larking about, and telling them stories about the foreign lands he'd been to. Sometimes the stories would scare her, but then he would make her laugh again. He always did. Still, he was due home soon, and he'd sort her brothers out all right. And who knows, perhaps he'd come home with enough money to get her a new bed. Perhaps. Some chance. As Dad always told her, 'Some people like meat pudden and some people don't. But you remember, my gel, some people never even get a dip in the gravy. Yer just be satisfied with what yer got.'

Jess tipped her washing water away down the cracked stone sink then dried out the enamel washing basin with a ragged piece of cloth. She folded the cloth neatly and draped it over the nail by the door. Then she put the bowl away on the rough wooden plank that served as a shelf under the sink. Rose liked things to be kept tidy and Jess wanted to keep her mum in a good mood; she didn't want her changing her mind about going hopping. She twirled her thick hair round her fingers into a smooth twist and pinned it up into place. Next she arranged her skirt so that the holes were hidden in the folds of the shabby black serge. Like Rose, Jess knew that even though they didn't have much, it was important to be respectable and to keep up appearances. And having a good wash of a morning, that didn't cost much either.

Grabbing her coat and hat off the banister rail, Jess had a final, luxurious stretch before her day started properly. Careful to avoid spoiling the job that her mother hadn't quite finished, Jess skipped nimbly across the front step, back into the bright, sunlit street. Rose didn't look up; she was rubbing hard at the boot scraper, polishing it up with a rag dipped in black lead. Bending over her to kiss Rose's cheek, Jess couldn't resist giving her mother a hug.

'Ta, Mum, I knew yer wouldn't let me down. I promise I'll save that money.' She squeezed Rose to her chest. 'Aw, I do love yer.'

Rose brushed her away, 'Yer great daft thing. Go on with yer. Anyone'd think yer was seven instead of seventeen.'

Jess grinned. The thought of being in Kent with all its green fields and fresh air, and no factories or dirt, made her feel wonderful, and she knew that Rose felt the same way. She couldn't fool her daughter.

'Go on and let me finish me scrubbin' and get yerself off to work. Yer'll miss yer tram, an' there'll be no 'opping for no one.'

'See yer tonight, Mum,' called Jess over her shoulder.

The tram ran just round the corner from the Mission hut, up towards the Commercial Road. As Jess walked past the scruffy little building she was determined not to feel sorry about missing the Saturday dances. There'd be plenty of fun to be had in Tilnhurst, there always was.

'Jess. 'Ere, Jessie, wait for us.'

Looking back down the street, Jessie saw a plump young woman running towards her. She was trying to put up her mass of wiry brown hair with one hand and hold a slab of bread and scrape, her breakfast, in the other.

'Come on, Lil, yer'll cop it if old Warner catches yer gettin' in late again.'

'Don't worry, Jess,' puffed Lil. 'Winnie'll cover for me. She's always early. Frightened she might miss somethin', the nosy cow.' Lil won the battle with her hair as she fell into step at Jessie's side. 'Anyway,' she said through a mouthful of bread, spraying Jess liberally with half-chewed crumbs, 'I've got a good excuse this mornin'. We got our letter.'

'So did we,' grinned Jess. 'Aw, I can't wait, Lil, can you? Gettin' away from all this muck.'

'An' from bloody Warner's.'

'Lil!'

'Well, I 'ate him. The dirty old pig. Can't keep his rotten 'ands to 'imself.'

Even in the warm summer sun Jess shuddered, thinking how their boss tried to get the girls alone in the storeroom so he could press his sweaty body against them. Warner seemed to think he was entitled to do as he liked with the girls, just because he was the governor.

'Still, 'oo cares, eh, Jess? It'll be us surprisin' 'im next month, when we all clear off down 'opping.'

'Never mind next month, Lilly Dorkin, there's our tram. Come on, Lil, run.'

Chapter 2

An Announcement

As Jess and Lil ran along the grimy London street to catch their tram, the staff at Worlington Hall were taking an early-morning break in the warm Kent sunshine.

Since first light, the estate servants had been busy in the house and grounds, getting everything ready for the evening's festivities. Nothing had been overlooked in the elaborate preparations. In the kitchens and cellars food and wines of the finest quality were being made ready. Lady Worlington had planned the meal herself. She had decided to present it in the buffet style. This was a daring innovation for a Kent country house, although, she assured the cook and butler, it was the height of fashion in London society. Lady Worlington also personally instructed Garnett, the head gardener, to choose blooms which would fill every room in the hall with their scent. Garnett, in turn, supervised the under-gardeners in gathering the flowers from the walled gardens and the orangery. A rough-looking elderly man, Garnett's appearance was at complete odds with his gentle manner and the way in which he cared for his beloved plants.

Lady Worlington also paid particular attention to the matter of entertainment. In this she had achieved a real coup. Rather than engaging the local, rather ageing ensemble, who did the rounds of balls and parties thrown by the neighbouring gentry, she had hired a professional orchestra from London. They were to play not only the ever-popular dance music from the Continent but also the very latest tunes in the foxtrot style. Like the buffet, the entertainment would be another first for Tilnhurst society.

All this intriguing innovation was a result of Lady Worlington's hard work, rather than any enthusiasm on her husband's part. No detail had been overlooked. Even the tree-lined drive had been dotted with braziers ready to light the way home for the departing guests. These weren't simply decorative, although everyone later agreed they did look most attractive. They also had a very practical function. The last party at the Hall had ended with an incident which had distressed everyone and had almost spoiled the evening. A coachman had actually lost his hand in full view of the guests. The unfortunate man had been struggling in the dark to remove an iron brakeshoe from the wheel of his master's carriage when his sleeve had become entangled between the wheel and the axle. The horses had suddenly pulled forward and the man's trapped wrist was crushed, tearing the flesh from his bones as though he was an overcooked fowl. His screams echoed through the still night air right across the lake. Some people claimed his cries could be heard right down in the village of Tilnhurst itself. Everyone had been terribly upset. The fire-lit drive was an attempt to ensure that no similar event would mar the celebrations for this evening's merrymakers.

It was details such as these which ensured the popularity of Sir George and Lady Worlington's galas throughout the Kent countryside. The Worlingtons' July Ball was considered to be the highlight of the whole summer season. The last real event, in fact, until the harvest celebrations were over and the first of the hunt balls began. The harvest suppers were, after all, thought by most of Tilnhurst society to be a duty rather than a pleasure: a gesture to reward the servants and farm labourers with dancing and cheap ale.

But tonight's ball was to be even more memorable than usual. Not just because Sir George was unveiling his new electrical lighting system – although the whole county was discussing it – but because the engagement of Sir George's elder son Robert was being announced. His future bride was Julia Markington, the only child of doting parents. The Markingtons were an Anglo-Irish family with massive land holdings and increasingly valuable shipping interests in North America, and they were very rich, very rich indeed.

Julia Markington, and her fortune of course, would make a most suitable match for Robert, thought Sir George as he sat in the library, hiding from his wife and her interminable party preparations. From the comfort of his armchair, the owner of Worlington Hall could see right across his rolling parkland, down to the fruit-laden orchards, and all the way to the hop gardens and the village of Tilnhurst beyond. What he saw pleased him: a scene of order, tradition and fecundity. He watched as the estate servants returned to work after their rest, raking gravel and sweeping, tidying and cleaning. He saw the small flock of ornamental sheep grazing picturesquely by the lake, and, in the mid-distance, he could see Robert and Paul, his sons, exercising the hunters they would ride to hounds later in the year. Then, for almost as far as Sir George could see, stretching into the distance, were his orchards and hop gardens, the most valuable part of the Worlington estate.

He sighed loudly. The hop harvest would soon begin and the glorious peace would be destroyed. He stood up, pushing his chair back noisily across the inlaid wooden floor. He walked over to the window and slammed his hand hard against the oak-panelled wall. All those damned cockneys would be arriving in a few weeks, infecting the countryside with their vile squalor and city ways. He felt the same every year. He detested the invasion but he needed their cheap, and, he had to admit it, efficient labour. Those London women and their brats could certainly pick hops faster than any other workers he could get. Even if they only did so out of greed. All hop farmers knew that greed was the pickers' only motivation, so they didn't give the women a wage but paid them according to the number of bushel baskets they filled. That ensured they picked at full speed, that the harvest was completed in the shortest possible time, and that the Kent countryside was rid of the vermin as soon as possible.

A knock on the library door pulled Sir George back to the present. He turned to see a young maidservant entering, her eyes cast nervously to the floor.

'Excuse me, sir,' she said, dropping a quick, bobbing curtsey, 'but Lady Worlington said she'd like to see you in the morning room.' She bit her lip anxiously. 'She said how she wants to discuss the, er, "boofhay" arrangements.'

When Sir George failed to respond, the girl's voice dropped to an embarrassed whisper. 'Least, I think "boofhay" is what she said. I'm not sure really, see.'

She laughed anxiously. Sir George wasn't known for his patience, particularly when dealing with servants.

He returned to his consideration of the view from the window. 'Go away, girl,' he bellowed. 'Can't you see I'm busy?'

The maid backed out of the book-lined room, wishing, as she always did after being shouted at, that she could find a way to escape what fate had seen fit to give her. If only she knew how to dress hair in all the new styles and to sew a bit better, then she could be a lady's maid, just like the snobs at the Hall who looked down on her for still living at her parents' cottage. One day she'd show them all; she'd run away from Worlington and she wouldn't have to put up with Sir George shouting at her any more.

Sir George had decided it was high time that he disappeared from the house too. He guessed a three-hour ride round the estate should keep him safe from any unwelcome discussions about buffet arrangements or other such nonsense. He strode out of the library and made determinedly for the stables.

After an infuriating and fruitless ten-minute wait, Lady Worlington abandoned all hope of getting any help from her husband. She should have known better than to have expected any. Arrangements for the party would, as usual, be her sole responsibility.

Leonore Worlington had realised long ago that most things were her responsibility, and not just the duties she had expected to carry out in her position as mistress of the Hall. As well as confirming the monthly menus and dealing with other house-hold matters, Leonore had increasingly been obliged to do things she had once expected her husband to attend to, such as overseeing the estate accounts and even conducting meetings with the farm bailiff. It was depressing, but true, that if some-thing didn't have a mane and four legs, or didn't come in a bottle, then Sir George Worlington simply wasn't interested in it. But it was no use wasting her time being angry; she had far too much to do, and she was rapidly learning more and more about how to get on with things alone.

By the time Sir George eventually got back to the house, after several detours to local taverns and the emptying of a number of bottles, the dancing was already well under way in the main ballroom. Lady Worlington was too preoccupied making sure that the Markingtons, the guests of honour, were introduced to everyone to bother with her husband's absence or his late arrival. As for the Markingtons, they had arrived from Kildare over a week ago, and had become almost used to Sir George and Leonore Worlington's rather eccentric marriage. At first they had been concerned at their daughter's choice of future in-laws, but once they had seen Robert ride and had had his connections with the English aristocracy confirmed, Julia's family had succumbed to her pleas for their consent. And, with the growing unrest in Ireland, they were actually rather pleased to think that their only child would be settled in England. Tonight's impressive celebrations had done nothing to change their minds.

It was still only ten o'clock, and yet, notwithstanding Sir George's usual difficult behaviour, the party was already being spoken of as a triumph by everyone present. Even those guests who were accustomed to Worlington hospitality, and those others who were perhaps a little jealous of its reputation, were as impressed by the opulence of the occasion as the Markingtons, who were experiencing it for the first time. The new electric lighting system added the final touch of enchantment to the glitteringly splendid spectacle of wealth and privilege.

Lady Leonore Worlington graciously accepted her friends' congratulations, and was feeling justifiably pleased with her efforts as she silenced the orchestra. It was ten-thirty precisely and she wanted all her guests to hear the announcement for which they had been waiting.

'My dear friends,' she began, her lovely face glowing not just with pleasure at the evening's obvious success, but with her hopes for the future. 'My husband Sir George and I would like to welcome you all to Worlington this evening.'

On hearing his name, Sir George awoke from his alcohol-induced stupor in the corner, and executed a drunken stagger across the dance floor towards the platform on which his wife was standing. His journey was greeted with good-natured cheering and encouragement from the happy company. Even the Markingtons produced amiable smiles as he joined them and Lady Worlington. Their smiles disappeared rapidly, when it became evident that one important person was still missing from the dais. Robert Worlington was nowhere to be seen.

After repeated calls for Robert to come forward, and with the Markingtons' only daughter close to tears, a rather inebriated search party was dispatched to find the fiancé-to-be.

Leonore was managing, thanks to years of experience in dealing with her always difficult husband and sons, to hide her true feelings.

'He'll be found soon enough. You'll see,' she reassured the stern-faced Markingtons with a bright smile. 'Young men of his age are so full of fun.'

But secretly Leonore was disappointed in Robert, saddened that he could behave so badly on tonight of all nights, when she had worked so hard to make everything a success. And her hopes that the engagement would tame his wild ways were rapidly disappearing. She was also more than slightly alarmed to see Robert's younger brother, Paul, reassuring Julia in such a friendly manner. Watching the young girl so readily accept his comforting attention, Leonore decided that Miss Markington was obviously in need of a discreet word of warning from her future mama-in-law about the behaviour of men in general, and of the Worlington males in particular.

The search party lurched drunkenly from room to room, half of them not quite sure what or whom they were seeking. If only they had looked in the orangery they would have found

Robert immediately. For there he was, with Milly Garnett, the young maidservant, who earlier that day had never even laid eyes on a 'boofhay', let alone engaged in what she and young Master Robert were now up to.

Chapter 3

They Say that Hopping's Lousy...

'I can't wait to see 'is face, Jess.' Lil was shaking so much from the effort of suppressing her giggles that she was barely able to fold the cardboard shapes into boxes. 'I've been waitin' for this for weeks.'

Jess was more cautious; she wondered what mood old Warner was in and how he would react when the girls announced they were going off to Kent to pick hops. She didn't have to wonder for long.

'What's all this noise about? What's wrong in here?' The loud male voice immediately caught the attention of everyone in the workshop.

'Nothing, Mr Warner,' said Lil. Always cheeky, she gave him an innocent smile and added another badly folded box to her lopsided pile under the bench.

'Well, there'd better not be. But if you'd rather waste your time chatting, there's plenty more girls'd be glad of the work. Now get on with it.'

Jess glanced along the row to Lil who was now fit to burst with the effort of looking serious.

Harold Warner hooked the arms of his spectacles around his big red ears and consulted his cheap metal pocket watch.

'Five past one,' he droned. 'Here's the wages.'

He sat down at the rickety, cup-ringed table which stretched the width of the long, narrow room. He placed a small tin cash box in front of him and lined it up precisely next to a maroon, cloth-bound ledger. Through one of the unwashed skylights in the roof, a single shaft of sun managed to break through the grime, illuminating the man bent over his money as he arranged it in piles on the shabby wooden table.

'That sunray makes him look like the Bible picture what I got from Sunday school once,' Jess whispered to her friend. 'Like the angel Gabriel in a shaft of 'oly light.'

'Do what?' said Lil, a bit louder than she should have. 'Angel 'oo? 'Ow can that ol' bleeder look like an angel?'

'Shhh!' Jess stilled her. 'It don't matter. Look, 'e's openin' the ledger.'

Warner found the place where the workers' names were listed. As each new girl was taken on at the factory her name was entered into the book in his mean, scratchy writing; thus they became part of Harold Warner's list of debits – drains on his greedily accumulated and regularly counted profits.

One by one the women and girls were called forward. They went and stood in front of their employer. Then, 'Thank you, Mr Warner,' they mumbled, taking their wages quickly before he could touch them with his clammy hands, and returning to their places at the bench. Finally, there were only three names on his list left uncalled: Lil Dorkin, Winnie Baxter and Jess Fairleigh.

'Lillian Dorkin.'

Lil moved away from the bench, and, giving Jess a nudge as she passed, walked the length of the room with her head held high and her boots clopping loudly on the dusty wooden floor. Most of her hair had, as usual, broken free of its pins, and was spilling round her fine, broad shoulders. Warner counted out her wages. Jess and Winnie held their breath and watched as he handed the coins to their friend. The silence was shattered by Lil's indignant shouts.

''Ere, now 'old on a minute. This is two bob bleed'n' short, this is. What's yer game?'

Now it wasn't just Winnie and Jess who were interested; all the other workers looked towards the table.

Warner didn't glance up from his ledger. 'Late four mornings. Two shillings forfeit.' He dismissed her with a loose gesture of his flabby pink hand. 'Next. Winnie Baxter.'

Lil wouldn't be dismissed so easily. 'It's nothin' to do with me bein' late, yer slimy ol' goat, an' you know it. It's cos I wouldn't let you touch me when we was in the storeroom. Yer dirty old pig. Anyway, see if I care, yer ol' bugger. I'm off down 'opping tomorrow, I am. So yer know what yer can do with yer boxes, don't yer? Stick 'em where the monkey keeps 'is nuts, that's what.'

With that, Lil flipped his ledger shut, leant across the table and pinched his cheek as though he was a great fat baby. 'See yer in October, sweet'eart,' she said. 'If yer lucky, that is.'

If they hadn't seen it with their own eyes the box-makers wouldn't have believed it: old Warner's face actually turned redder than ever. As Lil pranced saucily from the room, her wide hips swaying, Warner raised his voice, which he turned at full volume on his gawping audience.

'Out. Go on out. All of you. Out of my sight, before I dock someone else's pay.'

Jess, always more subtle than Lil, held up her hand to silence Winnie's protests. Then she took Winnie by the elbow and guided her to the table. When the others had filed out she spoke softly to her crimson-faced boss.

'We never got our money, Mr Warner. Me and Winnie 'ere. Sorry to be a nuisance, like.'

Outside in the street, their wages safely in their pockets, Jess, Lil and Win linked arms and made their way to the tram.

'So, what did 'e say when yer told 'im you two was goin' 'opping an' all?' asked Lil, eager for an account of the row that must surely have broken out.

'Didn't say nothin', said Win casually.

That wasn't good enough for Lil. 'Nothin'? Why not? I thought 'e'd go flamin' barmy once 'e knew all three of us was goin' down Kent.'

'I suppose 'e would 'ave done if we'd 'ave told 'im,' said Jess, straight-faced. 'Only when 'e started goin' on about never takin' on no more girls next October if they 'ad 'op stains on their 'ands, well, I thought we'd best keep it our little secret. Just between us, like.'

Jess then described to her two friends how old Warner would be sitting at his table on Monday morning, looking at his pocket watch, waiting for her and Winnie to arrive. Then he'd sneer and take great pleasure in entering the sixpenny late-comer's penalty next to their names in his ledger, not realising that all three of them had cleared off to Kent. The thought of it was almost too much for Lil. This Saturday afternoon was turning out to be a real lark. The fact that work finished at one o'clock made most Saturdays good, but this was one of the best she could remember.

'Come on girls,' Lil said, 'I think we'll 'ave ourselves a little song to celebrate.'

Winnie and Jess wouldn't have dreamed of doing such a thing usually, but somehow, when they were with Lil, lots of things they wouldn't usually do just seemed to happen. The three friends, still arm-in-arm, changed their step to match their tune as they danced and sang along the cobbled street.

They say that 'opping's lousy,
I don't believe it's true,
We only go down 'opping To earn a bob or two.
With a tee-eye-oh A tee-eye-oh A tee-eye-ee-eye-oh.

When they arrived at Jess's house, the front door of Number 8 Burton Street was wide open. Inside, women were crowded into the little kitchen, drinking tea, packing things into boxes and all talking at once at the tops of their voices.

Lil walked straight in, settled herself at the scrubbed wooden table, and started folding clothes and shoving them messily into a half-full cardboard box.

'Old Warner's boxes 'ave got some use then,' she said. 'I should 'ave nicked a few more.'

Rose took the blouse that Lil was clumsily attempting to fold and handed it to Jess. 'You get off 'ome, Lil, and 'elp yer own mum.'

Florrie Baxter, Winnie's mum, looked round the room at the others and mumbled, 'If she's back from the pub, that is.'

'What was that, Florrie?' said Lil, leaning menacingly across the table. 'Did yer say somethin' about me mum?'

'No,' said Florrie hurriedly, 'I was talkin' to my Win.' Winnie looked surprised, unaware that she had been spoken to. 'I said she can get off 'ome an' tell 'er dad I'll be 'ome in a minute.'

'That's all right then,' said Lil, straightening up her not inconsiderable bulk. 'So long as yer never said nothin' about me mum. Cos yer know what'd 'appen to yer if yer did, don't yer?'

'Go on, you two, off yer go,' said Rose, calming the situation. 'My Jessie takes up enough room without you pair 'anging round me.'

'Not my fault I'm tall, Mum.' Jess stood behind Rose's chair and bent forward to cuddle her. She was so excited. They'd be going hopping in the morning.

'Get off, Jess.' Rose tried to sound annoyed but she was just as exhilarated as the girls. 'An' go on you two. Do as yer told. I told yer to move yerselves.'

Rose stood up and shooed Lil and Winnie to the door, then turned back to her daughter. ''Ow'd 'e take it then?'

The other women looked up, stopping what they were doing to hear what old Warner had had to say for himself.

'Yer should 'ave seen Lil, Mum. What a laugh.'

'Never mind Lil's business, 'ow about you? What'd 'e say to yer? Can yer 'ave yer job back after 'opping?'

Jess was nervous, not knowing how Rose would react to the news. 'I never told 'im, Mum. I was worried 'e'd 'old back me money after Lil 'ad upset 'im. But I'm sure 'e'll take me on again in October. I'm a good, clean worker. An' 'e knows it.'

Jess needn't have worried. 'Gawd love yer. Yer a sensible girl, Jess,' said her mother proudly. 'No point in provokin' 'im into sayin' things 'e don't really mean. Now come on, let's get this finished before them boys get in from work and want their teas.'

Disappointed they weren't going to hear about a row, Rose's neighbours got back to their sorting and packing.

Ted was the first of the Fairleigh boys to get home. He was the youngest, only just fifteen, but compared to his two brothers he was also the most reliable. He hardly ever hung around street comers, getting up to goodness knows what, like his older brother Charlie did, and he wasn't always chasing girls, like Sammy, the eldest of the Fairleigh boys.

'Oi, oi, Mum, where's me tea then?' Ted stood in the kitchen doorway, surveying the busy scene, then made his way quickly towards the smell of food.

'Yer'll 'ave to wait, Ted, I'm still sortin' out all this gear for tomorrow. An' get away from that saucepan with yer dirty 'ands.'

'Ain't yer finished yet?' he moaned. 'Yer've been gettin' that lot ready for months.'

'Yer know me, Ted. I like everythin' done proper, like. I don't want everything chucked in any old 'ow.'

'What 'ave we got anyway?'

'Nice bit of neck o' lamb stew. A treat cos I'm off tomorrow. Gawd alone knows what you lot'll be eatin' for the next couple of weeks.'

'Cor 'andsome, Mum.' Ted lifted the lid off the big stew pan.

Florrie Baxter laughed. 'I remember the first time our Arthur was old enough to stay 'ome from 'opping. Thought 'e was such a big man. Well, when I come 'ome! Yer should 'ave seen the state of that boy. Honest. 'E looked fit for the work'ouse.'

They all joined in with the laughter, except Rose and Mabel Lawrence.

Mabel was a widow. She'd been in the workhouse only a couple of weeks previously, and would still have been in there if Rose hadn't got the neighbours to club together to get her and the children out of its punishing shame. Mabel wasn't the first from Burton Street to go in there, and she probably wouldn't be the last either. But the women weren't laughing maliciously; they were laughing about the workhouse for the same reasons that kids whistle in the dark, to stop them from being afraid of the bogeyman. Mabel knew that, but it was too fresh in her mind for her to join in.

The women of Burton Street knew all about poverty all right – only too well – but they also knew that there was much worse deprivation in other parts of the East End. They could see it all around them. Not that many streets away were the tenements, where whole families lived crowded into one rat-infested, some even splitting sleeping time in the lousy beds into shifts. Round there, the people had no water except what they fetched from the standpipe in the central stairwell, and food – if there was any – was cooked over makeshift fires. More usually, though, they lined up for hand-outs. The outside lavatories of Burton Street would have been a luxury to the poor souls who lived in 'The Buildings'.

And then there were those who didn't even have a roof over their heads, the ones who roamed the streets waiting until twilight when they'd be allowed into the flophouses to shelter for the night – if they could afford the couple of pennies entrance money.

And then there were the streets, the life that was known by none except those who had sunk into those hellish depths, those who had entered the downward spiral from which there was no return.

Mabel understood the importance of hanging on to her life in Burton Street all right. Once she let go of that there would be nothing to stop her sliding to the very bottom, into the gutter itself.

Rose's voice lifted over the women's chattering. 'I said to get away from that stove, Ted. Jess'll dish yer up a bit of stew if yer can't wait, but the pearl barley'll still be 'ard as old 'Arry.'

'I don't care, Mum.' Ted grasped his belly dramatically. 'I'm starvin'. Me belly thinks me throat's been cut.'

Jess stopped what she was doing and got a bowl down from the dresser. She scooped two ladlefuls of stew from the big pot on the range into the white china dish.

''Ere yer are, 'ungry guts,' she said fondly to herbrother. 'Get that down yer.'

'Yer've spoilt 'im,' said Florrie Baxter primly.

Everyone was used to Florrie, so they did what they did most of the time when she moaned or complained – they ignored her and got on with what they were doing.

Ted took the bowl of stew and went to sit on the front step to enjoy his tea in peace, away from the chattering women.

'Give us a lump of bread, sis,' he called along the passage.

'Yer chancin' yer luck a bit, ain't yer, Ted?' she called back.

'Go on,' he whinged.

Jess stood up again. She'd never admit it, but Florrie was right; as the youngest in the family, Ted usually got his own way without too much trouble.

''Old on,' she shouted, 'I'll get yer a bit.'

As Jess sawed a chunk of bread off the two-day-old loaf, Charlie and Sammy walked into the room.

''Ello girls,' said Sammy, the oldest of the Fairleigh boys, chucking his mum affectionately under the chin. ''Oo's got a kiss for me then?'

''Ark at 'im. 'E fancies 'is chances, don't 'e?' said Florrie Baxter. 'Yer might think yer a big 'andsome brute, but yer ain't too big for a clip round the ear'ole, yer know, Sammy.'

'Go on,' said Sam, 'yer know yer love me, darlin'. All the gels do.'

Florrie reached out across the table and caught him a sharp wallop round the side of his head.

'Oi! That 'urt.' He rubbed his temple sulkily.

'It was meant to. Now clear off and let's finish in 'ere. Or yer can 'elp get yer mother's gear ready, if yer like. An' I'll get off 'ome to me old man.'

'No thanks. Come on, Charlie, let's 'ave some of this stew then get down The Star for a couple of jars.'

'Don't yer go takin' that Ted down the pub,' said Rose. She didn't trust her two elder boys to look after young Ted. He might have been fifteen, but he was still her baby.

'Leave off, Mum.' It was Charlie's turn to aggravate Rose. 'If 'e's old enough to stay 'ome when all you old trouts go down 'opping, he's old enough to 'ave a few pints of mild, ain't 'e?'

Charlie was much quicker on his feet than Sammy, and Florrie's hand hit thin air instead of the back of his head. And he'd dished out two portions from the pot before Rose had even noticed.

'Cop this, Sammy boy.' Charlie handed his brother a bowl and spoon. 'Let's go out the front with Ted and leave these old gels to their natterin'.'

'Kids. They'll be the end of us,' said Florrie shaking her head.

Rose carried on folding and packing, letting the others get on with their chatting as she thought about her boys. They drove her mad some days, especially when Bill was away, and they could certainly do with acting a bit more sensibly at times, she'd be the first to admit it. But they could have been worse, a lot worse. She thanked her lucky stars when she thought about some of the things they could have been involved in. Like the trouble that was always ready to break out down by the docks. The boys could so easily have wound up down there. It was well known that the more dubious delights of Chinatown attracted a lot of the young fellers from the East End. It might only have been a few streets in Limehouse, wedged between Poplar and the docks, but that small area teemed with life and industry. The problem was that some of the businesses in Chinatown weren't too fussy about which services they provided: like the illicit gambling, fighting and whoring – all there to cater for the men fresh off the boats with their pockets full of money.

Rose looked round at the women in the room. She counted herself a lot more fortunate than some of the other mothers. Her Sammy was fixed up in a decent job down the woodyard – it was him putting in a good word that had got Charlie and young Ted their chances down there. She knew that Charlie could be a bit of a lad, but he was only eighteen, he'd learn. He might not like the woodyard much, but he'd do all right for himself when he settled down. Rose might not have been too happy about some of the blokes he knocked around with, but he'd never brought any trouble home to Burton Street, and that was the important thing.

Then there was Jess. She looked across the table at her daughter. She'd grown into a beauty all right, and with a nature to match, kind, considerate and a real grafter. Rose sighed contentedly to herself. She didn't have too much to complain about, and that was the truth.

She pushed back her chair and stood up. 'More tea, gels?'

As Rose poured the boiling water into the big earthenware pot, Ted slipped back into the kitchen.

'Drop more stew in there, Mum?' he asked sweetly.

Rose turned to look at him. His cherubic expression was marred only by the gravy on his hairless chin. She knew exactly how to deal with young Ted.

'Do yer remember when yer got yer first 'opping 'aircut, Ted?' she asked wistfully. 'A right little sweet'eart yer looked.'

'Bless 'im,' said Florrie, all sarcastic.

'Mum,' said Ted under his breath, his face flaming.

'I was so proud of yer as yer sat on the board across the arms of the barber's chair. 'Ardly grizzled at all. A right little darlin'.'

'Mum…'

'A little wooden monkey up a stick, the barber let yer 'old, to keep yer quiet.' Rose batted her lashes at her now excruciatingly embarrassed son.

'That's it. I'm off.' Ted fled along the passage to the street door, away from the women's laughter.

'Thought yer wanted some more stew,' Jess called after him.

It was ten o'clock, and the other women had long gone back to their own houses and families by the time Rose and Jess had finished their packing.

Rose put the final cup back on to the dresser and spread the drying cloth over the wooden draining board. They'd got through plenty of tea that night. She yawned and went over to the hearth, picking up the envelope containing their hopping letter from its pride of place on the overmantel. She touched it to her lips then slipped it into the deep pocket of her apron, as though she were afraid it might disappear if she left it alone.

'Come on, Jess,' she said with a yawn, 'let's 'ave a bit of a sit-down, a little blow.'

Mother and daughter each took a wooden chair from the kitchen and went outside on to the narrow pavement. All along Burton Street groups of people sat talking. Some had done the same as the Fairleigh women and had brought out their chairs, others sat on street doorsteps or leant against the stone window-ledges still warm from the late summer sun. The night air carried the reassuring sounds of children's laughter as they scrabbled in the gutters over games of marbles, or jostled each other in the side alleys, playing boisterous rounds of High-Jimmy-Knacker and British Bulldog. From the corner of the street louder voices could be heard shouting and singing along to the metallic twang of an untuned piano: the familiar sounds of The Star on a Saturday night.

'Don't yer wanna get a couple of hours kip before we go, Mum? I'll wait up for the boys if yer like.'

'Not worth it now, love. It's gone ten already. Joey said 'e'll be bringin' the cart round at about 'alf two. 'E'll be 'ere in a couple of hours. Wants to be off by three at the latest.'

'Yer sure? Yer look tired.'

'Yeh. I'm all right sittin' 'ere for now.' Rose could see that her daughter was too excited to sit with her. 'Why don't yer go along and see if that Lilly's ready yet?'

A voice from the group sitting outside the house next door joined in their conversation. 'The way they gas in that 'ouse I'll bet 'er mother ain't even got 'er beddin' sorted out yet.'

Rose chose to ignore her nosy neighbour.

'I don't think Elsie's ever been on time for anythin', 'as she, Mum?' Jess laughed fondly at the thought of her friend's mum and her slapdash ways. 'Lil's exactly the same. Always larkin' about. Nothin' gets 'em down. Smashin' family,' she added, looking pointedly at the now tutting woman next door.

'Well, like mother like daughter, they say,' said Rose, rearranging her apron tidily over her skirt.

'That why I'm so beautiful then, Mum?'

'Go way with yer. Go on. Go and sort that Lilly out.'

Rose landed a playful slap on Jessie's behind, sending a cloud of dust dancing up into the gas-lit night air, making them both cough.

'Blimey, look at that,' Rose spluttered. 'I'll be glad to get down 'opping. Get away from all this muck.'

'An' it'll do yer chest the world of good an' all, Mum.'

'Let's 'ope so, this cough's drivin' me bonkers.' Rose's eyes watered from the strain of choking on the dust.

'Yer sure it's all right if I pop down Lil's?' said Jess. 'I won't be long.'

'Course it's all right, darlin'. See yer later.' Rose leant back and closed her eyes, enjoying the chance of a rest. She suddenly sat bolt upright and opened her eyes.

''Ere, 'ang on, Jess,' she called, stopping her daughter. 'Did yer remember to tell Miss Feldman we're goin'? Better make sure she's got someone to turn on 'er gas an' light her fire of a Friday night. Don't want the poor old gel sittin' in the cold and dark with the nights drawin' in.'

'I've already sorted Ted out for that, Mum,' Jess called back. ''E's a good kid. 'E'll make sure she'll 'ave a fire for 'er Sabbath. 'E promised me.'

'All right, love,' said Rose, settling back and making herself comfortable.

Not for the first time that day Rose counted herself a lucky woman. Jess was such a good girl, thoughtful and caring. All that Rose could hope for in a daughter, in fact. All she hoped for now, she thought to herself, was that her Jess would find herself a decent bloke. She hadn't seemed to have any interest in blokes at all until that day when Jack brought the hopping letter. Rose nodded to herself. He was steady, Jack, sensible and reliable. Over the last few weeks, Rose had watched the pair of them, seen how they'd looked at one another, how they'd started acting all shy with each other. She smiled. It was a bit different from when they were kids playing rough and tumble in the street together. Yes, Jack Barnes would do fine. With Jess settled with a nice chap like him, Rose would have no worries about her daughter at all.

As she shifted, the familiar creaking of the old wooden chair soothed her; the sounds of the happy, busy street fading away, she closed her eyes. She thought of the day when she'd told her old mum that Bill Fairleigh had asked her to marry him. 'So long as he gives yer enough to pay the rent and to put a dinner on the table every day,' her mum had said. He'd always done that all right, Rose smiled to herself, the very best, in fact, that he could do – by her *and* the kids, even if it wasn't always easy. Bill Fairleigh was a good man. And that's what she wanted for her Jess. A good man.

–

From the activity in Burton Street anyone would have thought it was the middle of the day rather than three o'clock in the morning. Joey Fuller had tethered his wall-eyed black and white pony, Daddler, to the lamp-post and was loading the women's baggage on to his cart.

'That's it then,' said Joey. He stood upright, straightening his aching back. 'I don't know, though, it don't look enough to me somehow.' He scratched his head making his cheesecutter cap wobble from side to side.

'That's cos Elsie Dorkin ain't 'ere yet,' said Florrie Baxter, full of her usual spiteful sarcasm. 'Win, go and give 'em a knock. I bet the lazy so-and-sos are still in bed. Typical of them. All bone idle, the 'ole bloomin' lot of 'em.'

'All right, Mum. Yer comin', Jess?'

Winnie and Jess hitched up their skirts and ran along the road to find out what had happened to Lil and the rest of the Dorkins.

'Never known a mob like that Elsie and 'er girls,' continued Florrie through pursed lips, her arms folded and her head tilted to one side. 'Lazy? I should say so. Stay abed all day if they could. An' fat? When they ain't kippin' they're stuffin' 'emselves with grub.'

'Wouldn't do if we was all the same, now would it, Florrie?' Rose didn't like gossip, and, even if everyone agreed with Winnie's mum, she wouldn't hear her talking ill of anyone. 'An' yer'd better watch 'oo 'ears yer chatterin' an' all, cos 'ere comes Elsie an' the gels now.'

'At last. 'Oo-bloody-ray!' Joey Fuller gave a jokey cheer. 'Come on, you lot. Me old pony'll change 'er mind an' stay 'ere if yer don't get a move on.'

'Sorry, Joe. Yer know what it's like gettin' these girls sorted out of a mornin'.'

'Good Gawd, Elsie,' Florrie criticised her. 'Yer've only got four. Anyone'd think yer 'ad a big family the way yer go on all the time. An' we've all been standin' 'ere for ages waitin' for yer.'

'All right, Florrie, Mrs Bleed'n' Perfect. Leave off. I'm 'ere now, ain't I?'

Joey Fuller, Rose's three boys and Jack Barnes the postman worked together, stowing the last of the parcels on the back of the brightly painted coster's trolley.

'There yer are, Mum. All done.'

'Good boy, Ted.' Rose looked fondly at her youngest child, then turned to her eldest. 'Now, Sammy, I want you and Charlie to look after 'im. Do you 'ear me? I don't want yer even goin' *near* Chinatown, or Bow Common, or...'

''Ere we go,' said Charlie, rolling his eyes.

'Shut up, Charlie.' Jess jumped to her mum's defence. 'Yer know Mum's worried about leavin' Ted 'ere with you two 'ooligans. Sammy with 'is gels, and you with yer dodgy mates.'

Jess's efforts misfired.

'Aw, she's right,' said Rose, panicking. 'I can't leave me baby 'ere.'

'Mum!' Ted was mortified at the show being made of him.

'Say 'e goes down by them docks? Yer all know what could 'appen to 'im. All them gels 'anging round, waitin' for the seamen off the ships…'

Ted's mouth opened, ready to ask his usual awkward questions. Rose was too quick for him.

'Yer dad's different,' she snapped.

Jack saw his chance. He'd already stayed up all night to help load the luggage, even though Clara, his own mum, had never been hop picking in her life. And here was another opportunity to impress Jessie with his maturity. 'Don't worry, Rose. I'll keep an eye on the boys for yer if yer like.'

Rose was relieved. Jack might only have been eighteen, just a year older than Jess, but he was more sensible than her two eldest boys put together.

'Would yer, Jack? I wouldn't 'alf appreciate it.'

'Course I would,' said Jack, pleased to see Jess smiling happily at him.

'My Bill'll be 'ome from sea soon, so yer can tell 'im if there's been any nonsense,' Rose said. She turned to her now grimacing sons. 'Do you boys 'ear me? Any trouble and Jack'll tell yer dad. An' 'e'll have somethin' to say about it all right.'

The Fairleigh boys mumbled an indignant reply to their mother. The Dorkin girls and Winnie Baxter giggled, enjoying the boys' embarrassment.

'Anythin' for you, Rose,' said Jack.

'What yer after then, Jacko?' Sammy asked the postman, getting his own back by using Jack's schoolboy name – he knew he hated it. 'Tryin' to butter up me mum to impress me little sister, are yer?'

Before Jack could think of an answer for Sammy, Joey had untied Daddler's reins and was making ready to leave. A row was all he needed; they'd never get away once a slanging match started.

'Come on, ladies, it's time we was off.'

A relieved cheer went up.

''Ang on a minute there, Joe,' said Jack.

Joey dropped the pony's reins again. 'What now?' he said wearily.

''Ere, Jess. I brought yer something.'

The young postman picked up his sack and took out a cane birdcage. Inside, on a little swing, was perched a bright-yellow canary.

'Jack.' Jess couldn't believe the present was really for her.

'Go on, take it.' Jack nodded encouragingly. 'It's yours. To keep.'

Some of the bystanders whistled and laughed, others kept quiet, anxious to hear Jess's reply.

'It's the prettiest thing I've ever 'ad.' Jess took the cage by its red ribbon handle, leant forward and kissed Jack on the cheek. 'Ta, Jack. It's lovely.'

Jack and Jessie stood looking at each other, unaware of, or not caring about, the interest they were arousing. Jack touched Jess gently on the arm.

'I'll come down to Kent and see yer in a few weeks, when the rest of 'em go down, shall I?' He paused, not sure if he'd overstepped the mark. 'If yer like, that is.'

'I'd like that a lot, Jack, really I would.'

'Can we go now?' Joey tried to sound impatient, although he was as intrigued as the rest of them at witnessing the long-awaited romantic scene. 'Them 'oo's ridin' for the first hour get on the cart. An' watch them parcels. Yer'll 'ave 'em all on the floor again. An' them what's walkin' keep away from them wheels. We don't want no accidents before we even get there.'

Jess had been picked to ride for the first part of the long journey, but before she could climb aboard, Jack had put his hands around her waist and had lifted her up on to the back of the trolley.

''Elpin' up a great thing like 'er,' exclaimed Rose.

'She could've stepped up easy with them great long legs of 'ers. Don't yer go fussin' over 'er, Jack.'

But Rose didn't fool her neighbours; they all knew she was delighted with this sudden progress between her daughter and Jack Barnes. Jess had found herself a good bloke all right, and Jack would make just the sort of son-in-law she and Bill had always hoped for.

'An' yer make sure yer remember to keep an eye on them boys for me, Jack. 'Specially that Charlie. An' make sure they get up for work of a mornin'. An' watch young Ted. Make sure yer mind 'im. An' Sammy.'

Her sons groaned at the disgrace of it all.

'I won't let yer down, Rose,' Jack said, standing tall. 'Yer can trust me, yer know that.'

'I think I can, son,' said Rose, flushed with pleasure. 'I think I can.'

''Ere yer are, Jack, take this as a little keepsake,' said Jess. She untied the yellow paisley stock from around her neck and handed it to him. 'Keep yer neck nice an' warm of a mornin' when yer doin' yer rounds.'

Jack took the neckerchief from her and their fingers touched. Jess dangled her legs, swinging them back and forth from her place on the tailboard. They looked at each other, big soppy smiles on their faces.

'Oi, oi. 'Oo looks like the cat what's got the cream then?' hooted Charlie.

Joey decided it was time to part the new lovebirds. He clicked his tongue and shook the reins in encouragement and the sturdy little pony pulled away, making the iron-rimmed wheels of the coster's cart spark on the cobbles. The Fairleigh boys, Jack and aother sleepy males from Burton Street stood in the middle of the road, watching them go. Waving their hands and caps, they shouted their goodbyes through their yawns, bidding farewell to wives, children and sisters.

Jack called his goodbyes to Jess as he tied the yellow paisley scarf around his neck.

'Yer great big girl,' taunted young Ted. 'Fancy givin' our Jess a canary.'

Sammy ruffled his little brother's hair. 'Yer just wait, Ted. Won't be long before it's you buyin' girls presents.'

'An' gettin' a few little keepsakes of 'is own, eh, Jacky boy?' laughed Charlie.

The idea of ever wasting money on girls made Ted laugh, but the sight of Jack shouting up the street after his sister made him laugh even louder.

''Ark at 'im, Charlie,' he said. 'What a bleed'n' nit.'

'Oi, mouthy, an' 'ark at you, an' all,' replied his brother. 'Mum ain't 'ardly out of the street yet an' yer bloody swearin'.'

The cart disappeared into the darkness but Jack still called out his promises to see Jess in a fortnight.

'But yer right, little 'un,' said Charlie, ''e is a bleed'n' nit. Just look at 'im.'

'Leave 'im alone,' said Sam. 'The geezer's in love, ain't 'e. No finer feelin' in the world, mate.'

The motley group of cockney women and their street-raking offspring had gone. Their annual journey into the peaceful garden of England had begun.

Once the little band had crossed the familiar brown waters swirling beneath Tower Bridge and had departed the unfamiliar world of south London, the weather itself seemed to change. The sky grew lighter and the early chill disappeared. The roads were wider, just as dirty and covered with horse dung, but the houses were cleaner and taller and there was more grass and trees.

By the time they reached the Kent countryside the roads had become narrow again, but these were lanes, not the vermin-infested alleys that ran between the grimy terraces and tenements that were home to the East Enders. The smells were of grass, corn and earth. Even the animal smells from the farms were different from the cloying sickly sweetness of the stable yard behind Burton Street.

But it wasn't until they saw the first oast houses, standing tall against the blue summer sky, that the travellers really believed they were almost there. Once they'd spotted those, they could relax a bit and the women were glad to accept Joey's offer of a stop at the next pub.

They drew to a halt in Dowlhurst. The village was as good as a picture postcard. It had thatched cottages, each with its own front garden full of flowers and vegetables; a village green planted with wide, shady chestnut trees; a pond dotted with fat white ducks; and the most lovely church that Rose had ever seen.

Rose wasn't a religious woman, but while the others sat on the grass eating their bread and cheese and swigging down the glasses of beer and lemonade which Joey had fetched them from the Maltster's Arms, she strolled over to the arched doorway of the little Norman church. She pushed the heavy, studded wooden door until it swung back on its ancient. She blinked and squinted until her eyes got used to the light.

Inside it was strangely dim, not gloomy like at home, but soft somehow, with blue, red and gold shadows from the glorious windows set high in the stone walls. She stepped inside and closed the door behind her. She couldn't remember seeing anything more beautiful or peaceful. Rose wasn't used to being in church and wasn't sure what to do next, but she felt that it would be all right if she just sat down and said her thanks that life was being so good to her and her family. That her Jessie was going to be settled with a decent man.

Chapter 4

A Little Talk

'And, on this final Sunday in August, let us pray. Let us pray that, this year, the arrival of the hop pickers from London will not prove to be too distressing for us and for our beautiful village.'

The Reverend Henry Batsford, vicar of Tilnhurst, leant forward and grasped the front of his carved wooden pulpit with his long, spindly hands. He raised his eyes heavenwards, his Adam's apple bobbed in his scrawny throat, and his voice droned on.

'We beseech thee, oh Lord, to keep us safe from the immoral ways and vile habits of those who will be invading thy beautiful countryside this day. Keep us, oh Lord, safe from harm; safe from contamination from the heathen city filth and from the corruption of their dark souls.'

As usual, the Reverend Henry Batsford whittered on and on, but, for once, most of the congregation of St Mary's, Tilnhurst, were actually listening to the morning sermon. They were as alarmed as their pastor at the thought of the impending threat to their rural peace and morality, and if praying would help protect them, then pray they would. The exceptions, in the otherwise rapt congregation, were Sir George and Lady Worlington. Sir George hadn't been paying attention because, for the early part of the service, he had been complaining to his wife about a domestic matter, and now, during the second half, he was slumped back in the pew, snoring loudly, oblivious to the sermon and to those around him.

Lady Worlington had not listened to the vicar for reasons of her own. She considered the opinions of the Reverend Batsford to represent the very worst of backward rural prejudice, and chose to ignore them the best she could. Leonore had been born and had spent her girlhood in London, and then, when she was eighteen, had met Sir George at a friend's house party in Kent. Her initial infatuation with the young and handsome George Worlington had blinded her to his crass behaviour. But now she saw him for what he was, an old-fashioned boor who would have fitted in quite happily with the feudal brutality of his ancestors on their medieval estates. Leonore could not imagine her husband ever caring enough about her to discover her true feelings about living in the country, or her real feelings for him. Nor could she imagine what he would do if he ever found out what she actually did during her increasingly frequent visits to London. She doubted whether he would even listen if she decided to confront him, to simply raise the subject over breakfast one morning. In her heart she knew that even then she would never be able to discuss her life, her feelings or her hopes with the man she had grown to despise. If she had half as much courage as some women, she thought, she would have left her husband years ago. But she had neither the courage nor anywhere to go, so she stayed in Kent and lived the lie of being a dutiful wife to Sir George Worlington and mother to her equally arrogant sons, Robert and Paul.

It was the subject of their elder son's behaviour which had occupied the first half of the Worlingtons' morning in church.

'I won't have it, Leonore. I mean it.' Sir George didn't bother to speak in a respectful whisper; he didn't give a damn who was listening, and he was unstoppable once he had started.

'Garnett's been head gardener at the Hall since before that boy was born,' he boomed. 'I'm not having it. Do you hear? If Robert wants to play around with servant girls, why pick Garnett's bloody daughter? You'd better tell that son of yours that I will not have Garnett upset. Let him get himself a cockney girl if he wants some fun.'

Not one of the congregation turned to stare at him.

'I don't know why you're so upset about Garnett.' Leonore managed to slip in a few words, to have her say while her husband was preoccupied with blowing his nose. Her tones were at least subdued. 'How about Milly, his poor daughter? That's what I want to know. What's to become of *her* now everyone knows what they've been up to? And your shouting about it in church hardly helps, George. I cannot think it has been a very good start to an engagement. Whatever is Julia to make of all this?'

Sir George Worlington stuffed his handkerchief deep into his pocket, then twisted round slowly to look at his wife. His lip was curled in sneering disbelief. 'What the hell has it got to do with her?'

Leonore had decided that the Sunday service was neither the time nor the place to discuss her son's behaviour towards women, and, to her relief, her husband had turned away from her without waiting for an answer and soon drifted into a deep, if noisy, sleep – his rest equally undisturbed by organ, choir or sermon.

As the vicar intoned the final blessing, Leonore leant across and tapped her husband's arm, being careful to avoid the stale stench of his port-laden snores.

'George. George, the service has finished. Wake up.'

'Eh? What d'you want, woman? Damn you.' The master of Worlington Hall shifted his great bulk, trying unsuccessfully to find a more comfortable position in the ornately carved Worlington family pew.

'George, come along,' said Leonore, more loudly this time. 'It is time to leave.'

He opened his eyes reluctantly, shook his wife's hand from his sleeve and staggered to his feet, issuing a loud, alcohol-induced belch as he did so.

Not even the slightest smirk passed across the faces of the St Mary's departing faithful. In one way or another, Sir George Worlington owned them all, and the inhabitants of Tilnhurst certainly knew their place.

In the church porch, the Reverend Batsford was going through his weekly ritual of shaking hands with the more influential members of his flock and nodding briefly at those he considered to be lesser individuals. This morning the congregation weren't in their usual hurry to be off, either to the Hop Bine for a pint or to get back to work in their cottage gardens. This, the 'homedwellers', as they termed themselves during the time of the hop harvest, were reluctant to leave at all. They all wanted to discuss the impending arrival of the Londoners, the 'foreigners' as they called the hop pickers from the fog-bound streets of the capital. Not even the vicar's admonishments could get them to return to their homes and their labours. The gossiping continued as lively as ever.

'I do hope you have looked out your keys, my dear,' said one ruddy-faced woman, whose expression suggested she'd been sucking lemons. 'I do know as I'll be locking up at night from now on.'

'I have indeed, beaut,' said her equally grim-faced companion. 'They trains their young ones, you know. Soon as they can walk, they has them begging and stealing from the likes of decent folk such as us.'

'Dear oh dear!' The first woman shook her head with distaste and folded her arms more tightly across her ample bosom. 'Don't know the meaning of an honest day's work, none of them. Filth they are. All of them.'

'Only the Lord himself knows what their menfolk gets up to while their women are down here.'

'I can guess,' her companion replied. She looked round to make sure she wasn't being overheard. 'I do hear as there's "girls", if you takes my meaning, on every street corner in London.' She leant forward, lowering her tone conspiratorially. 'My Edwin's brother Cedric went up there once. To London. He could not believe his eyes. Disgusting he said it was. Real disgusting.'

'You don't say so, beaut?' This was better than she'd hoped for, real, juicy scandal. 'What do these "girls" get up to then?' she asked, narrowing her eyes.

'Well, I'll tell you all about it. Then you'll know exactly what to look out for when they gets here, won't you?'

And so it went on. Even after Sir George and his lady had bid the vicar a brusque good morning the villagers had still not departed. Vegetable rows went unweeded, pints remained undrunk as the villagers stood in the sun-drenched rural churchyard exchanging their dark tales.

By the time the grounds of St Mary's were finally emptied of the faithful it was almost time for evensong. And it was soon after that particular act of worship had been completed that the first 'foreigners' arrived in Tilnhurst to begin work on the hop harvest.

47

Worlington Hall was not the first farm in the area to extend its welcome to the seasonal labourers: that honour went to the neighbouring estate belonging to the Fanshawes. As Joey's cart moved slowly along the narrow, tree-lined lanes of Tilnhurst, the women and girls from Burton Street saw the welcoming yellow glow of candles and spirit lamps which the Fanshawe hop pickers had already hung outside their huts.

'Just think,' Jess whispered to Rose, 'we nearly went there, Mum.'

'Not really,' said Rose smiling at her daughter. 'I could never have fancied going to Fanshawe's, not with that lot from south London. I wouldn't know no one, would I?'

The evening light had almost faded before the field behind the hop gardens of Worlington Hall, known to everyone as the Common, finally began to come to life. Joey pulled on his right rein and the tired little pony turned on to the rutted track which led down past the orchards and on to the Common. The women who were riding on the cart climbed down to make the final part of their journey on foot and Joey joined them, leading the pony by her noseband.

The peaceful scene of tired but happy people making their weary way to their huts was shattered by Elsie Dorkin as she suddenly planted her feet, stood stock-still, and pulled her clay pipe out of her mouth to bellow angrily into the calm country air.

'Now I see it. That's what the greedy old bastard wanted all them two bobs off us lot for. They wasn't no deposits. They was to pay to get the electric put on. Just look at it.'

She stabbed her pipe in the direction of the Hall. As one, they all followed her instructions. And there, across the Common behind the orchards, was the big house for all to see, shining out like they had never seen before. It was certainly a wonder to behold. The Hall was ablaze with strong, steady light pouring out from every room.

'Yer wait 'hi I see 'im, the crafty ol' sod.' Elsie was now in full flow.

'An' what yer goin' to do then, Elsie?' Florrie asked contemptuously. 'Borrow a cup of electric off 'im to light up yer 'ut?'

'Yer can laugh, Florrie,' said Elsie, leaning threateningly close to her neighbour. 'It's only cos the likes of us graftin' for 'im that 'e's got the money for 'is fancy bloody electric in the first place. An' 'is big 'ouse.'

'An' it's cos of the likes of 'im that yer'll 'ave enough 'opping money to buy a bit of pork and a goose at Christmas time,' Florrie replied, equally belligerent.

'Aw, so yer sidin' with 'im now, are yer?'

'What's it to yer?'

'I'll show yer.'

At the sight of Elsie shaping up to her like a prizefighter, Florrie paled visibly, but she kept up the bravado. 'Get away with yer,' she jeered, 'yer couldn't knock the skin off a rice pudden.'

Joey looked at Rose and pulled a face, and Rose nodded in reply. They could both see that Elsie and Florrie were working themselves up to one of their rows. And, if they were on their usual form, it could go on all night and would probably wind up developing into a real stand-up fight. Then there'd be no rest for anyone. Joey walked the pony forward on to the Common, leaving Rose to speak.

''Ere we are.' The others looked round to see what Rose wanted. 'We're 'ere now.' Rose spoke in a jolly, pleased voice. 'Lilly, why don't yer 'elp yer mum start unpackin', love? Get yer belongings off the wagon,' she said enthusiastically. 'Joey'll want to 'ave a bit of a sleep before he gets off 'ome.'

'Yeh, come on, Lil.' Jess winked at her friend. 'If we get all our gear sorted, Joey can settle Daddler down, can't 'e?'

Lil was sensible enough to listen to Jess and Rose. Like them, she'd seen her mum and Florrie rowing all too many times before. 'Come on then, Win,' she said pointedly to Florrie's daughter.

The friends set to lifting boxes, bags and parcels off the back of the cart, carefully ignoring the challenging glares of Elsie and Florrie.

Although it had been a full twelve months since the women and children had last got the huts ready for their stay in Tilnhurst, the jobs had become so familiar over the years that it felt like they'd been there only yesterday. Outside on the Common, fires were lit, kettle props stuck into the ground, water boiled and tea brewed. Jam jars were half filled with a mixture of sugar and water and hung outside the hut doors to act as wasp traps. Inside the huts, beds were made up, pots and pans unpacked and tea chests, storing clothing and groceries, pushed into comers to double as tables.

The younger Dorkin girls were set by Lil to collect a supply of faggots – bundles of twigs, their main source of fuel, tied into manageable armfuls. The children knew, without being told by their big sister, to fetch enough for their neighbours. By the time they had finished they had collected enough faggots for all the four huts occupied by families from Burton Street.

The hut on the end was Rose's. It felt strange; this was the first year she'd be sharing it with just her daughter, the first year all the boys were old enough to stay at home in London and work. It would take some getting used to. But who could say, maybe Jess would have a young one of her own to bring down one day. Rose smiled to herself and carried on with her unpacking.

Next to the Fairleighs' hut was Elsie Dorkin and her four girls, although Lil was really a young woman now. Then there was Mabel Lawrence, the widow, her three children, all of them under five, the youngest still a babe in arms. The fourth in the row of ten hoppers' huts housed the Baxters: Florrie, her only girl Winnie, and her twin ten-year-olds, Sidney and Albert.

The twins had been sent by Florrie to fetch bales of straw to stuff the striped calico palliasses which served as mattresses. It was important to stuff them well, or the hard wooden shelf which acted as the bed base would provide an uncomfortable and sleepless night – even after the long, tiring journey.

'Joey, the bed's made in 'ere, mate,' Rose called from the hut. 'Come in an' get yer 'ead down for a while an' I'll get yer a bit of supper cooked before yer get off 'ome.'

'Ta, Rose,' Joey called over his shoulder. He was squatting by the bright, crackling fire. 'I'll just finish me cuppa tea an' give Daddler 'er nosebag, then I'll take yer up on that.'

With the pony settled, Joey stepped into the hut that would be Rose and Jessie Fairleigh's home for the 1913 hop harvest.

The wooden hut was about ten feet square, with a wide, waist-high shelf running the length of the far wall – the platform on which Rose and Jess would sleep. The right-hand wall, which separated them from the Dorkins, was almost concealed behind the painted pine dresser that Bill had made the first year he'd come down to her, after they'd got married. Rose was allowed to leave the dresser as a permanent fixture in the hut. Leaving such items was a privilege extended to only a few of the families, and depended not only on their reputation for reliability but also on the whim of the farm bailiff, Mr Audley. He had known Rose since she was a little girl and he respected her as a good and trusted worker. The rest of the space in the hut was taken up with the boxes and parcels that Rose and Jess had brought with them from Poplar. The only light came from two candles, stuck inside old jars for safety. There were no windows to give either illumination or ventilation, just cracks in the wooden roof and walls. But the huts were a big improvement on the bell tents that some farms still had for the pickers.

Joey, however, couldn't have cared less about the decor. He was just grateful for the chance to stretch out his stiff limbs and get a few hours sleep before the long journey back to London, and the start of another week's work.

'Joe. Joey.' Jess gently shook the sleeping man's arm. 'Mum's 'otted yer up a bit of neck o' lamb stew, Joe.'

Slowly he opened his eyes and levered himself up on to his elbow. 'Cor, I wondered where I was for the minute, gel,' he said, straightening his cap.

He swung his legs round and sat up. Taking the bowl of stew from Jess he started to eat.

'Your mum's a marvel an' that's a fact. 'Ot grub. I dunno. 'Ow's she got this lot sorted out already?'

'Yer know Mum, Joe, always organised, ain't she? She brought down a stone jar full of it. She knew yer'd want a bit of somethin' down yer before yer went 'ome.'

'I've always said it, an' I always will,' said Joey in between sucking the sweet meat off the lamb bones. 'She's a really good woman, your mother. A real good 'un. Bill Fairleigh's a lucky bloke an' no mistake.'

'What yer saying about my ol' man?' Rose came into the hut, shielding her candle from the night breeze. She busied herself sticking it safely into one of the empty jars, then rearranging boxes that didn't really need her attention.

"E's saying all sorts of nice things about yer, Mum. Make yer right blush, it would.'

'Well, Joe, yer can forget all that ol' nonsense,' Rose said, dusting down her apron. 'I don't agree with nothin' like that. I'm a respectable married woman. An' everyone knows it.'

'Only speakin' as I find, Rose.' Joey wiped the last of his crust of bread round the bowl, soaking up the remaining precious drops of rich gravy.

"Andsome,' he said, winking at Jess.

Jess took the empty bowl from him and handed him his boots. "Ere yer are, Joe.'

Joey pulled on his boots and stood up, his head nearly reaching the ceiling of the hut. 'Well, I'll 'ave to love yers an' leave yer, I've gotta get meself shifted. I'm down the market tomorrow.' He yawned noisily, and scratched at his chest.

'I made sure Daddler 'ad plenty to drink,' said Jess, 'so I reckon she'll be ready to get 'ome an' all.'

Joey reached out and touched Jessie's auburn hair. 'Blimey, I dunno. Two good women in one family.' He shook his head in wonder. 'I reckon yer both got the brains left over from them lot next door. An' their share of the looks.'

Jess couldn't help laughing, but, compliment or not, Rose wouldn't have any gossip in her home, even if it was only a wooden hut.

'Now don't start, Joey. That's enough of that. The Dorkins never 'armed no one. Now go on, off with yer.' Rose shooed him out of the hut like he was a bluebottle.

The women and children from the other huts in the row joined the Burton Street families to call their farewells to Joey and Daddler. Years spent hopping together had made them all old friends even though the short distance that separated their

East End homes meant they very rarely saw each other during the rest of the year.

Soon the cart had disappeared into the black Kent night. Jess went and sat by the dying embers of the fire, and Winnie and Lil sat down beside her, pretending they were eager to share their excitement about the weeks to come. What they actually wanted to know was what was going on between Jessie and Jack, and, as Lil put it, 'with that bleed'n' canary'.

Much to Jess's relief, Rose interrupted their interrogation. 'Come on, Jess, there'll be plenty of time for talkin' later. We've got work to do in the mornin', gel.'

'All right, Mum. Comin'. Goodnight, Lil, night, Win. Night, everyone.'

'Night, night. But don't think yer've got off that easy, Jessie gel,' Lil called after her. 'Me an' Win wanna know all the business. Even if we 'ave gotta wait 'til the mornin'.'

'We'll 'ave to see about that now, won't we, Lil?' said Jess, grinning back at her over her shoulder. 'An' I'm not really sure as I know what yer talkin' about, to tell yer the truth. Night night, you two.'

All the other cockney voices wishing each other goodnight soon faded and were replaced by the sounds of the countryside: owls, deer, insects, foxes and other strange noises, all unidentifiably mysterious to the city dwellers.

Rose blew out the candles and climbed into bed, her daughter cuddled up to her. They spoke softly, in whispers that wouldn't carry through the thin wooden walls and disturb Elsie's youngsters.

'Seems funny without our Ted, Mum.'

'Yeh, but more room without 'im sleepin' along the bottom, eh, Jess?'

'I wonder if Charlie and Sammy are lookin' after 'im.'

'They'd better be, or they'll 'ave yer dad to deal with when 'e gets 'ome.'

'D'yer suppose 'e'll come down with the boys?' Jess asked her mum.

''Oo? Ted or yer dad?' Rose paused, then said: 'Or do yer mean Jack?'

'Leave off, Mum,' said Jess shyly.

'Yer another one 'oo wants to be a bit less backward in comin' forward.'

'Do what? What yer talkin' about?'

'Nothin',' Rose said fondly, tucking the blanket round Jess's shoulder. 'Only somethin' I said to someone once. Anyway, yer could do a lot worse for yerself than Jack Barnes.'

'I know that, Mum. An' I really like 'im an' all. An' I love that little bird 'e give me...'

'But?' Rose was concerned to hear the doubt in her daughter's voice.

'It's just that I feel a bit shy with boys, that's all. I get, aw, I don't know, all mixed up about 'ow I feel. About what to do an' say an' that. An' Jack, well 'e's always been more like a brother to me, but now I feel different about 'im.'

'I know, love, I know.' Rose stroked Jessie's thick auburn hair, soothing her the way she'd done when Jess was a little girl. 'Tell yer what, me and you'll 'ave to 'ave a little talk about boys, I reckon. 'Ow's that?'

'I'd like that, Mum, I really would, but can it wait? I'm ever so tired.'

Rose hugged her daughter closer to her. 'Course it can, Jess. It's waited seventeen years, so I don't suppose a bit longer'll 'urt.' She coughed painfully, joining the chorus of choking sounds coming from the line of huts. Chests congested with factory soot and tar crackled and wheezed as they drew in the sharp, clean air of Kent.

'Soon 'ave all that muck out of yer lungs when we get on them fields in the mornin', eh, Mum?'

'Yeh, I reckon a lot of things'll be clearer in the mornin'. Night night, darlin'. God bless.'

–

The Londoners were not the only ones thinking about beginning work the next morning in the hop gardens. Many of the homedwellers were also involved in the harvest, and even those who would not actually be picking the hops had their own concerns about what would be going on during the coming weeks.

'Now I'm telling you, I do *not* want you hanging around none of them cockney girls, do you hear me?', or something similar, was to be heard in bedrooms throughout the village. In fact, more than a few of the wives of Tilnhurst spent a good part of the night keeping their husbands awake with their advice on how to behave when confronted with the immorality of the city temptresses. The women had learnt their lessons well from the gossips in the churchyard that morning. And what with the vicar's sermon and the tales passed on from Edwin's brother Cedric, the women of Tilnhurst had no intention of being shown up by their wayward menfolk.

The advice being given in the billiard room of Worlington Hall, however, was of quite a different nature.

'So, Robert,' Sir George said as he straightened up from the baize-covered table. He steadied himself with his cue and tried, with great difficulty, to focus on the face of his elder son. 'Take this as a bit of fatherly advice from your old man. From one who knows best, do you see?' Sir George swayed alarmingly as he wagged his finger instructively at his son. 'You just leave the maids alone for a while, understand?' He puffed out his cheeks and belched loudly, as bile rose in his throat and a rush of gas filled his mouth. Several more loud belches punctuated his words as he continued. 'Have fun. Yes. And why not? Good for a young fellow, a bit of fun. But not with the staff, boy. Not with the bloody staff. If you want a bit of totty, get yourself a cockney girl to fool around with.'

'What's all this sudden interest in the welfare of the servants?' Robert asked. He surveyed his drunken father with impersonal disgust. Then he took a sip from his glass and leant back against the white marble mantelshelf. 'Did the Reverend Batsford make you see the light this morning or something, Father? Remind you of your duty to those in your employ, did he?'

'Don't you take that impudent tone with me, Robert.' Sir George's body wavered as much as his voice as he struggled to remain upright.

'Well, you do have to admit all this is rather a change of attitude on your part, Father. You usually couldn't care less who we mess around with in the house, but you've always warned us to keep well away from the cockney girls.'

'Nonsense,' said Sir George, his eyes swivelling in and out of focus.

Robert nodded. 'Yes you did. You always reckoned they were dirty. Carry all sorts of vile diseases, you said. Now this year you're practically ordering me to marry one.'

'Are you being deliberately stupid, boy? Marriage has nothing to do with this.'

Paul Worlington found himself having to interrupt the argument between his drunken father and his brother. Up until now it had merely bored him, but suddenly it had become rather interesting. 'Nothing to do with marriage?' he said, raising his eyebrows. 'I wonder what Julia would have to say about that.'

'Shut up, Paul,' his brother dismissed him. 'I want to know what Father's up to.'

'Yes. What are you up to?' Paul was really beginning to enjoy himself.

'I've had enough of this damned questioning.' Sir George hissed the words through his teeth. 'Your mother's spoilt the pair of you. You're like bloody women the way you carry on. Nagging and whining all the time. Why don't you pull yourselves together. Act like men. And keep away from Garnett's daughter.'

'Good God. I've got it,' grinned Paul, jubilantly thumping the arms of his chair. He stood up, walked over to the table and confronted his father face to face. 'That's what all this is about, isn't it? You don't want Robert upsetting Garnett. Mustn't offend the head gardener, eh? I mean, we don't want to ruin the flowerbeds or the yew hedges, now do we? We have to have our priorities.'

Delighted to have solved the mystery of his father's sudden concern with the menials, Paul slapped his hand on the edge of the billiard table, knocking Sir George's glass of port on to the floor. The three Worlington men ignored the shattered glass and its contents as it ran quickly over the highly polished wood. A fourth man, who had been standing silently in the corner, moved forward and bent to clear up the sticky mess and the splinters of Waterford crystal.

Robert unfolded his arms, pushed himself away from the mantelpiece and took up position ready to play his shot. But he stopped midway through lining up the ball. He looked thoughtful, as though trying to recall some distant or insignificant event.

'Which one is Garnett's daughter anyway?' he said.

Chapter 5

The Cockney Girl

''E's all right with 'is two-bob deposit an' 'is bloody electric. Pity 'e ain't put up the rate 'e pays us.' Florrie was in full flow, chatting nineteen to the dozen, not caring who, if anyone, was listening to her. She had conveniently forgotten her previous defence of her employer's rights. 'I wouldn't mind a few more coppers a bushel, I can tell yer. Now a rise, that's somethin' as would be worth listenin' to. Not like this rubbish. 'Ark at 'im goin' on and on and on.'

'Sssh, Florrie, yer the one 'oo's going on,' said Rose, running out of patience with her noisy neighbour. 'I wanna listen to the bailiff even if you don't.'

'What's the matter with yer, Rose? We've 'eard 'im read out them rotten rules on the first mornin' of 'opping every year since we've been comin' 'ere. An' it still ain't got no more interestin'.'

'Well, Florrie, I wanna 'ear them again. Now if yer don't mind…'

'Suit yerself.'

The bailiff finished reading his list of regulations and restrictions, then folded up the yellowing sheets of paper and put them away safely in the leather countryman's pouch he wore at his waist. 'So,' he said, 'let's be sorting out these bins.'

The women walked over and selected the particular bins they favoured. The big hessian bags supported on wooden frames, into which the women threw the hops after they had plucked them from the prickle-covered bines, were actually all the same, but it was customary to select a particular bin, the one that took your fancy. So they chose their bins, and when they had cleared the hops from one set, 'their' bins would be moved with them to the next area to be harvested.

'Everyone settled?' called the bailiff.

'Yes thanks, Mr Audley,' was mumbled up and down the rows.

'Right then.' He raised a battered horn-like instrument to his lips and blew a rasping two-tone note. 'Let picking begin.'

The women loved to pick the first hops of the morning. Still wet from the dew, the bines were less tough on their tender fingers, which had become unused to the work during their year away from the countryside. With a great swoosh, their hands would run down the stems and the hops would fall into the bins.

The bins were soon swelling with their loads of plump hop cones and the air filled with the bittersweet smell of the plants; a smell so different from the stench of London, a smell so much part of being in Kent. The word was passed along the rows:

''Ere he comes, gels. Look lively, the measurer's on 'is way.'

And the song went up:

Our luwerly 'ops,
Our luwerly 'ops.
When the measurer 'e comes round,
Pick 'em up, pick 'em up off the ground.
When 'e starts 'is measurin'
'E don't know when to stop.

Aye aye get in the bin An' take the Weedin' lot!

Children didn't need to be told twice; they got down and scrambled around under the bins to collect any loose hops, which they added to their mothers' precious loads to make up the bulk for the measuring.

A miserable, hollow-cheeked farm worker and Mr Audley the bailiff were making their way along the rows between the hop poles up which the plants were growing. The two men walked along beside a horse-drawn wagon piled high with huge sacks – the pokes – in which they were collecting the harvested hops. They stopped by Rose and Jess.

'Only one bin this year, Mrs Fairleigh?'

'Yeh, Mr Audley. Me youngest stayed at 'ome this year, got 'imself settled in a decent job, so we've only got one bin. 'E used to work the other one with 'is sister 'ere.'

'Well, let's see how you two have done between you.'

The bailiff stood back for the farm worker to dip into the brimming hessian bin with his bushel basket. He poured the measured hops into the now half-full poke.

'Well, Mrs Fairleigh,' said the bailiff pleasantly. 'From the look of this lot you could easily manage another bin. What do you think? Do you want another one?'

'If 'e carries on measurin' as fair as that, I do. But's no good if 'e starts pushin' 'em down 'ard in the basket an' makes me lose 'alf me tally. We'll never get nowhere then.'

The farm worker glared at Rose. 'You saying I'm a dishonest measurer, missus?'

'No. No, I'm not,' Rose said evenly. 'I just speak as I find, that's all. Everyone knows that. An' they know yer ain't always that fair. 'Specially when Mr Audley ain't around.'

'Bloody foreigners,' he hissed under his breath.

''Ark at him,' exploded Elsie. 'We've only been down 'ere a day an' 'e's started.' She voiced the indignity all the women felt when dealing with the ferretfaced measurer.

Rose half wished she hadn't opened her mouth; she only wanted a fair measure, not a row.

Jess spoke quickly. 'I think I could manage a bin of me own, don't you, Mum? I'll work 'ard. An' the money would come in 'andy, wouldn't it?'

'It's up to your mother,' the bailiff said, smiling at Jess. Mr Audley appreciated Jess's efforts to halt the unpleasantness between Elsie and the surly measurer. Antagonised workers meant a slow harvest, which meant Sir George wouldn't be pleased and would be sure to take it out on him.

'We'll give it a go tomorrow, Mr Audley,' said Rose, proud of Jess's grown-up behaviour but keen to show she wasn't to be taken for a ride. 'After I've 'ad a chance to keep me eye on 'im an' 'is bushel basket for the rest of the day.'

'That's settled then.' The bailiff unhooked a notched stick from a metal hoop that he wore hanging from his belt. 'Here's your tally, Mrs Fairleigh. Five bushels, right?'

'Right,' Rose agreed. 'Mind yer,' she added, staring at the sour-faced measurer, 'yer could give us a proper 'opping book, yer know. We don't 'ave to 'ave tally sticks. Me daughter can read, see. An' do 'er sums. Yer could keep a written total for us if yer liked.'

'Well, she's one up on Theo here,' laughed the bailiff. 'No good asking him for a written tally, he can hardly make his mark.'

The measurer never answered, but he would have plenty to say when he went back to his cottage. He would make sure he told his wife every detail of what had happened; how Gerald Audley had made him look a fool in front of these low women. The bailiff siding with the foreigners against him – it wasn't right, it wasn't the natural order of things. The Reverend Batsford had called them 'heathen city filth' and that's what they were; vermin. What did Audley think he was doing taking the part of the foreigners against a homedweller, and being so friendly with them? What was in it for him? The measurer's wife would be very interested in all this, especially as Mrs Audley, the bailiff's wife, thought herself a cut above the labourers' families. She wouldn't be so fancy in church next Sunday if she could see her husband smiling and laughing with these harlots. Let her show off with her fancy ways then.

The first measuring of the day was also the signal for the women and children to stop picking and take a break. Faggot fires, miniature versions of those outside their huts, were started near the bins, and kettle props stuck in beside them. As the water was boiling, loaves were cut and jam or dripping spread on to the thick doorsteps of bread. The hoppers sat warming themselves in the morning sun, eating their bread and drinking their tea.

'Mum,' Winnie shouted, 'look at them twins' 'ands.'

Florrie looked at her sons, who were already on to their third bits of bread. 'Sidney, Albert, what yer been up to, yer pair of tripe'ounds? Yer 'ands are lousy. Where've yer both been?' Her voice rose ominously. 'Answer yer mother.'

'Nothin', Mum. Honest.' Sidney's innocent reply was spoiled when he added, 'Anyway, look at 'er hands. All covered in brown they are. Yuck!'

''Er 'ands are brown 'cos she's been 'elpin' yer mum with the 'ops,' said Lil, butting into the Baxter family's row. 'Not like you, yer lazy little devils. Yer look like yer've been in the pigsty. An' yer smell like it an' all.'

Albert jumped to his feet and thumbed his nose at his sister's friend, shouting, 'That's 'cos we 'ave been playin' in the pigsty, if yer must know. An' just like you they was, Lil. Big an' fat an' ugly.'

With that, Albert and his twin dropped on to all fours and started bouncing around, grunting and snorting like pigs.

'Yeh, just like yer they was, Lil,' echoed Sidney, 'big an' fat an' ugly.'

'Come on, girls.' Lil grabbed Jess's arm and Winnie followed as they chased the screaming twins through the hop gardens towards the orchards.

'Dunno where them kids get their energy from,' said Elsie, spluttering crumbs of bread and jam over everyone as she tore off another great mouthful with her cracked brown teeth. 'We've only been pickin' a few hours an' I'm bloody exhausted already.'

'Yer always exhausted, Elsie,' said Florrie. 'I've never seen no one always so ready for either a bit of kip or a bellyful of grub.'

Elsie ignored her and stretched out flat on her back on the sun-warmed earth, eating all the while.

'It's 'cos they're young,' said Mabel Lawrence wistfully. 'That's why they're so lively.'

Rose handed Mabel some of the cold toast she had brought with her from the hut. She had seen the young widow feeding her pale, listless children, and having nothing left for herself. It was something Rose herself had done often enough in the past.

'Try a bit of this toast and dripping, Mabel,' she said, nodding her encouragement. 'All jelly bottoms it is. Lovely. Put 'airs on yer chest, that will.'

'Ta, Rose.' Mabel bit ravenously into the bread. 'I could do with somethin' an' all. Just watchin' them young 'uns runnin' around makes me feel whacked out.'

'Yer ain't exactly a granny yerself,' said Florrie spitefully.

'I might as well be,' sighed Mabel. 'I feel like one.'

'That's 'aving three babies an' no old man to bring 'ome a few bob for yer. We know it ain't easy, Mabel.' Rose looked at the prematurely aged woman, not with pity but with concern as Mabel's youngest, a skinny, sickly baby, sucked at Mabel's flattened, almost milkless breast. 'Tell yer what, 'ow about if my Jessie 'elps yer, once they've finished their gallopin' about? Yer'll get plenty picked then. She's got enough energy for ten, that one.'

'Would she, Rose? That'd be smashin'. I could really do with a bit extra.'

'I thought she was going to 'ave a bin of 'er own, Rose,' said Florrie, relishing the opportunity to add her two penn'orth. 'That's what yer said to the bailiff, I 'eard yer. Yer said, "Mr Audley, Jess is gonna…"'

'No, Florrie. I didn't, as it 'appens. Yer must 'ave been earwiggin' for a change an' 'eard all wrong.'

Rose didn't want bad feelings with her neighbours but sometimes Florrie Baxter could really stick her nose in where it wasn't wanted. Quite deliberately, Rose turned her back on Florrie and handed Mabel a thick china cup of steaming tea.

'Jess'll be glad to 'elp yer, Mabel,' she said. 'An' I'll be glad to get 'er out of me 'air for a bit.'

Rose's last comment was a lie and all the women knew it, but they didn't say anything. Except Florrie Baxter, of course. Florrie couldn't resist rubbing it in; she had to say something.

'An' I always thought yer precious Jessie was the apple of yer eye,' she said huffily. 'Still, I suppose it's very generous of yer to do yer duty to Mabel.'

'What I do is out of friendship, not duty,' Rose said without bothering to turn to face Florrie. She poured herself a cup of tea, and topped up Mabel's to the brim. 'An' I'm proud to number Mabel amongst me friends, an' I 'ope she feels the same.'

Elsie grinned with pleasure at Florrie's discomfort and treated herself to another pipeful of her favourite evil-smelling tobacco, which she packed down hard with the end of her filthy thumb.

'Yer a nosy tart, Florrie,' she said happily.

Jess and Winnie finally caught up with the twins beyond the hop gardens, where the cherry orchards began. The girls held the unfortunate pair firmly by the wrists until Lilly came puffing up behind them.

'So, I look like a pig, do I?' Lil asked. She stood in front of the boys, hands on hips, feet apart. 'Did yer know that pigs bite? 'Specially little boys.'

The brothers struggled but were held fast by Jess and Winnie.

'Yer leave us alone,' wailed Albert, 'or our mum'll get yer. Then yer'll be sorry.'

'Don't bank on it, Albert,' said his sister menacingly, 'Mum said we was to give yer an extra four-penny one round the ear 'ole. Just for 'er.' Winnie raised her hand in threat.

'I bet she didn't,' Albert wailed. 'We're 'er favourites we are, me an' Sid. She 'ates you, Winnie. She told me.'

Albert's sauciness was a mistake. The three girls started the torture. They tickled the boys until they yelled for mercy and then tickled them some more. Their squeals sounded far more like piglets than their earlier efforts at impersonation had done.

'What the hell is going on here?'

At the sound of the authoritative male voice, the three girls and their prisoners stopped brawling immediately and turned to see who was speaking.

'I asked a question. Is no one going to answer me?' He pointed at Jessie. 'You. You can talk, I know that, I could hear the noise from right across the fields.'

The man who spoke to them was sitting on a tall chestnut horse. He was accompanied by another, slightly younger man riding a less impressive bay animal. A little rough-haired terrier trotted along behind them, trying to catch up with the horses.

'Yer dog looks thirsty,' said Jess, chin in the air. 'She needs a drink.'

'My animals are my concern,' he said unpleasantly, 'and so is this farm. Now what are you up to?'

'We didn't mean nothin', mister,' said Albert, wide-eyed with fear. He recognised trouble when he saw it; he and his twin were experts. 'We was only playin'. Truth.'

'You're not here to play. You're here to work. Now get back to those hops.'

''Ow do you know we're 'op pickers?' Lil demanded. 'We could be anyone. We could be visitors, or someone. Or...' Lil ran out of possible explanations for being on the farm.

'Speaking the way *you* do? And in those clothes? You're not exactly dressed to visit the Hall, now are you? Oh, let's see, maybe you've come for the job of scarecrow.' The man addressed his companion. 'Can you imagine Mother's face if they turned up at the house for afternoon tea?'

The other man laughed out loud at the idea of these ruffians meeting his refined mother.

Jess hid her hop-stained hands behind her skirt. 'There's no need to worry about us. We wasn't doin' no 'arm to no one. An' we was just goin', anyway. Come on you lot, let's get back. We've got work to do.'

The five Londoners, now considerably more subdued than before, walked back towards the hop gardens, through the plum-laden orchards.

'Wait,' the man on the chestnut horse called. 'You, the tall one with the red hair.'

Jess stopped and turned round. 'Yer talkin' to me?'

'Yes, you. Come here.'

'Now yer for it,' said Lil.

'Don't worry about me, Lil,' Jess said quietly. 'Go on, all of yer, get back. Go on. It's bad enough one of us bein' in trouble.'

'All right, Jess,' said Lil, her head down. 'But be careful. Don't own up to nothin'. He ain't got no right to tell yer off, we never did no 'arm.'

Glad to be free, Lil, Win and the twins ran off back to the safety of the hop gardens.

'I'm waiting.' He beckoned to Jess with his riding crop.

Jess took a small step towards the man, then stopped. 'I can 'ear yer from where I am, thanks.'

'You were worried about my dog,' he said.

'Robert, why are you bothering with her?' asked the other man impatiently. 'Don't start anything. Come on. Let's go.'

'Don't interfere, Paul. You go on. I'll catch you up.'

The younger man shrugged and urged his horse forward, 'You know best.'

'Now,' said Robert, leaning down from the saddle towards her. 'My dog?'

''Er tongue's 'angin' out,' said Jess. She hoped she sounded calmer than she felt. 'She wants a drink. It's 'ot out 'ere.'

'You like dogs, do you?'

'I like all animals,' said Jess. 'I've even got a canary of me very own.' She blushed, not knowing why she was talking like this to a stranger. A stranger who could send her and her mother back to London just because he felt like it.

'A canary. Have you now?' The man looked her slowly up and down, appraising her openly with no intention of concealing his interest. 'Tadger here had puppies a fortnight ago. How would you like to see them?'

'I can't. I've gotta get back to me mum. She'll be wonderin' where I am.' She half turned to go, then, 'But I do like puppies.' Again she didn't know why she had spoken out in that way. She could have bitten off her tongue.

'Right, later then.' Robert signalled his horse to move off in the direction of the house, the way the other man had ridden.

Jess walked off in the opposite direction, back to her work. She had almost reached Rose when the sound of horse's hooves pounding on the hard earth made everyone in the hop garden stop and look round.

'You. You there. You never told me. What's your name?' Robert called to her from the end of the row.

'Jess. Jessie Fairleigh.'

'Later then, Jessie Fairleigh.' The man spurred the chestnut horse and was gone.

Rose looked along the row at the gawping faces of her neighbours. She started plucking the hops from the stems more quickly than Jess had ever seen.

'That was the farmer's son, Robert Worlington, wasn't it?' Rose said flatly, throwing the stripped bine to the ground.

'Yeh, I think so,' said Jess. She half-heartedly plucked at the hop cones, her attention still on the man on the big chestnut horse. ''E seemed all right. Nice. 'E said 'e'd show me 'is puppies.'

Rose exhaled loudly. 'We'd better 'ave that little talk sooner than I reckoned, me gel,' she said. 'Tonight.'

'Are yer upset with me or somethin', Mum?' said Jess, sounding surprised.

'It don't matter,' snapped Rose. 'I'm too busy to chat. Now go and 'elp Mabel.'

'I thought I was gonna 'ave me own bin.'

'That's what I…' began Florrie.

'I don't 'ave to tell yer twice do I, Jess?' Rose stared down into the bin, not trusting herself even to look at Florrie. 'Now do as yer told. Go and 'elp Mabel, will yer.'

'Yeh, sorry, Mum. Course I will.'

–

Robert cantered up to his brother and checked his horse to a walk. They rode in silence until Paul eventually spoke.

'Julia said she wanted to ride this afternoon, Robert. Said she'd like to see the rest of the estate.'

'I won't have time for Julia, I'm afraid. I'm far too busy.'

'Too selfish you mean, Robert. The poor girl's all alone now her parents have gone back.'

'If you're so concerned, little brother, why don't you take her out?'

'If you like, but she is your fiancée.' Paul could hardly believe his luck; an afternoon alone with Julia and with Robert's permission. He did his best to hide his delight. 'What's so urgent anyway?'

'I'm going to be busy following Father's instructions,' said Robert, speeding up to a trot. 'In fact, you'd actually be doing me a favour if you would entertain Julia.'

'What instructions?' Paul frowned. What was going on? Perhaps things weren't so simple after all; he certainly knew better than to trust his big brother. 'Father was still sleeping

71

off last night's port when we came out this morning,' he said warily. 'He couldn't have given you any instructions.'

'No, you're right, Paul. He didn't leave any. Not this morning, anyway. It was last night. Remember? Or were you as drunk as Father?'

Paul snorted in reply.

'He told me to leave Garnett's daughter alone. Yes? Told me to get myself a hopping girl?' Robert dug his heels into his horse's side and surged forward into an extended gallop, leaving his brother far behind. 'Well, I think I've found one,' he shouted back into the wind.

–

The women had finished their day's work in the fields and were now chatting and laughing as they sat outside their huts, chopping vegetables and stirring pots, getting food ready for their evening meals.

'Way yer talked to that measurer, Rose,' said Elsie. 'I couldn't believe it was you.'

'I never said nothin' that wasn't the truth,' said Rose.

'Well, yer've got some guts, and that's the truth an' all. I was proud of yer.'

'Someone 'ad to say it, Elsie,' said Rose. ''E's always been a real demon for doin' us out of the full measure, that one. I thought it best to clear the air while the bailiff was around, that's all.'

'Yer right, Rose,' agreed Elsie. 'Mr Audley's not soft but at least 'e's fair. 'E'd never do us out of nothin'. Not like that bloody Feobald or whatever 'e calls 'imself. Feobald! What sort of a bleed'n' name's that when it's at 'ome?'

The talk continued as the women stirred and chopped, scraped and boiled, making the few ingredients stretch to feed their families. There was not much meat in evidence in the women's pots, but they all had their own ways of making a dinner out of what they did have. They scraped out the insides of marrowbones, collecting the fat to make suet puddings. Then the bones could be boiled and the fat skimmed from the top of the water. When it was cold it would set into creamy white dripping with rich brown jelly 'bottoms'. They still had use for the marrowbones; they were boiled up again and the water was used as stock, a tasty base for vegetable soup.

'Seen me boys, anyone?' asked Florrie as she threw sliced onions and potatoes into her pot. 'They need more eyes watchin' them than I've got. Drive me blinkin' barmy, them twins. All day long they're on the go. 'Ere, there and every-where. In and out of everythin'.'

'They went off with the gels,' said Elsie. She was sitting on the grass by her fire, sucking on her pipe and idly stirring the stew that bubbled away in her pot. 'They went to get a few apples to bake in the ashes.'

'I 'ope my Jess ain't gone with 'em if they're scrumpin',' said Rose, looking up from her chores. 'The Fairleighs 'ave never 'ad the name of thievin', an' never will if I 'ave anythin' to do with it.'

''Old yer 'air on, Rose,' said Elsie. 'They're after windfalls, that's all.'

'So long as that is all. I was disgusted enough when Worlington asked us for that two-bob deposit. We don't want 'im chargin' us even more next year to cover what's been nicked from 'is orchards. I don't want my Jess involved in nothin' like that.'

'D'yer really think 'e might charge more deposit, Rose?' Mabel sounded worried. 'I know we get it back after, but I wouldn't be able to find it in the first place if 'e put it up.' She patted her fretful baby as it snivelled into her skinny shoulder. 'If 'e does charge more I wouldn't be able to come, and that's that.'

'Course yer would, Mabel,' said Elsie loudly. 'We wouldn't 'ave yer stayin' 'ome at 'opping time, would we, gels?' Elsie addressed her neighbours, but she continued before they had a chance to reply. 'Mind yer, we could all go to Fanshawe's if 'e starts gettin' too saucy with 'is deposits an' that.'

'Yer'd be by yerself if yer went there,' said Florrie, butting in. 'Soapy load of buggers they are. Ain't never 'ad a wash most of 'em. Never even seen a bar of Sunlight. From south London, see? Not like us East Enders. Once yer gets south of the river, London ain't the same.'

'Oh! Hark hat her highness. Reckons 'ow she's better than the south Londoners,' jeered Elsie in a mock-posh voice. 'Tell yer what, yer could go down Uncle's an' pawn one hof yer tiaras from the crown jewels, me lady. Then we could hall come down 'ere no matter 'ow big the bleed'n' deposit was!'

'I bet Uncle misses us lot from Burton Street going down there with our bits an' pieces,' said Rose.

'I don't think Feldman depends on our couple of bob for 'is livin',' said Florrie nastily. 'Got 'undreds 'idden away, I've 'eard. Money's nothin' to the likes of 'im.'

'No, Florrie, yer wrong there. What Rose said's right,' said Elsie. 'You add all our two an' three bobs up an' yer've got a good few pound.'

'I dunno about that,' said Florrie, 'What I know I ain't never seen a poor pawnbroker. An' I bet none of you lot 'ave neither. That upstairs room of 'is, I bet it's' with gear.' She paused for breath. 'An' them Neaveses round Chris Street, they're rollin' in it, an' all. I've 'eard tell that they...'

'Aw look. 'Ere comes the kids,' said Elsie, managing to interrupt what threatened to become one of Florrie's marathon discourses on the ways of the world. 'Looks like they've found plenty of apples an' all. The girls 'ave got their aprons full of 'em.'

'I 'ope yer found them under the trees an' not still on the branches, Jess,' said Rose, leaving her cooking and walking over to her daughter. She wanted to know what was going on. 'Yer ain't been scrumpin', I 'ope.'

'What, Mum?'

'The apples, dopey. Blimey, yer in a dream.'

'She's thinkin' about Jacky boy,' teased Albert. ''Oo loves Jacko Barnes then?'

'The farmer's boy, more like,' chanted his twin. 'That's 'oo she loves. She loves the farmer's boy. Rode right by us again in the orchards, 'e did. Kept starin' at 'er. Like this, 'e went. All soppy.' Sid fluttered his lashes coquettishly. 'An' never said nothin' about us bein' there neither. Not a word.'

'You shut up, Sidney, an' you, Albert. Stop gettin' busy, the pair of yer,' said Lil, shoving the nearer twin with her elbow. 'Come on, Jess, Win, 'elp me dig the worms out of these apples.' Lil looked over at her mum who was still sprawled happily on the grass, half-heartedly attending to the cooking. 'They're better'n the specky ones they give yer down the market, Mum, but there's still plenty of crawlies in 'em.'

The three girls went and sat outside the Dorkins' hut and set about cleaning the windfalls.

Rose shook her head in disbelief and addressed no one in particular. 'To think a little while ago I was worried I'd never get 'er settled an' off me 'ands. 'Ad no interest in boys, she didn't. Now she's got them round 'er like flies.'

'Least she ain't like that tart from 'Awerley Street,' said Florrie, gesturing with a sideways nod along the Common. 'Yer know the gel. The family's in the last 'ut on the end. Right little madam. No better than she ought to be, that one. She'll wind up with a red 'at an' no drawers, mark my word. I never would 'ave dreamt of behavin' like that when I was a girl. Never allowed to, anyway. An' I knew what was right from wrong.'

'For Gawd's sake leave the gels alone,' Elsie Dorkin said, surprising everyone with her sudden animation as she dashed her spoon into her pot. 'Blimey, don't yer remember when yer was young yerselves? They're only gonna be young once. 'Ow can yer begrudge 'em a bit of a laugh? Won't be long before it's a baby a year an' their old man off down the pub every night. Thinkin' 'emselves lucky if 'e's too drunk to bother 'em for a bit of the other when 'e gets back 'ome. Washin', scrubbin', doin' what yer can to feed yer kids an' flightin' off the bloody rats an' bugs all the time. Why don't yer let 'em alone. Let 'em 'ave a laugh an' a few dreams.'

'Elsie's right,' said Mabel, looking at Rose with her deep-set, sad eyes. 'It won't last long.'

Chapter 6

A Bit of a Lark

'Sammy. Sam, wake up. Sam, what's that noise?' Ted shook his big brother, trying to rouse him.

'What? What's the matter?' Sammy sat up in the single bed that stood next to the double bed shared by his two younger brothers.

'Listen,' Ted whispered. The noise came again. Not quite a rattle and not really a scratching. 'I thought it was rats, but it ain't, it's out there.' He looked towards the small, curtained window from the safety of his brother's side.

'I know what that is,' fumed Sammy.

He threw back the grey wool blanket and straightened the baggy crotch of his dingy long-johns. Then he climbed first across his own bed, then his brothers' bed, the only route in the crowded little room, to the window. He pulled the threadbare material back from the glass and forced up the window on its sash.

'What the bleed'n' 'ell do yer think yer doin' down there?'

Down below in the street stood Jack, just about to throw another handle of stones at the bedroom window. 'Tryin' to wake you lot up,' he shouted. 'Yer'll be late for work if yer don't move yerselves.'

'An' what business is that of yours?' demanded Sam. 'Yer nosy bleeder. Bugger off an' leave us alone.'

'Shut up, you mob out there,' shouted a disembodied voice from somewhere along Burton Street. 'People are tryin' to sleep.'

'Me an' all, moosh, if I 'ad the chance,' replied Sam, leaning over the windowsill in the general direction of the complaint.

'Now yer listen to me, Sammy.' Jack lowered his voice but he couldn't conceal the anger behind his words. 'I promised Rose I'd keep an eye on the three of yer. Come on, get up. Don't mess about.'

'I'm up, Jack,' called Ted from the bedroom. 'I'm gettin' ready right now.'

'It ain't you I'm worried about, Ted, it's yer big brothers what need lookin' after.'

'Who's that 'ollerin' out there?' Charlie was awake now. He yawned luxuriously, stretching like a cat.

'It's Jack, Charlie. 'E's out in the street 'avin' a row with our Sammy in 'ere.'

'Gawd 'elp us, it's like a soddin' mad'ouse round 'ere. I'm goin' back to sleep.' Good as his word, Charlie turned on to his side and pulled the covers back over his head.

And so it became a morning routine: Sammy cursing Jack through the open window, Charlie burying himself under the blankets and Ted rushing around getting himself ready for work. And the neighbours adding their two penn'orth of complaints at all the row.

Eventually Sammy and Ted would leave the house and Charlie would stay in bed. Jack wasn't too unhappy; two out of three getting to work wasn't bad, and nobody had ever been able to do much with Charlie anyway.

In the evenings Sammy and Ted would walk home from the woodyard eating trotters and pease pudding, or fish and chips, or saveloys and mash from thick cones of newspaper.

They would make a cup of tea when they got in, and then plan their evening's entertainment. The beginning of the week had been a real laugh. They had been to the music hall to see the turns, and the picture palace, and even to Premierland to see the fights, but by Wednesday they had run out of money.

'What we gonna do, Sam? 'Ow we gonna get anythin' to eat?' Ted was scared. His mum had always been there to sort out things like food. His insides rumbled. 'I'm a growin' boy, me, I need me grub.' His voice sounded pathetic.

'I dunno, Ted. I never realised we was spendin' so much.' Sammy sat at the once scrubbed kitchen table that was now ringed with tea stains and sliced the last of the stale loaf in two.

'Ain't there even no drippin'?' Ted couldn't believe it had come to dry bread and tea with no milk. 'I'm starvin', Sam. I'll die, I will. An' then yer'll cop it from Mum, an' good job an' all.'

''Oo's starvin'?' Charlie swaggered into the kitchen, cap pulled well down over one eye, white stock tied neatly at his throat. It was the first time either of his brothers had seen him in two days.

'I am, Charlie. Proper starvin'. We ain't 'ad no tea. An' I've been at work all day an' all. I'm really 'ungry.' Ted gripped his guts and rolled his eyes. 'I think I'll pass out soon, honest.'

'Well, young 'un, we can't 'ave yer workin' on an empty Derby Kelly, now can we?' Charlie put his hand in his pocket and threw a handful of silver on to the table in front of his disbelieving brothers.

'Blimey, Charlie, what yer done? Robbed a bank?' Ted was impressed.

'Never yer mind,' said Charlie, winking at his little brother. 'Just get yerself up the corner and fetch the three of us some nice fish and taters. Plenty of cracklin' an' onion vinegar on mine.'

Ted, eyes like saucers at the thought of all that lovely grub, gathered up the coins enthusiastically.

'An' fetch a couple of quarts of mild from The Star an' all. Now go on, I wanna talk to Sammy.'

Sammy listened for the front door to close, then leaned across the table to his brother. 'What's all this about, Charlie? Where'd yer get that money from? Yer in trouble again?'

'I got meself a job,' said Charlie, rocking the wooden chair on its back legs.

'What d'yer mean? Yer've already got a job.'

'I don't mean down that poxy woodyard,' sneered Charlie. 'That's a load of shit if yer ask me. I mean a real job, with real money.'

'What's goin' on, Charlie?' Sammy was concerned that something dangerous was happening, and that he might somehow become involved. Sammy had never had the courage nor the brains of his younger brother, and it didn't worry him at all, not one little bit. He was a coward and proud of it.

'I went down Pennyfields…'

'Yer've been down Chinatown?' Sammy's eyes were on stalks. 'Mum'll kill yer if she finds out yer've been down there. Yer know what she told us.'

'So 'oo's gonna tell 'er then? You? Now, do yer wanna listen or not?'

When he was satisfied that Sammy would keep quiet, Charlie continued.

'Some bloke come up to me an' said 'e'd 'eard 'ow I could fight. So I said to 'im, "Aw yeh. 'Oo says?" An' 'e said it was none of my business, but if I could fight then 'e could offer me an interestin' business proposition. That's what 'e said, Sam, "an interesting business proposition".'

'What yer got yerself involved in, Charlie? It's a different world down there. It ain't for the likes of us.'

'Aw, leave off, Sam, it was a bit of a lark, that's all.' Charlie dismissed his big brother's concern with a wave of his hand. 'They was 'aving a bare-knuckle contest, see, down by the dock gates on a bit of waste ground. They wanted someone what could look after 'imself. Well, there was a lot of gamblin' goin' on. A real lot. Yer know what it's like down there, as bad as the spielers in Whitechapel. Worse, if anythin'. Big money, know what I mean? An', as it 'appens, a lot of the money was on yours truly, Charlie Fairleigh.'

Charlie studied his fingernails arrogantly then looked up to check Sammy's reaction to the story so far. He was pleased to see his big brother's mouth was wide open.

'Well, I won, didn't I? Mind yer, I got this for me trouble.' Charlie lifted his cap to display a deeply cut and bruised eye. 'Should 'ave seen the other geezer, though.' He grinned broadly, obviously delighted with his achievements.

'They paid yer then, did they? For gettin' that?'

Sammy screwed up his face, imagining the pain involved in being punched hard enough for it to do that much damage.

'Too right, my son. They certainly did that all right. Paid me an 'ole 'alf a guinea, if yer must know. Not bad for a nineteen-year-old, eh?' He winked at Sam. 'But that ain't all. This bloke I told yer about, 'e only wants to enter me for a fight at Premierland, don't 'e.'

Sammy didn't need to utter a word: his boggle-eyed expression said it all.

'Fifteen bob I'll get, whether I win or lose.'

'No!'

'Truth. But first I've got another bare-knuckle fight down Chinatown. In some private club where all the *big* gamblers go for a bit of the real action.'

'When's this fight gonna 'appen then?' Sammy was horrified, yet intrigued.

'Tomorrow. Yer comin' to cheer me on?'

'Couldn't if I wanted to, Charlie.' Sammy shrugged. 'No money.'

'Don't yer worry yerself about that, Sammy. 'Ere yer are.' Charlie took the rest of the coins from his pocket and handed them over to his big brother. 'An' there'll be plenty more where that came from an' all, my son. Now, where's that Ted? I'm starvin'.'

The next morning Jack didn't have the chance to throw any stones up at the boys' bedroom window. Before he had even collected his first handful, Charlie and Ted had opened the street door.

'Charlie?' said Jack, stepping back into the gutter at the shock of seeing them up so bright and early. 'What yer doing 'ere?'

'I live 'ere, Jacko, didn't yer know? An' I thought yer was meant to be a postman an' all.'

'Very funny.' Jack chose to ignore Charlie's teasing use of his old nickname. He stepped up to the street door and peered along the shadowy passage; he wasn't sure what he was looking for, but something was bound to be wrong. 'I ain't seen much of yer round 'ere lately, that's all,' Jack said, squinting into the darkness.

'No, well I've 'ad a bit of business to attend to, ain't I?' Charlie sniffed loudly, savouring the early autumn air. 'Now, if yer'll excuse me.'

With that, Charlie pushed past the astonished postman and ran off down the cobbled street, wearing nothing but a pair of baggy knee-length shorts and a greying, holey vest.

'Our Charlie's in trainin' see, Jack. 'E's fightin' in Chinatown, an' I'm gonna see 'im. An' guess what? 'E's only gonna fight at Premierland, ain't 'e? That's all. What do yer think of that then?'

Jack wasn't given the opportunity to comment on these amazing revelations. Sammy had appeared on the narrow stairs. His voice was tight.

'Ted, get in 'ere. I thought Charlie said yer wasn't to tell no one.'

'It's all right, Sam. It's only Jack.'

'Well, now yer've gone an' done it, Ted. 'E'll go and tell...'

Before Sam could finish, Jack had walked along the passage and into the kitchen. Sammy hurriedly followed him, taking the opportunity to swipe Ted a quick fourpenny one round the back of his head as he squeezed past.

''Oo will I tell, Sam? Rose?' Jack had settled himself at the table. 'That what yer worried about? Yer meant to be the oldest an' look at yer. Lettin' Ted go down Chinatown and Gawd knows what else.'

'I ain't been down Chinatown, Jack, not yet, but Sammy's takin' me. I'll be all right.'

Sammy's threat of another swipe round the head was not nearly enough to stop his excited little brother from babbling on about the great events.

'Our Charlie's got this big fight tonight an' we're both goin' to see 'im. Good, eh?'

'Thank you, Ted. Thank you very much. Now 'e knows the bloody lot.' Sam was angry. 'Shut up and get out of 'ere, can't yer. Go on, an' get ready for work.'

'No, yer wait 'ere a minute, Ted.' Jack held on to the boy's arm. 'I wanna talk to yer.'

Sam sighed deeply, knowing he was fighting a losing battle. He nodded for his brother to sit down at the table.

'I promised yer mum I'd keep an eye on yer an' I intend doin' just that. For a start, Ted, 'ave you been down the slipper baths yet? Rose said yer was to go once a week.'

'I ain't exactly been down the baths, Jack. But I 'ave 'ad me bath,' he added brightly.

This time it was Sammy who started questioning him. 'Where 'ave yer been then? I give yer the penny Sunday night.'

'I used that to buy the bag of peanuts we 'ad at the flicks.' Ted sounded injured. 'Yer should know, Sammy, you et most of 'em.'

'Yer little sod,' hollered Sammy. 'Yer ain't 'ad yer bath, 'ave yer?'

'I 'ave, Sam.' Ted's face was a picture of hurt innocence. 'I went down the Thames with me mates. We went swimmin' off the stairs down Wappin'.'

Jack shook his head at the bedlam he had come into. 'That's flamin' wonderful, that is. She ain't even been away a fortnight yet an' I'll be goin' down 'opping to tell yer mum yer've been drowned. That'll be 'andsome, that will.'

Ted dropped his head so that his chin nearly touched his chest. Sammy muttered to himself and shoved his chair back so hard it fell over, crashing loudly on to the bare wooden floor.

'I'll make some tea,' he groaned.

Jack lifted Ted's face, squeezing his plump adolescent cheeks, making him look him in the eye. 'Anythin' else yer wanna tell me, Ted? Yer ain't been 'angin' around with none of them gels from Whitechapel like Sammy does, 'ave yer?' Jack let go of the boy's face. 'What the 'ell 'ave I got meself into, lookin' out for you mob?'

''Ello, Jacko boy, yer still 'ere then?' Charlie entered the kitchen, sweating and panting from his exercise. He bounced around the little room, jabbing punches into the air, shadow-boxing his invisible opponent. 'I thought yer was the one what always worried about bein' late for work. This won't do, now will it?'

'Jack reckons I've been 'angin' round with birds, Charlie.' Ted was getting worried. He wondered exactly what Jack was planning to tell his mother.

'The only birds young Ted 'ere's interested in is 'is racin' pigeons. Ain't that right, young 'un? Not like our Sammy one bit, are yer, mate?' Still jigging around the room, Charlie paused to pat his little brother's cheek affectionately. Ted beamed up at him with relief.

'It ain't right, yer know, Charlie.'

'Yer talkin' to me, Jack?' Charlie had stopped skipping around. He was standing very still. He looked at Jack calmly, but he was agitated, they could all see that.

'D'yer want some tea, Chas?' Sammy asked quietly. He held out a cup to his brother, hoping to distract him. Charlie had a real temper on him when he got going.

'Later.' Charlie didn't take his eyes off the postman.

Jack swallowed hard. 'Yeh, Charlie, I was talkin' to yer. I don't reckon yer should be encouragin' Ted to go down that place.'

'I dunno what yer think goes on down there, Jack.' Charlie moved closer to the table where Jack was sitting stock-still, like a rabbit cornered by a terrier. 'But there's a lot of shit talked about Chinatown. They're people, just like you and me. An' jus' the same as anywhere else in this poxy world, there's respectable

85

geezers an' there's dodgy 'uns. An' if yer think I'd let young Ted 'ere get 'urt in any way then yer a bigger fool than I reckoned.' Charlie narrowed his eyes and leant even closer. Jack could feel his breath hot on his cheek as he spoke. 'An' they're just earnin' a livin', makin' a few bob, that's all. Just givin' people what they want.'

'An' yer gonna 'elp 'em do it, are yer?' Jack coughed trying to keep control of his quavering voice. 'Put on a bit of a show for 'em?'

'That's right. Now, as I said earlier, Jack, if yer'll excuse me, I've got business to attend to. An' I thought you 'ad letters to deliver.' Charlie swept out of the room and took the narrow stairs to his bedroom three at a time.

Jack let out a long, relieved sigh. 'I was goin' anyway,' he said. He stood up, scraping his chair noisily back from the table. 'But yer listen to me, Sammy,' he said, pointing a warning finger at the oldest of the Fairleigh brood. 'I'll be round 'ere tonight, directly yer've finished work. An' yer'd better not get no ideas about creepin' off without me.' Jack picked up his sack and swung it on to his shoulder.

'Yer think yer clever now our Charlie ain't 'ere,' said Sammy cockily.

'No, more like stupid to be botherin' with you lot,' he answered bitterly. 'Now, if yer really set on takin' young Ted to Chinatown, then I'm goin' with yer. At least I'll see 'e don't get in no bother that way. Look good, wouldn't it, if 'e wound up in one of them opium dens? Please Rose good and proper that would.' Jack walked out, slamming the door behind him.

'Sammy,' said Ted. 'What's an opium den?'

'Aw, shut up,' said Sam.

Ted had never been into Chinatown before, not right into the tight little maze of streets in which he now found himself. He walked through the twisting byways, staring down the fog-shrouded alleys and into the arches which led to places he couldn't even imagine down by the banks of the Thames. He had often ventured to the edges of the mysterious Oriental quarter when his friends had taunted each other, seeing how far they would dare go, but this time it was different. Ted felt brave. He was with his big brother Sammy and with Jack Barnes. And they were all going to see Charlie – the toughest bloke in Poplar, Ted reckoned – have a fight in some secret club. This wasn't scary, not really, this was more like an adventure.

Nearly every house they passed seemed to be involved in running a business of some kind out of its overflowing rooms. Over the doorways brightly painted silk banners fluttered, each one covered in strange symbols picked out in gold. Everywhere there were pictures of dragons and mountains, birds and trees, serpents and monsters, all illuminated by guttering lamps and candles. Pungent scents from open windows mingled with the musty smell of damp. Ted's senses were filled as he walked along wide-eyed and open-mouthed.

Boys of about his own age, with his same adolescent energy, ran through the streets shouting words to each other that Ted couldn't understand. They were dressed in a way that Ted had only glimpsed before. Now he saw them close up he could see they were wearing tight leggings and high-necked tunics, and, on their heads, little hats with tassels dangling down behind.

The older Chinese men moved much more slowly along the narrow, bustling streets. Their hands were tucked inside the wide, flowing sleeves of their richly coloured floor-length satin robes. They wore their hair in long pigtails and had even longer beards. Several times Ted was so preoccupied with the wonders which surrounded him that he knocked into the exotically garbed strangers and was admonished by them in their unfamiliar tongue. But nothing could put him off staring. Every few yards there was some new thing at which to marvel.

Sammy was not so delighted with the experience. 'I can't see many gels about, Jack,' he complained.

'They 'ave different ways, I suppose,' said Jack, shrugging. 'Perhaps they don't go about the streets by 'emselves. Anyway, yer should be worryin' about yer little brother for a change, not thinkin' about gels.'

'Aw, shut up, Jack,' scowled Sammy. 'Yer don't 'alf go on all the time.'

Jack shook his head in despair. Not for the first time he wondered how Sammy and Charlie could possibly come from the same family as Jessie and Rose.

'Look, Sam,' shouted Ted, bouncing around in front of his brother. 'Look, there's our Charlie. Look, Jack, over there 'e is. That must be the club. Come on.'

Ted ran off across the street, dodging in between the slowly moving locals. ''Ello, Charlie,' he said, breathless with exertion and excitement. 'We've come to see yer fight.'

''Ello, little 'un. Come to bring me luck, 'ave yer?' Charlie ruffled Ted's hair affectionately. 'Blimey, 'oo's this yer've brought with yer? 'Ow on earth d'yer get Jacky boy down 'ere?'

'Don't get no wrong ideas, Charlie. I'm 'ere for yer mum's sake, that's all.'

Sam strolled nonchalantly over to join his brothers in the sombrely lit doorway of the narrow terraced house. ''Ello, Charlie, mate. This the place then? Looks a bit poky to me.'

'Don't be 'orrible, Sam,' said Ted. 'I think it looks smashin', Charlie.'

'When's this fight supposed to start, then?' asked Sam, looking past Charlie into the hallway of the house. 'I don't want to 'ang around 'ere all night, yer know. I've got better things to do with me time.'

'Well, I wouldn't wanna keep yer 'ere an' disappoint all the gels in Poplar, Sam,' said Charlie sarcastically. 'I know what important work it is, thrillin' the gels. But it won't start 'til they've finished their game of Puck-A-Poo in there. An' don't ask, cos I don't know when that'll be.' Charlie became more serious, dropping his voice to a whisper. 'Honest, though, Sam, I've never seen gamblin' like it. Yer should see 'em. They don't stop. An' the money they lay out.' He shook his head in wonder at the amounts he had witnessed being exchanged.

Ted had his forehead pressed against one of the windows, and was shielding his eyes with his hands, trying to see into the dark interior of the little house.

'What are them men doin' layin' about on them beds, Charlie?'

'Come away, Ted,' said Jack. 'That's nothin' to do with us.'

''E'll 'ave to grow up some time, Jacko,' said Charlie. He folded his strong arms and leant against the doorway. 'They're smokin' opium pipes, son. The "Palace of Dreams" they calls that room. But don't see why they do it meself. Loungin' about for hours smokin' them pipes. Then they just goes off to sleep. Seems a waste of time an' money to me. But they seem to like it.'

'Cor,' was Ted's only response.

Charlie shoved himself upright and began sparring and jabbing the air. 'I like somethin' a bit more active meself.'

'Me an' all!' Sammy whistled loudly. 'Now, these are what I call gels.'

Sammy was always easily distracted by any possibility of female company, but the beauty of the two young Oriental women who were approaching the house was more than even he could have hoped for. Their thick black hair dropped straight to their shoulders, which were covered in feminine versions of the satin robes worn by the older Chinese men. Their eyes were highlighted by delicately painted lines, accentuating their exotic allure.

'Where yer off to then, darlin's?'

The women glided past as though Sammy hadn't spoken, as though he didn't even exist, and disappeared into the hallway of the house.

'Yer did well there, Sam,' laughed Ted.

'It's obvious, innit,' Sam said. 'They've come along to see the fight, or play that Puck-A-Poo game. Charlie said these Chinese are always gamblin'.'

'I don't think so,' said Charlie, laughing at his brother's feeble attempts to explain his failure. 'Those girls work 'ere, Sam. I reckon they thought yer couldn't afford their prices. They 'ave to make their livin', if yer know what I mean.'

Jack knew exactly what he meant; the docks were a notorious red-light district, serving newly paid incoming seamen with whatever they desired.

'Do yer really think this is the sort of place for young Ted to be 'angin' around, Charlie? What yer get up to is yer own affair, but Ted's different. 'E's only a kid.'

'We've 'ad all this before, Jacko. I told yer, don't worry so much. They ain't all villains round 'ere, nowhat people say.' Charlie put his arm round Ted's shoulders. 'An' Ted wouldn't come to no 'arm even if they was. Not while I'm 'ere to look after 'im, 'e wouldn't. Ain't that right, little 'un?'

Ted looked up at his brother. He was not really sure what was going on between the others, and he didn't care much anyway. It was all too exciting to start fretting.

Sammy was even less happy than Jack, and was beginning to wonder if he wouldn't be better off going home instead of wasting his time standing round dark streets while all the fun happened behind doors which were closed to him and his empty pockets.

'Charles. We're ready for you.' An elegantly dressed yet sinister-looking Englishman beckoned to Charlie with his silver-topped cane. Charlie stepped into the hallway. The man had a jagged scar linking the edge of his left eye to the corner of his mouth; it made him look as though he was always about to smile, but never quite fulfilled the promise.

'Me brothers 'ave come to watch me. That be all right, will it?' asked Charlie respectfully.

'As long as they don't get in the way, and they don't interfere. Yes. But they behave. Do you understand?'

'I understand.' Charlie turned to Sammy, Ted and Jack, who were still waiting outside. 'Yer 'eard what the gentleman said, an' 'e meant it. Yer be'ave yerselves.' Then he walked ahead with the man. 'Follow me, an' keep quiet,' Charlie said to them over his shoulder, touching his finger to his lips.

The narrow passageway, lit by red-shaded gas lamps, was thick with strange-smelling smoke. They walked past rooms with closed doors from which they heard muffled sounds and cries; then down two flights of stairs past other rooms with open doors, where they saw tense huddles of men throwing dice and flicking cards.

From the street the terrace had been left to look like a row of separate dwellings. To outsiders it looked as though they were entering a small two-storey house, but inside, all the houses in the terrace had been joined to form a complex of rooms and stairways running the whole length of the street.

'Blimey.' Even Jack had to admit he was amazed. 'Who'd 'ave expected this, eh, Sam? It's like another world in 'ere,' he whispered.

The most amazing sight of all awaited them behind the final door, through which they were ushered before Charlie and his companion left them. When the door was opened, they found themselves in a huge, noisy arena. The cellars of all the houses in the terrace had been joined up to make one enormous windowless, low-ceilinged, flagstoned space. The central area was quite bare apart from a roughly chalked circle, but around the walls of the flare-lit room stood a double row of chairs. The seats were nearly all occupied by groups of men talking animatedly to each other. They were mainly Chinese, although there were a few who looked English, and they all seemed to be dressed in clothes even more expensive than those worn by the scarred man who had led them down there. Behind the chairs stood raucous gangs of sailors wearing the uniforms of navies from all round the world.

'The ships in the docks must be empty,' hissed Sammy. 'All the seamen are down 'ere.' He lifted an empty chair to one side, making a path to the back of the room. 'Get round there, you two, and we can lean against the wall, be out of the way.'

Ted, Sammy and Jack slipped behind the rows of chairs and positioned themselves in the corner beneath one of the blazing torches which illuminated the room. The flames added to the already almost unbearable heat. The atmosphere was tense and thick, a mixture of anticipation, unfamiliar smells and sweat. Young Chinese lads, dressed in the pyjama-like outfits they had seen the boys wearing in the street, rushed around collecting money from the crowd. They scratched signs on small, hand-held slates and did dazzlingly rapid calculations on wooden framed abacuses. Suddenly all the noise and activity stopped. The room was silent. The boy bet-collectors sped away up the stairs.

The scarred man walked into the open space in the centre of the room. He was followed by Charlie and the other competitor. His opponent was slightly shorter than Charlie, with olive skin and dark, curly hair. He could have been any age between sixteen and thirty. The adversaries were dressed alike in ankle-length cotton underpants. Their hair was oiled back, their feet bare; the flickering torches made their skin shine as though their bodies had been burnished.

Charlie's brothers and Jack were surprised when the scarred man started speaking in the same language as the Chinese men. Those who could understand him obviously approved of what he was saying, for they roared their appreciation several times during his speech, clapping and laughing with pleasure.

'Wonder what 'e's on about, Sam?' said Ted.

'Sssh, just watch,' he replied.

Then the man spoke in English. 'Tonight we have two new fighters for your entertainment. A local boy, Charles Fairleigh from Poplar.' A few cheers came from around the room. 'And Miguel Lopez all the way from,' he paused for effect, 'the docks! Because he's just jumped ship.'

The English-speaking members of the audience burst out laughing at the joke, glad of even such a slight relief from the tense mood that had been building steadily in the stifling room. Most of them looked as tough as any other men who had business in this part of the docks, but unless they were Chinese they were in alien territory, and they knew it.

'I will keep you no longer,' the man concluded, 'as I know you all have money at stake. The rules are – as usual – the one who doesn't get up loses.'

As the man stepped out of the chalked circle Charlie gave a cheeky wave to the audience. He was still grinning at his brothers when Lopez aimed a flying kick to his guts. The crowd went wild. Everybody stood up and screamed and bayed for more as Charlie fell sideways to the ground and rolled over twice, almost crashing into the front row of the audience who ducked smartly out of the way. He turned, using the impetus of the roll to spring forward and grab Lopez round the calves, bringing him down flat on his back. The shocking, dull thud of Lopez's head hitting the flagstones could be heard even above the roaring mob. Charlie threw himself across Lopez and started smashing his fist against the jaw and cheekbones of his dazed opponent. The battered man's blood spattered high into the air, splashing against Charlie's bare chest and mingling with his sweat, running down his flesh in thickening rivulets. The crowd clamoured for more. They wanted Lopez to stand up, to fight back, to carry on.

Suddenly a voice called out Charlie's name from behind where Jack was standing. It was loud and demanding. Charlie looked round. That was the chance Lopez needed; with an extraordinary gathering of effort he arched his back and threw his head forward, butting Charlie directly on the eye he had injured in his last fight. The wound opened up like a mouth. Charlie's blood poured down to mix with his opponent's. This was more like it. The pack loved it.

Both men were now standing, circling each other slowly, trying to control their breathing.

'Look at Charlie's eye, Sam. Will 'e be all right?' Ted murmured.

It was Jack who answered him. 'It looks worse than it is, I reckon. Bleeds easy that part of yer face. Do yer wanna leave, Ted? I know I've 'ad enough.'

'No one leaves until the fight's over,' said the voice which had earlier distracted Charlie by calling his name. It was the scarred man who had introduced the contest. 'Understand?'

'You called 'is name deliberately,' said Jack, turning to face him, 'so that geezer could get 'im.'

'I'm in the entertainment business, young man.'

Before Jack could reply, or even think of a suitable answer, the noise in the room rose to an animal bellowing. The men were punching and kicking at each other again. Despite his horror at the brutality of what he was witnessing Jack did not look away. He could not. He was like the rest of them, excited and aroused at the barbarity, by the smell and sight of the blood.

The fight continued for an amazingly long time. The bruised and bleeding men fell time and time again, seeming to have lost the will to stand, but then one of them would somehow find the energy or the anger to strike out and the shattering blows would hit battered flesh once more. The action became slower and slower. The men, half blinded by the blood and sweat running into their eyes, made contact less often. Then, unexpectedly, with a short, sharp jab, Charlie rammed his fist, just once, full into Lopez's kidney. As Charlie's raw knuckles made contact, Lopez lurched forward, spewed a stream of vomit and blood across the men who were cheering for his fall, and collapsed to the ground. The contest was over.

Lopez was dragged unceremoniously to one side by his ankles while the scarred man walked over to Charlie and held his hand high in the air.

'Gentlemen. Our new champion. Charles Fairleigh of Poplar.'

Charlie was surrounded by men congratulating him, pushing each other away to get close to the man who, for the moment at least, was the centre of their interest, the winner of their bets.

'Did yer 'ear that, Jack? 'E called our Charlie a champion.' Ted was strutting with pride like a bantam cock. His brother was a hero.

'I never even 'ad a bet on 'im,' Sammy said furiously. ''E might 'ave told us 'e was gonna win.'

'I 'ardly think 'e knew what was gonna 'appen, Sam,' said Jack wearily.

'Course 'e did,' Sammy said, convinced at the injustice. 'They only put on all that show for the crowd.

Didn't yer see 'em. Loved it, they did.'

'Yer amaze me, Sammy, yer really do.' Jack rolled his eyes heavenwards. 'Yer own brother's nearly 'ad 'is block knocked off an' yer think it's all a game.'

'Well, it's like Charlie says 'imself,' said Sam, puffing out his chest. 'It's only a bit of a lark, ain't it. Yer worry yerself too much, Jacko, my son. Us Fairleighs know 'ow to look after ourselves.'

Jack didn't bother to answer him.

Charlie had elbowed his way through the applauding men to find his brothers and Jack Barnes.

'What do yer think of yer big brother then?' he asked Ted.

'I think yer great, Charlie. Honest, I'm really proud of yer. Wait till I tell all me mates. Me brother's the Champ an' that's a fact.'

Charlie's eye had swollen closed so he didn't notice the scarred man come to stand next to him.

'Your money, Charles.' The cultured, authoritative voice immediately got Charlie's attention.

'Thanks very much, that's good that is. Good. Look at this, Ted.' Charlie held out his bloody hand to show his little brother his winnings. 'Supper's on me tonight, young 'un.'

'You did well,' the man said. 'You deserved to win the purse. You have courage, Charles.'

'So yer think I'm good enough to 'ave that fight at Premierland then? I'd love the chance and I wouldn't let yer down.'

'You can forget that, Charles.'

Charlie was stunned; he had worked so hard for his chance and now it was being taken away from him.

'Don't look so distressed, Charles. Fighting at Premierland is small-time. That's for the likes of Lopez there to dream of. You don't want to finish your days with a broken face and a weakened mind. I've got something far more interesting for you, young man. Now come with me, I'd like you to meet someone.'

Charlie leant as close to the man as he dared and asked quietly, 'Can I bring me brothers?'

'Not this time, Charles. Another time maybe.'

'Seems like I'll be seein' you three later.' Charlie smiled at Ted, handed Sammy some money, clicked his tongue as though he were encouraging a reluctant pony, and then walked off to find out about his future.

Charlie's brothers and Jack jostled their way back up to the street.

'Cor, fresh air.' Sammy took a deep lungful of the cool autumn night. 'Like our Charlie said, supper's on 'im.' He spun a shiny coin high into the air. 'Now, what do yer fancy, lads? Pie and mash? Savs? Faggots and pease pudden?'

'I don't care what we 'ave, but put that money away and let's get back up to the East India Dock Road before we get ourselves coshed. We don't belong round 'ere, Sammy, an' we ought to be gettin' young Ted 'ome an' all.'

'Aw, Jack, don't let's go 'ome yet,' groaned Ted. 'I'm all right. Yer'd think I was a bleedin' baby the way yer all go on about me all the time.'

Four burly seamen pushed past Sammy to get into the house where the fight had taken place. The stink of rum fumes floated around them like a cloud.

'I think Jack might be right, Ted. It's gettin' late. Let's get out of Lime'ouse at least.'

'Can we 'ave fish and taters then?'

'What, again?'

Ted grinned appealingly up at his big brother.

'Course we can, son, an' a big juicy wally, an' as much cracklin' as yer can stuff down yerself. 'Ow about that?' Sammy winked broadly. 'Cos it's all on our Charlie tonight. Charlie Fairleigh, the Champ of Burton Street.'

Jack was invited in to share the victor's feast: a fish supper and bottles of India pale ale. It seemed a good idea to join them. He could make sure that Ted got off to bed at a reasonable hour; he had work in the morning, after all. And he wouldn't mind a bit to eat – he wasn't daft enough to think Clara, his mother, would have kept a hot meal waiting for him.

They sat round the table and spread the newspaper wrapping out like a tablecloth. If they had dined off a cloth of the finest Nottingham lace the meal could not have tasted better. The three ate and drank greedily, with grease and beer dripping from their fingers and chins. They talked both between and during mouthfuls about the marvels they had seen, the sounds they had heard and the smells that had filled the air of Chinatown. And about Charlie's fantastic success. Then they drank some more beer, a lot more.

'Listen a minute, Sam, what's that noise?' Ted cocked his head to one side, a handful of chips poised at his lips.

Sammy took another long pull from his quart bottle and lined it up next to the row of empties which already stood next to his chair. He attempted not to slur his reply.

'I can tell yer one thing, Ted,' mumbled Sammy, a stupid grin on his face. 'It ain't Jacky boy tryin' to wake us up with his stone throwin', and that's a fact.'

Sam reached out shakily and thumped the postman hard across the shoulders in what he felt was a suitably comradely gesture. Jack smiled cherubically back at him.

'An' 'ow do I know that, Ted?' Sammy continued. 'Cos ol' Jack is sittin' right 'ere next to me, 'is very best mate in all the world, that's 'ow. Ain't that right, Jacky, old son?'

Jack, who was only slightly less drunk than his newly found best friend, agreed that it wasn't him making all the racket, but that he too could hear the strange noise.

'Tell yer what,' he beamed at Sammy, 'I'll go and see 'oo it is, shall I?'

Jack rose unsteadily to his feet, knocking his chair over on to the kitchen floor, and stumbled tipsily along the passageway to open the street door.

'Blimey,' he shouted from the step, 'come and 'ave a look at this, you two. Yer'll believe it unless yer see it for yerselves.'

They certainly wouldn't have believed it, for there was Charlie, their Charlie, the Champ of Burton Street, paying a cabman. He had come home in a hansom, and he was smoking a cigar.

'Thank you, my good man,' Charlie said, 'an' take this little somethin' for yer trouble.'

He spun round on his heel, stepped under the streetlight and stood perfectly still, waiting for Jack and his brothers to admire his outfit. He wore a dark suit that could almost have been new, a white shirt a stiff, high collar and, to top it off, a bowler hat.

'I dunno what to say, Charlie,' Sammy sighed with respect. 'Look at yer, all cased up.'

'Good, eh?' Charlie flicked the brim of his hat with his finger. 'An' this, chaps, is just the start.'

'Not you lot again. Don't yer ever sleep in that bleed'n' 'ouse?' The unseen protester had been woken yet again by the Fairleighs. He shouted wearily into the night air, 'Yer wait 'til yer old man gets 'ome, that's all. I'll tell 'im such a tale about yer carryings on while 'e's been away. Yer arses'll ache for a week from the beltin' 'e'll give yer.'

'An' yer'll be quite welcome to tell 'im an' all, madam,' mocked Charlie.

From the upstairs window of the house opposite Number 8 a furious elderly man stuck his head out into the street. 'I'll give yer callin' me madam, yer cheeky bugger. Yer can stop yer ol' saucin' as soon as yer like, Charlie Fairleigh, or I'll...'

Before he could finish his threats, the man caught sight of Charlie posing in the glow of the gaslight. Despite himself, the man couldn't help laughing.

'I've gotta 'and it to yer, Charlie Fairleigh. I might 'ave known yer'd be the first one in this street to 'ave a bloody bowler 'at.' The angry neighbour spoke to an unseen person in the bedroom behind him. 'Yer should see the ol' bounce on that Charlie Fairleigh, Maud. Bloody bowler 'at,' he chuckled. But once he had got over the surprise of seeing Charlie in all his sartorial splendour he continued with his warning. 'But I'm tellin' yer. Yer might think yer Jack the lad but if yer don't get in that 'ouse and shut up – now, the lot of yer – I'll be down there to yer with this poker. Now shut up!'

The noise the man made slamming his bedroom window down was greeted with a further chorus of enraged shouts from the houses around him.

'An' yer can be quiet an' all, yer old bleeder,' was one of the politest suggestions as to what he should do.

'I think it's time we went in, lads.' They followed Charlie into the kitchen, eager to learn about this new turn of events.

'So I was introduced to this Mr Chen, see?' Charlie told them, settling himself down at the table.

'One of them ol' geezers in the long frocks?' asked Ted, stuffing the last of the cold chips into his mouth.

'That's right, yeh. Long red robes 'e's got. With all kinds of beautiful patterns and that. An' a pigtail an' everythin'. Mind yer 'e's a right powerful feller, if yer gets me meanin'. They all respect Mr Chen down there, everyone do. Everyone knows about Mr Chen.' Charlie fiddled with the unaccustomed tightness of the stiff collar. 'So anyway, I'm introduced to 'im. I'm the new champion, that sort of thing, yer know. And 'e spoke to me in English, right posh soundin' 'e is an' all. Said as 'ow I 'andled meself well and that 'e might 'ave a job for me.'

'What sort of job?' Jack was concentrating hard now, sobering up rapidly.

'I'd be like an 'elper really. I've just got to be there when 'e wants me to 'elp 'im, see? Make sure there's no trouble.' Charlie took a swig from one of the remaining bottles of pale ale. 'Say when someone't think they should 'ave lost at Puck-A-Poo. I'll be there to straighten things out. An' I'll see things don't get out of order, say if a customer gets a bit rough with Mr Chen's young ladies. See that the blokes pay for their pipes of stuff in the front room. That sort of thing.' Charlie was speaking very casually, but he kept glancing towards Jack, gauging his reactions to the news.

'Yer gonna work for a crook, yer mean,' Jack said.

Charlie paused, just a moment, but long enough to make Jack feel uncomfortable. 'If yer say so, Jack.'

'Don't yer care, Charlie?'

'Why should I?'

'Cos of Rose, that's why.' Jack leant across the table towards Charlie, his voice rising with anger. Sammy and Ted looked at each other. Sammy shrugged. He didn't know what to do. Jack continued, 'She don't even like yer goin' down Chinatown, let alone gettin' involved with filth like Chen or whatever 'e calls 'imself.'

'An' 'oo says 'e's filth?'

'Yer sayin' 'e's straight then, Charlie?'

Ted and Sammy had both turned towards their brother. For a brief moment the room was very quiet and still. Then the shouting started.

'An' what else is there round this dump, eh, Jack? Tell me that,' Charlie demanded. 'Graftin' down that poxy woodyard? Is that what yer think I should do?' He slammed the table with the flat of his hand. 'Slave down there all me life? Work all them hours for 'ardly nothin'? Wind up with no money and with all that dust on me chest, killin' me before I'm thirty? Or go down the brewery like Joey Fuller's ol' man? Yeh! That's a good idea, I could get killed even quicker that way. Or 'ow about goin' down the docks? Line up on the stones every mornin' like cattle, waitin' to get picked for work by some crooked bastard 'oo takes 'alf yer wages for the privilege. Or be like me dad and go off for months on end, stuck on a stinkin' ship miles away from me wife an' kids? Or maybe I should become a postman like you an' never 'ave *no* chance of gettin' out of this dump.

No, Jack. None of that's for me. There ain't many routes out of this 'ole. But I've found one. An' I'm gonna take it.'

'Yer dunno what yer talkin' about, Charlie.' Jack was red-faced and angry, but he also felt ashamed at what Charlie had said.

'Aw yes I do, Jack. Yes I do.' Charlie's lip was curled in contempt. 'It's like our bedroom, see. There's only one way out of there an' that's by climbin' over the others.' He gestured wildly towards his brothers. 'An' that's what I'm gonna do with me life. I'm gonna climb me way out of this dump, right over the others. If you wanna stay round 'ere and rot, yer welcome, but me, I'm goin' places, goin' to the top. No matter what anyone says. An' yer'd all better get used to the idea.'

Chapter 7

Silk

Fresh from his bath, Robert Worlington walked easily down the wide, curving staircase. He hesitated on the bottom stair. He could hear laughter and music coming from the room where the guests were due to gather before dinner. But it was still too early for that. He waited, straining to hear the conversation. He moved forward, then, with a single movement he threw open the double doors and walked in. The laughter stopped immediately. Julia and Paul stood in the middle of the floor, quite still. Their arms were wrapped around each other.

'Good evening, Julia,' said Robert.

'Wonderful dancer, this fiancée of yours,' said Paul. He sounded more relaxed than he looked. He moved his arms awkwardly from around Julia's modishly tiny waist and scratched the side of his head. 'Knows all the latest steps.'

'Good evening, Robert,' said Julia coolly. 'I haven't seen you at all today. I wondered about you.' She turned back to Robert's younger brother and smiled. 'Then Paul found me. He said you have been very busy. Occupied with business on the estate.'

Robert thought he noticed an edge to Julia's voice and decided this was not the moment to question her attitude. 'Yes,' he replied neutrally, 'the estate does take a great deal of my time.'

'So Paul said. He also told me it was on your suggestion that he accompanied me on my ride around the grounds this afternoon. It was delightful.' Julia smiled, keeping her eyes on Paul.

'Right,' said Robert. He was not really listening to Julia; he was far more interested in pouring himself a drink from one of the decanters on the side table. 'Anyone else?' he asked when his glass was full.

'No thanks, Robert,' answered his brother, returning Julia's smile. 'And I've looked after Julia already.'

Paul was amused and delighted to see that his brother was not concerned enough to pick him up on his obviously flirtatious manner with Julia; he was even more delighted to see Julia herself blush delicately and shyly bow her head. He was undoubtedly making quite an impression on Miss Markington and yet his brother was totally unaware of it. Tilnhurst could be boring for a young man like Paul, but with Julia around it might become a deal more interesting. Paul went to tend to the gramophone which had wound down to a slow, drawling whine.

'What do you say?' said Paul, raising his brows in question. 'Shall we have a little more music?'

Before they could answer, Lady Worlington entered the room, followed by her dinner guests.

'Boys. Julia,' she said pleasantly. 'Let me introduce everyone.'

And so another evening at Worlington Hall began. The family and their guests enjoyed an excellent dinner. Then the ladies played bridge and gossiped, while Sir George drank far too much, and the other gentlemen played billiards and put the world to rights, arguing about the various solutions to the Balkan problem and the German threat to British naval supremacy.

Paul's concerns, however, were far closer to home. He very much wanted to talk to Robert about the tall, auburn-haired girl who had so clearly caught his brother's eye, the cockney girl on whom he had evidently set his sights. But, disappointingly for Paul, Robert would not be drawn on the subject; he was momentarily more interested in defending the five guineas which he and the Reverend Henry Batsford had wagered on the outcome of their game of billiards.

Like his younger son, Sir George had had his hopes for the evening dashed. Things were definitely not proceeding as he would have liked. Instead of being left undisturbed to his port and cigars, his simple pleasures had been interrupted by the butler.

'So sorry to disturb you, Sir George,' said Tyler deferentially, 'but I thought you would want to know that Garnett is most anxious to see you.' The butler spoke softly, choosing his words carefully, recognising the signs of drunkenness which so often led to his master losing his unpredictable and violent temper.

'What does the bloody man want now?' shouted Sir George, loudly enough to make his guests wince, some with embarrassment, others with anxiety. His wife ignored him completely and carried on studying her cards.

'I am not sure, Sir George, but he really is most anxious to see you.'

Sir George hesitated for a moment but then thought about his gardens, and the wonders which Garnett worked upon them. He made up his mind to spare him a few moments. He heaved himself up from the winged armchair.

'Well, come on. Where is the bloody man?' he asked resignedly, striding out of the room in front of the butler. 'Haven't got all night, you know.'

Garnett was waiting outside the kitchen entrance to the Hall, nervously rubbing his freshly razored chin. At the approach of Sir George he took his battered felt hat from his head and bit anxiously on his bottom lip.

'This had better be important, Garnett.'

'Yes, Sir George, it is, sir. Very important, sir. I couldn't sleep from worrying about it. That's why I came up to the Hall to speak to you.'

'Get to the point, man.' Sir George intoned each word as though he had already run out of patience.

'It's about my daughter, sir. My Milly.'

Garnett flinched momentarily and stepped back from the blast of port-laden breath. He thought he was about to become the target of Sir George's flying fist, but the thick red knuckles landed harmlessly in the palm of his employer's own hand.

'That damned Robert,' fumed Sir George. 'If he's been hanging around your girl again, so help me, I'll string the little swine up from one of the oast houses. What's he been up to now?'

'It's not so much what he's doing,' Garnett explained, 'so much as what he's already done. If you see what I mean, sir.'

'What, you mean your girl's in foal?' blurted Sir George.

Shocked to hear his daughter described so crudely, it was a moment before Garnett could answer. 'No, Sir George, she's not in the family way.' The gardener paused. 'Least, not as far as me and her mother knows. It ain't that sort of trouble she's having.'

'Is this going to take much longer, Garnett? I have guests waiting for me in there, you know.'

'I'll get to the point then, sir. My Milly is not a happy girl. Ever since the night of the engagement, when she was "found" by all them young gentlemen what was searching for young Master Robert, well, she says she's too ashamed to show her face around here. Won't leave the cottage, she won't. Just moons around all day. Won't do a stroke of work neither. Says she's never going to get wed now everyone knows all about the carryings-on that night. And as how Master Robert...' Garnett looked expectantly at the man who could solve or increase his problems with a simple nod or shake of his head.

'You don't think Robert meant any of those things he said to the girl that night, do you, Garnett? You know what young men are like when they're roused. Promise them all sorts of things.' Sir George laughed lasciviously, forgetting he was addressing the girl's father. 'Did it myself. Still do.' He seemed to be enjoying a private memory that had managed to find its way into his mind through the alcoholic fug.

'No, sir,' Garnett replied coldly, 'I don't think that your son meant any of the things he said. But our Milly does. Or, at least, she half does. To tell you the truth, I'm not sure what she thinks no more. And, well, me and the wife can't have her hanging about the cottage not working, hoping for Master Robert to come and take her away. We can't afford to feed a mouth just for the sake of it, daughter or not. We was hoping as how you could have a word with one of your friends and find her work away from here. She's a good...' He stopped and reconsidered his description of his daughter's attributes. 'She's a willing, hardworking girl. Usually. She wouldn't let no one down, would Milly.' He looked pointedly at his master. 'She's been brought up different to that. But me and Mrs Garnett both think she'll be better off away from here.'

'That it then, Garnett?'

'Yes, Sir George.'

'Right.' He turned on his heel and walked back into the house, leaving the gardener standing alone, unsure whether his problems had been solved or not.

Sir George used the staff entrance, making the servant girls giggle with astonishment and the cook click her tongue in rage at the disruption as their master strode through the steam-filled room.

'Carry on. Carry on,' Sir George barked, gesturing nonspecifically around the kitchen, leaving as suddenly as he had appeared.

Instead of returning to his guests in the games room, however, Sir George first went into the library and rang for Tyler.

'Yes, sir?' Having been forewarned by the cook of Sir George's detour, the butler arrived almost immediately.

'Tell Lady Worlington I want to see her. Now.'

'Very well, sir.'

Accustomed to her husband's unsociable behaviour, particularly after dinner and its accompanying wine, Leonore apologised to her bridge partner, assuring them that she would return as quickly as possible, and left the room for the library. The rustling of her long skirts could not quite hide the whispers which accompanied her exit.

'You wanted to speak to me, George,' she said as she closed the library door behind her.

'Milly Garnett,' he said, as though that was the only explanation required.

'The gardener's daughter. Yes?'

'Find her a position away from that bloody son of yours. Garnett's not happy. I don't want my yew hedges to suffer.'

With that, he stepped around his wife, opened the library door and returned to the billiard room and his port.

'Of course, my dear,' said Leonore to the empty, book-lined room. 'But not because you've asked me. Oh, no, not because of that. I'll do it to get that young woman away from you damned Worlington men.'

—

The next morning, Leonore, accompanied by Julia and their ladies' maids, left for London to spend a week with her cousin Amelia.

During the journey, Leonore was not surprised to discover that her pretty future daughter-in-law's topics of conversation were limited to those they had already exhausted in the drawing room. From the moment they got into the brougham for the journey to the station, Julia chattered and giggled about the froth which filled her head. She spoke about the latest fashions, her new riding habit, her preference for a spring wedding, the bounce of her fair curls. It was to drive Leonore to distraction, but she managed to nod and smile in the appropriate places, whilst never actually engaging in the trivial chatter that Julia seemed able, and happy, to carry on endlessly.

Inwardly Leonore sighed; she was making the journey to London to rescue Milly Garnett from Robert's clutches, and here was this silly, privileged girl offering herself as yet another willing lamb ready for him to slaughter. She had no personal dislike for Julia; rather she was frustrated by the girl's complete lack of interest in anything not to do with her own closed, silly little world. Soon after they had been introduced, Leonore had made tentative enquiries about Julia's interests; she had even asked her thoughts on political affairs. Her questions had been met with either puzzled silences, or Julia's charming but disappointing giggles.

Before they had met, Leonore had hoped that her future daughter-in-law might share some of her own concerns, that it would be like having a daughter at last, an ally against the overwhelmingly male household at Worlington. But it was not to be. Maybe when Paul met someone it would be different. Maybe. She could always hope.

Leonore was not entirely gloomy, however. During the week they would be spending in London, she would take the opportunity not just to ask her cousin Amelia for help with the 'Milly problem', but also to go with her cousin to the place they went whenever they could manage to steal some moments from their usual wifely duties. Leonore was relieved that this time she did not have to go through the tedious motions of inventing yet another feeble excuse for her journey into town. Not that George ever appeared to notice or care about her absences, but her work was too important for her to take even the slightest risk of George discovering the true reason for her increasingly frequent trips to London.

As Julia and the train both went on and on in their monotonously relentless rhythm, Leonore studied the girl's lovely yet vacant face. She remembered how she too had once been blissfully unaware of the realities of the world which surrounded her.

It had been quite by chance that she and Amelia had found Liza lying in the gutter. They had been choosing silks for their new spring gowns and they, like Julia, had been totally absorbed in the vanities of their own comfortable lives as they made their way from shop to exclusive shop. At first Leonore had thought it was a heap of rags which someone had dumped in the street. Then she had seen the pool of blood spreading darkly on the ground. Holding her lace-trimmed handkerchief to her nose, Leonore went closer to the wretched bundle.

'Careful, Leonore,' warned Amelia, 'I think it's a beggar. They carry all manner of diseases.'

Leonore ignored her cousin's cautions and gingerly poked the rags with her parasol, which she held at full arm's length in her gloved hand. The shapeless lump gave a pathetic moan and moved stiffly. The sudden realisation that she was looking into the dull eyes of a child of barely thirteen years old made Leonore gasp with horror.

'For God's sake, Amelia, quick, help me.'

—

By promising him a substantial tip, Amelia finally persuaded a hansom driver to accept them as passengers. Their luck continued. He knew of a place where 'the likes of 'er', as he referred to the child, were welcomed.

He drove them down dirt-strewn thoroughfares and shadowy back alleys populated by huddled, shabbily dressed figures, doing whatever they could to scrape a living from the streets of London. Being unaccustomed to the smells of sick, unwashed flesh, the cousins found the journey in the closed confines of the cab difficult to bear, having the wretched girl slumped miserably between them. The driver seemed to be taking an extraordinarily long time to reach their destination. Eventually they stopped in a side road off the Covent Garden market.

Amelia threw open the cab door with an undisguised exclamation of relief. But once the cousins saw where the driver had actually brought them, they would gladly have remained in the hansom with their malodorous fellow passenger. They were in a place that was so different from the London they knew, they might have been in another world.

The cabman climbed down from his perch and knocked at a small, badly painted wooden door set in a high, blank wall. Two women came out and, without asking any questions, gently lifted the exhausted child from her seat, half carrying, half walking her through the door into the mysterious building.

'What do you think we should do now, Leo?' asked Amelia, keeping her arms close to her sides, as though it would protect her from the surrounding grimness.

Leonore paused for just a moment. 'In for a penny.'

She shrugged her shoulders, paid the cabman his fare and the promised bonus, and led her protesting cousin inside.

–

That afternoon, as they sat in the dingy little office drinking tea from thick, ugly china, the cousins' lives were changed for ever. They learnt from Charlotte, a helper at the hospital-cum-soup-kitchen, that Liza, the girl they had found, was in no way a unique case. She was just another one of the many young prostitutes driven by need and desperation to the probings of the filthy knitting needles and the hot, emetic gin of the backstreet abortionists.

'The lucky ones finish up here with us,' Charlotte said, offering the two astounded women more tea from a large, plain brown pot. 'It doesn't bear thinking what happens to the others.'

'But she's only a child,' protested Leonore, unable to take in the enormity of what she was hearing. 'It isn't possible.'

'In your circles, maybe not,' said Charlotte. 'But where she comes from she's probably been looking after herself since she was a lot younger than she is now. And God knows how many brothers and sisters she has to feed.'

'And you?' said Amelia, unable to conceal her curiosity. 'What circles do you come from that you know so much about these girls?'

'What is a "lady" like me doing in a place like this, do you mean?'

Amelia flushed. 'I did not mean to be impolite. I apologise.'

'No, please, don't be embarrassed,' said Charlotte.

'I realise I seem out of place in these surroundings.' She cast her eyes around the dull, cramped room. 'It's been a strange journey.' She paused, picking nonexistent fluff from her skirt. 'Like several of my friends I became involved with the suffrage movement. Now I'm sure you've both heard all about that.'

'Of course,' said Amelia, glancing anxiously at Leonore from under her lashes.

'Well,' said Charlotte, smiling and relaxing a little for the first time since they had met her. 'Don't believe all you've heard, or read, about us. We are not all crazed monsters.'

Unlike Charlotte, Amelia did not feel at all relaxed. She shifted in her seat, thinking up excuses to leave as quickly as possible.

'Are you saying the newspaper stories about your exploits are untrue?' asked Leonore, more interested than her cousin would have liked.

'What I am saying,' said Charlotte, 'is that the newspapers choose not to tell the whole truth. Rather they offer their own version. The version which suits their own ends. The truth of what things are really like is, thus, so often lost.'

Leonore nodded uncertainly. She was most definitely not convinced by Charlotte, but something about this intriguing young woman's sincerity made her keen to hear more.

Charlotte was happy to continue. 'I have brothers, you see…'

'This is absolutely fascinating,' said Amelia, 'but I really think we should be going. The shops will be closing soon, Leo, and we've so much to do.'

'Please, Amelia, let her finish.'

Charlotte looked at Amelia. Amelia replied with a noncommittal but resigned shrug.

'Thank you,' said Charlotte graciously. 'My brothers. You see, one day they will become powerful men. All of them. They are the sorts of men who will run this country. They will have the power and influence to make decisions which will affect us all. They are no cleverer than I. And no wiser. And they certainly have no greater understanding of what goes on in this capital of ours. But they will have the opportunity to run things. To change things. Maybe for the better, but probably for the worse.' She looked questioningly at Amelia. 'And what is there for me? Marriage, perhaps, to someone just like them?'

'Would that be so bad?' asked Amelia, attending unnecessarily to the fingers of her kid gloves.

'No, maybe not. But it wouldn't be enough,' continued Charlotte passionately. 'I wanted the vote more than I have ever wanted anything in my life. Not that I've ever had to want for anything very much,' she laughed. 'In material terms I have never wanted for anything, in fact. Not personally. But I wanted to have the chance to say how things should be. What is right and wrong in this world of ours. So I became involved with the WSPU. The Suffragettes.'

'Quite,' said Amelia sharply.

Used to such reactions, Charlotte went on with a thin smile. 'One day, at a meeting in the East End, in a tiny room behind a shop, I had the great good fortune to meet Sylvia Pankhurst. A truly amazing woman. It was she who changed my views.'

'Are you saying she is not one of your campaigners?' asked Leonore, clearly engrossed by what she was learning.

'It is not that straightforward,' explained Charlotte.

'Through Sylvia I became involved in the work here. Sylvia's campaigns go far wider than battling for the vote.'

Even Amelia became stirred as Charlotte began to tell the stories of the women and girls who came to the centre. Neither cousin interrupted; they sat quite still and listened to Charlotte's chronicling of the poverty, hardship and cruelties, as she described, all too accurately, the existence endured by the people from the slums.

She told them about the tragically short lives of women worn down by work, childbirth and brutality; of men too weak to earn a crust even if they could find a job; of the criminal path that was, for so many, the only way out. They learnt, that afternoon, about injustice.

They also heard about the people who, like Charlotte, had dedicated their lives to improving the lot of others – no matter who they were, or how they lived – people who offered no moral judgements, just their help and comfort.

At last, Charlotte put down her cup and saucer on the shabby, overcrowded desk.

'You must forgive me,' she said diffidently. 'I do preach rather when I get the chance.' Charlotte need not have worried. She had quite won over both the cousins with her moving words.

Since that first day when they had met Charlotte, their lives had been transformed. With their newfound understanding, they gradually peeled away layer after layer of deceit, unveiling to themselves the inequalities which supported their comfortable lives, unmasking the everyday hypocrisies which tricked privileged ladies such as themselves into thinking that all was well with the world.

The once complacent cousins were now committed to their newly discovered cause of righting injustice. On more than one occasion they wondered how they had once been so blind to what was under their very noses, their fervent, if naive, enthusiasm making them impatient for change. Not only did they work as volunteers at the centre, but Leonore determined to improve the conditions in which the hoppers worked at Worlington Hall and Amelia wanted to rescue all the girls from the streets surrounding her London home.

They both did what they could, but soon realised the strength of opposition to even what they considered the most insignificant of proposals. But it was not until they attended a public suffrage meeting and witnessed the hatred and physical violence directed at the Suffragettes that they fully realised the enormity of the situation in which they had become involved. To see women being struck to the ground with truncheons, simply for stating their beliefs, terrified them. It also made them determined to continue with their part in the struggle.

'I said, do you think it appropriate to wear ivory rather than white silk with my complexion.' Julia's insistent, almost petulant voice pulled Leonore back to the present.

'I am sorry, Julia, I'm afraid I didn't hear you properly. What did you say, my dear?'

Leonore looked from Julia to the soot-streaked train window, and watched the rows of grubby houses pass by. She could imagine the deprived lives of their, ruled by the noise, stench and dirt of the railway. She looked back at Julia and saw she was still talking, her pert, rouged little mouth forming each word into a sulky pout. Leonore closed her eyes – a moment longer than a blink. She sighed. She must keep calm. Amelia would be waiting for them at the station. Then she had the whole week to look forward to. Amelia would help Leonore sort out a position for Milly, and they would share all the latest news about the centre and their work.

Leonore could put up with Julia's nonsense for a bit longer.

–

Rose leaned forward over the bin, bent almost double with the racking cough which convulsed her whole body.

'Mum. Yer all right?' Jess put her arm round her mother's shoulders, trying to still the spasms that were shaking her.

Rose got her breath back at last. 'I'm fine, darlin'. Fine. Yer go back an' 'elp Mabel for a bit.'

'Yer sure I can't do nothin', Mum?'

Jess was worried. It was usual to have a cough for a few days, as the filth and muck from the London smogs cleared out of the hoppers' lungs, but they had been down there for over a week now, and Rose was still coughing. If anything, she sounded worse. It wasn't right.

'Honestly, Jess. Go on. It's a real pleasure seein' Mabel an' the kids perkin' up. Yer go over an' 'elp 'er a bit more.'

'If yer really sure, Mum.'

In an effort to convince Jess she could cope just, Rose stood herself upright and began picking like it was the first day of hopping. She knew that coughs like hers, caused by living in the foul and filthy atmosphere of the East End, got harder to shift as the years went by. And she was no spring chicken any more, even if she didn't like admitting it. Like plenty of other women from her neighbourhood, she'd just have to put up with it. It was no use feeling sorry for herself, there was plenty worse off. Mabel Lawrence for one.

Rose spoke gruffly to her daughter. 'I've told yer enough times, 'aven't I, Jess? Go an' 'elp 'er.'

Reluctant as she was to leave her mother to pick alone, Jess had to agree that it was true what Rose said about Mabel and her children. The four of them were blooming. The combination of clean country air and the diet of fresh eggs and milk, which Winnie's twin brothers seemed to keep 'finding' for the Lawrences, had worked a kind of magic on the family. Even the baby had a bit of colour in its thin, pinched little face.

When the nurse had come round on the second day of picking to inspect them all, Mabel had been terrified that she would be singled out and sent home. No farmer wanted to risk a sick hopper causing an epidemic amongst his pickers and ruining his harvest. Any sign of infection usually meant instant dismissal and being sent back to London without even having the chance to earn the fare home.

Mabel had been lucky. The nurse who had checked her was an elderly woman who knew the difference between the sickness that came from disease and the sickness that was the result of sheer poverty. She had decided to take the risk of giving the Lawrence family the benefit of the doubt, and so Mabel was passed fit for work.

It was Rose who had caused the nurse most concern. While she was queuing outside the little bell tent on the Common, waiting to be examined, it had been agony for her trying to control the coughing the best she could. When her turn came at last she sat down opposite the nurse on a rough wooden stool by a makeshift trestle table.

'Don't want to worry you, my dear,' said the nurse, her big hands folded in her wide lap, 'but has there been any illness in the family recently?'

'What sort of illness?' Rose whispered, anxious that Jess, who was next in line outside the flimsy canvas wall, should not hear.

'Nothing in particular.' The nurse looked into Rose's troubled face for what seemed an eternity. 'It's a nasty cough you've got there, that's all. Bit of a bad chest. Had it long?'

'Ain't as nasty as what some of 'em gets,' said Rose defensively. 'I'll get over it in time. I always do.'

'We're none of us getting any younger, Mrs Fairleigh,' said the nurse, with the best of intentions. 'You should try and get some rest, you know.'

'This *is* me rest, coming down 'opping.'

'I hear that from the hop pickers every year,' said the nurse amiably, shaking her head in wonder. 'But I must admit, it doesn't seem much like a holiday to me.'

Rose found herself smiling at the kindly woman. 'You ain't never 'ad to live in Burton Street,' she said.

The nurse smiled back and patted Rose on the arm.

'I suppose not. Anyway, you'll do, my dear.'

The nurse wrote something on a card, put it away in a cardboard folder and then handed Rose a dark green, tightly corked bottle. 'Pop that in your apron pocket,' she said, 'and see you take a spoon of it a couple of times a day.'

Rose nodded her relieved thanks and went back to work in the hop gardens.

Jess was given a clean bill of health immediately. From the top of her shiny auburn hair to the tips of her firm, agile feet, Jessie glowed with youth and vitality. The nurse had seen so many like her pass through the farm; yet within a few years she hardly recognised as the same girls the coughing, careworn mothers of two or three pallid, undernourished offspring. Life might have been hard sometimes in the Kent countryside, she thought to herself, but it must seem like paradise on earth to these women used to the hardships and squalor of the East End.

'Pull no more bines,' the call that signalled the end of the day's picking echoed through the fields, as the early evening mist began to reach into the hop gardens from the river bank.

''Bout bleed'n' time an' all,' grumbled Elsie, miserably pulling the remaining cones from what she was pleased to know was her last bine of the day. 'I thought the bailiff 'ad forgotten us down 'ere. The bloody damp's soaked right through me boots. Look at 'em.'

'It's been a long ol' day,' agreed Rose, yawning.

'I'll go an' 'elp Mum finish off 'er last few 'ops, Mabel, if yer don't mind.'

'Course I don't, go on. Yer've finished my lot anyway. Ta, Jess.'

Jess went over to her mother and started stripping the untouched bines piled by her bin. 'Yer've not picked many today. Mum.'

'Bit tired, that's all, Jess. I'll be glad to get back to the 'ut an' that's the truth. Be a good girl for me an' sort out our bit of laundry an' tea an' that tonight. I'm gonna 'ave a little rest. Get me 'ead down for a while.'

'Get yerself back now, Mum. I'll sort everythin' out.' Jess paused. 'Mum?'

'Can't it wait, love? I'm ever so tired.'

'It's nothin' really. I just wondered if I could go and see them puppies later on. That's all.'

'I dunno, Jess. Goin' up there to the 'All...'

'But, Mum...'

'Look, don't bother me now, Jess, all right?' Rose rubbed her rough, hop-stained hands over her face, knocking her turban sideways. 'I ain't up to it.'

'Mum. Go on.'

'Shut up, Jess, an' leave me alone, can't yer?' Rose sighed wearily. 'An' don't look at me like that, I can't think. I'm goin' back to the 'ut.'

'Sorry, Mum.' Jess continued picking the hops into the bin, shocked to hear Rose sound so angry with her, and disturbed to see her usually strong mother looking so weak and dishevelled. 'I'll wait for the last measure then I'll be right back.'

Rose was exhausted. Just bending to pick up her basket needed an almost impossible effort. She held on to the side of the bin to get her breath. She felt so old lately. It never usually took her so long to get over the change of air from the filthy London smogs. Her chest really did feel sore. A bad chest. She thought of her mother. Rose had lain in her bed listening to her old mum's coughing and wheezing. Her father had called out the doctor, even though her mother had insisted they couldn't afford it. 'A bad chest,' the doctor had said. Just like the nurse had said to her. 'She needs fresh air and some decent food,' he'd said. When her father had told the doctor they were going hopping soon, the doctor had sounded pleased. 'Finest thing for her,' she'd heard him say. But hopping hadn't come around soon enough that year. Rose's mother had died on a warm August afternoon. It hadn't seemed right, with the sun shining and everything. Tears filled Rose's eyes as she took shallow, rasping gulps of air.

'Yer all right, Mum?' Jess dropped the half-stripped bine on to the ground and rushed to her mother's side.

'Course,' Rose lied, giving Jess a gentle push away from her. 'I was thinkin' about somethin' Elsie and Mabel said earlier, that's all. They reckoned you girls deserve a bit of fun while yer young an' daft enough to enjoy it. That's what they said.' Her breath was coming a bit easier now.

'I ain't complainin', Mum.'

'I know yer ain't, darlin'.'

'An' I didn't mean to make yer cry. I ain't never seen yer do that before.'

'I ain't crying, me eyes are waterin', that's all. 'Ere, tell yer what, Jess, yer get them few jobs done for me, then yer can see them puppies. 'Ow'd that be?'

'Thanks, Mum!'

The sight of Jess's smile lighting up her face made Rose feel she had probably made the right decision, but still she worried about her only daughter going up to the Hall. Even if it was only to the stable block, it still wasn't right somehow, cockney girls hadn't been invited up there in her day.

'Make sure yer ain't too long, mind. A quick look an' then back to the 'ut. D'you 'ear me?'

'Yes, Mum, I 'ear yer. An' thanks, Mum.'

'An' we don't need no more animals bringin' 'ome. So don't get no ideas. Right?'

'Right.'

Jess had laid the faggot fire and lit it, fetched two pails of water from the pump, put the kettle on to boil, set Rose's hop-stained blouse to soak in a basin, and started a stew cooking in the pot, quicker than even she would have thought possible. Then she changed into a clean apron and tidied her hair. She looked into the hut. Rose was stretched out on the bed, sound asleep. Her breath made a coarse whistling noise as her chest rose and fell. Jess lifted the stiff grey blanket to cover her legs.

'Won't be long, Mum,' she whispered. 'You 'ave a sleep.'

To get to the Hall, Jess had to walk across the Common, past all the women and children outside their huts as they did their domestic chores before their evening meal.

''Ere, look at 'er in 'er clean apron,' said Florrie to anyone prepared to listen. 'I wonder where she thinks she's going?'

'Goin' to mind 'er own business, I shouldn't wonder,' said Elsie, spitting out a stream of tobacco-thickened phlegm as she tapped out the ashes from her blackened pipe. 'An' that's somethin' a few more people round 'ere could do with learnin' about. Mindin' their own business.'

Jess was too set on her destination to even realise that she was being talked about. In all the years she had been hopping at Tilnhurst, she had never been up to the big house. Worlington Hall and its stable block were strictly out of bounds to the hop pickers. Even though she had been invited, she still approached nervously, worried that she would get into trouble for just being there. The closer she got to the stables, the slower she walked.

'Hey, you. You there. Wait.'

Jess spun round at the loud command. 'I wasn't doing nothing, honest. I…' She stopped. It was Robert Worlington. 'Yer said I could come up and see the puppies. D'yer remember?'

'So I did.'

Robert surveyed Jess slowly, arrogantly, letting his eyes wander over every part of her. He dismounted from the big chestnut horse with a single confident movement, tucked the reins under the stirrup leather and slapped the huge animal on its quarters. The horse trotted off back to its stall and its evening feed.

Eager to break the uncomfortable silence Jess asked about the horse. 'Will it be all right goin' off by itself like that?'

'The grooms will be around,' answered Robert indifferently. 'Now, let's see if we can find those puppies.'

He judged that it might be too soon to actually touch the girl, so he walked briskly in the direction in which the horse had gone, seeming to almost ignore her presence.

When they entered the immaculately clean stable yard, it was empty. The only sound was the rhythmic munching of oats and chaff coming from the black and white painted stalls that bordered three sides of the yard.

'Yer 'orse must 'ave got 'ome then,' Jess said quietly.

'Of course he did,' said Robert. 'I give orders and they're obeyed. Even by animals.'

Robert was standing very close to Jess. Her unusual tallness meant that he was looking straight into her eyes. He had chosen well. She was beautiful.

'Can I see them then?'

Robert could hardly believe it was going to be so easy. His father obviously knew more about these cockney girls than he'd let on.

'In here,' he said, unbolting the top and bottom doors of one of the stables.

Jess stepped into the stall. The contrast with the evening light made it seem very dark, and the sweet smell of hay filled her nostrils. She closed her eyes and sniffed the air. It was so warm and clean.

'You sound like a little pony snorting round for food,' whispered Robert. 'Come over here. To me.'

In the corner where Robert was kneeling, Jess could just make out the outline of an apple box, surrounded by bales of straw. 'Look. Come over here and see them.'

Jess bent down next to Robert, near enough to feel the warmth of his body. She reached into the hay-lined box and lifted one of the little creatures from the heap of slumbering bodies.

'It's ever so soft. Feel its little ears and belly.' Jess held the sleepy pup to her cheek. It whimpered gently in protest, wanting to get back to the comfort of its brothers and sisters. 'Aw, I didn't mean to 'urt it or nothin'.'

Robert took the puppy from her and put it back into the box. 'You couldn't hurt it if you tried,' he breathed, close beside her again. 'You're just like the puppies, soft as silk.' He ran a finger down her cheek, then reached for her hand.

Ashamed of her work-worn hands, Jess backed away from him until she could go no further, her path blocked by the manger. 'I ain't never touched silk but I don't reckon it feels like these.' She held up her hands shyly for his inspection. They were scratched and stained brown, the nails ragged and broken.

'Never mind your hands.' Robert ran his fingertips up and down her throat. 'Your face and your hair. They're beautiful. You're beautiful.' His fingers moved lower, outlining where the smooth skin of her neck disappeared under the coarse cloth of her dress. The contrast made him gasp with pleasure. 'And your body.'

Before Jess knew what had happened he had covered her mouth with his and was tracing her lips with his tongue, forcing them open. She wasn't sure what to do, she knew it must be wrong to be doing this, but it was so exciting. She twisted her head, responding to his kisses.

'Lie down,' he gasped.

Jess shook her head, but Robert pushed down on her shoulders and she sank back slowly as though she was in a dream. Her hair came loose, veiling their faces as she half fell, was half pushed, back on to the straw-covered ground. Doubts about what she was doing faded as Robert kissed her again.

'So, where are these puppies I've heard so much fuss about, Paul?'

The unmistakable reality of Julia Markington's upper-class voice crashed its way in from the stable yard outside and into

Jess's confused mind. She woke from her dream. Horrified by what she was doing, Jess shoved Robert away from her and struggled to her feet.

'Robert seems absolutely obsessed with the pathetic little creatures,' Julia continued. 'While I was away in London with your mother he apparently moved them down here from the gardener's shed. All by himself. Can you imagine? You'd think they were pedigree show animals not some smelly mongrels. I wonder what the fascination is.'

A male voice answered her. 'Robert has always been very keen on puppies, Julia. Enjoys showing them to people, I've heard. And Milly, the gardener's girl, was as fascinated by them as Robert, by all accounts. Spent a lot of time with him in her father's shed, just looking at them.'

'What can you mean?' Julia burst into suggestive laughter as Paul threw open the stable door.

'Robert!' he shouted, in a wildly exaggerated imitation of shock. 'Mother said you were out riding. Can that really be you rolling about in the hay? And what's this? Is there someone in there with you?'

Jess was huddled in the comer by the puppies, picking straw from her clothes with one hand and attempting to rearrange her hair with the other.

'I ain't nobody,' she said.

'So we can see,' said Julia, and laughed loudly again. 'Come on, Paul, I think I've seen enough farmyard creatures for one day.'

Paul and Julia departed arm in arm, leaving the door swinging on its hinges behind them.

When she was sure they had gone Jess made a move to follow their example and leave the stable yard.

'And where do you think you're going?' demanded Robert harshly. He was still sprawling on the straw-covered ground.

'I've got to get back,' she said, looking down at him. 'Me mum's sick.' Realising immediately what she'd said, Jess panicked, afraid they would be sent home to Poplar. 'No, I don't mean she's sick, I'm mean she's really tired, and I promised I'd 'elp 'er.'

'Surely you don't have to go yet. Come on.' Robert reached up for her. 'Stay a bit longer.'

'No. No, I can't. I won't. It ain't right what we're doin'.'

'We've done nothing wrong,' he said. He smiled winningly up at her.

Jess hesitated by the half-open door. 'Yer shouldn't 'ave kissed me like that. It ain't right.'

'You didn't seem to mind.'

'I was mixed up. Yer got me all confused. Yer shouldn't 'ave done it.'

'You can't fool me, you little tease. You know what you want, don't you?' With that he lunged forward to grab her.

Jess dodged neatly out of his reach out into the yard and ran as fast as she could back to the Common.

Robert cursed Paul. He wasn't used to anyone getting the better of him, especially not his brother. He stormed back to the house, determined to get revenge for Paul's interference.

–

'Sorry I've been so long, Mum,' gasped Jess breathlessly as she reached the hut.

Rose was sitting on the grass, poking the fire under the cooking pot with a short, gnarled stick.

'I didn't realise it was so late. I ran all the way back, though. I'm sorry, Mum.'

Rose lifted her head to look at her daughter. 'Yer look all 'ot and bothered.'

Jess was shocked at how pale Rose looked, even in the firelight.

'I was runnin', Mum. I told yer.'

'Oh yeh, so yer did.' Rose returned to poking the fire.

'Mum.'

'Yeh.'

'Nothing.'

Robert took the wide stone steps at the front of the Hall three at a time. As Tyler opened the front door, he was shoved out of the way for his trouble. Robert stood in the middle of the marble-floored entrance hall and bellowed at the top of his voice.

'Where are you, you damned idiot? Paul, come out here. Now.'

'Master Paul is in the Chinese room, sir.'

Without acknowledging the butler's assistance, Robert tossed his riding coat to the floor and strode off to find his brother.

The calm atmosphere of the bright, airy room into which Robert threw himself couldn't have been more in contrast with his turbulent anger; the room being tastefully decorated in the pale-yellow silks and lacquered furniture of the eighteenth century's chinoiserie fad, while Robert was almost purple with apoplectic rage.

Julia was sitting writing at a small, ornate desk, and Paul was leaning over her.

'What a charming bloody scene.'

Paul turned his head. 'Robert. What a coincidence. We were just talking about you, weren't we, Julia?'

Julia smiled her agreement at Paul, then moved to stand up. But before she could do so Robert launched himself across the room and grabbed Paul by the throat.

'You bastard. You made me look a complete fool.'

'I think you did that yourself,' said Julia.

The surprise of hearing his fiancée speaking in so composed a manner made Robert momentarily loosen his grip on his brother's throat, though not long enough for Paul to escape.

'So you've been poisoning Julia's mind against me too, have you?' Robert said through gritted teeth. Then he began shaking Paul like a terrier trying to dispatch a particularly persistent rat.

Paul struggled and squirmed but still Robert had him fast.

'Don't, Robert, don't, you'll kill him.' Julia clutched at her fiance's arms, trying to drag him off. 'Leave him alone.' Paul's eyes began to roll up into his head. 'Robert!' Julia screamed. 'Leave him alone. Please. Please. Oh, I'll get help, Paul.' As she fled into the hallway she ran straight into Lady Worlington.

'Please, you must stop him.' Grabbing her astonished future mother-in-law by the sleeve, Julia rushed her into the Chinese room.

'Stop that immediately,' Leonore insisted. 'Whatever are you thinking of? My own sons behaving in this barbaric way.'

Robert dropped his hands to his sides. He scowled at Paul. 'Don't think I've finished with you, little brother,' he panted.

Paul rubbed his bruised throat, trying to ease the pain.

'Can neither of you look me in the eye? Are you too ashamed?' their mother demanded. 'I thought you might have learned something from the way your father behaves.' Neither replied. She shook her head sadly and left the room.

Paul and Robert looked at each other in disbelief and then burst out laughing.

'Stop it, you two,' sulked Julia, angry at being left out of the joke. 'I don't understand. What's so funny?'

The only reply was a further gale of laughter from the suddenly reunited brothers.

'You're impossible. Both of you.' She stamped her delicate little foot with surprising ferocity.

'You mustn't be cross, Julia,' snorted Robert, trying to keep a straight face. 'We only want to please Mother. So we're doing our best to learn from Father. Exactly as she wants us to. Isn't that right, Paul?'

The brothers' new roar of laughter could be heard throughout the Hall. It even woke Sir George.

Chapter 8

A Real Opportunity

When Ted and Sammy got home from work, Jack was sitting on their street-door step.

'Nothin' better to do than lay about in the afternoon sun, Jacko boy? Or won't Clara let yer in for yer tea?'

Jack ignored Sammy's attempt to make him look a fool in front of young Ted. 'I ain't sittin' 'ere for the fun of it, Sam, I'm waitin' to see your Charlie.'

'I wouldn't waste yer time, mate,' said Sam, sniffing cockily. 'We 'ardly see him ourselves lately. 'E come round yesterday for a couple of minutes. Dropped a few quid on the table for me an' Ted, like. Then cleared off again. Too busy nowadays to 'ang around this poxy dump.'

'When yer expectin' 'im back then?'

'Yer tell me.'

'Let us in, Sam,' Ted interrupted, hopping from foot to foot. 'I'm dyin' for a Jimmy Riddle. I'm gonna piss meself in a minute.'

''Ang on, Ted, let's find me key.' Sammy fumbled around in his pocket.

'Yer sure yer don't know when 'e's comin' 'ome?' Jack persisted. 'Yer ain't lyin' to me, are yer?'

'For Gawd's sake, Jack, why should I bother lyin' to yer? I told yer, didn't I? No, I do *not* know when Charlie is comin' back to Burton Street. That clear enough for yer? Now if yer don't mind, young Ted 'ere 'as to answer the call of nature.' Sam unlocked the door and Ted rushed into the passage and straight through to the lavatory in the back yard.

'Listen to me, Sam.'

Sammy looked down contemptuously at Jack's hand gripping his arm. 'Don't touch me, Jack,' he said.

Jack let go. 'Sam, I mean it. While Ted's out of the way, is there anythin' yer wanna tell me? Anythin' I should know? Is somethin' up?'

'Yer don't 'alf go on, Jack. Yer like a bloody ol' woman.'

'Sam, is Charlie in bother or somethin'? Where's 'e stayin' for one thing?'

Sam folded his arms and leant back against the rough brick wall of Number 8. He took his time pondering what Jack had said, then he answered. 'For a start, Jack, no, there is no bother as far as I know. In fact, Charlie is doin' very nicely for 'imself, thank you. An' for another thing, it's 'ardly none of your bleed'n' business, now is it, even if 'e did 'ave some bother.'

'Don't be like that, Sam,' Jack said. He didn't want to row with Jess's brothers, any of them. 'It's just that I promised yer mum. Yer know I did.'

'Yeh, yeh, we all know. An' we all know what yer promised an' all.' Sammy looked heavenwards. 'It's all we've bleed'n' 'eard round 'ere for the last two weeks. Now if yer don't mind, Jack, I've just got in from work an' I don't wanna stand out 'ere chattin' to no nursemaid.'

Sammy turned his back on Jack and stepped into the passageway.

Whatever Jack said in protest was lost on Sammy, who shut the door firmly in his face.

Jack waited outside, perched on the windowledge, weighing up what he should do next. He wasn't really interested in Charlie and his dodgy dealings but he had made a promise to Rose and he intended keeping it. He didn't want her and Jess thinking he was unreliable.

After a few minutes going over the options, he knew what he had to do. He'd have to go and find Charlie, find out what he was up to, and that, he knew, meant going back into Chinatown.

It took Jack only about fifteen minutes to walk down to Penny-fields, but by the time he'd reached the Thames-side quarter, the autumn twilight had faded into another damp and almost impenetrable fog-shrouded night.

Jack was no coward, but walking around Chinatown without the company of Sam, or even young Ted, was a nerve-racking experience for an outsider – even though the area bordered on his own home territory of Poplar. There were many stories and rumours about what went on in that part of Limehouse. It was widely accepted as fact, if rarely discussed openly, that the power and ferocity of both the English and the Chinese gangs in the area made even the police prefer to avoid that part of the docks. Everyone knew that prostitutes were able to ply their trade at the dock gates and outside Charlie Brown's, the notorious pub used by visiting seamen, without any fear of interference from the law. Thus it was that the stories grew up and were added to. Tales were told of how, unmolested by the authorities, the gaudily made-up women could lure their unsuspecting customers into the mist-cloaked courts and alleys. There they would be coshed and robbed by the prostitutes' accomplices. It was well known that coshes were a favoured piece of equipment in the forbidding, ill-lit riverside streets. So were hatchets. And even guns.

As far as he was able, Jack kept to the most brightly lit parts of the unfamiliar warren of alleyways in his search for the club where he had seen Charlie fight just the week before.

He hurried past the garish tattoo parlours; the boisterous drinking clubs; the occasionally noisy, but usually silent, gambling dens; and the stinking doss-houses full of seamen and the women whose company they had bought for the night.

'An' I reckon these are the safest parts of this rats' nest,' he thought nervously to himself as he passed a particularly fetid doorway leading to God alone knew where.

The sudden tap on his shoulder made his heart race.

'You want some fun, mister?'

Jack turned round cautiously, expecting the worst. He let out a small gasp of relief when he saw a small Chinese boy of about ten or eleven years old looking up at him expectantly.

'I know plenty of girls you can meet, mister. You want to come with me?'

'Not tonight, son. I'm busy, see.' Jack brushed the boy playfully on the chin with his fist and continued on his way. But then he changed his mind. He turned round and called, ''Old on, kid.'

'Yes, mister.' The eager youngster could sense a halfpenny to be earned. 'What do you want? Girls? Opium?'

'No. It's a bloke I'm after. A pal of mine. Tryin' to find 'im round these parts. Charlie Fairleigh. Know 'im? English feller. 'Bout my age. Red sort of 'air.'

The boy shook his head. 'No. I know no Charlie.'

Jack bent down closer to the child. Checking that no one was listening to their conversation, he said, as calmly as he could manage: "'E'll be with another man. Chinese bloke. A Mr Chen.'

'Goodbye, mister.' The boy disappeared into the crowd and down one of the narrow passageways before Jack had the chance to stop him.

So Jack was right, Chen was as dangerous as he had thought. He would have to be more careful whom he spoke to.

–

Jack had been walking for what felt like hours; although the area was actually quite small it was easy to go in circles in the unfamiliar streets and back alleys. He was tired and he was hungry. The windows of the food shops were filled with things that, though they looked strange, smelt delicious. Seeing two sailors in English uniforms about to go into one of the shops, Jack thought he would chance following them.

'Mind if I join you blokes?' he asked matily.

'No. Sit down, man. Glad of ya company,' said the squat, pale-haired one in a blunt Geordie accent. His shiny, ruddy face stretched into a grin of welcome.

Jack slid on to the bench next to the two seamen.

'Been round here before, like, have ya?' asked the other man in the same northern tones.

'No, I'm a stranger 'ere,' Jack said quickly. 'But I'oping to bet a few shillin's on the bare-knuckle fights they say go on round these parts. In some cellar, or somethin' or other.'

'Ya mean the fights they put on down old whatsisname's place.'

The pale-haired sailor dug his shipmate hard in the ribs to silence him. 'Shut up a minute, Bert. Here's the wee girl.'

'What can I fetch you gentlemen?' she asked in an unexpectedly English accent.

136

'I don't know, hen. Why don't ya surprise us,' said Bert. 'Tell ya what, fetch us enough grub for six. That should do us.' The waitress nodded demurely and left their table. 'Now, as I was saying before Horace here so rudely interrupted me. It'll be Mr Chen's establishment ya looking for. And it just so happens we're off there tonight, wer'selves. We'll have our bit of grub then ya can join us, if ya like, man.'

'Ta, Bert,' said Jack, 'I'd like that very much.'

'What's ya name then?' asked Horace.

'Walter,' said Jack.

After their meal, Jack's two companions took him directly to the club which he had earlier been unable to find.

'Here we are, Walter, man,' said Horace to Jack, 'Chen's place. Now how about seeing some of that boxing and winning wer'selves a few shillings?'

'Yer on,' said Jack, following Horace and Bert into the narrow doorway which concealed the true size and complexity of the building.

As they went deeper into the network of passages and stairways that linked the terrace of houses, Jack glanced into every open door, hoping for a glimpse of Charlie. The club was alive with people, mainly men, of every size, shape and colour, but Charlie was nowhere to be seen.

'This is it,' said Bert. 'The arena. We'll get wer'selves seats before the next fight starts.'

They squeezed past the young boys who were collecting bets on the outcome of the contests and found three chairs in the back row, at the far end of the massive room.

'It's bloody hot in here, man,' moaned Bert. 'I could really do with a drink.'

'Call one of the boys over, Bert,' said Horace. 'He'll nip upstairs and fetch us some ale.'

One of the boys was dispatched on the errand. He quickly returned with three bottles of beer. Bert greedily snatched one of the bottles and unscrewed the stopper. He was already guzzling the warm, foaming liquid when the boy tried to take it back from him. 'You no pay, you no drink.'

'Don't worry, I'll pay,' said Bert, wiping his mouth with the back of his big, tattooed hand. 'What's the damage?'

'Two shillings, mister.'

'What?'

'Two shillings.'

Bert rose to his feet. 'Two bob for three rotten bottles of beer?'

'No, mister, two shillings each bottle.'

Now Horace joined Bert in standing over the impassively insistent boy. 'Ya taking the piss out of us or something, son?'

'No. Two shillings. That is the price.'

Horace carefully placed his unopened bottle behind him on his seat, leaned forward and took hold of the boy's shoulders. 'I don't mind paying a fair whack, but I won't be taken on by no snotty-nosed kid, do ya understand?'

'Two shillings is the price. No pay, no drink,' the boy repeated.

'I'm getting fed up with listening to ya whingeing little voice,' said Horace and started shaking the boy violently.

'Leave 'im alone, 'Orace,' said Jack, trying to stop him from hurting the child any more. 'It ain't the kid's fault. That's the price. This is a club, not a street-corner boozer.'

'Ya keep ya nose out of it, Walter,' said Horace, concentrating on the boy.

Two Chinese men from the row in front started shouting. The now alarmed child did his best to reply, but failed. The two Chinese men ran from the room.

'Bloody cowards. Won't even help one of their own,' jeered Bert.

He looked round the room, challenging anyone to take him on. Everybody had eyes only for Horace and the boy; they shouted and complained, but nobody moved. Suddenly the room went quiet and everyone except Horace and his young victim turned their attention to the other end of the big room.

'I think yer'd better stop that, moosh, don't you?' said a calm, menacingly quiet voice.

'Oh yeh,' said Horace. 'And who's gonna make me?'

'Do as 'e says,' said Jack, looking not at Horace but at Charlie, who was standing in the doorway next to a bearded Chinese man.

Charlie held a heavy, leather-covered cosh, which he slapped rhythmically against the palm of his hand.

'Come near me, man, and I'll punch ya lamps out for ya, both a them,' spat Horace comtemptuously.

'Shut up an' leave the kid or 'e'll knock yer block off,' Jack warned him. 'An' I ain't kiddin', neither.'

'Good advice,' said Charlie, acknowledging Jack with a polite nod. 'If yer'll excuse me, Mr Chen.'

Charlie strolled slowly towards the sailor. His lack of haste added an even more sinister ingredient to his already threatening appearance.

'Going to knock my block off, are ya, man?' said Horace, letting go of the boy, ready to confront this new challenge. 'You and whose army?'

'I don't need no army, mate,' said Charlie gently. 'Just this.' He raised the cosh and gave Horace a sharp rap to the side of his head. 'Now, move.'

Momentarily stunned, Horace dabbed his finger at the blood which was beginning to seep from the wound on his temple. 'Ya've cut me, ya dirty cockney bastard. I'll have ya for that.'

'No yer won't,' said Charlie, all friendly intimidation. 'Now don't be a silly boy. Yer can choose. Do yer wanna leave 'ere walkin', or would yer rather be carried out?'

Horace drew back his arm, ready to smash the smile off Charlie's face. But Charlie brushed the fist away as if it was an annoying fly.

'Get him out of here, Charles. He is becoming a nuisance,' said Mr Chen as he turned to leave the room.

'You 'eard the gentleman. 'E wants yer to leave 'is club.'

'Can't ya get a job working for a decent Englishman?' taunted Horace. 'Got to work for foreigners, have ya?'

'Leave it,' said Bert, fidgeting with the back of his chair. 'He's not worth it, man.'

'Right, Bert. Why should I bother with the oily rag when I can deal with the engineer himself?' Horace snatched away the startled Bert's chair and threw it with all his force at Charlie. The unexpected blow knocked him sideways, giving Horace the chance to run for the door, swiftly followed by Bert.

'Nice company yer keeping nowadays, Jacky boy,' said Charlie as he picked himself up off the floor and made after the two seamen. 'Lovely friends, I don't think.'

'They ain't nothin' to do with me,' panted Jack, doing his best to keep up with the much fitter Charlie. 'Yer the one with the dodgy mates.'

As they reached the street Jack glimpsed the two seamen disappearing into a side road. 'There they go, Charlie. Down there.'

Despite the situation, Charlie couldn't resist teasing Jack as he sprinted after his quarry. 'This is a turnup, Jack. Yer 'elping me out. Wouldn't 'ave thought yer'd approve. Mind yer, yer almost family now, I suppose.'

Jack didn't have enough breath both to answer and continue pursuing the two men, but he was pleased that Charlie seemed to have accepted his relationship with Jess. Charlie's disapproval would have been more than a major obstacle for them.

'Down there,' shouted Charlie, 'the steps down to the river.'

'Christ,' said Jack, gulping air painfully into his heaving lungs, 'they've got Chen with them.'

'Mr Chen to you,' said Charlie without a moment's pause or a hint of irony.

'Mr Chen,' repeated Jack.

They stopped at the head of the steps and squinted down into the darkness, their eyes growing accustomed to the murky light.

'Don't make a sound,' whispered Charlie. 'We'll surprise them.'

'Say they're armed?'

'Sssh.' Charlie crouched and moved silently down the stone steps. He tapped Jack on the arm and pointed to the water's edge. Bert had the Chinese man held firmly from behind. Horace stood in front of him running a long, thin knife teasingly up and down the man's body.

'Where shall we start then, Bert?' asked Horace. 'How about this reet girly pigtail? Or this tatty old beard?' He flicked Chen's beard with the slim blade.

Charlie crept forward, staying hunched over until he was standing directly behind the little group at the water's edge. 'Why not start with me?' he asked. 'Or do yer only fight unarmed men?'

The surprise of hearing Charlie so close to him made Horace drop his guard just long enough for Charlie to grab the knife.

'Dear oh dear oh dear. Tut, tut,' said Charlie, waving the stiletto in Horace's face. 'What a clumsy boy yer are. Yer wanna be more careful with a dangerous chiv like this. Now be a sensible lad,' he said to Bert, 'an' let the gentleman go, eh?'

'Ignore him, Bert. Ya keep hold of the Chinese bastard.'

'Ttttt! See, that was another mistake,' said Charlie. 'Yer've gotta learn some manners. An' I'm gonna 'ave to teach 'em to yer, ain't I?'

Before Horace could protect himself, Charlie had drawn the knife down his cheek, leaving a thin streak of blood.

'An' now perhaps yer'd like to apologise to Mr Chen for yer bad manners?'

Bert let go of his prisoner and rushed to his friend's side. 'Horace. Come on, man. Let's go back to the ship.'

'No. Yer don't understand, son,' said Charlie, explaining slowly, as if he was talking to a child. ''E ain't goin' nowhere. Not 'til 'e apologises to Mr Chen.'

'Let 'em go, Charlie. Eh?' said Jack. 'It's finished. Come on,' he coaxed. 'No point carryin' on with this. Let's go an' 'ave a drink.'

'You keep out of this, Walter,' said Bert. 'This is nothing to do with you, man.'

Charlie turned his head and looked questioningly at Jack. 'Walter?'

'Look out!' yelled Jack, throwing himself forward to protect Charlie from Horace, who had taken his chance to grab a slime-covered rock from the mud. Jack rammed his shoulder full into the seaman's broad chest, knocking him off balance. Then Charlie threw himself down on top of him and began punching the sprawling man over and over again with sickening repetition.

'Don't, Charlie, don't. Yer'll kill 'im,' yelled Jack.

Even the combined efforts of Bert and Jack pulling together weren't enough to drag the incensed Charlie away from the object of his anger. Grunting and panting, the four of them rolled and scrabbled around in the black Thames sludge.

'Leave him. He must do his job.' Chen spoke with such detached authority that Jack and Bert both stopped immediately. They slithered unsteadily to their feet, leaving Charlie to batter the exhausted Horace into the mud.

'I dunno about do 'is job,' said Jack, his voice slow from the shock of what he was witnessing. 'But this ain't the sort of work 'e should be doin', I know that.'

Chen disregarded Jack and spoke to Charlie. 'Finish him,' he said simply.

'Get out of 'ere, Jack,' said Charlie as he raised the knife above his head, ready to plunge it into the cringing seaman.

'No!' screamed Jack and pitched himself forward. He wouldn't let Charlie become a murderer. No matter what.

He was too late. He couldn't stop Charlie bringing down the knife. But he made him miss his target. Instead of stabbing the semi-conscious sailor, the knife came down and went straight into the side of Jack's throat.

Jack twisted away, swooning from the pain. He fell on to his knees and rolled over until he was face down at the water's edge. The knife, still deep in his flesh, acted like a brake, stopping him from rolling any further. He moaned, barely able to make a sound. His mouth and nostrils filled with the soft, cloying muck left behind by the tide, his life-blood pulsing from him.

'Jesus Christ, he's done him in...' Bert half dragged, half kicked his shipmate into the safety of the shadows, out of the murderer's reach. He would get them both back on board before anyone missed them; before anybody could associate them with Walter or whatever his name was. He was too busy manhandling his stunned, heavy load to notice Chen signalling to one of the Chinese boys who had appeared silently out of the Thames fog.

'Jack. Come on, Jacky boy.' Charlie had forgotten the man he had just been trying to slaughter; he could think only of Jack. He knelt beside him in the mud, unaware of the incoming tide, cradling the dying man in his arms. Not just any man, but Jack Barnes, good old Jacky boy, the feller who was going to marry their Jess. A decent bloke. 'Don't mess around, Jack,' he pleaded. 'Come on, mate.'

'Leave him. There is no more you can do.' Chen stood behind Charlie and spoke in the composed manner which told so eloquently of his power over others. Even the power of life and death.

''E's dead, Mr Chen. I've killed 'im.' Charlie looked up at his master imploringly.

'Nonsense. It was an accident. He was brawling with those drunken sailors. My people will deal with the details.'

'But, Mr Chen…'

Chen lifted one satin-draped arm and Charlie was silent.

'This unfortunate man will be found tomorrow; yet another lamentable victim of too much drink and too little control.'

He raised his arm again. Another boy stepped forward from the shadows. Chen spoke to him in his own language, and then in English to Charlie.

'You are very wet, Charles. You should get out of those things. The boy here will take you back and get you some fresh clothes. He will dispose of your bloodstained garments.'

Charlie looked down at himself. He was smeared with the blood of two men, foul river water and slime. He retched. ''E should be buried proper,' he managed to say.

'The river will be his final resting place,' said Chen and walked towards the steps. Two men stepped forward and walked with him, one on either side. Without looking back he said to Charlie, 'The boy will take you through a rear entrance to the club. Be as quiet as possible.' Then he stopped. 'You did well, Charles. You proved your loyalty. I will not forget.' Before he climbed the steps he turned right round to face Charlie. 'You will need to go away for a while. I shall have a word with an associate of mine. You will be found a position with him; an occupation where you will be well rewarded.'

'Thank you, Mr Chen,' whispered Charlie into his chest.

Before he left Jack to the mercy of the tide, Charlie stroked the mud-caked hair away from the young postman's face.

'See yer sometime, mate,' he said gently.

With one swift movement he pulled the knife from Jack's throat and threw it with all his strength into the greedy depths of the river. Then he untied the yellow paisley stock from around the dead man's neck.

'Just a keepsake, Jacky boy,' he said through the tears running down his bloodstained cheeks. 'Just a keepsake.'

–

'Mum. Mum, it's me, Charlie. Come on. Open up.'

'For Gawd's sake, whatever's going on 'ere? It ain't even light yet.' Rose stood squinting in the doorway of the hop hut, her black serge coat draped round her shoulders, covering her long underclothes. 'What the 'ell are yer doin' 'ere? Whatever's 'appened?'

'Long time since I've seen yer with yer 'air down loose, Mum,' Charlie said, reaching out his hand to her. 'Yer still a good-looker and that's the truth.'

'Ne' mind none of that ol' nonsense, Charlie,' Rose sighed. 'Yer get yerself inside 'ere. An' keep yer noise down before yer wake everyone up.'

'Who's there? Mum?' Jess's voice, thick with sleep and scarcely audible came from the back of the pitch-dark hut.

'It's all right, love, it's our Charlie,' Rose whispered. ''E's come to see us, that's all. Yer go back to sleep.'

''Ello, Charlie,' she yawned.

'Do as Mum says, Jess. Yer go back to sleep.'

Jess snuggled deeper down into the straw-filled mattress, pulled the scratchy wool blanket over her head and smiled contentedly to herself, happy to go back to sleep.

'Now, will yer tell me what's 'appened? An' look at yer face, all swollen. Yer been fightin' again, ain't yer? Yer wasn't meant to come down 'til the weekend with all the others. Yer in trouble, are yer?'

'All right, all right, let's get a word in edgeways, Mum.' Charlie took his mother's hand. 'Sit down an' listen to me.'

Reluctantly, Rose sat down on the tea chest by the half-open door. Charlie squatted down on his haunches next to her. She was looking old. He hadn't noticed that before. In the first glow of early morning sun, he could just make out the lines on her tired face. They were deeper than he remembered.

'If yer can stop rabbitin' on for a minute,' he said gently, 'I've got some good news to tell yer. Yer'll be right proud of me, I reckon, when yer 'ear.'

'Don't mess around, Charlie. Spit it out. What's up? What yer been up to this time? Tell me.'

'Mum. Listen to me. I've been given a big chance. A real big chance.' He squeezed her hand, trying to reassure her. 'I'm gonna become a manager of a club.'

'You?' Rose shook her head, trying to understand.

'Well, an assistant manager. Gonna learn all the trade proper and everythin'.'

'You've already got a trade. Down the woodyard,' said Rose stiffly.

'Yer know I always 'ated that place, Mum.'

'Don't I just, all yer ever went on about was bein' a professional boxer.'

'Exactly. That's why I thought yer'd be pleased about the club. I've given up fightin' for good. No more knockin' geezers around on street comers earnin' pennies. I'm gonna be someone. It's a real opportunity for a bloke like me from Burton Street.'

''Oo'd want you for a job like that then? You look a real state with yer face all bashed up.'

'Should 'ave seen the other geezers.' Charlie laughed.

Rose didn't. 'Why do I think yer 'iding somethin' from me, Charlie Fairleigh?' she said. ''Oo is it givin' yer this big chance, anyway? 'Oo yer gonna be workin' for?'

'That's the really good bit, Mum. I'll be goin' to a place called Chicago. It's in America.'

'America! Oh, Charlie, whatever will yer dad 'ave to say? Yer'll 'ave to talk to 'im before yer agree to somethin' like that, boy.'

'I can't. See this geezer, 'e's gimme a contract thing. I 'ad to sign it an' all that. It's now or never 'e said.'

'What geezer?' Rose raked her fingers distractedly through her hair. It was still thick and glossy, though odd strands of grey were beginning to show through the rich auburn tones.

'Charlie, yer'll 'ave to speak to yer dad and that's that. 'E's due 'ome any day now. Yer won't 'ave to wait long.'

'Sorry, Mum, but I'm sailin' from Tilbury on Thursday mornin'.'

Rose took Charlie's face in her hands and pulled him towards her. She looked straight into his eyes, desperate to read the truth she was sure he was concealing. 'Yer remember Ivy, son? Ivy Jennings from down Barchester Street?'

'Yeh. What's she gotta do with it?'

'When 'er Archie died, the welfare people sent 'er kids to Canada. Said they was gettin' 'em good work an' that. Well, she never saw 'em again. Never. Not even a letter. Gawd alone knows what 'appened to them poor little devils.' Rose made no attempt to hide the tears that were rolling down her sunburned cheeks. 'Why America, son? Yer are in trouble, ain't yer? Tell me.'

Charlie stood up. 'Don't yer worry yerself, Mum. I'll make yer right proud of me, yer'll see. I'll work 'ard an' save, an' one day I'll 'ave a club of me own. 'Ow about that?' He opened the door wider and stepped out into the chilly morning air. ''Ark at them bleed'n' birds singin',' he said, breathing deeply andhis arms high above his head. ''Andsome down 'ere, innit? Don't get that in Poplar, eh, Mum? The sparrers can't sing for coughin' back 'ome.'

He made a real effort to look happy, to smile for his weeping mother. But he couldn't coax even the ghost of a smile from her. She really was looking old.

'Tell yer what, Rosie Fairleigh,' he said, almost his old cheeky self. 'When I've made me fortune I'll buy yer a bloody great big mansion. Better than them Worlingtons 'ave got up there. An' yer can invite that old bugger Sir George, an' 'is missus, round to tea. 'Ow about that, eh, Mum?' He wrapped his arms around her and kissed the top of her head. 'Yer've always been a duchess to me, Mum. An' yer always will be. Always.'

'Charlie, why don't yer wait, son?' Rose stood up to try and stop him. She didn't notice the cold, or that her coat had fallen from her shoulders on to the damp, dewy ground. 'Just 'til yer dad gets back, eh, boy? I promise I won't try to stop yer after that. Please, son, just a couple o' days.'

'I can't, Mum, honest.' He bent forward and kissed her again, then picked up her coat and draped it round her shoulders. 'Yer should keep yerself warm, Mum. Look after yerself. We're all big enough an' ugly enough to take care of ourselves now.'

Charlie took a roughly wrapped brown paper parcel from inside his jacket and handed it to Rose.

'Now 'ere's something I want yer to look after for me.'

Rose took the package without looking at it, clutching it to her chest as though it was the last she'd ever have of her boy.

'There's a few quid in there,' he said, winking. 'Emergencies, see? I mean, 'oo knows what's gonna 'appen to any of us in this ol' world, eh, Mum? An' there's a little secret in there an' all, just between you an' me. Yer might wanna look at it one day.'

'Charlie, don't go, son. Please.'

'Be 'appy for me, Mum.'

Rose held on to the door frame of the mean little hut, watching her son walk away across the Common and out of her life. Chicago. All she had left of her child, her Charlie, was a brown paper parcel. She sat back down on the tea chest and untied the knotted string. Inside was a filthy, stained cloth that looked like it might once have been yellow. It smelt horrible, stale. She unfolded the stiff material. Inside was more money than she'd ever seen in her life. She looked more closely at the cloth. She could just make out its paisley design. Her hands flew to her mouth, trying to stifle the gasp that escaped from her lips.

Jess stirred. 'Mum? Is it time to get up yet?' she asked, still groggy with sleep.

Rose hurriedly tucked the parcel under the patched folds of her threadbare petticoat. 'Go back to sleep, Jess,' she said quietly through her tears. 'I'll tell yer when it's time.'

Chapter 9

Bring Us Back a Monkey

'Jess.' Winnie poked her head inside the hut. 'Yer comin' over for a bath? Dunno about you, but I could really do with one. I feel lousy. Sweatin' out in them fields all week, and sleepin' on that dusty straw. Me frock's stiff.'

'I'll come with yer if yer'll shut up gassin', Win,' snapped Jessie. 'If not, yer can go by yerself.'

'Charmin',' pouted Winnie.

'Oi, Jess, there's no need to be rude to Winnie,' frowned Rose. 'What's got into yer, talkin' like that?'

'Thank you, Rose,' said Winnie, all offended. 'At least one of the Fairleighs has some manners.'

'Well, she gets on me nerves going on all the time,' Jess answered her mother.

Rose didn't reply, she just stared at Jessie. Whatever had got into the girl? she wondered. It wasn't like her to be unkind to anyone.

'An' if yer both don't stop chatterin',' said Lil, joining her friends in the doorway of the Fairleighs' hut, 'the Mission ladies'll 'ave gone, then there'll be no baths for no one.'

'Blimey, 'ello, Lil,' said Winnie, back to her old sarcastic self. 'Fancy seein' you this early on a Saturday mornin'. I didn't know yer 'ad it in yer.'

'I want to get a nice bath, don't I? Before we 'ave to start pickin'. Wanna posh meself up for the weekend, an' all the fellers.'

Win, getting more like her mother every day, found a reason to complain about the bathing facilities. 'Well, I think it's a right shame we can't 'ave our bath at dinnertime. At one o'clock, when we've finished pickin' for the week. Then we'd be proper clean for the weekend.'

'Yer should think yerself lucky the Mission ladies fetch the bath tent on a Saturday at all, Win,' said Lil, glad of the opportunity to get her own back on her moaning friend. 'Down Fanshawe's they get 'em there of a Friday night after pickin'. They 'ave to tear back from the fields, get their baths, get their tea, do the washin', an' all before it gets too dark. It's a right turn-out down there. An' anyway, Win,' Lil added, warming to her subject, 'listenin' to the way yer talkin', anyone'd think you Baxters was used to 'aving regular baths.'

'Aw shut up, Lilly Dorkin,' said Win. 'I don't need no sermon. 'Oo do yer think yer are, the bleed'n' vicar?'

'Shut up, yer moanin' cow,' spat Lil.

'Least I ain't got a fat arse,' sneered Winnie in reply.

'Why don't yer stop rowin', the pair of yer. I'm right fed up with all this,' said Jess irritably. 'If we're goin', let's get down there an' start queuin', or no one'll 'ave no bath.'

'Yeh,' said Lil, 'if she shuts 'er gob I will.'

'An' 'er an' all,' said Win. 'If she shuts 'ers.'

'I've 'ad enough of this. I'm going' down the bath tent, Mum,' Jess called into the hut, 'before war breaks out with these two. I'll save yer a place in the queue.'

Jess strode off across the grass.

'All right, Jess, leave off,' said Lil, rolling her eyes at Winnie. 'Wait for us. We're comin'. What's the matter with yer this mornin'?'

'I'm just fed up with you two rowin' all the time.'

Winnie didn't say anything; she simply raised her eyebrows and nodded at Lil, acknowledging that Jess's behaviour was confirming all the rumours Win had been busily passing around about her.

The three young women, with Jess keeping slightly ahead of her two still bickering friends, walked across the Common towards the big field next to the pub. It was there that the ladies of the 'Missionary League for the Hop Pickers of Kent' set up their big bell tent and offered weekly baths for a halfpenny, a dab of ointment for wounds, and spiritual advice for the misguided.

'I'll bet Jess is lookin' forward to the weekend, eh, Lil?' said Win, nudging Lil behind Jess's back. 'Or d'yer think it might be a bit awkward for 'er, like?'

'You two mates again then, are yer?' said Jess. She lengthened her stride, leaving her friends further behind. She kept walking determinedly towards the tent, head high, flicking her ragged scrap of towel at the lush, fruit-laden branches overhanging the hedgerows.

''Ow's that then, Win? 'Ow do yer mean?' asked Lil, feigning innocence. 'Yer said it might be a bit awkward for Jess?'

'Well, Lil,' explained Win expansively, 'what I mean is that if Jack Barnes comes down, like 'e promised 'e would, well, what's 'e to think when 'e sees young feller-me-lad, Master Robert from the big 'ouse, makin' eyes at our Jessie 'ere? An' them practically goin' out an' all. I mean 'e did give 'er that canary.'

'Yer shut up, Win,' said Jess, turning on them. 'I've 'ad enough of yer rotten comments. Yer've got a big bloody gob an' that's a fact. An' as for you, Lilly Dorkin, I'm surprised at yer joining in with 'er.' Jess took them both aback with her sudden outburst and the furious look on her face.

Win was the first to find her voice. 'Temper, temper,' she said, all hurt.

'Well, yer nosy cows,' said Jess. 'Yer know gossip like that causes trouble. An' it's all lies, anyway.'

'Sorry, yer ladyship,' mocked Lil dropping a wobbly curtsey. 'We never meant no offence, ma'am, I'm sure.'

The sight of the grubby, plump girl, with her hair tumbling from its pins, aping the starched manners and speech of a parlourmaid had Winnie spluttering with laughter.

'It ain't funny,' said Jess. 'Yer know 'ow stories get out of 'and. What would 'appen if me mum 'eard yer talkin' like that?'

'Leave off, Jess,' said Win. ''Oo'd believe Robert Worlington would really 'ave anythin' to do with the likes of us?'

'Yeh, forget it, Jess, we was only 'aving a lark,' said Lil. 'Now do yer want this bath or not?'

Saturday's half-day picking seemed to drag on forever as the women and girls waited eagerly to see their menfolk. Then, at last, 'Pull no more bines' was called, and Theo came round to do his final, reluctant measuring of the week.

'That old sod's gettin' worse than ever,' said Florrie Baxter to no one in particular. ''E drives me blinkin' crackers. I'd like to...'

'Ignore 'im. We're finished now,' said Rose. 'Don't let 'im spoil yer weekend, Flo.'

'Well, Rose, I've gotta speak fair,' said Elsie. 'I agree with Florrie for once. 'E really is an ignorant old bastard. 'E nearly knocked Mabel over, pushin' past 'er just now.'

'It's all right, Elsie,' said Mabel nervously, her head lowered. ''E never hurt me or nothin'.'

'No, but it's 'is bloody aggravatin' attitude.' Elsie shook her head, thinking about what she'd like to do to Theo and his rotten bushel basket. 'Still, this won't buy the baby a new bonnet, will it, gels? Come on, all of yers, back to the 'uts.' Elsie wiped her hands on her coarse sacking apron and tapped out her pipe on the corner of the bin. She collected up her things from the ground and gladly left the hop gardens until Monday morning.

The rest of the pickers followed her example and made their way back to the Common in an untidy procession, accompanied by children, emptied food baskets, and fire-blackened kettles.

'Ted! Sammy!' Jess lifted her skirts and broke into a run when she spotted her brothers basking in the sun on the grass outside the huts. 'Look, Mum, they've got 'ere.'

'Only just,' said Sammy, standing up to greet his sister, and dragging his little brother up by the ear. 'Ted 'ere only wanted to 'ire them penny-a-day bikes. Wanted to bike all the way down 'ere. 'E's drove me flamin' bonkers this last fortnight. I'm sure 'e's crackers or somethin'.'

'Yer shut up, Sammy, an' leave me alone. Mum's 'ere now. I'll tell 'er of yer if yer don't leave off.'

'Yer meant to be a grown-up worker now, Ted, not a snotty little snitchin' kid. Carry on like that an' instead of going back to work on Monday I'll 'ave to send yer back to school.'

'Aw yeh, big 'ead. 'Oo says? You?'

'Shut up, the pair of yer,' hissed Jess under her breath. 'Yer've only been 'ere five minutes an' yer fightin' already. Now be quiet before Mum 'ears yer.' Jess lowered her voice even more.

'She's not been too well. An' I don't want you pair upsettin' 'er. Right?' Jess stuck her fists into her hips. 'I said, right?'

'Yes, Jess,' said Ted.

'She ill or somethin'?' asked Sammy.

''Oo's she, the cat's mother?'

'Leave off, Jess, stop yer moanin',' whined Sammy. 'What's up with 'er then?'

'It's 'er chest. It ain't cleared up yet.'

'But yer've been 'ere two weeks.'

'I ain't stupid, Sammy. I know 'ow long I've been 'ere. Sssh, 'ere she is. Just be quiet. An' don't say nothin' about it,' Jess warned both her brothers with a look that showed she meant it. 'She'll only get upset.'

''Ere's me boys. Come an' give yer old mum a great big kiss.'

Ted and Sam threw their arms around Rose. Ted started sniffling.

''Ark at 'im, Mum,' tutted Sammy. 'I was sayin' 'e'll 'ave to go back to school if 'e can't behave like a proper bloke.'

'Leave 'im alone, Sammy. Yer pleased to see yer ol' mum, that's all, ain't yer, me little love?'

'An' we've got a real good surprise for yer, Mum, yer wait an' see,' sniffed Ted. 'Yer go in the 'ut, go on. You an' all, Jessie.'

Rose pushed open the hut door. 'Bill!'

'Wotcher, me old darlin',' said Bill, coming out of the hut towards her, his arms stretched wide.

''Ow've yer been, girl?' He wrapped his arms round his wife and kissed her. Then he hugged his daughter. 'An' look at this beauty. Blimey, Jess, yer a young lady now and no mistake.'

'Dad!' Jessie hugged her father tight.

'Gimme another go,' beamed Rose, and she moved forward to take her place again in her Bill's arms.

Jess went over to her brothers.

'Sam, Ted. Where's Jack?' she asked quietly.

-

All the huts at Worlington were buzzing with the excitement of the arrival of the weekend visitors. Even Mabel Lawrence's children were infected by the atmosphere of celebration. And their mother was glad to accept Elsie's invitation to join the Dorkin family and Joey Fuller 'for a bit of tea' – the pie, mash and liquor that Elsie's husband Percie had brought all the way from London in a great big china mixing bowl covered with a piece of old sheet.

By the late afternoon a party mood had developed and the pickers and their guests started thinking about decamping to the Hop Bine, the pub in the village.

Rose, however, chose not to go. She was content to sit round the fire drinking tea and listening to her Bill telling his stories about the jungles and beasts of South America.

'If only our Charlie was 'ere with us, eh, Bill?' she said wistfully. 'Then it would be all of us. All the Fairleighs together again.'

'I know, love, but it sounds like it was an opportunity 'e couldn't miss. 'E's a man now, Rose, nearly nineteen. We was married at that age. 'E 'as to make 'is own way in the world some time.'

'Talk about a chip off the old block,' said Rose, smiling and shaking her head. 'D'yer know, Bill, that's exactly what 'e said to me: "A real opportunity" 'e said.'

Rose looked into the far distance, sipping her tea, thinking about Charlie walking away from her across the Common, and his big opportunity, his new life. She bit her lip, praying in her own way that he'd be safe. That maybe one day he'd come home to her.

'Yer quiet, Jessie love,' said Bill, putting his arm round his daughter's shoulders. 'Miles away, yer are. Sittin' starin' into that fire like it was gonna tell yer fortune or somethin'.'

'I was wonderin' where 'e was, that's all, Dad.'

'Gawd, Jessie, wash yer ear'oles out, gel. Yer mother's been tellin' us for the past 'alf-hour. 'E's gone to work in a club, in Chicago, ain't 'e? In America.'

'No, Dad. I know about Charlie, Mum told me in the week. I was wonderin' where Jack was.'

'Jack?' Bill frowned, confused by this new turn in the conversation.

'Jacko Barnes,' piped up Ted, 'the postman.'

'I know 'oo Jack is, dopey,' said Bill. ''E spent so much time in our 'ouse as a kid 'e might as well 'ave moved in. But what would 'e be doin' down 'oppin'? Clara 'ates even the idea of it.'

''E's sweet on our Jess.' Ted ducked niftily as Rose stretched out to cuff him.

'Is 'e now?' said Bill, smiling and turning towards his daughter.

'Yeh,' continued Ted. ''E was the one what give 'er that canary.' He nodded towards the birdcage hanging outside the hut. 'Right in front of all of us 'e did. Didn't care 'oo saw 'im or nothin'. An' she give 'im a little yellow scarf to keep his skinny neck warm. Bleed'n' whistlin' all the time that bird is,' he added for what he thought was a grown-up effect.

This time Ted was not quick enough. Rose landed him a sharp wallop round the back of his head. 'I'll give yer bleed'n' whistlin'. What's all this swearin' lark? What'll yer dad think of yer?'

Ted rubbed his head pitifully. 'Can't be much of a bloke anyway if 'e don't even bother to turn up.'

'Right. That's it.' Rose was angry and Ted knew he'd gone too far. 'Get in that 'ut an' get to bed. Now.'

'Aw, Mum,' he snivelled, thinking he might as well push his luck a bit further. 'I wanted to go down the pub with all the others.'

'Yer start actin' like a man an' that's 'ow yer'll get treated. Now. Bed.'

Ted went grudgingly to the hut. 'Sorry, Jess,' he murmured.

'What was that, Ted?' asked Sammy, cupping his hand to his ear. 'Did yer say somethin'?'

'Leave 'im alone, all of yer,' Jess burst out suddenly. ''E's only a kid. But 'e's right. 'E can't be much of a bloke if 'e let me down like that. An' it ain't Ted's fault Jack Barnes is a rotten liar.'

'Don't cry, love,' said Bill, taking his daughter in his arms as she began sobbing uncontrollably. 'It ain't worth gettin' upset over 'im if that's what 'e's like.'

'But yer could see 'e really cared for 'er,' said Rose. She couldn't get the scrap of yellow cloth that Charlie had left her out of her mind. 'An' it ain't *like* 'im, actin' like this. It's right out a character.' She turned to her eldest son. 'Yer ain't 'eard nothin', 'ave yer, Sam?'

'Nothin'. In fact, 'is ol' man come round Number Eight lookin' for 'im only yesterday. Clara crept off back to Ireland last week, see, an' Cyril was wantin' a few bob sub off Jack to go down The Star.'

'Jack wouldn't 'ave gone to Ireland with 'is mum, would 'e?' asked Bill. Even he didn't sound very convinced by his own question.

'No chance,' said Rose. 'Clara likes to travel light.'

Ted slunk back from the hut to his place by the faggot fire and said in a wheedling voice, 'Dad. Why don't yer give our Jessie 'er present? That'll cheer 'er up.'

'Good idea, son,' said Bill, bending his head down to smile at Jess. 'I forgot all about it. Go in the 'ut an' get it for me, Ted.'

'Yer see, Jess, yer'll love it,' said Sam.

Ted returned from the hut with a large square container covered in a green chenille cloth. He placed it carefully on the ground behind Bill and Jess. Rose and Sam moved closer, eager to see Jess's reaction.

'Now. What do yer always say to yer old dad whenever 'e goes away to sea?'

'Bring us back a monkey,' said Jess through her tears. Then her eyes opened wide. 'Dad, yer 'aven't? Not really?' She raised herself up on to her knees. 'Aw, yer only 'ave, 'aven't yer? Yer've brought me back a monkey. Aw, Dad, let's see, let's 'ave a look.'

Bill uncovered the brass cage and opened the little door. He reached in and handed Jess the tiny golden marmoset. 'It's called a ginny monkey, love. Least, that's what the sailors call 'em. Don't know what the proper name is.'

The diminutive creature stared up at her with an almost human expression. It opened its minute jaws and yawned, then blinked at the bright firelight.

'Aw, look at it, Dad.' She turned to her father. 'I don't know what to say.'

'Yer'll 'ave to take care of it, mind. They don't like the cold. That's why it 'ad that cloth over it.'

'It'll be like a bleed'n' farmyard, what with that an' Jacko's canary whistlin' all day,' said Ted, without thinking.

Jess swallowed hard and bowed her head.

'Thank yer, Ted,' said Sammy, acting very superior, 'but I think we've 'eard enough from yer about canaries for one night.'

'For Gawd's sake, Sammy, take that boy down the pub and keep 'im quiet,' said Bill. ''Ere. Take this couple o' bob. Go on. An' you, Jess. Yer go with 'em. Go and 'ave a laugh, gel.'

'I'd rather stay 'ere, Dad.'

'No, go on. They'll all be down there. Think yer back 'ome in Burton Street, yer will.'

'Dad, I don't want to.'

'Listen to yer father,' said Rose levelly. 'Do as 'e says.'

'All right, but only cos 'e wants me to.' Jess stood up, brushing the grass from her skirt. ''Ow 'bout you and Dad. Yer coming with us?'

'No, gel,' said Bill. 'Me an' yer mum's stayin' 'ere on our own like. We've got a lot of things to catch up on. A lot to tell each other. An' don't worry, we'll look after yer monkey for yer.'

Reluctantly, Jess walked slowly away across the Common. 'See yer later, then,' she said miserably.

Sammy and Ted, keen not to miss valuable drinking time, were already halfway up the lane leading to Tilnhurst before Jess caught up with them.

'That's them gone,' said Bill, holding Rose close to him as he poked a long hazel twig into the brightly glowing embers. 'Fancy our Ted gettin' so tall, eh? I can 'ardly believe 'ow grown-up they all are.'

'An' I can't believe what's 'appened to our poor Jess,' Rose responded a bit sharper than she'd meant to.

'All right, gel. Calm yerself. It won't kill 'er, bein' stood up by a bloke. All part of growin' up.'

'But, Bill, you of all people should know that Jack ain't like that.' Rose held her hand up to her face, shielding herself from a piece of wood that spat from the fire. ''E's a good 'un, reliable. Wouldn't let no one down. It's obvious that's somethin's 'appened to 'im.'

'Prob'ly just scared 'imself. Realised 'e was gettin' in a bit deep per'aps? Bit too serious too quick?'

'No, Bill, yer don't understand. 'E was serious. Yer never saw 'ow 'e was moonin' about. An' 'e was definitely comin' down with the boys to see 'er. 'E was right taken with Jess.'

'Yer worryin' yerself over nothin', Rose. 'E'll 'ave found somethin' better to do. Yer know what young fellers are like.' Bill looked down at her sitting by his side on the grass. 'Or maybe 'e was barmy enough to think he could find a gel prettier than a Fairleigh.' He kissed Rose tenderly on the cheek.

'I think there's more to it than that, Bill,' said Rose, looking up into his eyes. 'It's no good, I've gotta talk to yer about it. I'm that worried. I'm sure that our Charlie…'

'Look, Rose, can't yer forget the kids for now, eh? Just this once? Come on, gel, give yer old man a cuddle. I ain't seen yer for months.'

–

The landlord of the Hop Bine finally managed to persuade the Londoners that he was closing the pub and that they should all get back to the farm.

'Goodnight, everyone,' he called as he shut the front doors. 'I'll be open again in the morning.'

As soon as they had left, he unlocked a narrow door at the back of the bar and welcomed in the locals who had spent the evening drinking in his kitchen.

'You can all come in now. The riffraff have gone, you'll be pleased to hear.'

''Bout time as well,' complained Theo, rubbing the back of his hand across his narrow lips. 'It's bad enough having to spend the day working near them without being kept out of the pub by the foreign scum.'

'Calm down, Theo,' grinned the landlord. 'Here, have this one on me.' He handed the sour-faced man a foaming tankard of beer.

'It's all right for you,' said the measurer, snatching the free pint with no attempt at thanks. 'You earns plenty of money out of them.'

'I certainly wouldn't be mixing with them otherwise, now would I, Theo?' said the landlord, outraged at the very idea that he would welcome such people for motives other than profit.

Oblivious to the hatred they inspired back in the pub, the 'foreigners' were making their way happily back to Worlington Hall Farm.

'Come on, Joey, give us a tune to 'elp us on our way,' came a shout from the rear of the wavering column of people winding its unsteady way along the pitch-dark country lane. It was Wally Baxter, chancing life and limb by having a good time.

It was well known that Florrie Baxter wasn't usually too keen, to say the least, on public displays of pleasure where her Wally was concerned, but unaccountably she had decided to join in the spirit of the thing – she hadn't even mentioned Jack's absence for at least a quarter of an hour. 'Yeh, Joe,' she giggled girlishly. 'Give us a song.'

Joey Fuller, who had been hired by the menfolk of Burton Street to drive them to Kent in his cart, produced his tin whistle from his jacket and began to play.

''Ere, Ted, Ted,' slurred Sam, digging his brother in the ribs with his elbow. 'Get out yer Jew's 'arp an' play along with 'im.'

Ted gave his brother a lopsided drunken grin for an answer and attempted to produce the instrument from the depths of his trouser pocket. ''S lost, Sam,' he said.

''S lost? Can't be. 'Ere, let me look for yer.' Sam began rifling ineffectually through his brother's tatty garments.

'Yer disgustin', the pair of yer. Look at yerselves, gettin' drunk,' snapped Jess tearfully from further along the lane. 'Serve yer right if yer get left behind. Yer'll never find yer way in the dark an' the grey lady'll get yer. Good job an' all.'

'She's got the 'ump,' said a woman's voice close to Jess. 'Been mopin' all night, she 'as.'

'What d'yer expect? She's been let down by that Jack Barnes, yer know,' answered another voice, which sounded very like Florrie Baxter back to her old form.

'Blimey, I thought they was in love an' all,' laughed the first voice.

Jess closed her eyes and cringed with shame, wishing she could crawl away into a ditch and hide from them all. Why had Jack done it to her? He hadn't even bothered to send her a message. And in front of everyone. She'd really thought he'd cared for her. She'd believed him.

''E's lost it, Jess,' persisted Sam, 'an I've gotta 'elp me little brother look for it, ain't I? I gotta…'

Jess didn't hear the last few words as Sam had managed to trip himself over and fall sideways into the hedge, pulling Ted down on top of him.

'Yer a disgrace, both of yer,' she sobbed at her sniggering brothers. 'Now get out of there before I go an' fetch Dad and let 'im sort yer out.'

'Don't be rotten, Jess,' chuckled Ted as he tried unsuccessfully to clamber to his feet. 'It ain't our fault Jacko's let yer down.'

'Shut up, Ted. Why don't yer just shut up?' Jess shouted through her tears. 'I don't care if I never see that no-good bugger Jack Barnes again. An' I don't care 'oo knows it neither.'

''Ark at 'er,' said someone disdainfully. 'Little Miss Perfect's lost 'er temper.'

All the Londoners, even the stragglers of the group, eventually arrived back at the huts. Some called their goodnights, others threw another faggot on their fire and sat around the bright flames, reminiscing, singing and laughing.

'Go an' ask Mum an' Dad if they wanna cuppa tea,' said Jess icily to Ted as she hung the kettle on the prop over the flames. 'No, wait, I'd better go. The state yer in yer'll probably go in the wrong 'ut by mistake.' She shoved Ted unceremoniously out of her way. 'I'd 'ate to think what Florrie'd do to yer if yer caught 'er in 'er drawers. Mind yer it might teach yer not to get drunk again, yer little fool.'

'Shall I bring yer a cuppa tea?' whispered Jess from the doorway of the hut, in case her parents were asleep.

'We'll come outside with yer, love,' said Bill. 'Come on, Rosie, let's go an' cheer our girly up a bit.'

Jess swallowed hard; her father's kindness seemed to make her feel worse, guilty that she was spoiling his leave.

He stepped out of the hut and smiled at her, his lovely, wide smile, with his little moustache all neat and trimmed. Jess looked up at him and decided she would stop crying and that was that. Jack Barnes might have done a runner, but that was too bad. If he didn't want her, then there was nothing she could do about it, she'd have to get used to it. She wasn't going to have Jack Barnes upsetting her or her family any more. Her dad was home from sea and they would all be happy together.

Rose and Bill sat with their children by the fire.

'Do yer remember 'ow when I come 'ome yer used to sit on me knee an' look into the flames, Jess?' said her father. 'When yer was little yer used to say, "Tell us them stories about ghosts an' witches." Used to love being scared, yer did.' He ran a calloused hand over her thick auburn hair, watching how the flickering light made it glow. 'An' just look at yer now. Me

165

little gel's turned into a real beauty. Too old for fairy tales, I suppose?'

'I'll never be too old to listen to yer stories, Dad,' said Jess.

'Well then, we'll 'ave a story, shall we? The scariest one I can think of. Cuddle up, you lot.' Rose and Jess made themselves comfortable on either side of Bill, resting against his strong seaman's body. 'Where's the boys got to?'

'Sam's fell asleep on the grass, Dad, but I'm 'ere,' said Ted from the shadows. 'Can I tell a story? It's a real good 'un.' He sat down, squeezing in between Jess and his father, like he used to do when he was little. 'Right scary it is. An' it's true an' all.'

'What do yer think, Rosie? Is our Ted old enough to be the storyteller?' asked Bill, obviously amused by it all.

'If 'e knows a good un, then I reckon 'e is,' said Rose. 'An' I wouldn't mind 'earing a story meself.'

'Dunno about no stories, but 'e's old enough to get keye-eyed down the pub with Sam all right,' said Jess moodily.

'Don't start, Jess. Yer father don't want to 'ear no squabblin' on 'is first night 'ome with us, now does 'e? Go on, Ted, tell us yer story. But take yer time; yer ain't exactly easy to understand tonight after being out with Sammy. An' nothin' rude.'

Ted began his tale. 'Well, it was like this. I was down by the Thames—'

'What was yer doing down there?' interrupted Rose immediately. 'Yer know yer not allowed down there.'

'Let 'im get on with it, Rose. It's only a story,' said Bill.

'It ain't a story, Dad, it's true,' insisted Ted. 'Honest.'

'If I thought…'

'Leave it, Rose,' said Bill. 'Like yer said, 'e ain't exactly sober.'

'As I was sayin',' Ted continued, 'I was down by the river with me mates. Met 'em after work I did, Dad,' he added proudly. 'An' guess what? What do yer think I saw? A body.

A real one. Floatin' down the Thames it was. All bloated an' 'orrible and purple. An' it stunk. Cor! Rotten as a pear it was. Well, me an' Jimmy found a big stick an' dragged it in to the bank.' He hesitated, his face blood-red reflecting the flames of the fire. 'Then we saw it. All the throat was cut open.' He made a dramatic slashing movement across his own neck. 'Like that!'

Rose was horrified. 'Body? What body? 'Oo was it? Ted? Ted? You answer me, boy.'

'Dunno, Mum. But it was all 'orrible an' the face was all kind of, yuck, I dunno. Jimmy ran off an' got the rozzers, while I watched it so no dogs got at it. The rozzers reckoned it was the crabs 'ad 'ad it. They'd 'ad a good feed off 'is face. Et it all away they 'ad. Tore it all with their claws. An' there was eels inside 'is belly an' all. Been eating all 'is guts out.'

'If yer telling me lies, Ted…'

'No, Mum, I ain't. Honest,' he said, a wide-eyed picture of truth and innocence. Then he started laughing. 'An' there was somethin' else.' He looked slyly at Jess to see her reaction. 'No one could guess 'oo 'e was, cos even all 'is clothes was missin'. Naked like a newborn baby 'e was.'

'That's it.' Rose stood up. 'Bed all of yers. Jess, Ted. Get that Sammy in the 'ut. I've made up a bed on the floor for the boys. An' you, Jess, yer going in with Mabel. An' don't wake 'er kids up neither.'

'Do as yer mother says,' said Bill. 'I'll speak to yer later, Ted.'

Jess dragged the protesting Ted away by his ear.

—

'Come to the Mission, will you come? Will you come? Free tea and buns.'

'What's that soddin' noise,' groaned Sammy, holding his throbbing head in his shaking hands.

'It's them Mission ladies singin', an' the vicar,' said Ted, apparently none the worse for the five pints of beer he had drunk the night before. 'If yer go an' join in the 'ymn singing they gives yer a free cuppa tea an' cakes. Right good it is. Yer comin'?'

Ted was the only member of the Fairleigh family who received the spiritual and prandial benefits of the missionary workers that Sunday. Sammy turned over on his makeshift bed and slept away the rest of the bright autumn morning. Jess helped Mabel with the children and her chores. And Rose prepared the Sunday meal, using a lot of imagination and her single pot suspended over the faggot fire. It was left to Bill to organise a group of the visiting men for a walk down to the village, where those who needed it could have a recuperative hair of the dog.

By midday some of the women had joined their menfolk in the pub, but not all of them by any means. The women who considered themselves respectable wives and mothers knew that Sunday lunchtime visits to the pub were an exclusively male affair, unless a woman was 'no better than she ought to be', of course.

After eating their varyingly appetising meals of pot roast, braised liver, sheep's head or sausage stew, the older visitors and their wives settled down in the straw-filled beds for a 'Sunday afternoon nap'. Many such naps would result in a new mouth to feed come May or June – in other words, the birth of yet another hopping baby.

The younger visitors were left to their own devices, so, having to sort out their own entertainment, they arranged a football match between Worlington's and Fanshawe's hop farms.

The pitch was an unconventional, crudely fashioned affair on the Common, with apple boxes marking the goalmouths. The teams were no more traditional in their make-up than the ground. The sides were neither limited to specific numbers in each team, nor to just kicking the ball with their feet. The game was governed by a far more relaxed set of rules which ensured an exciting event for the spectators – mainly sisters and sweethearts of the players – and a release for the youthful energies of the teams themselves. The match had been going for almost twenty incident-packed minutes when a disputed foul threatened to cause a fight between the opposing camps.

'Sam, don't 'it 'im. 'E never meant to kick yer,' pleaded Jess as her brother gestured menacingly at a stocky dock worker who was visiting his mother at Fanshawe's. 'Anyway, look at the size of 'im. 'E'll pulverise yer.'

'I ain't scared of the fat bastard,' sneered the usually cowardly Sam, uncharacteristically. If only his opponent hadn't hurt Sam's head, the trouble would never have started, but what with his hangover, Sam's temper had just snapped. 'I'll give 'im a right larrupin'.'

'Dad'll do 'is crust if yer do, Sam. Why don't yer forget it?'

'A very good idea, Miss Fairleigh.' Jess blushed at the sound of her name being spoken in the cultured voice of Robert Worlington. 'Get on with the game, there's good fellows. Tell you what, I'll be referee. Keep some order here.'

It was as though the dispute had never happened. Sam and the docker were immediately united against this intruder from the big house. They shook hands spontaneously and the docker addressed Robert Worlington in tones of undisguised hatred.

'We don't need no toffee-nosed ref round 'ere, thanks all the same. We look after our own affairs where we come from.' With that he slapped Sammy matily on the back and ran off to the centre spot of the field. 'Go on, Sammy, yer take the kick-off, moosh.'

Sammy bowed low. 'Why, thank yer very much, ol' chap,' he said in a mocking imitation of Robert's voice. 'I don't mind if I do.'

And with that, the game was again under way.

'They don't mean nothin', yer know,' said Jess to Robert, all the while keeping her eyes firmly on the football match. 'It's only their way.'

'They don't interest me, Jess,' Robert replied, outwardly concentrating on the sport, but brushing his arm deliberately against hers. 'I came over here as an excuse to be with you.'

'Don't talk daft,' she said. They stood in silence for a while, Jess increasingly aware of the closeness of Robert's body.

'Which one of those chaps is your suitor then?' he asked eventually, not even bothering to hide his obvious contempt for the assorted male specimens before him.

'What?'

'Your suitor? You must have one. Beau? Paramour?' Robert looked at Jess meaningfully. 'Lover?'

''E couldn't come,' she said abruptly.

'I see,' Robert said.

Jess turned to look at him. He was grinning broadly.

–

'See yer next weekend, gel.' Bill held Rose in his arms and gently kissed her on the forehead. 'If I don't get meself a bit of casual down the docks, that is. An' if I don't get down next week, I promise yer, it'll be the week after. All right? I'll be down then, no matter what.'

'Whatever else 'appens, Bill, promise me yer'll keep an eye on them boys. Don't let Ted go down that river again or nothin'.' She made sure that no one else could hear. 'An' let me know if there's any word of Jack.'

'All right, Rosie, don't go on at me. Yer know I'll stop 'em from gettin' in any trouble. An' I dunno 'ow many times I've said I'll see if I can find out about Jack. I don't know what's up with yer, yer ain't stopped worrying about them bloody boys all weekend. I'm 'ome now. Right? The old man's back.' He moved his hands up her back and rubbed the still soft skin at the nape of her neck with the pads of his rough working-man's thumbs.

'I don't mean to go on at yer, Bill. But they worry me so much. Yer know what they're like. Always up to somethin'. No matter 'ow 'ard I try to keep 'em in order. An' it don't seem to get no easier as they get older. We'll 'ave to 'ave a talk about 'em soon.'

'Yeh, I know, Rose. An' I know yer've 'ad an 'ard time bringin' 'em up with me being away so much.'

'Don't say that, Bill. I weren't 'aving a go or nothin'. I can't 'elp meself worryin'. That's all.'

'Well, yer to stop worryin'. D'you 'ear me? Start lookin' after yerself for once. Leave the boys to me. Yer make sure yer keep takin' that jollup the nurse give yer, an' get that chest of your'n better.'

Rose rested her head against her husband's chest, trying to think how to tell him about her fears about Jack and Charlie. But she couldn't begin to put her thoughts into words. Speaking about them would make them real. 'This old waist-coat could do with a bit of a darn,' she said instead. 'Want to leave it 'ere an' I'll see to it for yer?'

'Always gotta find yerself a job, ain't yer, Rosie? No, I won't leave it. All right? Sailors ain't useless, yer know. 'Oo d'yer think dams me gear when I'm at sea? The butler?'

'Go on, yer great daft lump.' Rose pushed Bill gently away from her. ''Urry up or yer'll miss yer lift with Joey. Then yer'll 'ave no chance of gettin' down the docks for the mornin' call. An' I don't want no idle layabout for an 'usband.'

He chucked Rose affectionately under the chin. 'Yer a gel,' he said.

'Bill,' she said, 'would yer do somethin' for me?'

'D'yer need to ask?'

'See if yer can find out what 'appened with Jack.'

Bill was about to answer when Jessie came up to them.

'Thanks for me monkey, Dad,' she said. She had waited until her parents had finished embracing before stepping out of the hut to join them. 'I really love it. Ta, Dad. I'll look after it proper.'

'Make sure yer do, darlin'. An' cheer up, eh, love? I don't want no geezer breakin' me baby's 'eart.' He spoke in a loud pretend whisper, 'An' try and cheer yer mother up a bit while yer at it. She's got the right 'ump on 'er about Charlie goin'.'

'We'll be all right, Dad,' said Jess, trying to sound brave for her father.

'Course yer will, Jessie. An' sod the postman, eh, love? A beauty like you. Wouldn't surprise me if yer found yerself a prince.'

–

Scenes of goodbye were being enacted on hop farms throughout the county as menfolk prepared to return to London. Some farewells were as loving as the Fairleighs', but some, like the one in Florrie Baxter's hut, were considerably less so. Wally's departure from his wife included him being lectured on a list of duties which was delivered to him as though he was a particularly unfortunate and downtrodden servant. And some women had nothing at all to say to their departing husbands; they were simply glad to see the back of the drunken nuisances, whose presence threatened them with yet another unwanted pregnancy, yet another mouth to feed come next spring.

Whatever the feelings accompanying those partings, by ten o'clock on Sunday night the hoppers' huts had once again become the domain of the women and their children, exhausted, ready for bed, and for another week's work in the hop gardens.

Chapter 10

Fair Rates for a Fair Bushel

As picking got under way on Monday morning, all the conversation and the gossip in the fields was about the weekend.

'That Wally Baxter,' laughed Elsie to Mabel. 'My Perce'd knock me from 'ere to Christmas mornin' if I give 'im orders like that Florrie do. Wouldn't mind but she's no bigger than 'apporth of coppers. An' the size of 'im. 'E's like the side of an 'ouse.'

'An' 'e's a good man an' all,' said Mabel. 'Give me a couple of shillin's to buy the kids some grub before 'e went.'

'Blimey, don't let Florrie know, she'd muller 'im. An' *you'd* never 'ear the end of it. She'd give yer a right ear'ole bashin'. Cor, imagine 'er 'avin' that to go on about.'

'I ain't barmy,' laughed Mabel.

Further down the row of bins, Florrie was talking to, or rather, at, Rose. 'Did yer see 'ow that one down there, the one from Awerley Street, was performin' in the pub on Saturday night? All round the blokes, she was. Common little tart. Thought she was gonna show 'em 'er drawers, way she was carryin' on. Mind yer, I doubt if she wears any, that one.'

'No, Florrie, I can't say as I did see 'er,' said Rose carrying on picking into her bin. 'I was too busy spendin' me time mindin' me own business with me 'usband.'

'Pity yer don't spend more time keepin' an eye on your Jessie an' that Worlington boy,' mumbled Florrie.

'What was that?' spat Rose, flinging the half-stripped bine on to the ground. 'Say that again, so's I can 'ear yer proper this time.'

'What's up with yer?' said Florrie innocently. 'I only said...'

But Florrie did not have the chance to finish her outraged defence as her twins, Sidney and Albert, came running up full pelt into the side of her bin.

'Oi, watch out, you boys.'

'Mum, quick, come an' see,' said Albert, dragging Florrie by the sleeve.

'All the pickers from Fanshawe's,' panted Sidney, 'they're on strike, an' they're all marchin' over 'ere. Got a big sign they 'ave. They're carryin' it right up in the air, on two big 'op poles.'

'Yeh,' said Albert. 'The banner says, "Fair rates for a fair bushel". They're all shoutin' an' everythin'. Come on. Come an' see 'em.'

Florrie did not have to leave her bin to witness the spectacle. The Fanshawe strikers had marched into the Worlington hop gardens. Their cry of 'Fair rates for a fair bushel', accompanied by the beating of sticks on kettles and tin cans, brought picking at Worlington to an astonished standstill.

A stout, grey-haired woman at the front of the procession handed the pole she had been carrying to one of her companions and started speaking in a loud, confident voice.

'We 'ave proclaimed an 'oppers' strike,' she bellowed. 'It's bad enough our men back 'ome 'avin' 'ad their wages cut. But us workin' women won't stand for it no more. We ain't askin' for what ain't ours by rights. We wants fairness, that's all. Fair rates for a fair bushel. We won't take the measurers, them farmers' lackeys, cheatin' us no more. An' we won't take bein' treated like animals. We wanna be able to use the well, not walk the quarter of a mile to the river. We wants our rights. Come an' join us.'

The Fanshawe strikers cheered their support for their spokeswoman, but Florrie would not have such disruption in 'her' hop garden.

'You Fanshawe mob,' she yelled back at them. 'Yer all the bleed'n' same. Strike every year at the drop of an 'at. An' it's always you, Bessie Shea, up the front leadin' 'em. Yer an' yer big gate shoutin' the odds. Well let me tell you somethin' for a change: Fanshawe might treat you lot badly over there. Well, perhaps yer deserve it. All I know is, we're all right 'ere thank yer very much. An' if it's all the same to you,' Florrie looked Bessie Shea up and down, "ladies", there's some of us wants to get on with our pickin'.'

This time it was Florrie who was cheered by the Worlington pickers. Encouraged by the support, Florrie stuck her hands on her hips and glared into Bessie Shea's furious face. 'What d'yer make of that then, Bessie bloody Shea?'

Rose stepped forward from her bin and took the neutral ground between the two bristling women. 'I ain't used to gettin' involved in this sort of thing,' she said, 'but if Bessie 'ere an' 'er mates 'ave got an argument with Fanshawe, that's their business, an' they're entitled to do as they see fit. But I don't reckon it's nothin' to do with us.'

'Yer tell 'er, Rose,' shouted Florrie, surprisingly briefly.

'But,' continued Rose, 'I don't reckon arguing amongst ourselves is right either. Even if we don't agree with the strike, us Londoners should stick together as much as we can. Don't let's 'ave no bad feelin's; we should 'elp each other out if we 'ave to.'

'An' yer ain't bloody wrong there, Rose,' said Elsie. 'Look over at the oast 'ouses.'

As one, strikers and pickers all turned towards the great drying sheds, to see yet another procession heading towards the field.

''Oo the 'ell are they?' asked one of the strikers from Fanshawe's.

'It's our bastard measurer,' answered Elsie, 'Theo. An' it looks like the little toerag's brought the 'ole of the village with 'im. 'Ere, 'e's even got that bloody Batsford, the 'Oly Joe, with 'im.'

'What do they want, Mum?' asked Jess.

'Dunno, girl, but they don't sound very friendly. Yer keep by me, an' keep yer mouth shut.'

The marchers were drawing close enough for the Londoners to make out their cries and chants.

'Like the troublemakers in the docks and in the mines. They're all the same. Bringing trouble to our village. Get back where you came from, city filth,' jeered Theo's wife from the approaching crowd.

'City filth! City scum!' they heard.

'But we ain't even strikin', Mum,' Jess protested.

'Don't matter to them, by the looks of it, Jess. They reckon we're all the same,' said Rose.

'Damned foreigners,' yelled a woman who was marching alongside Theo's wife.

'Ladies, please. Blasphemy is quite unnecessary.'

'That's a good 'un, vicar,' shouted Elsie, 'callin' them old cats "ladies". What's that make you and Theo? The toms?'

The first blow came from a rock, thrown by a villager at the Worlington pickers; it coincided with a squawking voice calling, 'That's for making up to our husbands, you foreign muck.'

Even the regular pickers were shocked by the venom of the curses which then flowed from the homedwellers' mouths. It was as though they had been saving poison and bile all their lives with the sole purpose of directing it at the Londoners.

'I ain't puttin' up with this shit,' said Elsie, pushing her sleeves up above her elbows. ''Oo's with me?'

Worlington and Fanshawe pickers were united. They fell on the offending village women with flailing fists.

Name-calling was one thing, but as soon as the violence became physical, Theo rapidly followed the Reverend Henry Batsford's example and slipped away, anxious not to be caught up in the bloody fighting.

'Mum, where are yer?' called Jess.

'Don't worry about me. Look after yerself. Some of 'em 'ave got broken 'op poles. Watch out!' Rose dodged a flying clod of earth. 'See if yer can find Mabel.'

'Mabel?' called Jess, narrowly avoiding another well-aimed throw.

'Ssh. She's over 'ere with me, Jess,' hissed Winnie from behind the thick tangles of growing hops. 'We're gettin' 'er kids back to the 'uts.'

'I'll be there with yer when I've found Lil. Ouch!' Jess felt a stinging pain as the thin end of a long chestnut pole was swiped round her cheek. 'Yer ol' cow.'

'Harlot!' shrieked her attacker, the woman who had supported the measurer's wife. 'Your red hair shows you for what you are. Jezebel!'

'An' I'll show yer what you bloody are,' shouted Lil, leaping to Jess's defence and knocking the pole from the woman's grip. 'Now show us 'ow clever yer are, yer snooty-nosed ol' bag.'

The two women circled each other, ominously silent in the yelling, fighting melee.

'Don't, Lil. Don't lose yer temper,' reasoned Jess. She'd seen Lil fight full-grown men outside The Star on a Saturday night. She knew how she could completely lose control. But Lil was deaf to Jess's pleadings. She sprang at the woman who had injured her friend, interested only in revenge for the insults. The combatants fell in an undignified sprawl between the hop bins.

'Lil, please. Don't.' Jess did her best to drag her champion away, but succeeded only in grabbing a handful of the village woman's hair. The woman screamed. Jess's confused attempts at apology were silenced by a thick length of wood hitting her hard across the back of the neck. She collapsed unconscious, and unnoticed by the fighting women, behind a half-full bin of hops.

'Oi! The rozzers are 'ere. Quick, leg it!'

Most of the Londoners, used to reacting quickly to such shouts, did not need a second warning. They did not wait to see the local police officer and his two mounted reinforcements, the so-called hopping coppers, who had been fortuitously summoned by the vicar before he left the village. The cockneys had no interest in watching the men rush along the rows, truncheons at the ready. Instead, they grabbed the younger children, regardless of family ties, and fled back to their huts. Only Bessie Shea and a few of her allies from Fanshawe's stood firm, surrounded by their village adversaries.

'Not you again, Bessie,' groaned PC Clarke. 'I thought we were going to have a peaceful harvest this year.'

'We'll 'ave peace when we 'ave justice,' said Bessie as dignified as her dishevelled appearance would allow. 'If yer gonna arrest me, yer'd best get on with it, or else I'll be gettin' back to me kids.'

'Go on. Out of my sight.' PC Clarke jerked his thumb over his shoulder in the direction of Fanshawe's. 'And if you know what's good for you. I'd suggest you ladies all go back to the village.'

The sight of Bessie Shea walking away without so much as a crack over the head from a police truncheon was more than Theo's wife could tolerate.

'They've bamboozled you as well,' she gasped. 'You men. You're all the same. Show you a glimpse of their filthy city ankles and you're useless. Useless.'

'Bessie Shea's ankles?' PC Clarke asked incredulously. He was a man out of his depth. 'I think you'd better let us escort you ladies back.' The constable gestured to his fellow officers. Wearily they coaxed the women into a disgruntled line and accompanied them back to their cottages.

–

'Elsie,' said Rose, knocking on the hut door, 'is Jess in there with your Lilly?'

'No, Rose. Not seen 'er,' said Elsie, sticking her head out of the hut, her pipe bobbing as she spoke.

Rose rubbed her tired eyes. 'I've looked everywhere. There was such a turn-out when the coppers come, I didn't know what was 'appenin'.'

'Not 'elpin' Mabel with the kids or nothin'?' suggested Elsie.

'No.'

'Don't worry, Rose. Jess'll look after 'erself. Them village women couldn't fight their way out of a paper bag. Daft old cows. An' that copper ain't a bad old boy. She'll be all right.'

'It ain't the women I'm worried about,' said Rose to herself.

–

Jess whimpered. Her head swam, her neck was stiff and bruised, her face smarted.

'It's all right, Jess. You're safe.'

Jess's eyes flickered open. She could make out the blurred face of Robert Worlington. He was kneeling over her, tenderly swabbing her wounds. Cautiously she touched a fingertip to the cut on her forehead. The pain made her draw in her breath sharply.

'No, don't touch it,' he said. 'Leave it to me. I can see what I'm doing.'

Jess closed her eyes again and let Robert get on with it. His hands were so gentle, and if she didn't move she hardly felt any pain at all.

'Where are we?' Her voice was hoarse with the effort of speaking.

'Sssh. We're in the stable block. I found you in the hop gardens after those rampaging women had been packed off by the constable. You must have taken quite a blow. You were out cold.'

'I... I don't remember.' Jess tried to sit up.

'It doesn't matter. Lie still.'

'It does. I... I was tryin' to stop Lilly. She was...' Jess bit her lip, willing herself not to cry with the pain. 'I 'ope she ain't got 'urt.'

'Listen to me. I told you, everything's going to be all right. You're safe.'

The cloth felt so cool as Robert wiped and dabbed at her skin. She let herself sink back into the hay as comfortably as she could.

'You're going to have quite a few bruises in the morning.'

'What?' Jess's head was spinning.

'Bruises. On your face.'

'Oh.'

'Try and rest. I'll take care of you.'

'Me 'ead. It 'urts so much.'

'I know,' he whispered.

Jess felt him loosen her blouse and slowly undo the buttons, one by one.

'Don't do that,' she moaned.

'Why?'

With a great effort she opened her eyes for a moment and looked up at him. His face was very close to hers. She flushed. 'Me underthings,' she managed to say. 'They ain't very nice. All 'oles in 'em.

'You rest,' he assured her, and slipped his hands into her blouse.

She closed her eyes, letting the smooth coolness of his hands soothe her hot skin.

'Does that feel good?' he said, running his hands over her breasts.

'Don't,' she said weakly.

'I'll be gentle,' he whispered. 'I won't hurt you.'

'Don't,' she managed to say again, 'it ain't right. Me mum and me. We 'ad a little talk. She said...'

Jess never finished telling Robert what her mother had told her in their little talk. Instead she floated back into blissful, pain-free unconsciousness.

—

'Hardly picked a damned thing for two days. Lazy blighters. This harvest will never be finished. Damn them. All of them.'

'Shouting at me won't help, George,' said Leonore, cutting her mutton into manageable mouthfuls. 'You must calm things down out there after the trouble. Get the pickers back to feeling happy about their work. Don't bluster around antagonising everybody.'

'And what exactly do you suggest, Leonore? Invite the vermin into the Hall for dinner?' Sir George's eyes were bulging with fury. His voice rose with his temper. 'Perhaps we could have a few rubbers of bridge after? Or why not a masked ball?'

'You'd like that, Robert, wouldn't you?' smirked Paul. 'An opportunity to dance with all the girls.'

'You never dance with me,' complained Julia, nibbling at the tiny morsel of meat impaled on the end of her fork.

'No, but Paul does, doesn't he, my sweet?' retorted Robert through a fixed, ugly smile.

'And I don't think your squabbling helps either,' said Lady Worlington stiffly.

Paul and Robert glowered at each other. Julia looked down at her plate.

'But George, you might have an idea there,' Leonore said pensively. 'About putting on a ball, I mean.'

'Put on a ball for the buggers? You're out of your mind, woman.' He turned to his sons in disbelief, nodding with alarming vigour. 'She's out of her mind. Same as her father. And her mother. Batty as coots, the whole family. And that cousin of hers, Amelia. Worst of the lot. All mad. Need certifying, the lot of them.'

'If I might continue,' Leonore said.

Sir George rolled his eyes at his wife's reprimand. His sons laughed impolitely at their mother. Julia continued to stare down at her plate.

'I did not intend, as you well know, George, to suggest that you should organise a grand ball. I rather thought we could have some kind of social occasion at which the locals and the Londoners might make their peace.' Her husband looked slightly more interested. 'It would hardly cost a thing,' she added.

That settled the matter as far as Sir George was concerned. A supper dance was to be held the coming Friday in the big barn, and Leonore could organise it.

—

'What's their game then?' asked Florrie suspiciously, cutting a fat hunk of cheese to go with the bread and pickles she'd already piled high on her plate. 'We don't never 'ave no party until the end of the 'arvest. An' what're all that lot doin' 'ere?' She jerked her head towards the glowering villagers who were grouped at the other end of the barn. 'An' 'avin' it all done out like this. Why ain't we sittin' down proper? Like we always do. An' them pies look a bit overdone to me an' all.'

'Seein' 'ow they've invited us an' all the locals, I reckon it's obvious,' said Rose. 'They're tryin' to get us to make our peace.'

'What? Us an' the 'omedwellers? 'E's got some chance,' said Florrie, still piling up her plate with more food.

'Well, Sir George has gone to enough trouble,' said Mabel, awestruck by the huge tables groaning under the weight of pies, cheeses, fruit, ale, cider, cakes, buns, breads, pickles and sauces.

'Aw yeh, did all this lot with 'is own fair 'ands, I don't think,' griped Florrie. ''E's got 'undreds of bloody skivvies to do all this for 'im. Don't even wipe 'is own arse, I'll bet.'

'Shut yer cake 'ole, for once, Florrie, an' stop complainin', will yer. Why don't yer just tuck in,' said Elsie, pouring her moaning neighbour another jug of cider. 'Way yer goin' on, yer'd think there was somethin' wrong with it.'

'Probably is,' said Florrie, emptying the tankard in two gulping swallows.

'Well, I think it's beautiful,' said Mabel. 'I ain't never seen nothin' like it in all me life.'

'Make sure yer sticks plenty in yer apron to take back for later on,' advised Elsie wisely.

'Cor. Don't yer think they'd mind?' Mabel was truly in paradise.

The women eventually fell into silence and got on with the serious business of eating and drinking their fill.

''Old up, there's the fiddler startin' up for the dancin',' whooped Lil, wiping her mouth on the back of her hand. 'Come on, Jess, let's show these yokels 'ow it's done.'

'Careful, Lil, yer'll make me spill me cider.'

Jess managed to hand her half-empty jug to Winnie before she resigned herself to being yanked around the makeshift dance floor by the less than elegant, but very enthusiastic Lilly Dorkin.

'My Lil's a gel,' said Elsie fondly.

'Pity she ain't a feller,' said Winnie. 'We could do with a few blokes to 'ave a dance with.'

'There's plenty of lads over by the beer barrels if that's what yer want,' said Rose, nodding towards the end of the barn.

A group of wary-looking young men stood by the bar which had been rigged up from planks and hay bales.

'Them! They're carrot crunchers,' said Win, spraying cake crumbs over Rose in horror. ''Oo'd wanna dance with them?'

'Mabel, for one,' said Florrie fondly. 'Just look at 'er.' Mabel was indeed dancing with one of the locals – a large, robust farm worker who towered over the skinny little Londoner. 'She's 'aving a right old time an' all, bless 'er. An' she deserves it, with what she's been through.'

'Blimey, yer in a good mood, Florrie,' said Elsie, obviously impressed by her friend's extraordinary frame of mind. 'Must be all that cider, 'Ere, gel, get another one down yer.'

'Thank yer, Elsie, I don't mind if I do.'

Winnie stifled a laugh. 'Don't get me mum too tiddly, Elsie. There's pickin' to do in the mornin'.'

'Sod the pickin',' yelled Florrie. With that, she took up the hem of her skirts in her hands and spun off round the floor in a solo polka, scattering any dancing couples who dared stray into her path.

'She's better drunk,' observed Elsie seriously.

–

'It seems to be going very well, George,' said Leonore, clapping her elegantly lace-gloved hands to the stirring rhythms of the fiddle music. She was sitting with her family and Julia Markington at a table which had been set out for them at a safe distance from the very popular beer platfrom. 'Boys, why don't you dance? It looks such fun.'

Paul seized the opportunity, and his brother's fiancée. 'Julia. May I?'

Giggling like an adolescent, Robert's betrothed allowed Paul to guide her on to the floor and around the room in a whirl of skipping steps and leaps.

'And how about you, Robert?' asked his mother. 'Won't you dance?'

'Leave the boy alone,' said Sir George, pouring himself another large glass of port from one of the bottles he had had brought over for himself from his cellars. 'It's bad enough we had to come tonight.'

'No, Father,' said Robert graciously, 'Mother is right. We must all do our bit for good relations with the workers.'

George Worlington did not notice his wife wince as Robert made directly for the tall, auburn beauty, one of the Fairleighs, who was twirling around the dance floor with a rather plain, plump girl with untidy hair. Neither did he notice his wife shake her head sorrowfully, as she predicted that yet another poor young woman was about to become the target of a Worlington male.

'Is this an excuse me? May I?' enquired Robert respectfully, tapping Lil on the shoulder.

'May yer what?'

'Take over with your partner?'

'Suit yerself, mate. I could do with a drink any'ow, I'm sweatin' like a pig.' Puffing noisily, Lil slouched off the dance floor towards the beer.

'Yer might 'ave asked me, Lil,' called Jess to her departing friend, but the music drowned her reply.

'Why? Don't you want me to take you in my arms again, Jess? Like before?' Robert asked.

'I told yer, it weren't right kissin' me like that.'

'You say no to kissing after what we've done together?'

She stopped dancing and pulled away from him, confused. 'What're yer talkin' about?'

'We'd better keep dancing, Jess,' he said, drawing her towards him again. 'People will wonder.'

'They're all lookin' at us anyway.'

'No, not at us, Jess. They're looking at you. And why shouldn't they? You are the most beautiful woman in the room.' He held her at arm's-length, appraising her unashamedly.

'Please. Don't, they'll 'ear yer. Let's dance.'

'Wouldn't you like to come outside with me, Jess?' he breathed into her ear. 'We could do it again, like we did in the stables.'

Jess felt heat rising from her throat until her face blushed scarlet. 'I dunno what yer talkin' about, but I don't like it.'

'Don't be a tease, Jess. That's not what you said when I looked after you. When I stroked your body all over, when we...'

'I ain't got a clue what yer talkin' about. I think yer'd better tell me what yer mean.' Jess's mouth was dry. She could hardly say the words.

'We can't talk here,' he said. 'Let's go where it's quiet. To the stable block. And I can show you what I mean.'

—

Like most of the other hoppers, Rose had succumbed to the festival atmosphere. In fact, it was because she was too busy keeping in time with the steps of Gerald Audley, the farm bailiff, as they took a turn together round the floor, that she failed to notice her daughter slip quietly away. The floor was so crowded with laughing, prancing couples that not even Florrie realised that Jess and Robert were missing from the barn for well over an hour. And even the local women didn't notice the developments between the young master and the cockney girl, since they were more concerned with keeping a watchful eye over their own menfolk, making sure that they didn't succumb to the obvious temptations put in their way by this ridiculous idea of Lady Worlington's.

'No good will come of such things, you mark my words,' as the measurer's tight-lipped wife was heard to remark more than once during the festivities.

'Thank you for so much for making the evening such a splendid success,' said Lady Worlington, balancing precariously on the beer platform. 'Sir George is too tired to thank you personally' – a few bold souls stared openly at the drunken man slumped over the table at the far end of the barn – 'but he wants you all to know what a pleasure this evening has been. For us all.'

'I thoroughly agree,' whispered Robert. He was standing behind Jess, nuzzling into the back of her neck. They were at the back of the crowd, having got there just in time to hear Lady Worlington's goodnight speech.

'Don't,' said Jess half-heartedly, 'they'll see yer.'

'Let the world see,' he replied, squeezing her waist. 'Let them all know how I feel about you.'

'Listen. Yer mum's talkin'.'

'I told you. I don't care about anyone but you, Jessie Fairleigh. I love you. You're going to be mine forever.'

Jess unclasped his hands from around her waist and turned to look at him. 'Yer said that before. Before we… Aw, yer know what I mean. But yer do really mean it, Robert, don't yer?' She closed her eyes. ''Cos I ain't never done that with no one before. Never. Even though yer thought I 'ad.' She opened her eyes and looked at him earnestly, imploring him to believe her. 'I didn't know we was doin' it the other time, honest. No matter what yer think.'

'If you say so, but there's no need to play games with me, Jessie.'

'I ain't playin' no games. I mean it. I didn't know. I was 'it over the 'ead, an' yer know I was. It's important to me, Robert, that yer believe me.'

'Sssh. Calm down. We've gone over all of this. It doesn't matter any more, Jess. You're mine now. I told you. I love you.'

''Ow about yer intended then? Julia whatever 'er name is. 'Ow about 'er?'

'And how about your intended? Jack, isn't it? How about him?'

Jessie turned her back on him.

Almost everyone present, with the exception of a few determinedly po-faced homedwellers, were clapping and cheering, thanking the Worlingtons for their generosity.

''E let me down,' said Jess. She was glad Robert couldn't see her face. ''E ain't nothin' to me no more.'

'That's my girl,' Robert said, wrapping his arms round her waist again. 'My very own hopping girl. Let's go back outside for a while.'

–

'Leave the bottle there, Tyler. We won't be needing you any more tonight.'

'Thank you,' said the elderly butler, inclining his head, not quite humbly. 'Goodnight, Master Paul. Master Robert.' He backed out of the billiards room and closed the big double doors after him.

Paul loosened his collar, kicked off his boots and fell back into one of the winged armchairs by the fireplace. 'God, I'm tired.'

'I'm not surprised. You did spend the whole evening dancing with my fiancée.'

'You can talk,' scoffed Paul. 'What you were up to with that red-haired girl takes far more energy than a few turns round the dance floor.'

'Well, you know what Father says,' said Robert, dropping into the chair opposite his brother.

They were now so familiar with Sir George's advice that they actually spoke the words in scornful unison:

'If you boys want a bit of fun, get yourselves a cockney girl. Save the decent girls for marriage.'

'Well,' said Robert, raising his glass in salute to his father's portrait over the mantelshelf, 'the old bugger was right for once.'

Chapter 11

I Didn't Realise

'Aw, no. When did it 'appen, Mum?' Bewildered by the news, Jess stopped picking to look at her mother.

'In the night,' said Rose simply.

'Why didn't yer tell me earlier?'

'Yer got in so late again yer was in no fit state to listen.'

Jess blushed and looked away, avoiding her mother's gaze.

Rose carried on plucking the hops from the thick, prickly bine, throwing them into the bin one after the other; there was no speed or enthusiasm in her actions this morning.

'Mabel woke up an' the poor little mite was gone,' she said, her voice dry and toneless. 'Dead in 'er arms it was.' She paused. 'Blessin' really. It 'ad got right bad again, God rest its little soul. It would never 'ave lasted the winter in London.'

'I can't believe it,' said Jess. Listlessly she began to toss hops into her bin. 'I thought it was gettin' stronger, doin' well, with the fresh air and milk and that.'

'Poor little thing, it was only six months old. Didn't stand a chance.' Rose tossed the bine she'd finished stripping to the ground, without bothering to look where it fell. She picked up a fresh, heavily laden stem and slowly began to remove its fruits. 'Yer know 'ow it is,' she said. 'Sickly babies like that. They ain't strong enough to get over it when they get ill. Even bein' down 'ere can't 'elp the likes of them.'

'It's 'elped you though, Mum, ain't it?' Jess asked anxiously. 'Yer gettin' a bit better now, ain't yer? Yer look better.'

'A bit, I suppose. I ain't as tired as I was. But I'm surprised yer've 'ad time to notice.'

'Don't be like that, Mum.' Jess couldn't meet her mother's gaze.

'Why not? Way yer've been behavin' lately, yer ain't 'ad time for no one but yerself. It's like yer've turned into a stranger.'

'I'm sorry, Mum. I didn't mean nothin'. I never realised the baby was so bad, honest.'

Rose looked at Jess. Her tone became hard. 'There's a lot of things yer 'aven't realised lately. Yer know yer ain't even bothered to ask me 'ow I've felt for days. Do yer know that?'

'Sorry.'

'Look, Jess, I know yer right cut up over Jack goin' missin'.'

'No, I...'

'Don't bother lyin' to me, Jess. I know 'ow it's got yer down, but it don't 'elp runnin' round actin' like yer've been doin' these last couple a weeks.'

'No, Mum. Sorry.' Still she kept her eyes downcast, focused only on the bin that was still almost empty.

'An' so much for yer 'avin' a bin of yer own, eh? That would've been a right waste a time, wouldn't it?'

Jess bit her lip. She kept mechanically picking away at the hops.

'An' yer do know I 'ad to feed that monkey an' the canary again last night? Well? Don't yer?'

'No, Mum. I didn't think. An' I said I was sorry.'

'Yer all right goin' off gallivantin' with them gels every night, ain't yer?' Rose looked across at her daughter, trying to see her reaction. Giving her the chance to answer her truthfully. 'Yer think about that all right.'

Jess kept her head down, and a lock of hair fell on to her face. She swallowed hard. She had to change the subject on to safer ground. 'Can we do anythin' to 'elp Mabel?' she asked.

'No, we can't do nothin' at the minute, but there'll be plenty to do when we get back to Burton Street next week. Lady Worlington's sorted 'er out for now. She let 'er pack up early an' go 'ome.'

'I didn't realise she'd already gone.'

'No, course yer didn't. Yer was still asleep. Yer got in late again last night. Remember?'

'Sorry, Mum.'

'So yer should be an' all.'

'I don't mean to upset yer or nothin', Mum.'

Rose stopped what she was doing and took hold of Jess by the shoulders, forcing her to look at her. 'Yer've never done nothin' to upset me in the past, Jess. Nothin'. Yer've always been a good kid. An' I've always been proud of yer. But I've got enough trouble worryin' about them boys gettin' in bother without you startin' an' all. Jack Barnes let yer down, an' everyone knew all about it. Yer felt ashamed, I know. But a lot of people get let down. Yer young an' yer pretty, yer won't 'ave no problem findin' yerself a bloke. If yer pull yerself together, that is.'

'I'm sorry.'

'So yer keep sayin'. But sayin' it's easy. I only 'ope yer mean it, that's all. Get yerself sorted out.'

'I do mean it, Mum, really.' Jess fought back the tears that were threatening to spill on to her cheeks.

Rose shook her head sorrowfully, then let go of Jess and went back to picking the hops. 'I've 'ad enough of all this lark for now,' she said. 'It's over, right? Let's forget it. Just yer be'ave yerself.'

'Yes, Mum.'

'An' yer can liven yourself up an' all. Yer ain't picked 'ardly anythin' this mornin'.'

'Right, Mum.'

Mother and daughter stood by their bin, silently picking the hops, side by side in the bright autumn sunshine. Children ran along the rows shouting and whooping, enjoying the simple pleasures of the countryside, which all too soon would be coming to an end for them. Women called to each other, exchanging stories and wisdom, gossip and laughter.

'I was tellin' yer about Lady Worlington,' said Rose as cheerily as she could manage. She couldn't stand the atmosphere between her and Jess any longer. 'I'd never 'ave thought it of the likes of 'er. D'yer know what she's gone an' done for Mabel?'

Jess didn't answer; she could only think about the harvest almost being over and about Mabel returning home to the filth and dirt of the East End with two children instead of three. And that she too would be going home. Away from the green fields and the bright, smokeless skies of Kent. But worst of all, she'd be going away from Robert.

'Jess. I'm speakin' to yer.'

'Sorry, Mum.'

'Gawd 'elp us. With all yer sorrys, Jess, yer gonna drive me barmy. I said, "Do yer know what Lady Worlington's done for Mabel?"'

'No. What's she done?'

'So yer are listenin' then,' Rose said sharply. Her patience was beginning to wear very thin. 'Well, she's not only paid Mabel a good whack – right fair *an'* without taking off any of 'er subs. But she's gone an' paid their train fares back to London, an' all. Out of 'er own pocket. An' she's arranged to 'ave the baby buried in the churchyard at St Mary's down in the village. Mabel really liked that. She said it was better than layin' the dear little scrap in some pauper's grave in London. An' she'll be able to see it every year when she comes down 'opping.'

'It's so sad, Mum. Poor Mabel.'

'That's life, girl,' said Rose, pulling a fresh bine from the tangled bundle at her feet, and wondering if she would ever hear from Charlie again. 'Losin' them yer love.'

–

'Get a move on, Jess. We'll never get packed up before Joey gets 'ere if yer don't 'elp.' Like the other women, Rose had all their belongings spread out on the grass outside the hut. They were all airing and sorting, swapping and passing on clothes to one another before they bundled everything up into crates and boxes for the journey home.

'She ain't caught lazyitis off that Elsie's mob, 'as she?' butted in Florrie.

Rose ignored her neighbour, straightened up from her task and rubbed her hands deep into her back. 'Yer ain't ill, are yer, gel? Yer lookin' a bit peaky.'

'I'm all right, Mum.'

'I 'ope so. That's all I could do with, you goin' sick. I'm a bit better, but I won't be able to do that much for a while yet. Yer gonna 'ave to pull more than yer fair share for a while when we get 'ome.'

'I told yer, didn't I? I'm all right.'

'Don't yer raise yer voice to me, Jessie Fairleigh.' Rose wagged her finger at her daughter. 'If it's that Jack yer still mopin' over…'

Jess turned away from her mother and ran inside the hut. Even from outside Rose could hear her trying to stifle her tears. She shook her head and went inside to her daughter.

'Don't know what all the fuss is about,' said Florrie to anyone who cared to listen. 'Jack's gone missin', yeh, but she's 'ardly been short of company now, 'as she? An' she won't be alone for long in Poplar neither, way she's carryin' on. Yer mark my words if I'm...'

The sight of Elsie drawing back her fist ready to punch Florrie in the face had a remarkable effect on her. It stopped her talking instantly.

–

'Come on, dopey, stop cryin'. Give yer ol' mum a cuddle.'

Glad of the chance to release her feelings, Jess sobbed uncontrollably into her mother's shoulder.

'Don't break yer 'eart, Jess. I know it ain't been easy for yer. Yer've been right let down over Jack, but yer've gotta get over 'im. An' runnin' around all hours with them gels ain't gonna get yer nowhere. Just get yer self a bad name, yer take it from me. Look at that one from Awerley Street. Right reputation she's got 'erself, an' no real fault of 'er own. Few vicious tongues waggin' an' that's it – ruined. Yer'll just 'ave to get yerself another feller, that's all. Now come on, yer big lump, we've got things to do.'

Rose still wasn't completely fit, but it wasn't her health that was worrying her now. She was frowning as she and her daughter went outside to get on with packing away their things for another year. She so wanted to tell Jess she didn't think it was Jack's fault that he had let her down; that something terrible had happened to him, and that somehow their Charlie knew all about it. But she neither knew where to begin, nor what she would be unleashing if she even mentioned it. Anyway, all she really had to go on were a bit of yellow cloth and a few unfounded suspicions. Suspicions that, if she was only half right, could do terrible damage to them all. More terrible than telling a few white lies ever would. But she wanted desperately to know the truth about Jack and her Charlie.

And Jess wanted the truth as well. She wanted to stop lying to her mother, wanted to tell her what she had really been doing when she'd said she'd been out baking potatoes in the oast houses with Win and Lil or hanging around with the young girls from the other huts. She wanted to tell Rose that she and Robert loved each other, and that she didn't care about Jack any more. She didn't care if she never saw him again, in fact. She had Robert now, he was the only one she cared for. She wanted to tell her mother that Robert had promised he was going to come for her last night, and even though he hadn't, he would still be coming for her any minute now. He would come for her as they were about to leave, and she would have to say goodbye to Rose and explain what had happened in front of all the others. But she would understand. Jess knew she would. She had to.

–

'It's a rotten turn-out over Jack Barnes all right, Rose,' said Joey Fuller, as he leant in the doorway of Rose's hut drinking a tin mug full of tea. 'She was like love's young dream on the journey down 'ere, going' all soppy over 'im. Pity, eh? She's such a smashin' gel.' He flung the dregs of his tea on to the grass outside and handed Rose the mug for packing. 'Don't look like she even wants to go back now. Look at 'er moonin' about over there. Upset an' shown up rotten at the same time, poor kid. Anythin' I can say to 'elp?'

'Don't ask me, Joe,' said Rose, wiping out the mug with a bit of rag. 'Yer know 'ow these young gels carry on nowadays.'

'It's all a mystery to me, Rose.' Joey lifted the tea chest Rose had finished packing and set it outside the hut. 'I thought Jack was right gone on 'er. But not even a word. I ain't surprised Clara don't know where 'e is, but even Cyril ain't got a clue.'

'Well, I ain't surprised either, Joey. Us mums an' dads are the last to know anythin'. I ain't 'ad a word from my Charlie. Not a word. I really don't understand 'em at all sometimes.'

Rose went around the little hut aiming final flicks of her coarse apron at any stray cobwebs and dust she'd missed up in the dark corners.

'Could eat yer dinner off this floor, Rosie Fairleigh. Yer a good 'un an' that's a fact.'

'Yer know me, Joe, clean 'ome an' clean livin',' said Rose primly. 'Right.' She shoved Joey outside and stepped out to join him on the grass. 'Take these cages off me.' She took a last look into the dark interior, slipped the padlock on to the door latch, and turned the key. 'That's that job jobbed for another year.' She took the dusty turban from her hair, folded it and pushed it deep into her apron pocket. 'An' that's me fit, an' all. I'll just go an' liven Jessie up, then we're ready.'

–

Even Elsie Dorkin and her brood were ready to leave before Rose could persuade Jess to take her place on Joey's cart.

'The sooner we're back in London with my Bill the better,' said Rose to no one in particular, shoving her daughter unceremoniously on to the wagon. 'I've got enough on me plate without all this.'

As the little coster's cart bumped its way along the farm track to the lane which would take them towards home, Jess kept her eyes fixed on Worlington Hall. Any minute now Robert would come galloping towards her, shouting his love for her in front of everybody, begging her to stay with him in Kent. He couldn't be like Jack. He couldn't. She couldn't have been fooled twice by lies, could she? Not after what she'd let Robert do to her.

—

Robert urged his tall chestnut horse to go faster still. The animal extended its stride until it was galloping, going flat out. Sweat lathered in white flecks from the friction of the reins rubbing on its golden sorrel neck. The animal did not hesitate at the hedge, but flew over it with a huge surge, landing easily in the next. Robert reined the horse in harshly, turning it round to face the fence it had just cleared.

'Woah. Steady. Steady,' he commanded. A smaller, bay horse took the jump and landed beside them.

'Not quite so confident as you, Robert,' laughed Paul, cantering off across the meadow, 'but we get there.'

Robert whipped his horse forward and quickly caught up with his brother.

'You'll have to do better than that, Paul, if you're going to hunt that old nag this season,' he mocked.

'Oh, I forgot,' panted Paul, desperately trying to keep his horse level with his brother's mount. 'You're the expert in hunting, aren't you? Always catch your prey.' His words came in short, panting gasps as the wind took his breath. 'Especially little red-haired vixens,' he puffed. 'Mind you, you seem pretty keen to let the quarry go once you've caught it.'

'Too right I do. What use would I have for a wild animal?'

'Especially once you've tamed it, eh, Robert?'

'Especially then, Paul,' grinned Robert. He curbed his animal brutally, making it skid to a halt. 'Come on. Race you back to the Hall. I seem to remember I have a fiancée waiting for me.'

Chapter 12

Old Granny Rawlins

''Ow did ol' Warner take it, then?' Rose fed the corner of the soaking-wet sheet into the rollers of the big iron-framed wringer. Her fingers were numb with the cold.

''E took me an' Win back all right,' said Jessie, dragging the rest of the bed sheet from the little tin bath as her mother turned the heavy handle, squeezing the water from the clean white cotton. 'But 'e wouldn't entertain Lil, though.'

'Elsie won't be very 'appy.' Rose nodded for Jess to catch hold of the sheet as it came out the other side of the rollers, while she continued to work the handle, turning the wheel.

''E said she'd 'ave to find something else, but 'e'll give in, I reckon. Anyway, me an' Win start back tomorrow.'

'Good job an' all. Yer dad's back pay won't last us much longer an' Gawd alone knows when 'is next trip'll be over. An' if it stays as cold as this we're gonna get through plenty of coal this winter.'

Rose and Jess took two comers each of the sheet and draped it over the washing line that ran the length of the tiny, smut-filled back yard. Rose bent down and picked out a pillowcase from the tin bath of rinsing water, wringing it out with her hands before putting it in the mangle. Jess made no attempt to help.

'Sammy an' Ted'll just 'ave to work a bit 'arder an' give yer a bit more money then, won't they? Or perhaps Charlie'll be so kind as to write at last, from Chicago or wherever 'e is, an' send us a few bob.'

Surprised at the bitterness in her daughter's voice Rose stopped turning the mangle, leaving the half-wrung cotton dangling between the worn wooden rollers. Wiping her raw, red hands on her apron, she said, 'Let's 'ave a cuppa tea, Jess. I've 'ad enough of this for a while. An' I've got plenty to do indoors.'

Jess followed her mother into the house from the back yard and sat at the kitchen table while Rose poured boiling water from the ever full kettle into the pot.

'Yer gonna tell me what's up, Jess?'

''Ow do yer mean?'

'With you, gel. What's up with yer? Face like a kite, yer've got. Jumpin' down everyone's throat all the time. Right misery yer've been lately.'

Rose went over to the hearth. She spat on the flat iron she'd picked up from the fireside. It sizzled back at her. The little kitchen was filled with the smells of fresh laundry as Rose worked at the table next to Jessie, coaxing creases from the damp laundry with long strokes of the hot iron.

'Leave me alone, eh, Mum,' Jess said. She rubbed her hands, still stained from the hops, over her pale, drawn cheeks, her elbows resting on the only corner of the scrubbed white surface of the table not covered in piles of clean washing and ironing.

'I ain't never 'ad yer behavin' like this, Jess, an' I mean it, I don't intend to start. Now, I'll ask yer again, Jessie. Are yer gonna tell me what's up?' Rose rested the iron on its heel and picked up the teapot. She poured a stream of boiling tea into her daughter's cup and pushed it towards her.

Jess took one sip and her face drained of its final traces of colour. She stood up unsteadily and rushed back into the yard. Rose could hear her being sick from the kitchen. She slammed the teapot down on to the table, splashing the clean washing with brown stains.

'Dammit, I bloody well thought so,' she snapped to herself. She went outside to Jess. 'Better now?' she asked, rubbing her daughter between the shoulder blades.

Jess was bent double, still choking and spluttering on to the patch of dirt that was the only bit of garden anyone living in Burton Street would ever have. She put her hands out and supported herself on the soot-engrained bricks which formed the boundary with Number 10 next door.

'Aw, I feel so ill, Mum,' she groaned pathetically.

'Yer ain't ill, yer silly little cow. Yer pregnant.'

–

'We'll 'ave to get yer round to ol' Granny Rawlins's an' get rid of it,' said Rose. She and Jess had settled themselves back at the table, Rose drinking her tea, and Jess sipping at a cup of water.

'No, Mum. Not that.'

'Don't be daft, Jess.' Rose did not feel as calm as she was trying to sound. ''Ow do yer think I only 'ad four kids?' She reached out and took Jess's hands in. 'An' 'ow about Mabel? I know she wishes she'd done somethin' about 'er last one before it was too late. Poor little mite, dead before it was a year old. An' I wouldn't be surprised if 'er oldest don't last the winter out neither. That the life yer want, is it, like Mabel's? I know yer can be proud, an' yer can be stubborn. Yer too like me, gel. But this ain't the time for none of that.'

'I ain't stupid, Mum.'

Rose raised a cynical eyebrow at her daughter's claim. 'Aw, no?'

'I mean I ain't bein' stupid now.' Jess gulped as her tears began to flow. It was all she seemed to do lately, she thought, cry and be sick. 'I've seen what 'appens to girls who've been there. To Granny Rawlins's. That's 'ow Maggie down at Warner's copped it. Eighteen she was, that's all. Eighteen. Bled for days, then got a fever an' died. I won't do it, Mum. I mean it.'

'It ain't always like that, Jess.'

'No, Mum. No matter what yer say, I ain't lettin' 'er touch me.'

'It's up to you. Yer ain't a kid no more. But if yer wanna 'ave it, yer gonna 'ave to write to Sir George an' see what 'im an' 'is precious Robert are gonna do about it.'

A look of real panic came over Jess's pale face. ''Ow d'yer mean, write to Sir George? An' what's it gotta do with Robert?'

'I ain't stupid either, Jess. An' I certainly ain't blind. Once I'd got over me bad chest a bit, I knew exactly what was goin' on down there. Let's 'ope not too many others worked out what yer was up to.' She poured herself another cup of tea. 'An' I can tell yer this much, Jess, I was right disappointed that yer lied to me. Right disappointed.'

'But, Mum, it wasn't like that, it was…'

'It ain't no good sayin' nothin' now. It'll only make it worse. Yer lied to me, an' that's that.'

'But it wasn't like yer think, Mum.'

'It never is, darlin'. It never is. Now, if yer wanna spend next year pickin' oakum in the work'ouse instead of 'ops down in Kent, then that's up to you. Yer the one 'oo's gotta choose. Worlington or the work'ouse?'

By the middle of December Jess had written five separate letters, dictated by her mother, to Sir George Worlington. There was no reply to any of them. Jess was feeling physically better – the sickness had stopped, and her belly was gently swelling – but she was becoming more and more depressed. Her father was due home at Christmas. She couldn't imagine how she would explain things to him. He'd be so hurt.

And then there were all the rumours going round about Jack that were upsetting her. Most of the stories were started, or at least embroidered and spread, by Florrie Baxter, of course. Florrie was only too keen to broadcast the poison. When they'd all got back from Kent, and she found out that Jack still hadn't shown up, she'd revelled in it. It was too good an opportunity for Florrie to miss. She didn't care if she upset Cyril Barnes, and she wasn't even scared what Clara would say. She just couldn't resist it. Some of the tales reckoned Jack had got someone in the family way and had run off to sea to escape his responsibilities. Others claimed he had found some money in one of the letters he was employed to deliver, and that he had stolen it and gone off to start a new life up north – Manchester or somewhere, they said. There was even wild talk of him being the victim of one of the cosh gangs who made their living down by the docks, but nobody really believed Jack Barnes would have any business down in Chinatown, no matter whatever else he got up to.

Sammy and Ted weren't having a very good time either. They weren't entirely sure what was going on indoors, although they guessed that it might have something to do with Jack Barnes having it away on his toes like that, but they knew well enough to keep their heads down. And at least they did still have their jobs – there were plenty didn't have work in Poplar

– so they could go to The Star of a evening. And what with Jess moping about and Rose ready to have a go at them for nothing all the time, they were only too pleased to go there and escape, although it was working out a bit pricey, and the novelty of going to the pub every night was wearing a bit thin.

In fact, the only real ray of light in the whole Fairleigh household was a scribbled five-line note they'd got from Charlie the week before. It said that he was doing all right for himself, more than all right if they must know; that he was working and saving hard, and that he wished them all a happy Christmas and promised to write again soon.

–

'Seems there might be even more trouble before Christmas is out,' said Robert.

The Worlington family sat eating their breakfast, their post and the newspapers. Leonore shaded her eyes from the bright winter sun as she looked across the table to her elder child. 'What was that, Robert?'

'Seems they're taking this business in the Balkans seriously again,' he said holding up his copy of *The Times* for his mother to see, as though the printed word would somehow prove his point. 'There's even talk of reserve officers assembling. Implications for the rest of Europe and all that.'

'I've heard nothing,' said Paul, forking another slice of kidney and a heap of scrambled egg into his mouth.

'This is men's business, little brother,' said Robert, shaking the crisp pages and folding them back on themselves.

Paul glared at Robert, and was furious to see Julia giggle. 'I'm only two years younger than you,' he snapped petulantly.

'More like twenty-two from the way you act,' said Robert coolly.

'Hardly a subject to argue over,' said Lady Worlington. 'You boys really do drive me to distraction at times.' She looked towards her husband, hoping that he might support her, or maybe contribute to the conversation in some way. 'Do you take this threat in Europe seriously, George?' she asked, trying to involve him.

'Load of damned nonsense over a load of damned fool foreigners, if you're really interested,' he barked, and stood up from the table.

His napkin fell to the floor, where he left it. He also left his letters and envelopes strewn around his plate – all except one, that is, which he was careful to slip, unopened, into his pocket.

'Can't sit here all morning talking about such rubbish. Lots to do.'

He strode purposefully towards the big double doors which opened into the main hall. He grabbed the door handle and spoke without bothering to turn round.

'But if there is a possibility of war,' he patted his pocket, checking that the letter was still there, 'better get this marriage thing organised pretty damn quick. Don't want young Julia waving goodbye to her fiance going off to battle. That's a wife's job. Need to be a wife for that sort of thing.'

Sir George left the room without worrying about shutting the doors behind him. The butler, Tyler, moved from his position behind Lady Worlington's chair and soundlessly closed them. Only he and Paul had seen the momentary look of horror on Julia Markington's face when Sir George had mentioned matrimony.

–

When he had shut himself safely away in the library, Sir George sat at the elegant partners' desk and opened the letter that he had secreted in his pocket. He scanned the contents briefly. He had been right; it was another letter from the Fairleigh woman, the fifth she had sent to him about her daughter's 'condition', if he remembered correctly.

He read it through again, more carefully this time. He was barely able to stifle his amusement that the ridiculous woman could imagine he would respond to her pleas for Robert to do the 'decent thing', whatever she thought that might be.

As the door opened and Julia and Paul walked in, they saw Sir George hurriedly push the letter and envelope he had been studying under the blotter on his desk. Paul smiled to see his father hastily affecting a most uncharacteristic interest in the toppling pile of papers in front of him.

'Father,' said Paul very firmly, addressing the back of his father's head, 'Julia wishes to say something to you.'

–

'And what exactly does Robert have to say about all this?' asked Sir George when Julia had said her piece. He was still feigning a deep fascination with the heap of unanswered correspondence before him.

'He agrees with her, Father,' said Paul, speaking for Julia, who had nodded her consent for him to do so. 'It would be best all round to postpone the wedding. At least until all this business in Europe is sorted out. The situation is very uncertain at the moment, as everybody is aware. If war really were to be declared Robert would be worrying about Julia all the time. Most distracting. And it wouldn't be fair on Julia either. She wouldn't want to be an army wife. But she'll be perfectly happy to stay here. With us at Worlington, I mean.'

Sir George waited a moment, then slowly turned round to face his busybody of a younger son and the wealthy girl whom he was banking on becoming his future daughter-in-law by marrying his *elder* son.

'Now let me see,' Sir George began in an ominously quiet and controlled tone. 'As far as I can tell this marriage business has very little to do with you, Paul. Nothing at all, in fact.'

He leant back in his chair and formed his fingers into a steeple over his big, round, tweed-clad belly. He tapped the tips of his fat fingers together with a slow rhythmic patting.

'But you appear to know a damned lot about it all.'

Sir George's now quavering voice gave away the fact that he was nearing the point when his temper would finally be lost. Even the merest possibility of Worlington Hall having to sacrifice the Markington dowry, because of his sons' idiotic ideas, was enough to make him very angry indeed.

'So what the hell are you doing here, Paul? Would you explain yourself to me?'

'I'm here because Robert asked me to come along with Julia, actually,' Paul said confidently. 'He had a previous engagement, you see. Had to go and see someone.'

'Exercising his hunter, you mean,' said Julia tartly.

'Exercising his hunter?' Sir George's red-veined cheeks engorged to an alarming degree as he rose to his feet, pushed past his younger son and rushed out of the library to get his hands around the throat of his elder son and heir.

'Goodness me,' was the only comment Julia made, as she fanned herself with her pretty milky-white hand and glided around the room looking fleetingly at the titles which lined the shelves.

'Ignore him. He goes off like that all the time,' said Paul, going over to the desk. He picked up the letter and envelope he had seen his father slip underneath the blotter.

'Now here's something far more interesting than the old man's temper tantrums,' he said, smiling at Julia, who didn't actually seem very interested in much at all. 'Let's see, what do you think Father would want to hide from us? A mistress? Gambling debts?'

Paul looked quickly through the carefully formed lines of writing, letting out a long, slow whistle as the contents of the letter became clear to him. 'Oh dear, Robert,' he said, grinning like a fool. 'Oh dear, dear me. You have been a very silly boy. Very silly indeed. I wonder what Mama will make of this.'

Unwittingly following his father's example, Paul slipped the letter into his pocket.

Julia had not listened to Paul; she was too busy admiring her reflection in the long windows which overlooked the gardens. Nor had she noticed the beauty of the pale blue shadows on the deep drifts of snow, nor the breathtaking sight of the bare oak trees standing tall and magnificent against the December sky. All she could see was her trim figure silhouetted in the glass in front of her.

She spoke in her light, girlish voice. 'I think yellow suits me very well. Don't you, Paul?'

Chapter 13

Justice

Rose pulled back the red plush curtain that was drawn to keep out the winter draughts and peered round the crowded, smoke-filled public bar.

'Joey, can I see yer a minute?' she called to him from the doorway.

'Excuse me, chaps,' Joey said, laying his hand of cards face down on the beer-stained table. 'I'm wanted.'

He was well aware of the whispered ribald remarks made by his card-playing companions as he went over to Rose.

'Sorry to bother yer, Joe,' said Rose apologetically.

'That's all right, gel, any time. Yer know that.'

'Put that curtain back. It's perishin' in 'ere,' shouted the barman.

'Sorry,' called Rose, stepping into the pub and straightening the heavy material over the door behind her.

'Ne'mind 'im, Rose. What d'yer want?'

'I've got a favour to ask yer,' she said, leaning close so that no one could hear.

'Course,' he said immediately. 'Anythin' for you.'

'Not 'ere, Joe. Outside, eh?'

Joe pulled back the curtain again and opened the door, gesturing for Rose to go out first.

'All right, all right,' he said before anyone had the chance to complain, 'I'm closing it as quick as I can.' As he pushed the door shut behind them, the cold hit him. 'Christ, we can't stand out 'ere and talk, it's freezin'. Come over to mine an' I'll make yer a cuppa tea.' He saw Rose hesitate. 'Don't worry. I ain't gonna eat yer up. An' yer know Mum's always there.'

Rose smiled, grateful for the chance to talk to such a kind, uncomplicated, undemanding man. 'Ta, Joe. I'd like that a lot. If yer don't mind.'

As they walked along Burton Street, the contrast between the cold night air and the warm cosiness of The Star made Joey shiver. He turned up his jacket collar and stuck his hands deep in his pockets.

'I don't think this snow'll ever clear. It's murder of a momin' gettin' the cart 'itched up.'

'Yer wanna get yerself some gloves,' said Rose, her breath coming out in white cloudy puffs.

Joey laughed, a gentle, regretful chuckle. 'Me ol' Mum's knittin' days are over, Rose. Art' I never got the 'ang of it.'

'I could make yer some if yer like.' As Rose turned to look at him, she missed her footing on the frozen cobblestones and slipped against him.

Joey grabbed her, and held her arms till she righted herself. Only a moment, but long enough for them both to be embarrassed by the unfamiliar contact.

'Ta, Rose, I could do with some to keep me 'ands warm when I'm seein' to Daddler.'

They walked on in silence. Joey was puzzled. Rose was a good neighbour, one of the best, but she usually kept herself to herself. Always there to help, of course, whenever anyone needed her, but she'd never offered to do anything like that for him before, nothing so personal.

'I'd like that a lot, Rose,' he said.

'It might pay yer back a bit for what I'm gonna ask yer,' she said.

Joey Fuller lived in the last house in Burton Street, at the opposite end to The Star. He had lived there all his life, since the day he had been born in the little front bedroom. His father, Joseph, had been the foreman of the cooperage yard at the brewery, where most of the neighbours who weren't dockers earned their living.

One morning, for no reason that anyone had ever discovered, a stack of barrels had crashed forward and fallen on Joseph, crushing his body against the cold flagstoned yard. He had survived the accident to live for five terrible days in agonising pain, until death did for him what the doctor couldn't by mercifully releasing him from his suffering.

Since that dreadful day Joey had looked after his mother. They had received no money or help from the brewery. It was an accident and that was that. A foreman could easily be replaced. And so Joey had become the breadwinner, the man of the house. He had been thirteen years old.

His mother never recovered from the shock of losing her beloved Joseph, and never left the house again. Lately she had become more and more confused. Sometimes she thought Joey was his father, other times she thought she was a little girl again. Mostly she just sat by the fire, staring into the flames. But Joey coped; he had to. He had never married. Once, however, he'd told Rose that when she had married Bill Fairleigh, that was it, he was not interested in anyone else. He would have to stay a bachelor for ever. She was never sure if he was joking or not.

Joey blew on his freezing fingers before he turned the key carefully in the lock.

'Don't wanna drop the key an' wake Mum,' he explained. 'Yer know 'ow she gets all mixed up.'

Rose followed him through the pitch-dark passage and into the little kitchen out the back. She sat at the table and looked round while Joey made the tea. It was the first time she'd ever been inside there.

The Fullers' house was exactly the same as the Fairleighs', the same, in fact, as every other house in Burton Street, and as many others in that part of Poplar – two up, two down, including the small kitchen which was the centre of most households in Poplar, and a tiny stone-floored scullery in the little back yard.

But Joey's house differed in one way from Rose's: though it was clean – yes, very clean; Joey worked hard to earn a living and keep the place nice for his mum – it didn't have the warm, cosy feel of Number 8. It didn't have the homely touches that made Rose's place so welcoming; the little ornaments and pictures that every family seemed to accumulate over the years were missing. That was it, she thought. Rose knew that Joey worked long, lonely hours with his pony and cart, doing the rounds of the markets, delivering and picking up whatever gear he was asked to. It choked her to think of him coming home to such a bare little room.

'There y'are, Rose,' he said, sitting opposite her. He handed her a thick china cup. 'That'll warm yer up.'

'Ta, Joe.' She sipped gingerly at the steaming tea. 'I reckon I've drunk enough of this over the years to float one of my Bill's ships.'

Joey laughed. 'Me an' all. But yer can never 'ave too much of a good thing, eh, Rose?' He looked at her over the rim of his cup. 'Like good company. Yer can't beat 'avin' friends. 'Specially if yer worried about somethin',' he added.

Rose didn't say anything, but carried on drinking her tea.

'Ol' Cyril was in The Star earlier. Drunk as a tiddler, 'e was. Seems to 'ave forgotten all about his Jack goin' missin'.'

Rose set her cup down on the table more heavily than she'd meant to. The tea splashed on to the scrubbed pine surface. 'Aw, I'm a silly cow. Sorry, Joe. Yer got a cloth?' she asked, jumping to her feet.

'Don't worry yerself.' Joe touched her shoulder, making her sit down. He got a rag and mopped up the spill. 'Now, Rose,' he said, 'this favour yer was talkin' about; to do with Charlie, is it?'

Rose frowned. She felt confused and guilty; for the last few days she'd hardly thought about Charlie, or Jack Barnes for that matter. Not since she'd made up her mind what she had to do, in fact.

'No, Joe, not Charlie. Not this time anyway.' She managed a smile. 'I 'eard from 'im the other week, funny enough. Reckons 'e's doin' all right for 'imself.' She sipped at her tea. 'I 'ope so. I worry that 'e's 'eadin for some sort a trouble, yer know. But then I think, no, not our Charlie. 'E'll be all right. 'E's a survivor.'

'I reckon 'e is, Rose,' said Joey, laughing as he topped up their cups. ''E's got a lucky streak, that boy of your'n. Strokes 'e used to pull as a nipper an' 'e always come out on top.'

'That's what I try an' tell meself,' said Rose. 'Yer know, barely a couple a pound born 'e was, didn't think 'e'd make it through the night. Now 'e's such a great 'ulkin' lump. No, I should stop worryin' about 'im. 'E'll land on 'is feet. Please Gawd.'

'So, it's not Charlie.' Joey waited, letting Rose take her time.

'Joe, I've gotta take Jess down to Kent. She ain't keen to go, but we've got no choice. I know the weather's bad an' that, but it can't be 'elped. It's gotta be done.'

Joey did not ask her for reasons, he simply asked, 'When do yer wanna leave?'

–

Early the next morning, well before dawn, Rose, Jess and Joey Fuller set off for Tilnhurst. The journey was not easy, the cart slithering and sliding through the slushy London streets and the snowbound lanes of Kent, but they arrived at last, late that night.

Joey stopped his pony outside the main entrance to the Hall. The gravel drive had been completely cleared by the outdoors staff. It was as though no snow had fallen on it at all. Rose got down from the cart, stiff with sitting for so long. She climbed the broad stone stairs and rapped on the big wooden doors, her knuckles numb with cold.

Tyler opened the door. At the sight of Rose and the shaggy coster's pony he took a step back.

'I've come to see Sir George,' she said as plainly and bravely as she could manage.

'Sir George does not give charity to beggars,' said Tyler down his nose. 'Try the kitchen door round at the back. Cook may have some scraps.'

'Tell 'im Rose Fairleigh's 'ere,' she said, straightening her aching body. ''E'll see me all right.'

Tyler raised a disbelieving eyebrow but went to inform his master anyway. Sir George had been known to agree to all sorts of things when he was less than sober.

Rose stood in the doorway, looking into the brightly lit hallway. The electrically powered chandelier threw its glittering lights on to the black and white chequered marble floor. She looked back to the drive and saw Jess huddled on the back of the cart, a snow-dampened blanket draped around her hunched shoulders. Rose knew that Jess would rather be anywhere but Worlington Hall, but she would have to learn that the likes of them had few choices in life. Joey was tending to Daddler. He'd thrown an old sack across her back and was feeding her oats from a hessian nosebag. The pony's munching and snorting were the only sounds in the still, frosty air.

—

'Who?' bellowed Sir George.

'Rose Fairleigh, sir,' said the butler for the third time. His attempts at remaining discreet were being increasingly hampered by his employer's drunken failure to comprehend even the simplest of statements.

'Is there a problem, Tyler?' asked Leonore, walking into the billiards room. Even though she had been insitting room working on a tapestry, she had heard her husband shouting at the butler. 'Is there some way in which I can be of help?'

Tyler decided to throw caution to the winds, and anyway, he reasoned that Sir George's present state would prevent him from recalling any indiscretion on his butler's part. And he wanted to get this over with and get to bed.

'There is a…' He hesitated, unsure of which description to employ. 'A person, m'lady. At the front door. A Rose Fairleigh.'

The effect of those few words made Tyler entirely unsure as to whether he had said the wrong or right thing after all. On hearing the name, Lady Worlington had gone quite pale and fled from the room out into the hallway.

'Mrs Fairleigh?' she said. She knew it was her immediately, as soon as she saw the poorly dressed woman standing at her door. Her worst fears were confirmed. Paul had not invented the letter he had shown her after all. He had been telling the truth for once. More trouble, and Robert was right in the middle of it, yet again.

'Yeh,' said Rose. 'That's me.'

'You come here for the hop picking, don't you?'

'Yeh. An' now I've come to speak to Sir George.'

Leonore held out her hand in welcome. 'Won't you come in. Please. You must be very cold out there.'

Rose remained on the steps, firmly outside the door. 'I don't wanna leave me daughter. An' me friend who brought us 'ere. They're cold an' all.'

'Your daughter.' Leonore swallowed hard, struggling to retain some semblance of composure. 'And your friend, of course. They must both come in.'

She opened the door wider and stepped out. Welcoming light flooded from behind her out on to the porticoed entrance.

'Won't you both come in?'

–

Rose stood in the corner of the large, high-ceilinged room. Logs blazed in the biggest fireplace she had ever seen. Joey stood protectively behind her. Jess lingered in the doorway. She felt she would die from the humiliation. Then she reconsidered: no, she wouldn't be lucky enough for that to happen.

As the warmth worked on their bodies they tingled and itched. Their rough woollen clothing felt harsh against their skin.

Leonore Worlington entered. 'I've spoken to my husband. He will be joining us shortly.' She sat down in a winged armchair by the fireside. 'Won't you sit down?'

'We're all right as we are. Thank you very much.' Rose answered for all three of them.

The passing of each awkward moment was marked by the tick-tocking of the tall ormolu clock on the ornate mantelshelf. Eyes were trained on anything but each other. When the door finally opened, they all looked round in relief.

'Five pounds and that's my only offer.'

Even Leonore, used to her husband's boorish behaviour, was astounded by his callousness. 'Five pounds, George? You are talking about your future grandchild as though it were a calf at the market.'

Joey shuffled his feet uncomfortably, still keeping up the pretence that he had no idea as to the purpose of the visit. 'I'm going outside to see to me 'orse,' he said and left the room.

''Ow can she raise a kid on that?' Rose demanded. 'She'll need more than that just to clothe 'erself an' keep 'erself warm while she's expectin'.'

It wasn't like Rose to speak out like that, but she was fighting for her Jessie, for her daughter's survival.

Sir George merely sneered in reply.

Rose looked desperately at Leonore, appealing to her as a mother. 'Honest. I ain't being greedy. Where we live, see, it's really 'ard. Our Charlie ain't around any more to 'elp us out with a few bob. An' me other boys, they eat like men but bring in kids' wages, what with all the problems with work back 'ome. Another mouth would mean…'

'Ten pounds, if you'll shut up talking, woman. If not, it goes back to five.'

'None of yer is gonna put a price on me baby's 'ead. None of yers.'

Sir George laughed at the audacity of the pathetic attempt at dignity coming from the shabby girl standing by the door.

'Go on, 'ave yer laugh. I don't care. But yer can keep yer money. I don't want it. I don't want nothin' off yer, not for meself. All I want's a name for me baby. I don't want it to be no bastard.'

Leonore bowed her head, hiding her shame as her husband's laughter echoed around the room. 'Want to have a little Worlington, do you?'

'Yeh, I do. An' I will an' all. Yer son said 'e'd marry me. Said 'e loved me. Now I know 'e don't, but I don't care about 'im no more. I just want me baby to 'ave a name.'

'You will regret taking that tone with me,' said Sir George stonily. 'We'll have to see what the court has to say about all this.' He looked her up and down, his expression one of contempt. 'Yes, I really think you will live to regret tonight, young woman. Five pounds is more than you'll ever get out of me now.'

Leonore stood up and faced her husband, her hands formed into tight, angry fists by her side. 'You are being unspeakably cruel, George.'

'Don't yer worry about us, lady,' said Rose. 'We know we're in the right. We'll go to court if that's what 'e wants. 'E won't get away with treatin' us like that. The court'll see to that.'

'I'll see you in court then,' said Sir George, making his way to the door. 'At, shall we say, eleven tomorrow morning.'

'Where do we go?' said Rose, feeling stronger and more hopeful than she had in weeks.

'The local court is conducted here, actually,' he replied from the doorway. 'Here, in the Hall. Now if you'll excuse me, I'll bid you goodnight, ladies.' With a deep, mocking bow, Sir George left the three women alone.

Fear slithered its way down Rose's spine, making her shudder. 'Someone's walked over me grave,' she muttered.

Leonore pretended not to hear. What could she say? She must try to act normally, keep control of herself. She rang for the butler.

'Tyler, organise some food for Mrs and Miss Fairleigh and for their companion. And somewhere for them to sleep.' She reached out a hand to touch Jess, but withdrew it, still not knowing what she could say.

'Goodnight,' she said noncommittally. 'Please excuse me, but I must speak to my husband before he retires for the night.'

—

After their supper of broth and stale bread which the cook had blatantly scooped from the leavings in the pigswill bin, Tyler escorted the three Londoners from the kitchen to the bam. Like the cook, the butler did not bother to hide his distaste at being in close proximity to such people, to foreigners.

'Better than the 'oppers' 'uts,' whispered Rose as they lay in the warm darkness of the hayloft. 'An' this 'ay's more comfy than the straw they usually gives us an' all. Lovely an' warm an' cosy.'

'More'n yer can say for that butler,' said Joe.

'They don't like us East Enders down 'ere,' said Rose. '"Foreigners" they calls us 'oppers, don't they, Jess?'

Jess's only reply was a trembling sob which tore at her mother's heart.

Anxious to sound calm for her daughter, Rose spoke into the darkness. 'These country bumpkins could learn a lot from us cockneys, I reckon. Didn't 'ave to ask Elsie twice. Straight away she said she'd look after yer mum, didn't she, Joe? Mind yer, they ain't treatin' us too bad tonight. What more could we ask, eh?'

The pretence became too much for her. Rose rolled over, wrapped her arms round Jess's tense, shuddering body and cried with her.

Joey rolled himself one thin cigarette after another, smoking them to keep himself awake, until he was sure Rose and Jess had finally dropped off to sleep.

He didn't know whether they would want him to do anything for them, but he wanted to be there and ready if they did.

-

The next morning, the maid who had been charged by Lady Leonore to take a cooked breakfast to the Londoners in the guest cottage was redirected by Tyler to take a jug of thin gruel and some stale bread to the foreigners in the barn.

At a quarter to eleven, Jess and her mother were shown into the court. It had been set up in the long, vaulted-ceilinged room which ran the full length of the Hall. They were instructed to stand by a low, plain wooden bench, which was set at right angles to the large, highly polished table which dominated the room. The table itself was dominated by a thronelike seat, placed in the middle of a row of eight less formidable chairs. A man, not unlike Sir George, occupied the main place at the table. The other places were occupied by the Reverend Henry Batsford and seven men of similar social standing and authority in the Tilnhurst community. Sir George himself sat in a plump brocade armchair in front of, and slightly to the side of the table. Lady Worlington sat in a smaller armchair behind him.

As she sat there, her hands gripped tightly in her lap, it hardly seemed possible to Leonore that this room had been the scene of so many happy gatherings in the past; a place where guests had laughed and chatted with the Worlingtons before going in to dinner. Robert, her handsome, dashing son, had often been the centre of attention at such evenings. But there was no sign of him today.

Nor was there any sign of Joey, but for very different reasons. He had been denied entry to the proceedings and, much to the butler's annoyance, had insisted on waiting with his pony and cart on the gravel outside the front entrance to the Hall.

The man at the centre of the table, the magistrate, was Arthur Fanshawe, the owner of the neighbouring estate. As the longcase clock in the corner of the room struck eleven, Fanshawe opened the session. He conducted the proceedings at such a fast pace and with such long and complicated words that Rose quickly became totally bewildered.

But Jess was unaffected by his performance. She was not listening to him. He had nothing to say that could be of any interest to her. All she could think of was her child growing in her belly. It had been Robert's child, but not now. Now it was her child. Only hers. If he didn't want it, then she would look after it herself. She didn't hear the Reverend Henry Batsford's speech either, in which he expounded on the immorality of the London labouring classes. Nor did she attend to Sir George's invective on the subject of moral degeneracy in girls who made the trapping of decent men their life's work. He even expanded on his theme by explaining to all present that the girl's mother had tried to get money out of him – a price for the bastard.

'That is why the trollop got herself in this state in the first place,' he boomed, looking portentously round the room, 'and by God alone knows what poor fellow. Maybe someone in this very village.'

Rose tried to protest that it was Sir George himself who had first mentioned money, that Jess had refused it, and that he knew full well who the father was. But she was silenced.

Leonore never opened her mouth. She remained silent throughout. She did not tell those present that the girl had only wanted her child to be recognised by its father, her own son, Robert Worlington. She never said a word, even though she also wanted the child, her grandchild, to be made legitimate, even though she had seen for herself the vile reality of women living alone with their children in the back-streets of the East End. Yes, she knew all about that. But she also knew what her husband was capable of. She kept silent as it was the best way she could think of to protect Jessie Fairleigh. She would go to her after the farce of the court hearing was over and they had sent her back to London, to starve for all they cared. And she would find a way to help her. Leonore knew that she would, she must, do all she could to make up for the behaviour of the man she was now ashamed to call her son. She was so preoccupied racking her brains for a scheme to help Jessie and her unborn child that she was scarcely aware that Arthur Fanshawe was drawing the proceedings to a close.

'On the basis of the proof of her moral degeneracy,' he droned, 'Jessie, er...' he checked his notes for her name 'Jessie Fairleigh is committed to the county asylum for lunatics until such time as she can prove her sanity.'

Rose screamed her denial of what she was hearing. Shocked, Leonore buried her face in her hands. Jess stood impassively by the hard wooden bench.

'Perhaps after the birth of her bastard she will come to her senses,' suggested the Reverend Henry Batsford.

It was not quite a quarter past eleven. The whole proceedings had taken just twelve minutes.

The butler was instructed by his master to see that Rose left the grounds of Worlington Hall immediately. Tyler dragged her cursing and shouting from the room and dumped her brutally on the stone steps where she had stood so expectantly the night before.

'You should have listened to me,' Tyler said sarcastically, looking down at her. 'I told you. Sir George doesn't give charity to beggars.'

Joey dropped Daddler's reins and rushed to help Rose to her feet. 'Rose?'

'They've put her away, Joe,' Rose wailed disbelievingly. 'They've put my Jessie in the bin.'

Joey did not say anything. He lifted Rose on to the cart and covered her legs with a rug. Then he started up the stone steps, two at a time. He had not quite reached the top when Theo the measurer came up behind him and stuck the muzzle of a double-barrelled shotgun in his back.

'Master says as how he wants you to leave. Now.'

Joe still did not speak, but turned round and slammed the full force of his fist into the man's face, sending him somersaulting down the steps. He stepped over the unconscious measurer and climbed rigidly on to the cart and shook the reins, signalling Daddler to walk on.

They were almost at the turn in the drive, the point where the Hall disappeared from the view of departing guests, when Leonore shouted to them from the porch.

'She'll be all right. I promise you,' she called after them. 'I really promise. I promise there will be justice.'

Whether they heard her or not she didn't know, but they didn't look back.

Chapter 14

A Taste of Better Things

The Gothic architecture of the county asylum, standing high on the Kent hillside, dominated the skyline for miles around. It had been designed that way in order to impress and intimidate those who were committed to be contained within its walls. And impress and intimidate them it did. The design and the running of the interior of the establishment were equally successful at their task of imposing authority on the unfortunate inmates. From the bare, cold walls to the hard, ungiving dormitory beds, the asylum inflicted its rigours of routine and harsh discipline on its stiffly clad prisoners. Few of the staff ever bothered to adhere to what they considered the pretence of calling them patients.

A sense of blame ensued from every rule, regulation and punishment thought up by the stony-faced matron who wielded most of the power in the institution. It was she who decided on rations, workloads and accommodation. It was she who was feared by inmates and staff alike – all, that is, except the visiting doctors and the more senior resident staff, who saw nothing of the real Mrs Roberts. They saw only the mask, her pretence of being an enlightened believer in treatment and cure.

Mrs Roberts did not particularly enjoy being cruel, although she had no qualms about being so; she simply saw it as the most efficient way in which to run the establishment. And efficiency meant profit. She had been accumulating an increasingly large nest egg, siphoned off from the economies she introduced into the asylum, since the first day she had been employed by the county. And as long as she kept the board of governors happy with her neatly scripted accounts ledgers, there was no one who would challenge her system.

Jess quickly learnt, like the others who had on admittance protested and resisted, that there was no escape from the regime except by retreat into blank passivity. That was the only way any of them had found to avoid the worst of the viciousness of the staff.

At first Jess could not understand why, as far as she could tell, so few of the women with whom she shared the long, bleak dormitory, appeared to be suffering from any form of madness. She soon came to realise that what they were actually suffering from was poverty, desperation and a lack of power. But she also came to know about the other wards, those with extra guards at their double-locked doors, where the real lunatics were incarcerated. And she also found out about the existence of the prettily decorated individual rooms where the discarded wives of rich men languished in madness-inducing isolation.

Nobody knew where the information about the other wards came from, and nobody talked of those other places in front of the asylum staff. Somehow these things just became common knowledge. The women in Jess's ward considered themselves well off compared to some, and did not want to risk being punished or losing the few privileges that they did have. So they did their work as instructed, without complaint about the harsh toil in the fierce heat and steam of the laundry rooms. Day in, day out, they washed and mangled, starched and ironed the never-ending mountains of soiled sheets and clothing. They laundered not only their own and the staff's uniforms and bedding, but also the linen and lace of many of the wealthy families in the district – yet another ingenious way which Mrs Roberts had found to add a few extra pounds to her miser's hoard.

It gave the matron intense, almost sensual pleasure to slip into the asylum chapel late at night and take the chest from its secret place hidden beneath the altar cloth. The feel of the key turning in the lock and the lid of the coffer opening silently on its well-oiled hinges made her draw in her breath with pure delight. Sometimes she would count her treasure over and over again. At other times she was content merely to add her latest coins to those already stacked in neat piles. That cash box represented everything in which Mrs Roberts believed.

It was the public face, the benevolent, caring version of Mrs Roberts, however, who received Lady Worlington in her immaculately ordered matron's office on a cold January morning. She might, after all, become a new customer for her very reasonably priced laundry service.

'I am afraid that unless you are a relative of the girl,' Mrs Roberts explained with sweet rationality, 'you will not be able to visit. The rule is there to prevent sightseers. I'm sure you understand.'

'Sightseers?' Leonore was not sure she had heard correctly. 'But this place is so…' She tried to find the least offensive term in which to describe the horrific surroundings in which she had so unexpectedly found herself. Even the asylum's forbidding exterior had not prepared her for what she had seen so far of the inside.

'Oh yes, Lady Worlington,' Mrs Roberts continued, 'there *are* still those who believe these unfortunate souls to be merely a source of amusement. Usually, if I might be so bold, it is ladies who are bored and who think that visiting the lunatics is an appropriately Christian act of charity. With a little – how can I put it – diversion? yes, diversion, thrown in for good measure.' Mrs Roberts allowed herself a thin-lipped smile. She was pleased with herself, feeling she had achieved the right balance between putting off a potential busybody's prying into her strictly ordered regime, without offending a potential customer for her laundry services.

Leonore did not return her smile. She raised her chin and addressed the unpleasant woman before her with all the aristocratic aloofness she usually abhorred. This woman brought out the worst in her.

'If I might clarify my own interest, Matron. I am not here to pass some idle moments. I am here with a very specific interest. Jessie Fairleigh.'

Mrs Roberts ran her finger down a list in one of her ledgers. She nodded.

'She was a seasonal worker at Worlington Hall, a hop picker. There was, as I am sure you know, a hearing which resulted in her being brought to this place.'

Mrs Roberts nodded again. She said nothing but she was assessing the possible impact of this woman's visit to the smooth running of her asylum.

'I have been shocked, deeply shocked, by the villagers' indignation against the girl. I have heard that there has been much vicious gossip about her and her unborn child. She has no one living locally who might support her, so I simply wanted to see if I could help her in some way. You appeared to be questioning the motives behind my visit, but believe me, Matron, I am no meddling do-gooder. Merely a wellwisher who would like to do her duty to a past employee.'

Mrs Roberts nodded her head yet again. 'An admirable sentiment, Lady Worlington. If only there were more people showing such concern about our unfortunates.' She had decided to let the silly woman have her say; she didn't want to risk antagonising her. She could never tell who these rich women might know. It wasn't worth making an enemy of her, and thus a potential threat to her profits.

'It was during the harvest that she became pregnant and, as I am sure you know, she is a Londoner. Her family are poor. She has no one to visit her. The purpose of *my* visit is to ensure that all is well, so that I can write and reassure her mother.'

Mrs Roberts's eyes flashed. It had only been for a moment, but Leonore had seen her bristle at the hint that something might be other than well in her establishment.

'I really don't know what you're implying, Lady Worlington, I'm sure,' she said hurriedly, confirming Leonore's fears. 'What could possibly be other than well?'

'You seem rather put out, Mrs Roberts. Is there some other reason why I may not see her?'

'Rules are rules,' said Mrs Roberts, standing up from her desk and fussing with an already orderly pile of papers. 'I am sorry, but I have explained to you already. And, as you are not related to the girl...' She shrugged regretfully, indicating that the matter was out of her hands. 'Now if you would excuse me, I have to see to my many administrative duties.'

'I see,' said Leonore, not even attempting to leave the depressing little room. 'In that case, I would like to speak with Sir Ralph Hamley.'

'Sir Ralph?' The colour faded from Mrs Roberts's already pallid cheeks.

'A family friend,' said Leonore. She smiled to cover her growing suspicions that there was a hidden, and not altogether pleasant, side to the good matron's character.

–

'Leonore, how good to see you. Come in, come in.' Sir Ralph Hamley, the county medical officer in charge of the asylum, welcomed Leonore into his luxuriously appointed office, with its delightful views over the extensive grounds. 'Thank you, Matron, that will be all.'

Mrs Roberts hovered in the doorway, her reluctance to leave obvious to Leonore. It only added to her suspicions that all was not well.

'Perhaps,' he began.

'Yes?' Mrs Roberts said eagerly, hoping for even the slightest chance to stay and hear what this woman was really doing in her asylum.

'Perhaps you could arrange for some tea for us, Mrs Roberts? I'm sure Lady Worlington would like some. And some of those excellent shortbread biscuits.'

'That would be lovely, Ralph,' said Leonore, settling back into an armchair beside his very grand desk.

Mrs Roberts left without comment. The next official rounds were not due for another three days. If this woman was going to poke her nose around, she would have to get to the laundry, the kitchen and the dormitories. She would have to arrange things, hide things away, and all because this nuisance of a visitor had turned up. And she had to 'arrange for some tea' into the bargain. Why did people have to interfere, why couldn't they leave well alone?

'I really cannot begin to think what you are doing here, Leonore.' Sir Ralph smiled. 'But, as ever, I am enchanted to see you.'

'How very gallant you are, Ralph,' said Leonore, extending her gloved hand for him to touch to his lips. 'I was wondering if you would give me the benefit of your experience.'

'My professional experience?' he said, settling into the imposingly large leather chair behind his desk.

'Yes. I would like to discuss in particular a case of moral degeneracy.'

'Heavens,' he teased, raising a neatly clipped grey eyebrow. 'Trying to get your rake of a husband put away, are you?'

'Ralph, you are wicked!' Leonore smiled charmingly at him from under the wide brim of her fashionably large hat. She knew how to flatter men like him. She had even dressed especially for the occasion. 'No, it isn't George's behaviour I wish to discuss.' She lifted her chin and looked directly at him. 'I'll be blunt with you. There was a girl brought in here about a month ago. Jessie Fairleigh.'

'Can't say I know of her,' he said, shaking his head. He reached across his desk to the carved ivory humidor. 'Mind if I smoke?'

'Of course not. I've always loved the smell of a good cigar.' She let him cut and light the long Havana, waiting for him to relax. Then she said, 'She'll be about five months pregnant.'

'Ah. One of those cases,' he said carefully. 'Don't really come into my jurisdiction, I'm afraid. Mrs Roberts – the matron – tends to run things in that area. Not a lot we can do for them, you see. The mental degeneracy is more a product of poor breeding than any curable condition.'

The rapping on his office door prevented Ralph Hamley from noticing Leonore's expression of anger at his easy dismissal of Jessie Fairleigh and 'those cases' like her.

'Come,' he called officiously.

'Mrs Roberts sent me with the tea, sir.'

–

As they sipped their Earl Grey, Leonore tried to persuade Ralph that Jess Fairleigh would benefit from leaving the asylum and becoming gainfully employed as a servant at the Hall.

'There are plenty of opportunities for a girl like her, Ralph. It could be arranged so easily.'

'Your interest in your employee, and a casual labourer at that, is commendable, Leonore, but, quite frankly, I don't think you know what you're talking about.' Ralph leaned back in the big leather chair and linked his hands across his considerable waistcoated belly. 'Not only would I find it very difficult, very difficult indeed, to simply let the girl free, but you'll be doing her no favours by taking her on, even if it were possible.'

Ralph Hamley swivelled his chair around and looked down on to the rolling parkland, seeking inspiration, the words to explain such complex matters to a woman. He turned back to face her.

'You'll just be giving her a taste of better things. She'll see it as a reward for her behaviour. Simply encourage her to do more of the same. Believe me, does more harm than good to show kindness to girls like her, once they've gone wrong. You have to have an understanding of their inbred, diseased minds, their corrupt attitudes.' He gestured to the shelves of books which lined the office. 'It's all in there. Believe me. I know about these things.'

'Well, I have different beliefs,' said Leonora coolly. 'Poverty and ignorance, they're the real diseases. The poverty of girls like her and the ignorance of men like you.' She placed her still half-full cup on to the silver tray and stood up. 'Now, if you wouldn't mind arranging it, Ralph, I would like to see her for myself.'

'You always were plucky,' said Sir Ralph, grinning at Leonore. 'Why not? Can't do any harm.'

He picked up his cigar from the crystal ashtray, took a leisurely draw at it, then blew the richly scented smoke up towards the elaborately beamed ceiling.

–

The walk to the dormitory through the long, bare corridors echoing with the anguished cries of men and women suffering from the unthinkable and unknowable secret terrors of the mind, made Leonore even more determined to rescue Jess and her future grandchild from that hell. And when she saw Jess, standing hollow-eyed and grey-faced by the mean, narrow bedstead in the seemingly unending row of similar cots, Leonore knew she would not rest until the girl was set free.

'Hello, Jess.'

'Answer Lady Worlington,' snapped Mrs Roberts, who was furious at having been ordered to accompany this nuisance of a woman to the ward.

'Don't speak if you don't want to, Jess,' said Leonore gently. 'And I won't be needing you here, thank you, Matron. Sir Ralph said it was in order for me to be alone with Miss Fairleigh.'

Mrs Roberts shook her head at the disruption to her routine, but knew she was powerless to question her superior. 'I'll be in my office if you need me, and there's a warder at the double gate there,' she said, pointing to the barred glass and wooden doors at the end of the room. 'The other girls will be back in an hour,' she said, consulting the fob watch pinned to her starched white apron. 'You'll have to be gone by then.'

Leonore waited for the matron to leave, then spoke to Jess again. 'Please don't be scared to speak to me. I've come to help you.'

Jess still did not respond, but just stood there, staring down at the bare stone floor, hands clasped in front of her.

'I know you have no reason to trust anyone with the name of Worlington, but I assure you, Jess, I mean you no harm. I mean only to help you.'

Jess shifted slightly, readjusted her position.

'You look uncomfortable. Why don't you sit down, Jess?' said Leonore patting the bed. 'Next to me.'

Silently, Jess did so.

–

Leonore talked for almost half an hour. She told Jess about how she had spent her girlhood in London, and about her cousin, Amelia, who still lived there. It was only when she said that she found living in the country so very difficult at times that Jess reacted at all. It was barely perceptible, but Leonore noticed her raise her eyes disbelievingly.

'I know my life must seem impossibly luxurious to you, Jess, but I know what it is like to feel alone,' she said.

Jess looked at her more openly, directly. Then she spoke for the first time. 'I dunno why yer being so nice to me, Lady Worlington, but me mum's always said that the kindness of strangers can mean more than the love of friends.'

'Oh, Jess,' said Leonore, her voice shaking with emotion. 'How can I be a stranger when the baby you're carrying has my blood? Is my own grandchild?'

'Yer believe me then? About the baby's dad?'

'Yes, I believe you, Jess. Of course I do. I know the baby is Robert's. I have never doubted it.'

'So why d'yer let 'im do this to me then?'

'I had no choice, Jess. No, don't turn away from me, please. I am making no excuses – for any of us.' She gestured around the forbidding room. 'For any of *this*. I fully admit that it is my family's fault you are in this place, but it was not Robert who put you in here, it was his father.'

'It weren't 'is father what did this to me, was it?' said Jess, looking down at her swollen middle.

'Of course not. What I meant was that Robert is...' Her voice trailed off. They sat silently for a while, then Leonore spoke again. 'I would have stopped my husband if I could, Jess, please believe me. If I had known how, I would have done anything I could to have stopped him. But I'll make up for all of this. I won't let this go on. I'll get you out of here. I'll take you back to the Hall.'

'Aw, no yer don't.' Jess became agitated at the very thought. 'Yer ain't gettin' me back there. Never. Yer 'eard the things them people said about me in the court.'

'It'll be all right, Jess, I promise. We'll find a way for you to have the baby and to be safe from all of them. No one need even know you are there.' Leonore looked around. 'And it's got to be better than this place for the baby.'

'It ain't that bad. There's plenty lives in worse.' Jessie still had her pride, even in there.

'Have you seen where the babies are kept while the mothers work, Jess? I have. I have a friend who works here, you see. He has told me about the "system" they have for unwed girls with babies.' Leonore shuddered involuntarily. 'It is...' she took a deep breath '... uncivilised. You would be used as free labour, just as you are now, but your baby would be left all day in their so-called nursery. Believe me, you would both be far better off at the Hall.'

'All right then,' said Jess flatly. 'I'll come, if that's what yer thinks's best for the baby.' She stood up. 'I ain't got nothin' to pack, they took me clothes away from me. So I can come right away. As I am.'

'I didn't mean immediately,' said Leonore, flustered by Jess's sudden decision.

'Changed yer mind?' she said, dropping listlessly back on to the bed. 'I thought yer would. Must run in the family.'

'No, Jess. No, I haven't changed my mind,' said Leonore, taking Jessie's rough, worksore hand in hers. 'I want you to come with me. To let me care for you. But,' she searched for the right words, 'it won't be that easy. I have to convince the authorities here that it would be for the best.'

'I see,' said Jess, her voice dull with disappointment, yet resigned to being let down.

'Don't look like that, Jess. I promised you I would help and I will. I promise I will get you out of here.' The sound of footsteps approaching made both women looked towards the doors. 'The matron told me to go before the others came back,' she said, touching Jess's cheek. 'We don't want to upset anyone, do we? I've got to prove I'm a responsible person. That I'm making a sensible decision.'

Jess nodded. 'As yer like,' she said.

'And I'll get a message to your mother telling her that I'm going to sort out this mess,' she called as she opened the doors.

'But me mum can't read. I always read 'er letters for 'er,' cried Jess frantically after the departing figure. A sudden feeling of loss overwhelmed her. Not for the first time since she had been incarcerated, Jess wondered if she should have gone to Granny Rawlins's after all. Could anything be worse than this?

Leonore stood looking at her from the doorway, the gateway to freedom, the big, surly warder by her side.

'Don't worry, Jess,' she said, 'I'll find a way of letting her know.' Leonore smiled; she had thought of a solution to that small problem at least. 'You have brothers, don't you? One of them will be able to read it to her.'

'No! Please.' Jess was frantic. 'Don't do that. They'll tell me dad. 'E mustn't know.'

'Look, I won't do anything you don't agree to, Jess.' Leonore contemptuously brushed aside the warder's attempts to take her arm, to escort her from the ward. 'I'll go and see her myself, if you'd prefer.'

'Would yer?'

'Of course.'

'But not yet. Would yer wait? 'Til yer've sorted it out. Like yer said.'

'Whatever you say, Jess.'

Jess watched Leonore walk away along the corridor. Would things really be easier now that she had someone who said she was her friend? She felt that things might come out right, somehow. They had to. She couldn't stay here, not with the baby. She wouldn't.

Leonore became a familiar figure at the county asylum, going once a week to visit both Jess and Sir Ralph Hamley.

239

At first the visits were merely frustrating for Leonore, as Sir Ralph repeatedly refused to even consider reversing the court's order of committal. But then, once Mrs Roberts realised that Leonore was only interested in Jess, that she didn't intend using the laundry service, and that she represented no threat to her profits, the difficulties increased. The matron not only became less helpful, she became positively obstructive, often allowing Leonore to see only one of them, either Jess or Ralph, and sometimes allowing her to see neither. Mrs Roberts did not even bother to make plausible excuses to Leonore. The matron acted as the fancy took her, and playing games with Lady Worlington made a change from the everyday routine. But Leonore would not be deterred, even by the senseless barriers constructed by Mrs Roberts. She refused to give up on her mission. It didn't matter that no one else would help; she would not renounce her responsibility to free Jess and her future grandchild.

—

One afternoon early in June, Leonore was arguing, yet again, with Mrs Roberts in the matron's poky, depressing little office. She had long gone beyond the irritating pretence of sympathising with the matron's difficulties.

'And why, pray, can I not see her this time, Mrs Roberts? I suppose there has been a plague outbreak in here, or some other nonsense you've decided to concoct.'

'She's in the hospital ward actually,' replied Mrs Roberts without once glancing up from her ledgers.

'The baby?'

'Mmm.'

—

Sylvia Rose Fairleigh was born on the 6th of June 1914. Rose for her grandmother, and Sylvia after a friend whom Leonore was always talking about to Jess. Leonore had been so kind to her, Jess was glad to be able to please her, even in such a small way.

The birth had not been difficult, and mother and baby were both fit and healthy, but Jess was becoming increasingly distressed. Every day she had to be dragged protesting to the laundry, where she sweated from early morning until late each night. It wasn't the work she minded, even though it was hard and relentless – East End girls were used to hard graft. It was leaving Sylvia that was so painful. Each morning she had to be forced to leave her baby with the other infants in the vast, bleak nursery. There they were left, without comfort, alone and screaming except for the breaks when their mothers were allowed to go and breastfeed them.

Jess cried herself to sleep at night thinking about her baby, and about her mother who didn't even know that Sylvia existed.

Seeing Jessie's agony, the decline in her spirit, and the lack of light in her once lovely eyes, Leonore entered a fresh phase of her campaign. She pestered Ralph Hamley with a renewed vigour.

–

No one, not the matron, not Leonore, not Jess, nor Ralph Hamley himself, would have been able to predict the day when Jess was finally released into Leonore's keeping. It was the middle of July and Leonore was sitting in Ralph's office waiting for him to return from a meeting in London. She was idly flicking through a newspaper she had brought with her; she had learnt to prepare herself for a long wait each week.

'Good afternoon, Ralph,' she said pleasantly as he entered the room.

'Leonore.'

'You seem agitated. I hope you're not going to be difficult with me again.'

'Please, Leonore, not today. I have serious matters to consider.'

'And what can be more important than the welfare of one of your charges, Ralph?' asked Leonore sharply.

'If you must know, Leonore,' said Ralph, flopping down exhausted into his chair, 'the outbreak of war. That is what is more important than some bit of a girl from the London slums.'

'Is that all?' Leonore tossed her newspaper on to the desk in front of him. 'If you've been reading *The Times* lately, you'd think war had already broken out.'

'It almost has, I'm afraid.'

Leonore studied his face carefully. He was serious. 'You mean it, don't you, Ralph?'

'I'm surprised you don't know about it yourself with those sons of yours,' said Ralph. 'If they're like most young men I've met lately they'll be completely overexcited by the whole ugly business. Relishing the prospect of being heroes. A chance to show Germany that Britannia still rules the waves and all that.'

His sarcastic tone alarmed Leonore. She needed Ralph on her side. He would be a very dangerous enemy. She had to lighten the atmosphere. As she avoided discussing her own family whenever possible, she enquired about Ralph's instead. 'Why is the possibility of war of such concern to you personally, Ralph? You have only daughters.' Leonore tried a wide smile. 'And I do not wish to be impertinent, but you are hardly soldiering age.'

'The war is no longer merely a possibility, Leonore,' he answered wearily. 'It is a matter of when it will begin, not if.'

He paused to take a cigar from the humidor on his desk. Leonore watched him go through his well-practised habit of cutting and lighting its end. The routine pacified him.

'I have been instructed today – this is, of course, in confidence.' He looked at her through the blue clouds of smoke which curled lazily between them.

'Of course, Ralph.' Leonore frowned. He really was very serious indeed.

'Good. Well,' he sighed loudly, 'this asylum is being requisitioned. As from next week, work – secret work, mind,' he emphasised, pointing his cigar at her, 'is beginning here. We are being turned into a military hospital, whether we like it or not.'

Leonore looked puzzled. She had been following the interminable newspaper articles about the German threat, of course – everyone had – but what had all this to do with the hospital?

'Near the Channel, you see. Word is that Belgium might be the scene of some pretty rough fighting.'

'Belgium?' Leonore almost laughed with relief. 'Surely, Ralph, we won't get involved to that extent?'

'If we want to sort this lot out as quickly as possible, then there are going to be some casualties. We have to be prepared.'

'It doesn't seem possible on a glorious day like this to be speaking of war. No, Ralph, I can't believe it.' As if on cue, a blackbird, perched in the tall elm close to the open window, burst into an enchanting trilling song. 'And what will this mean for the people in the asylum, Ralph? What will happen to them?'

'Most of them will be shifted inland, to other institutions. A few will be lodged out to locals as labourers and domestic...'

When Leonore clapped excitedly, Ralph did not bother to finish the sentence.

'I'll sign her over to you first thing Monday morning.' He raised his hand to still her protests. 'Can't do it before then. I'll be doing it unofficially as it is, and if Mrs Roberts becomes suspicious, well, she'll never get out. Matron won't want to lose one of her laundry workers.' Ralph almost smiled. 'I'll miss these meetings, Leonore.'

Leonore didn't go to see Jess, but, leaving the asylum immediately, went straight to the gardener's cottage at Worlington Hall.

–

'Oh m'lady,' said Mrs Garnett, bobbing politely and wiping her flour-covered hands on her crossover pinafore. 'I thought you were my husband home for his dinner.'

'Don't let me keep you from your baking, Mrs Garnett. I'm not here to disturb you. I've come to ask a favour.'

Leonore sat at the table and put her proposition to Mrs Garnett while the amiable middle-aged woman got on with her kneading, rolling and cutting. The gardener's wife listened patiently, not speaking until she was satisfied that Leonore had finished.

'I don't want to speak out of turn, Lady Worlington,' said Mrs Garnett, as she took a tray of scones from the shining black-leaded range and set them down on the long deal table. 'But I don't see as how I can have that girl here in the cottage. There's enough talk in the village about our Milly still.' She sat down at the table, facing Leonore. 'What would it look like? Stranger in the place. And with a baby and all.'

'I understand your concern, Mrs Garnett, I honestly do, but it wouldn't be like that. I should have explained. You see

244

Jess's presence here will be a secret. You're very secluded, that's one of the reasons I thought of you. No one need ever know she's here.' Leonore looked down into her lap. 'Unless you or Garnett told them, of course.'

'We're not gossips in this house, m'lady,' Mrs Garnett said as she eased the scones, one by one, from the tray on to a cooling rack.

'Precisely,' said Leonore triumphantly. 'One of the other reasons I thought of you, Mrs Garnett.' Leonore sniffed appreciatively. 'They smell wonderful.'

Mrs Garnett stood up and fetched two pretty blue and white plates from the gaily painted dresser.

Leonore held up her hand, 'Oh please, I didn't mean you to do that.'

'Hospitality, that's all,' said Mrs Garnett as she put two of the warm scones on each plate, with generous helpings of jam, then spooned out big measures of thick yellow cream from a white china basin. She placed one of the plates in front of Leonore. 'Then there's the baby,' she said.

The women were outwardly calm, breaking open their scones and spreading them with the rich cream and fruit-laden preserves. Inwardly their minds were racing; neither was used to such delicate negotiations.

'Nearly two months old,' said Leonore, dabbing at the corner of her mouth with her lace-trimmed handkerchief. 'Sylvia. A beautiful little girl.' She did her best to make everyday conversation. 'These are excellent, Mrs Garnett.'

The gardener's wife nodded her thanks. 'And the baby's father,' she said. 'He'd be wanting to visit, I suppose.'

'No,' said Leonore, avoiding Mrs Garnett's questioning look by pretending to concentrate on her scones. 'It isn't like that.'

'Poor girl,' said Mrs Garnett, standing up. 'I'll pour us some tea to have with these.' She went over to where the pot stood on a trivet at the side of the range. 'Been abandoned by some no good, has she?' she asked over her shoulder.

'Something like that,' said Leonore quietly.

'I don't know,' said Mrs Garnett, shaking her head. 'It's a tough life and no mistake.'

'Especially for a girl like her, with nowhere to go.' Leonore didn't care about playing shamelessly on the kindly woman's emotions; she was doing it for Jessie and Sylvia. She was sure Mrs Garnett would give in to her better nature sooner or later. 'Won't *you* help her, Mrs Garnett?'

'No disrespect, m'lady, and I don't want you to think I didn't appreciate you sorting out a position for our Milly. But now all the children have left home, it's hard enough feeding ourselves on Garnett's money.'

Leonore blushed at George's meanness. He kept all his workers short of cash. 'You would, of course, be well paid for your trouble. And Jess is tall and strong. She'll be able to help you with all sorts of jobs. Think about it. The extra money. And her helping you about the place.'

'I suppose it is a waste our Milly's room being left empty,' said Mrs Garnett, taking the dirty plates and cups over to the deep stone sink by the window. 'And I wouldn't mind some help.'

'Splendid.' Leonore could have sung with joy. She stood up before Mrs Garnett could ask any more questions, and walked over to the door. 'The scones were wonderful, Mrs Garnett, thank you. Thank you very much indeed.'

Leonore stepped outside into the warm summer sun and took a deep breath of sweet country air. 'She'll love it here, I know she will. So different from the place she is in now.' As though it was an afterthought she added, 'Oh, I should have mentioned, she'll be arriving on Monday. I'll make sure she has everything she needs for the child.'

With that she made her escape, before the gardener's wife could change her mind.

As Mrs Garnett closed the bottom half of the cottage door behind Lady Worlington, she wondered whatever her husband would think. But then she thought about having some company around the place again. She'd like that. Although she was pleased Milly was settled and happy in London, she really missed having her daughter to talk to. Perhaps it wouldn't be so bad.

She went back to her baking. As she shaped and pummelled the bread dough with her firm countrywoman's hands she grew more and more to like the idea of Jessie staying there with them. And it would brighten up the cottage no end having a baby around the place.

Mrs Garnett set the bread to rise by the range and wondered at how the world was changing around her, and whether she would ever have a grandchild of her own. She shook her head and sighed. Things were certainly different to when she was a girl. There was her Milly in London, the first one in the family ever to go that far from the village, and now a stranger was coming to live with them. A young girl with a baby and no husband.

She poured hot water from the kettle into the deep sink and got on with washing the baking tray and the dishes. She wondered if either of the young women, Milly or Jess, realised how fortunate they were to have been employed by the Worlingtons. Lady Worlington was a real lady, who cared about what happened to the people who worked for her, even casual labourers like Jessie Fairleigh.

Garnett was not as sure as his wife about having a lodger at the cottage, especially a foreigner with a baby. But he let himself be persuaded for his wife's sake; she had had a hard time lately, suffering from the harsh tongues of the village busybodies. So it was for his wife that he was finally prepared to give the girl a chance, to see if a bit of young life around the cottage would cheer up his beloved Susan.

Like Matthew Garnett, Jess was also unsure about she and Sylvia living in the cottage. No matter what Leonore Worlington said about them, the Garnetts were country people, homedwellers when all was said and done. Jess had had enough experience of the villagers of Tilnhurst not to trust any of them. And when Leonore explained that she would be paying the Garnetts for Jess's board and lodging, she was even more anxious about the arrangement. But in the end she knew she had no option: rather than set eyes again on Mrs Roberts and the asylum, she would even prefer the shame of going to the workhouse and throwing herself on the mercy of the Board of Guardians. At least Leonore had saved her from that indignity.

But it was still with much trepidation that on the Monday morning Jess climbed into the little carriage and sat down next to Leonore. Lady Worlington had engineered things so that Garnett drove them – the fewer people who knew about her not entirely official arrangements with Ralph Hamley the better.

As the carriage drove through the hated gates of the asylum, Jess tore off the loathed starched uniform cap, the mark of her so-called immorality, and flung it with all her strength high into the air. She didn't turn round to see where it landed. She refused to look back; she was on the road to her new home, going towards a future that would be better – it had to be – for her and her little daughter. But she still couldn't help worrying what new hell she might be letting herself in for.

Jess needn't have worried. From the moment she saw the little thatched cottage with its neat garden full of flowers and vegetables growing in orderly, well-tended rows, and the brightly painted green shutters standing out against the freshly whitewashed walls, Jess was sure everything would be all right. Then when Mrs Garnett came rushing out to greet them, her round face full of smiles and kindness, she knew that her life could begin again.

Jess and Sylvia quickly became honorary members of the Garnett household. It soon felt as though they had lived there for years, as though the asylum had been part of a bad dream Jess had woken up from and had almost forgotten.

Jess was a clean, willing worker and her singing made the whole place come back to life, just as Mrs Garnett had hoped it would. It was a real pleasure for her to see the young mother and baby flourishing on the fresh air and freedom.

Jess woke every morning full of thanks that she did not have to wait for the wardress to unlock the doors and make her leave her baby in that dreaded dungeon of a nursery. But she still had two regrets, two places of darkness in her life: the places which were filled with remorse about Rose and sadness about Robert. She so wanted to be with Rose, to show her the granddaughter she knew she would love, but she understood that her release had been irregular, and that she must wait until Leonore said it was safe before she could contact her mother.

And then there was Robert. She would often see him in the distance, riding around the grounds on his big chestnut horse, dressed in his finery. He never saw her; she always kept well hidden from him. She still couldn't understand his callousness. How could he have abandoned her so cruelly? How could he have forsaken his own child?

And so Jessie's days passed, happily enough, but still with the sadness deep inside her.

—　　　—

Leonore shaded her eyes with her hand and peered into the cottage window, hoping to see the baby; instead she saw Jess sitting at the table, crying.

'Jessie. What's wrong?' she asked, pushing open the door.

Jess looked up at her baby's grandmother, her eyes red from tears. She hurriedly dried her face on her sleeve. Sniffing loudly she said, 'I didn't expect nobody to be about. Mrs Garnett's gone to the market, see. I'll finish these spuds right now. I've nearly done 'em.'

'I'm not that hateful matron, Jess. I'm not trying to catch you out.' Leonore moved closer. She put her hand gently on Jess's shoulder. 'I don't want to see you upset like this. It's not Sylvia, is it? She's not ill?'

'No, she's beautiful. Really beautiful.' Tears began to flow down her cheeks again. 'I'd love my mum to see 'er. An'…' She couldn't help it, she had to say it, even though Leonore had been so good to her. 'An' I don't understand why Robert don't want us.'

'Oh, Jessie.' Leonore sat down next to her. She reached out and stroked Jess's hair, then rocked her until she had cried out all her tears. 'Listen to me,' she said, lifting Jess's face until their eyes met. 'I admit I do not understand the behaviour of my sons, either of them. But I also want you to know something about Robert.' Leonore swallowed hard. The words did not come easily. 'Jess, Robert still does not know about Sylvia, nor does he have any idea that you were even pregnant. I swear to you.'

'What?' Jess gasped.

'And, I am ashamed to say, I feel he isn't worthy of knowing about her, even though he is her father. He is too much like his own father for you to trust him.' Leonore bowed her head. 'Jessie, I am telling you this although it shames me to do so. He would disown all knowledge of you. Both of you. That would suit him. And you would be back in that place. Worse, you would be moved to somewhere far away from here. But there's something else I have to tell you. Robert has accepted a commission in the army. He is preparing to join his regiment shortly. It seems that war will be declared on Germany.'

Leonore watched Jess go to the corner of the comfortable, neat little kitchen and take her sleeping daughter from the crib. She felt so terribly sad for Jess, for all her pain and suffering, and she felt almost unbearably angry at her son. She could see how much Jess loved the child, and knowing how badly Robert had treated her was agony for Leonore. Leonore too felt pain all right, she felt the pain of a mother who knows her son to be a bad man, just like his father.

Jess kissed Sylvia tenderly on her forehead and handed her to Leonore. 'I want me mum to know that me and the baby's all right. That I'm out of that stinkin' place. Please. Please find a way to tell 'er for me. 'Specially if there's gonna be a war.' Jess rubbed her hands over her salty cheeks. 'I know yer ain't meant to tell no one about us bein' 'ere an' everythin', but please I want 'er to know. Will yer go to see 'er for me? Yer did promise me once.'

'Yes, Jessie. I'll tell her for you.' Leonore kissed Sylvia and handed her back to Jess. Then she stood up to leave.

'Ta,' said Jess quietly.

Leonore was halfway down the path when Jess called out to her, "As 'e married that Julia girl then?'

'No, Jess,' said Leonore simply, 'he hasn't.'

—

Lady Worlington instructed her chauffeur to drive her to the station. He was a recent employee of the Hall, an outsider, and far less likely to gossip than the coachman. She told him that she was going to London where she had some shopping to attend to. He was to meet the 11.20 at Tilnhurst station the next morning, as she would be staying the night in Belgravia with her cousin Amelia.

As Leonore had hoped, Sir George was as uninterested as the driver had been in the minor details of her excursion into town. It was quite usual for her to go on shopping expeditions with Amelia. At least, that's what he thought. Over the years, shopping had provided a very useful cover for Leonore and Amelia to continue their clandestine work in the London slums. But today's shopping masked a very different venture, even though it was in the same locality in which she and her cousin did much of their work. Today, Leonore was going to Poplar to see Rose Fairleigh.

—

With the help of a sketch map provided by Jess, Leonore took a cab to the comer of Burton Street, then made her way on foot to Number 8.

The sight of such a grand lady walking past her window was more than Florrie Baxter could bear. Peering from behind the curtains at the stranger, like most of the other residents of Burton Street were doing, wasn't good enough for Florrie. She went right outside to discover what was going on.

'Can I 'elp yer, dear?' she enquired, tripping down her front doorstep in her anxiety to speak to the woman. 'Yer lost or somethin', are yer? Yer ain't from round these parts, I know that.'

'No, I'm not. And thank you, but I'm not lost.'

'Visitin' someone then, are yer?'

'Yes. Yes, I am.'

'What?' Florrie was almost bursting; she really couldn't imagine what was going on – a posh lady like her in Poplar? 'Visitin' someone, yer say? In Burton Street? You?'

'Yes.' Leonore did not want to be rude to the woman, but equally she did not want to broadcast her intentions to the whole neighbourhood. She was all too aware that if the wrong person were to find out about Jessie, then her safety at the Garnetts' would be in real danger.

'Well, yer've found the right person 'ere, all right,' said Florrie enthusiastically. 'I know everyone around 'ere. Everyone. I can tell yer if yer goin' to the right 'ouse. If they're 'ome and that.' She paused briefly for breath. 'If yer like, that is.'

Florrie was staring, unable to take her eyes off the woman's clothes. They were the most beautiful things she had ever been so close to. The most wonderful things she had ever seen before. She smelt lovely as well. All fresh and flowery. And her hat. It was pale blue, big and broad-brimmed, with great sweeping feathers and a heavy lace veil. In fact, that was the only thing Florrie was not too keen on. The veil was a bit thick for her liking; she could hardly make out the woman's features at all. Perhaps she had a horrible scar or something.

'D'yer always wear a thick veil like that?' Florrie asked, peering alarmingly closely at the woman.

When Leonore did not answer, Florrie decided she must be really badly disfigured to not want to talk about it. She was lucky she had money though, so she could afford to wear posh clothes and hide it. Florrie returned to her earlier, more promising line of questioning.

'Go on, let me 'elp yer find the 'ouse. Yer tell me 'oo lives there, what their name is an' that. An' I'm bound to know 'em. I know everyone around 'ere.'

In her desire not to draw any more unwelcome attention to herself, Leonore relented under Florrie's pressure. Anything to get away from the woman. 'Thank you for your offer of help,' she said graciously. 'I'm looking for a Mrs Fairleigh.'

'Rose?' shrieked Florrie. 'Gawd blimey!'

Leonore looked around, embarrassed at the volume of the woman's exclamation. 'This is Burton Street, isn't it?'

'Yeh,' said Florrie, barely able to keep her mouth closed with the amazement of it all. 'This is Burton Street all right.'

'Then I have the right place.'

''Ang on,' said Florrie slowly. 'Don't I know yer voice?' Florrie moved even closer to Leonore in her efforts to place her. 'Let's see, ain't yer one of them charity ladies or somethin'? Is that 'oo yer are?'

Leonore fiddled with her veil, making sure her face was covered from prying eyes.

'Somethin' 'appened to 'er ol' man, 'as it? Bill 'ad an accident at sea? Been drownded dead, 'as 'e?'

Leonore grasped at the opportunity to quieten the woman's escalating suspicions. 'Well, yes,' she said slowly. 'I am from a charitable organisation. But I've not come about Mr Fairleigh. I've come about,' she paused, looking for inspiration, 'a private matter.' She decided that was the most innocent of explanations. She couldn't have been more wrong as far as Florrie was concerned.

'Aw! That'll be their Charlie then,' said Florrie, delighted that she had solved the puzzle. 'I knew they was lyin' when they said 'e'd gone abroad. America they reckoned, if yer don't mind. Bloody America.'

Leonore could not convince Flonie otherwise as she proceeded to launch into a knowing round of regret and recrimination directed at all ungrateful sons and their suffering mothers, most of which concerned her oldest child, Arthur, and her twins, Sidney and Albert.

'Always knew 'e'd end up comin' to no good, that one. Trouble to Rose from the day 'e was born.'

Leonore consulted her fob watch again. She was unused to standing about in the street, particularly when accompanied by someone as voluble as Florrie Baxter.

'Yer keep lookin' at the time,' said Florrie, arms folded purposefully across her chest. 'Yer in an 'urry, are yer?'

'Well, actually I am rather.'

'Tell yer what. 'Ow about if I goes an' fetches 'er? 'Ow would that be? I could do that if yer want.'

'Would you?' asked Leonore, relieved at the prospect of a rest from Florrie's incessant talking.

'Yeh. She'll be round ol' Miss Feldman's. Does for 'er, yer see. Jessie – now that's Rose's girl – used to light 'er fires an' 'er gaslights for 'er of a Friday night. Before she went off into so-called service. Mind yer, believe that an' yer'll believe anythin'.' Florrie spat venomously into the gutter, making Leonore wince. 'Service,' she sneered. 'Do me a favour, don't make me laugh. Tell us the old, old story, eh? Anyway Friday night's the start of their Sabbath, see. Don't do no jobs or nothin'. It's their religion. Jewish lady she is. Got a few bob an' all, I've 'eard. Sister of the bloke what owns the pawnshop. I dunno about you, but *I've* never seen a poor pawnbroker.'

Desperate that Florrie should not launch into another life story of one of her neighbours, Leonore closed her ears, opened her bag and took out her purse.

'You'll need some fare money to fetch her,' she managed to butt in quickly, as Florrie paused to draw breath.

'No, I won't,' said Florrie, put out by Leonore's gesture. 'I just told yer, Miss Feldman only lives round the corner. Wasn't yer listenin' to me?'

At that moment, Rose turned into Burton Street. When she saw Leonore Worlington standing on her doorstep being talked at by Florrie Baxter, she did her best to hide her bewilderment at what was going on.

''Ello,' she said simply, taking out her key. 'Yer'd better come in.'

'I'll come in with yer, if yer like,' offered Florrie, stepping in front of Leonore, blocking the way between her and the door. She was now almost bursting with anxiety to find out what was going on, and manners would certainly be no barrier to her. 'Case it's bad news about your Charlie.'

'No thanks, Florrie, I'd like to speak to the lady in private. And,' she added sharply, 'Charlie's just fine.' She nodded a brisk thanks and goodbye to her neighbour, unlocked the street door and elbowed Florrie unceremoniously out of the way. 'In 'ere.'

The last Florrie was to see of the meeting was Leonore stepping inside Number 8 and the door being closed firmly in her face.

Leonore followed Rose blindly along the dark, narrow passage.

'Mind yerself on the mat,' said Rose. 'It's a bit raggy.'

The kitchen was stiflingly hot. Rose threw open the back door, letting in a fraction more light and air from the tiny back yard. 'It's the range. I 'ave to keep it going to 'eat up the water, an' for cookin' an' that,' explained Rose.

'And it has been so very warm again today,' said Leonore, dabbing her face with a cologne-scented handkerchief.

'I don't suppose yer used to sittin' in back kitchens, an' I don't suppose yer 'ere to chat about the weather neither,' said Rose, hiding her trepidation by busying herself with the kettle, and being unusually curt. 'Why don't yer sit yerself down. I'll make us a cup of tea an' then yer can tell me whatever it is yer've got to say. An' then yer be on yer way.'

Even though she felt she had every right to speak in that way, Rose felt ashamed at her rudeness.

'Let me say first that we all appreciated round 'ere what yer did for Mabel Lawrence when she 'ad 'er bit a trouble. But that apart, I'd still rather yer got it over with, whatever yer've got to say, an' left. I ain't got a lot of time for the Worlington family at the minute.'

Leonore forced herself to look at Rose, not to drop her head in shame. 'Mrs Fairleigh, I would also like to make something clear before I say what I came here to say. You may not believe me but I share your feelings entirely about the Worlingtons. I too have grown to loathe what my husband and sons stand for.'

'That ain't my business, now is it? 'Ow many sugars?'

'None thank you. Just a little milk.'

Rose poured the tea and sat at the table opposite Lady Worlington. 'So. What it is then?'

Leonore turned her cup round and round in its saucer, studying the steaming liquid as though it were an intricate work of art. 'Jess has had her baby,' she said.

'I figured she would 'ave. Is everythin' all right? They well, are they?' Rose did her best to keep the excitement from her voice. She didn't want this woman having anything to hold over her or use against her.

'Yes, very well. Sylvia Rose. She was born on the sixth of June.'

'My little Jessie, a mum,' said Rose. Unable to help herself, she began crying.

'Don't distress yourself, Mrs Fairleigh, please.' Leonore put down her cup and went to reach her hand out in comfort to Rose. But she couldn't. She had no right. 'I've brought you good news. Please, calm yourself.' Leonore clapped her hands together in exasperation. 'I'm finding all this *very* difficult. You see, the whole thing has had to be arranged in a rather unorthodox manner, and I do not want the people who have helped me getting into trouble for their generosity.' She leant forward. 'Do you follow me?'

'I 'ave to tell yer,' said Rose, wiping her eyes on her apron, 'I don't understand a word yer sayin'.'

Leonore laughed with relief at Rose's refreshing candour. She wasn't used to such things at Worlington, and she sometimes forgot how much easier it was to be honest. She decided to follow Rose's sensible example and explain truthfully and directly about all the circumstances and negotiations which had finally resulted in Jess and Sylvia being lodged with the Garnetts.

Rose too was relieved. She was relieved that Jess had had her baby, that her daughter and grandchild were well, that they had a clean place to stay, and that Leonore Worlington was obviously making sure that they would not suffer because of her no-good son.

'I nearly forgot. I have something for you,' said Leonore, taking a small tissue packet from her bag and handing it to Rose.

Rose unfolded the paper and took out a lock of pale golden hair.

'She is not as auburn as Jessie, or you, but she has a mass of curls,' said Leonore, smiling at the image she had of her beautiful granddaughter. 'I wanted to have a photograph taken for you, but it wasn't wise for Jess to take her to the studio. People gossip so in the country.'

'Not only in the country,' said Rose, wiping a fresh lot of tears away with the edge of her cuff. 'An' don't think I ain't appreciated yer comin' 'ere. Thanks. It can't 'ave been easy for yer.'

'Compared to what Jess has been through over these last few months, it has been simplicity itself.' Leonore was near to tears herself. 'I've had an idea,' she said, brightening at the prospect of doing something useful. 'Why don't you travel back with me? Come and see Jess and the baby. She'd love to see you, I know she would.'

'Wouldn't really be a good idea yet awhile,' said Rose regretfully. 'It might 'ave been 'ard enough for yer to 'ave come 'ere an' seen me, but it'd be an 'ell of a lot 'arder for the likes of me to travel down there.'

'I am sorry, I didn't think. If it's money,' Leonore picked up her bag, 'I could help.'

'No, it ain't that.'

'Mrs Fairleigh, I have offended you.' She let the bag slip to her feet. 'I am truly sorry.'

'No, I ain't offended,' said Rose, trying a smile. 'An' me name's Rose.'

'Thank you, Rose. And please, you must call me Leonore.'

'Well, Leonore,' said Rose, sighing loudly and topping up their teacups. 'It's like this. 'Ow would I explain where I was goin'? Or where I was? We don't do a lot of travellin' round these parts. Mind yer, 'opping'll be startin' next month. I could've gone down then and no one would've blinked an eye.'

'Is something preventing you, Rose?'

'I ain't 'ad me letter this year, 'ave I?' she answered, unable to keep the bitterness from her voice. 'An' I don't suppose Sir George will be welcomin' none of us Fairleighs to Worlington no more.'

Leonore drained her cup resolutely. 'Things are changing at Worlington, Rose. The birth of young Sylvia has made me a very determined woman. Very determined indeed. I do not intend to let my husband cause any more difficulties for my granddaughter. For our granddaughter, I should say. I will ensure that you get your letter. I'll go to the bailiff myself and instruct him to send it immediately. George doesn't have a single idea what goes on on the farm anyway. I even oversee the farm accounts nowadays, you know.' She smiled wondering at how she herself had changed so much over the years, and how she was talking so freely to this woman. 'My husband is either too drunk or too busy with his horses to worry about little details like the running of the estate.'

'There's plenty of men round 'ere like that,' said Rose sympathetically. 'Too busy boozin' to do a decent day's work. That'll *never* change, but yer right, some things *are* changin'. I don't understand what's 'appenin' in the world 'alf the time. D'yer know they was actually celebratin' round 'ere when they 'eard war 'ad broke out? The copper stood on the corner of Burton Street an' announced it, an' they all went barmy. Dancin' an' singin' all night down The Star they was.' Rose shook her head sadly. 'Celebratin' cos their 'usbands an' sons are gonna go off to war.'

'It was the same at Worlington, Rose. And in the village.'

'Thank Gawd our Ted ain't old enough to go. But our Sammy, that's me oldest boy, signed up straight away. When 'e saw the girls goin' mad for the blokes in uniform, that was that. All 'is mates from the woodyard joined up together, Pals Battalion they called it. An 'ole lot of fellers from round our part of Poplar all joinin' up together. Yer'd think they was goin' off on a beano way they was actin'. An' I know for a fact that some of 'em wasn't nearly old enough. Yer know I don't think they even thought about them poor so-and-sos in Belgium they're meant to be 'elpin'. I don't know.' Rose looked at the little curl of golden hair nestling in her hand. ''Ark at me.' She laughed unconvincingly. 'I sound like Florrie the way I'm leadin' off.'

'My elder son has gone to Belgium.'

'Robert?'

'Yes,' said Leonore quietly.

'It ain't easy, is it?'

'Rose, when I think about the pain he has caused you and your family, I feel so... Oh, I don't know. I feel that I shouldn't care about him. But then I feel so guilty. About my own feelings, and about what he has done.'

'None of it ain't yer fault, Leonore. We've all 'ad trouble with our kids at one time or another. My Charlie for one. Right cowson 'e was as a kid. Now 'e's livin' in Chicago. In America, if yer don't mind. 'E writes every now an' then. When 'e remembers. Doin' all right for 'imself an' all, 'e reckons. Savin' 'ard to open a business. It's a real dream 'e's got. I 'ope 'e manages it one day. It'd be a right disappointment for 'im if it went wrong. Still, whatever 'e does, least 'e's safe from this stinkin' war, eh?' Rose refilled the kettle from the single cold tap over the sink and set it on the range to boil. 'Yer know I never thought of yer as a woman before,' she said, looking at Leonore. 'Not like the rest of us, some'ow. 'Cept when yer 'elped Mabel, I suppose. But now look at us. Sittin' 'ere gabbin'. Just a couple of women worryin' about our kids. Who'd 'ave thought it, eh?'

—

When Rose had waved her goodbyes to Leonore from the doorstep, she looked over towards the Baxters' house. Sure enough, there was Florrie, pretending to polish up the knocker on the street door.

'Get a good look, did yer, Florrie?' Rose called to her neighbour. 'Or shall I get Ted to write down all the details for yer?'

Chapter 15

Gossips

Rose was glad to have Mabel Lawrence sharing her hopper's hut. Mabel was company for her. She couldn't have stood sleeping in the straw-filled bed all alone.

At first Ted had been talking about going with his mum, but finally they had both thought it best if he stayed at home in Burton Street to carry on with his job. During the weeks since war had broken out, the woodyard had lost a lot of workers, and now, for the first time since he had started there, Ted wasn't only the kid who did the sweeping up and ran errands; he was now a valued employee. But despite his new status, he was still Rose's youngest, and she was as worried about him as ever, so he was placed very firmly under Joey Fuller's supervision while his mother was away.

The arrangements also suited Mabel, who was more than pleased to be sharing with Rose. She'd been dreading going back to Tilnhurst for the first time since her baby had died. And even though it hadn't been easy, she had gone, as soon as they'd arrived, to visit the little grave with its tiny wooden cross. But at least Rose had been there with her. She'd been a real help to Mabel, not just like a neighbour, but like a friend, a good friend. She was always there if Mabel wanted to have a chat, and always willing to keep an eye on the children without being asked. Rose was a good, kind woman, and Mabel appreciated it.

It was the evening of the first Monday of the harvest. They had only been in Kent since the night before, but once the two women had settled down into the routine of picking hops and doing their chores, it was almost as though they had never been away, as though nothing had changed. Everything seemed to be as it always had been. Indeed, for most of the Londoners staying in the Kent countryside, nothing *had* changed, even though the country was now at war.

But for Rose there were many big differences in her life. And one of them was that she was now a grandmother.

'I'm goin' off for a little walk, Mabel,' whispered Rose, picking up her shawl from the foot of the bed. 'Gonna get a bit o' fresh air, an' blow some a this muck off me chest.'

'All right, Rose,' said Mabel, tucking the blanket round her children. 'I'll see yer later.'

Rose pushed the hut door open. 'Leave that bit of washin', Mabel. I'll see to it when I get back.'

'Don't worry yerself, Rose,' said Mabel. 'These two 'ave nearly gone off, they're exhausted, bless 'em.' Mabel stroked the hair of her two precious children. 'I'll be finished in 'ere then. So I can go out and do the laundry. Go on, yer take yerself off. Yer could do with a bit of time to yerself.'

So as not to disturb Mabel's youngsters, Rose mouthed her goodbyes and closed the hut door softly behind her. She walked across the Common towards the path through the orchards, pulling her old knitted shawl more tightly round her shoulders against the chill of the dewy autumn evening.

'So where d'yer think Rose's off to, Elsie?' asked Florrie, craning her neck to get a better look as she squatted by her fire, stirring her pot of stew.

'I dunno, Florrie, but if yer don't stop gawpin' at 'er and watch yer frock yer'll be up in flames, yer nosy cow.'

Florrie pulled her skirts clear of the crackling faggots but chose to ignore Elsie's other remarks. 'Right mystery that Rose is lately. Ask 'er about Jessie an' all yer get is, "She's gone into service." Service, if yer don't mind. Well, if yer ask me, it was all a bit sudden. Never even mentioned to our Winnie that she was goin' into no service. Never said nothin'. Did she say anythin' to yer Lilly about it? Mind you, since Lil lost 'er job at Warner's I don't suppose she saw that much of Jessie before she left.'

'Florrie,' said Elsie, apparently fascinated with the task of repacking her pipe bowl with matted strings of dark brown tobacco. 'I can't even begin to think 'ow many times yer've tried to pump me about Jessie. Now I'll tell yer again. I don't know nothin', right. An' even if I did, I'd 'ardly tell a bleed'n' big gob like you, now would I?'

'Flippin' charmin', I'm sure. I'm only interested.'

'Aw, shut up, Florrie, an' keep yer nose in your cookin' pot, an' out of everyone else's soddin' business.'

–

When she was sure that no one had followed her, and that she was completely alone, Rose opened the little wooden gate to the garden of the Garnetts' cottage. The top half of the kitchen door stood open.

Rose looked over the top into the cosy room, aglow with lamplight. She saw a scene of contentment: the big wooden table set with a vase of bright flowers, the cheerful plaited rugs in front of the range, and Jess, sitting in the rocking chair next to the crib, singing her baby to sleep.

Rose stood there silently watching, waiting until Jess stood up. Then she spoke.

''Ello, Jess, love.'

'Mum!'

Rose rushed in and grabbed hold of her daughter in her arms. They didn't say anything else, just held each other close and cried. Mrs Garnett looked down from the landing to see who had come to visit. When she saw who it was, she smiled, and, not wanting to disturb the reunion, went back into her bedroom, quietly closing the door.

Eventually Rose held her daughter away from her at arm's-length. 'Let me look at yer. Me little Jessie. A mum. 'Oo'd believe it, eh?' Rose walked over to the crib and gently stroked the sleeping child's downy hair. 'An' she's so beautiful. A little angel. Just look at them little fingers. She's the image of yer when yer was a baby, Jess.' Rose bent forward and placed a tender kiss on her grandchild's forehead. 'I'll leave 'er be till she wakes. Let 'er get 'er rest, eh?'

Jess stood next to her mother, looking down into the crib at her sleeping baby. 'I'm so pleased yer 'ere, Mum. I can't tell yer. Mrs Garnett an' 'er 'usband, they've been real kind to me. An' Leonore.' She paused, glancing sideways at her mother. 'Lady Worlington, I mean.'

'Leonore. Yeh, I know. Go on.'

'Well, she's been real good to me an' all, but I've missed yer so much, Mum, I really 'ave.' Jess gripped the side of the crib, her knuckles white, her face tense with the pain of remembering. 'All the time I was in that 'orrible place I thought about gettin' out and runnin' back 'ome to yer at Burton Street. I didn't know 'ow I'd ever get away from there, but I knew if I didn't I really would go mad.' Jess's voice faded to a hoarse whisper. 'That 'appens in there, Mum. I've seen it for meself.'

'Jess.' Rose bit her lip, trying desperately to stop herself from crying again. 'If only I could 'ave 'elped yer, love. Yer know I would 'ave, don't yer?'

'Don't blame yerself, Mum, I know 'ow 'ard it is.' Jess turned to her mother. ''Ark at me goin' on about all me troubles. What 'ave I got to complain about, eh? Tell me, 'ow's things at 'ome?'

'Same as ever, I suppose,' said Rose shrugging. 'Yer Dad's away on a trip still, an' with all this war lark, Gawd only knows when 'e'll be back.'

Although she was wrapped up well enough, Jess fussed with the baby's blanket, hoping to hide her concern. 'No one's 'eard nothin' from Jack Barnes then?' she asked casually.

'No,' said Rose flatly. 'Not a word. But there is somethin' I've gotta tell yer.'

Rose stopped and looked hard at her daughter. She had the words on the tip of her tongue, the secret words that until now had only gone round in her head. The words that spoke her worst fears about Jack's disappearance being something to do with their Charlie going away. But when she looked down into the crib at the baby sleeping so peacefully, she changed her mind. She'd settle for telling her daughter the other bad news.

'I've gotta tell yer, Jess,' she said uneasily. 'It's our Sammy. 'E's gone an' joined up. Gone to Belgium with the army.'

Jess looked away from her mother's anxious face, unable to bear seeing her so worried. She wondered how much more Rose could take.

'Don't get upset, Mum,' she said as briskly as she could. 'Yer know what our Sammy's like. 'E'll be all right, same as our Charlie. They're like a couple a big ol' ginger toms runnin' wild over the rooftops an' always landin' on their feet, no matter 'ow they fall.'

Rose jerked her head up in an attempt at looking cheerful. 'At least Charlie's written a couple of times. An' I've gotta speak as I find – *if* Ted's not been makin' it up when 'e reads the letters to me, then Charlie's as 'appy as Larry over there. I never reckoned 'e'd make it, Jess, but I really think 'e will. I've got this feelin'.'

'There y'are, Mum, I told yer things'd work out all right.'

'Let's just 'ope 'e don't get too many big ideas, eh? That Charlie's vain enough as it it.'

'See? That's better. It ain't like yer to be so morbid.'

'Yer right. We've got a lot to be grateful for. Yer know I wish I could tell Charlie about the baby, 'e'd be ever so proud. Imagine 'im, an uncle.'

'I don't think that'd be a very good idea just yet, Mum.'

'No, I suppose yer right.' Rose sighed. 'I don't mean to be a misery, but there's so many things I wish I could do. Yer know. Things I'd like to put right. I feel so useless sometimes.'

'Don't be daft, Mum. We all know yer'd do anythin' for us kids. Yer've always 'elped all of us whenever yer can.'

'I didn't do much for yer when they took yer away, did I?'

'It was 'ard enough for Leonore to sort out, an' she knows all sorts of people. Yer know, I still ain't sure 'ow she swung it.' Jess managed to laugh. 'I'm still on the run, mind. Like a convict I am. If Leonore's 'usband found out,' she paused, 'or anyone else in that family, for that matter, I'd be done for.'

Rose frowned. ''Ow much do these people yer stayin' with know?'

'Mr an' Mrs Garnett know almost everythin', Mum.'

'Christ, Jess, yer sure that's safe?'

'Don't worry, it's all right, an' Leonore said it was for the best in the end. It was gettin' right complicated tellin' lies all the time. An' I know all about that from me own experience, don't I, when I lied to you? I should 'ave listened to yer. Yer brought me up to always tell the truth, remember?'

'But is it safe, them knowin'? I couldn't bear nothin' more to 'appen to yer, Jess.'

'Nothin' will, Mum. They're as good as gold, the Garnetts. They 'ad a bit of trouble 'emselves, see, so they know what it's like.'

'Yer sure yer can trust 'em?'

'I'm sure. An' they know I've gotta keep my 'ead down for a while. 'Til it's all died down, like.'

'Let's 'ope that'll be soon, eh, darlin'?'

'Yeh. P'raps that's the one good thing to be said about this war. It'll make everyone forget about someone as unimportant as me.'

'Yer'll never be unimportant, Jess. Never.'

'Don't start cryin' again, Mum. Yer'll set me off. Be 'appy for me. It's all right 'ere. Really it is. I 'elp Mrs Garnett with things, an' get paid a bit an' all. An' now,' Jess threw her arms around Rose, 'I've got you 'ere with me. What more could I want?'

'Did I hear my name being mentioned down there?'

'Mrs Garnett.' Jess let go of Rose and went over to the foot of the stairs. She took Mrs Garnett by the arm. 'Come an' meet me mum. Mum, this is Mrs Garnett. She's been right good to me an' little Sylvie.'

'Pleased to meet yer, Mrs Garnett, I'm sure,' said Rose formally.

'And I'm very pleased to meet you, Mrs Fairleigh. Your Jess here has told me so much about you. All the stories about living up there in the big city.'

Rose flashed a worried look at her daughter.

'Don't go worrying yourself, she's told no family secrets,' said Mrs Garnett, smiling pleasantly. 'And you're a very special lady according to your daughter here. Very special indeed. Now, sit yourself down and I'll make us a nice pot of tea.'

Rose relaxed a little. 'I don't know about being special, Mrs Garnett. But I know I never say no to a cuppa tea.'

'Jess, why don't you go out to the pump and fetch in some more water, my dear?' suggested Mrs Garnett.

'There's plenty in the kettle. I got some in earlier.'

'Jess,' said Rose, gesturing towards the door with a nod. 'I think Mrs Garnett wants yer to go to the pump.'

Jess took the hint. She gave her mother another hug and almost danced out of the cottage, swinging the empty bucket by her side.

'We're in no hurry for that water,' called Mrs Garnett.

–

When she returned, Jess found the two women talking across the table like old friends.

'Mrs Garnett 'ere tells me they 'ave their Florrie Baxters in Tiln'urst as well as in Poplar,' said Rose laughing.

'Just like 'ome,' said Jess, topping up the big black kettle.

'An' I always thought country people were too busy complainin' about us Londoners to find time to gossip about each other.' Realising what she had said, Rose apologised to Mrs Garnett. 'No offence, of course.'

'None taken, I'm sure.'

'We don't get involved with none of that lark, Mum,' said Jess, putting down the empty bucket outside the door. 'Do we, Mrs Garnett?'

Mrs Garnett smiled her agreement.

'That's why I'm so 'appy stayin' 'ere in the cottage, see. It's just like bein' at 'ome with you, Mum. Won't 'ave none of their nosin' and tellin' tales, will yer, Mrs Garnett?'

'I'm glad to 'ear it,' Rose said to the kindly countrywoman. 'I did me best to bring Jessie up to be a good girl, an' not 'ave nothin' to do with bad talk about no one. There's enough of that without us joinin' in.'

'There's good and bad all over, I reckon,' said Mrs Garnett. 'Town or country. Good and bad.'

'Yer right there, Mrs Garnett,' agreed Rose. 'It's like in the 'op gardens. We've got a real good 'un doing the measurin' this year. Talk about chalk an' cheese. Yer wouldn't think 'e was even the same breed as that Theo, or whatever 'is name was. I know we've only been pickin' a day but yer can tell already that's 'e's really fair, this new bloke. Polite an' all. Says "good mornin'" an' everythin'. What 'appened to that Theo anyway?'

Mrs Garnett beamed with pleasure as Jess answered her mother.

'Theo's not around any more. 'E joined up. So Mr Garnett took over the measurin'. It's 'im what's so nice. 'E's much too old to join up, see.'

'I'm not that old, Jessie.'

The three women looked round to see the gardener standing in the doorway.

'I was expecting you to come and see us, Mrs Fairleigh. You're very welcome.' He stepped out of his mud-caked boots and walked in his stockinged feet to join them at the table.

'Keep your voice down, Matthew,' his wife scolded him playfully. 'The baby's asleep.'

'Sorry,' he whispered.

'She's fine,' said Jess, smiling at the gentle gardener. 'Sleeps like a log she does, Mum,' she added proudly.

Matthew Garnett kept his voice lowered anyway. 'I came back to tell you I won't be finished for a while yet, Susan.' He looked at Rose. 'In all truth, I wasn't sad to see the back of Theo and his meddling ways. We don't approve of that kind of thing in this family. But with all the other jobs I have to do now, I'm working from dawn 'til it's pitch-dark.' He turned back to his wife. 'I'll have a quick cup of tea, then I'll have to get back.' He swallowed the hot tea amazingly quickly and stood up to leave. 'Good job we've got your Jessie here to help us, eh, Mrs Fairleigh?'

'I'm glad she's doin' 'er share, Mr Garnett. An' before yer go I wanna thank yer for takin' 'er in. An' for not sayin' nothin' down in the 'op gardens.'

'There's no tittle-tattlers in this cottage, Mrs Fairleigh,' he assured her.

-

By the time the harvest was in full swing, Rose had become a familiar face at the Garnetts' cottage. And, like Leonore Worlington, she took every opportunity to slip away to the Garnetts' to see Jess and Sylvia.

Susan and Matthew Garnett made Rose as welcome as any member of their own family, although they found Leonore's visits rather more of a strain. They just didn't know how to treat the mistress of the Hall in such unfamiliar circumstances, and found themselves acting awkwardly and shyly with her.

Sylvia's reactions were far less complicated to the two women. She had learnt to recognise her grandmothers and delighted them both with her cooing and gurgling whenever they visited.

But Rose's visits to the cottage were a source of real anxiety for one person. And that was Florrie Baxter. She suffered horribly, fretting and worrying herself about where Rose could be disappearing to all the time. She had tried to follow her on more than one occasion but the twins spoilt her plans every time. They just would not cooperate with her efforts at secret snooping, and had given her away with their noisy questioning about where she thought she was going and what she thought she was doing. Unfortunately for Florrie, nosiness was a definite Baxter family trait.

–

Rose could hardly believe it when the harvest came to an end. It was as though it had only just started. She had never known hop picking fly by so quickly. It had been such a strange time: all the joy and happiness at seeing her beautiful granddaughter, and seeing for herself that Jess was doing so well. Even the weather had been glorious. But all the time, there in the background, were the worries nagging away at her. She worried that Jess would be found out and get put away again to keep her quiet. And she fretted over whether Bill and Sammy would come home safely from the war. And she was still concerned about Charlie; no matter what his letters said, it wasn't like having him at home with her. And as for Jack, well that didn't even bear thinking about.

Rose went one last time to the Garnetts' cottage, to say her farewells to Jess and to little Sylvia, and to say thank you to the Garnetts.

Susan and Jess had made special cakes and sandwiches and Matthew had brought flowers from the garden to decorate the kitchen table. Leonore had arrived early with a new dress for Sylvia, to make her look pretty for Nanna Fairleigh's goodbye tea. She was sitting holding her granddaughter when Rose arrived.

'There you are, my beauty,' said Leonore as she handed Sylvia to Rose. 'Go and see your grandmama.'

An hour later, the food, so lovingly prepared, was still hardly touched. Nobody had much of an appetite.

'I'll just go upstairs and get a box to pack some of these cakes in for your journey, Rose,' said Mrs Garnett. 'Be a pity to waste them.'

'Thank yer, Susan. I'd like that. Sorry I didn't eat much. It was such a lovely spread yer put on as well.'

'No need to explain. I understand, my dear. Now I might be a little while finding a box, so you can sit there and have a nice chat. And, Matthew, didn't you say as how you wanted to dig up a few vegetables for Rose to take home with her?'

'What? Oh yes, yes. That I did,' said Matthew, pulling on his boots and taking his wife's hint to leave their guests alone.

'I wonder if I might stay for a while?' asked Leonore.

'I'd be glad if yer would,' said Rose.

The three women talked as they watched Sylvia rolling around on the rug in front of the range, biting at her fists and gurgling away in the busy little language that made sense only to her.

'I'll miss seein' 'er take 'er first steps, Jess,' said Rose sadly.

'Don't be like that, Mum. Be 'appy for me.'

'Yer said that before, darlin' – be 'appy for me. So did our Charlie.' Rose buried her face in her hands. 'Just before 'e left. Yer sound just like 'im.'

'Is that your son who joined the army?' asked Leonore sympathetically.

'No,' said Rose looking up at her. 'That's me oldest – our Sammy. Charlie's the one who went off to Chicago. That's in America, that is. The one 'oo wants to open a club. What a way to earn a livin' for a kid from Burton Street, eh? Yer know, 'e's worried the life out of me at times.' Rose bent down and picked up the baby. She held Sylvia closely to her, feeling the comfort of her life and warmth. 'When yer see 'em like this, yer wouldn't believe it, would yer? Yer wouldn't believe they could grow up to be such bloody nuisances, an' break yer 'eart.'

Leonore bowed her head. 'Robert has gone with the British Expeditionary Force to Belgium. I hear from friends who know about such things that it might be dangerous.' She looked at Rose, then at Jess. Her voice shook. 'I hope you can understand. Even though he behaved so abominably, I still worry about him. I am his mother, when all's said and done.'

Sylvia produced a loud, throaty chuckle as Rose tickled her dimpled knees. 'I can understand all right, Leonore,' she said. 'No matter what they do, yer still love 'em.'

Jess did not say anything. She just looked at Sylvia and wondered if she would always love her child as unreservedly as these two women loved theirs.

–

'Yer gonna get down, Rosie Fairleigh, or what?' asked Joe softly. 'Everyone's waitin', an' me poor ol' pony's nearly a-kip.'

'Do what?' Rose opened her eyes and looked around her. They were in Burton Street already. She felt for a moment as though she had never been away.

'You, Rosie Fairleigh,' butted in Florrie loudly. ''E said, are yer gettin' down or what? Gawd blimey, gel, yer ain't said nothin' for the 'ole journey 'ome. Now yer in a bleedin' dream. Whatever's the matter with yer?'

'Sorry, I was miles away.' Rose climbed down from Joey Fuller's cart and began half-heartedly unloading her bags and boxes from the back.

'That's more like it,' said Florrie huffily. 'Now perhaps I can reach some of my gear. If nobody minds, that is. Gettin' in people's way. I think it's a liberty.'

''Ere she goes, Lil,' said Elsie Dorkin, nudging her daughter. 'Found somethin' else to bleed'n' moan about for a change.'

'There's some of us, Elsie, as wants to get 'ome to see to our 'ousework an' our jobs an' that. Wanna sort things out after bein' away. We ain't all like you Dorkins, yer know.'

'An' what's *that* supposed to mean, yer bigmouthed old tart?' Elsie yelled at the top of her booming voice.

'Ladies, ladies. Please.' Joey decided it was time to intervene, before physical violence took over from verbal abuse. 'Do us a favour. We've only been back in Burton Street for five minutes. What're yer old men gonna think, eh? They'll be sittin' there waitin' for yer with open arms, an' all they'll get is a load of screamin' an' 'ollerin'.'

''Er old man'll be down at The Star out of 'er way, if 'e's got any sense,' spat Elsie, pointing aggressively at Florrie.

'That's it,' said Joey. 'I've 'ad enough.' With two sweeps of his arms he calmly sent all the remaining bags and baggage tumbling on to the pavement at the astonished women's feet.

Despite the emptiness she felt, Rose couldn't help laughing as Elsie and Florrie set to fighting over ownership of the pile of parcels. They even continued squabbling over one of the packages as they walked along the road back to their houses, not giving a damn as to who saw or heard them.

'Will yer look at 'em?' said Joey. 'That's my brown paper parcel, that is, give it 'ere,' he whined, in a very creditable impersonation of Florrie Baxter.

'Yer a caution, Joey Fuller,' said Rose.

'More like a bleed'n' 'eadcase puttin' up with this lot every year,' he said, sitting down on the kerb and rolling himself a cigarette.

'Joey?'

'Yeh, Rose.'

'Can I talk to yer?'

'Course yer can, mate.'

'Not 'ere though. Indoors, eh? In me 'ouse. I won't keep yer long.'

'Sure.' Joey stood up and slung Daddler's reins over her neck. 'Stay there, gel,' he said to the little pony. 'Come on then, Rose.'

The sight of Joey Fuller going into Number 8 Burton Street with Rose Fairleigh had a miraculous effect on Florrie. She had, until that moment, still been straddling her doorstep and screeching abuse at Elsie as they struggled over possession of the parcel. But now she stood stock-still and stared along the road.

'Gawd 'elp us, Florrie, whatever's the matter? Yer look like someone's 'it yer with an 'addock,' said Elsie, backing away.

Florrie pointed towards Number 8. 'Look at 'em. Just look. Carryin' on in front of everyone,' she gasped. 'An' with 'er old man away at sea an' all. Bloody disgrace. No shame, the pair of 'em.'

Elsie, for once, did not get the opportunity to tell Florrie to shut up. This time, that honour went to Mr Baxter who had come out to investigate the source of the row. 'Why don't yer shut yer mouth, Florrie? Rose Fairleigh's a good woman,' said Wally to his wife. 'A bloody good woman. Yer could learn a few things from the likes of 'er. Now are yer comin' in, or what? I want me tea.'

'Welcome 'ome to you an' all, yer ol' bastard,' answered his wife.

Rose pushed the teacup across the table to Joey. 'Sorry there's no ale or nothin', Joe. Don't look like Ted's done a lot of shoppin''

''E's been over ours mostly. That's where 'e is now, I'll bet, with Mum. They've been playin' cards an' that of a night. Funny, she doesn't usually take to people much. But young Ted seems to get through to 'er. An' that little ginny monkey. She loves it. Fascinates 'er, it does. She talks away to it.'

'Lookin' after me kids *an'* their bloody zoo. I dunno, yer've been a good friend to me, Joey Fuller,' said Rose.

'Leave off, Rose, yer'll make me go all soppy.'

'Don't joke, Joey, I mean it. That's why I wanted to talk to yer.' Rose wrapped her hands around her cup, took a sip of the tea, then stared at the kitchen wall. 'I can't keep it all to meself much longer, Joe. What with Bill away an' everythin'. See, I've gotta tell someone about my Jessie, an' yer know most of it anyway.'

'Yer talk away, Rose. I'm right flattered yer trust me, but don't tell me nothin' yer'd regret.'

'Yer a mate, Joe. There's nothin' I'd regret tellin' yer. Nothin'. An' that's the truth.'

Chapter 16

Letters Home

Dear Mother,

I hardly know where to begin. When I picked up my pen, I realised that this is the first real letter I have ever written to you – or anyone, for that matter. There never seemed the need before, but out here everyone writes letters home. It gives one a feeling of contact with the real world, with a world that hasn't gone entirely mad. So here it is, a letter from your son...

At night, if nothing is happening and I am sitting here with the sky so dark and no shells exploding, it's then that the boredom sets in. It's strange; when the bombardments are happening, all you want is for them to stop, but the boredom is even more terrible, because it's then that you begin to think, and that is the worst time of all.

It's then, in those quiet moments, that I am really affected. It's then that I feel this overwhelming need to tell you how I feel. Yes, Ma, you read correctly, I did say 'feel'. Don't be too shocked, and no, I haven't gone totally insane, not yet anyway.

I'm not sure how to explain these feelings to you yet, but I'm certainly learning how to try. I work through them again and again in my mind, while I sit out there waiting alone in the dark. One of the things I feel most strongly is a need to ask your forgiveness for all the things I have done in the past. Not only the important things which I now know must have hurt you so badly, but all the ridiculous, stupid little things I did because I didn't bother to think about anyone but myself.

I hope I don't sound too much like one of the Reverend Batsford's Sunday specials. Those awful sermons of his! Thinking about them is enough to send me to sleep. I couldn't think of anything more horrible than becoming like that dreadful pinch-nosed little man. I want you, please, Mother, to believe that I am speaking to you from my heart, and not from hypocrisy like that so-called man of God. Being the good woman you are I am sure you understand what I am trying to say. But know that I wouldn't blame you if you simply screwed up this letter and threw it in the fire before you've even finished reading it.

Do you know, that is how I imagine you? Sitting there at Worlington, warm and snug by the fire, logs crackling. Looking through those splendid windows in the Chinese Room (which I hardly noticed when I was at home and now I think of them constantly) at the fields outside glistening with fresh snow, unspoiled by mud or the burnt stumps of trees. There's no sound out there but the geese as they fly across the lake, their wings beating in the still, crisp air, the scene untainted by hatred and despair.

I cannot tell you exactly where I am, but you know it is in Belgium. It used to be farm land around here, just like the Kent wold when we first arrived. Rich and fertile. A place of living things and beauty. That's how it used to be. It isn't any more. How I wish I was there with you at Worlington.

War is not as I had thought it would be, Ma. That arrogant young officer who came here all that time ago – when was it, three, four months ago? – he no longer exists. I have seen and done things which I never imagined, not even in my worst childhood dreams. I have seen men, incredibly brave men, stunted by an existence of poverty and hardship. I was totally bewildered when I first met them. I had seen the farm labourers and the men who came to stay with the hop pickers, of course, but never have I seen so many sickly, bedraggled-looking men together at one time. It is as though these working men of Britain are from a different race. Yet they are stout-hearted, willing to give up their lives for men like me. And why? Just because we are officers and have ordered them to go forward. To go over the top into hell. I am ashamed to say that I find it extremely unpleasant to be in such close proximity to these my fellow men. I hadn't realised until now what a very special privilege it is to have a room of one's own. The sties at Worlington smell sweeter than a dug-out full of men.

I wonder if this letter will be left unmarked by the censor's ink, or if someone will scratch out lines as I do for those brave young men who want only to tell their loved ones that they are alive. I intend to slip this in with the rest when I have finished, and hope that it will go unnoticed. Another undeserved privilege.

We get the newspapers here, you know. It seems unreal. Not only because we are living in a different world from which the newspapers, and we, once came, but also because of what we read in them. It makes everyone so angry. Those reports of glorious victory and success, while we live in dug-outs sharing our squalor with rats, disease and mud, death, lice and more mud.

Someone is calling me. I will write more later.

I have just returned, wet through and exhausted. I have reread what I wrote earlier. It simply doesn't say what I feel. If only I could tell you how I have changed, explain the paradox of how I have been renewed by this hell. It is not only land frontiers which I have crossed, but frontiers in my mind and in my feelings. The old world will never be the same again. But I don't know how to write the words to explain myself.

Please be patient with this son of yours, he is newborn and needs his mother. And no, I repeat, Ma, I really haven't gone mad. Nor have I suffered a blow to the head, well, not so bad a one that I have gone completely dotty.

I have changed, that is all I can say. This place changes us all.

I will tell you what happened at Christmas. Thanks for the parcel, by the way, my manners have been rather left behind in Kent, I'm afraid. You can't believe how important it is to get such things from home. Whisky and chocolate and socks! I am truly a rich man. It arrived yesterday, too late for Christmas but just in time for our New Year celebrations tomorrow. A time when many resolutions will be made. They said this lot would all be over by Christmas, and here we are, going into 1915 and still no sign of it ending. But I digress – I really don't have the hang of this writing

282

game yet, Ma. Back to Christmas. We all started singing carols, to cheer ourselves up. You know the sort of thing. 'Holly and the Ivy', 'Silent Night'. Then, what do you think? Fritz started singing back from across no man's land. Same tune as ours, different words of course. We were actually singing together. It might sound unbelievable, but it seemed so natural, so right. We were shooting at each other one minute and singing together the next. Even telling you about it makes the hairs on the back of my neck tingle. No one fired any guns that night. There were even stories from further along the line of the men meeting and shaking hands, playing football and showing photographs of their families. That didn't happen here, but the singing did. High Command on both sides were pretty damned angry about the whole thing apparently. But none of us cared. For that moment we were all human beings. Men. Far away from home, cold and lonely.

And that's really what I wanted to say to you. I know now what matters in life. We are all here together, and all the same when all's said and done. We aren't so very important as individuals after all. It's what we are to each other that counts, we work together and support our fellow men. That is how we survive. It might have taken me twenty-four years to find that out, but better late than never, eh, Ma?

Please write soon. I am sorry for not writing to you before, but you will not be able to stop me now. I do seem to have written rather a lot, but I have so much I want to tell you.

Give my regards to Father, Paul and Julia.

With my very fondest love, from your son, Robert

Leonore sat by the fireside as Robert had imagined her, reading his letter for the third time. Still she could hardly take in the words. Could this really be from the same Robert, the man who had behaved so unspeakably to all those young women? The man who had left a young girl pregnant without even caring enough to realise he had done so?

Leonore stood up and went over to the window. She looked out across the fields. It looks exactly as he described, she thought. The gently rolling ground covered in bright, fresh snow, sparkling in the clear January air, the wisp of blue smoke rising from beyond the orchards. It would be coming from the Garnetts' chimney, she supposed. Sylvia was probably having her breakfast in the neat little cottage sitting in the special highchair that Garnett had made for her from elm wood. Leonore smiled, counting herself fortunate that her grand-daughter would learn about the ways of countrymen from such a kind, gentle person as Matthew Garnett. Her smile quickly faded. It was certainly a more auspicious introduction than Jessie, her poor abandoned mother, had had at the hands of Robert Worlington.

Leonore sighed. Her mind was filled with confusion. She had known for a long time that life was not clearly divided into good and bad, kindness and evil. But did she really have any reason to hope that her son was changing, that he was growing into a better man? She looked down at the letter in her hand and read it yet again. The new year had begun only a few days ago, and yes it was a time for resolutions, but was she fooling herself? Why should she feel even a little optimistic about her son's true intentions when the civilised world seemed to be crumbling around them all? Was Robert simply reacting as anyone in his position might? Making promises to be good so that he might be saved, a childlike talisman against his own destruction.

Leonore leant forward and breathed on the icy-cold windowpane. When her breath had clouded the glass she wrote in the mist with her finger: *Sylvia Worlington*.

She stepped back and read what she had written. There was nothing so very extraordinary about the words, so was it *really* so improbable that her grandchild might one day take her rightful name? Leonore looked at the words for a moment longer, then rubbed the pane clear with her hand. She hesitated no more; she went over to the desk, took up her pen and began to write.

My dear Robert,

Such a very welcome letter. I admit I cried tears of joy when I first read it (I have read it many times since) because now I know my son is alive. Such a blessed relief when the newspapers are daily so full of those horrifying lists, only words, I know, but words which can destroy a mother's world.

I also cried tears of sadness as I read it. I grieve that you are not here, safe with me at Worlington. I am also more than a little concerned that you speak so lightly of having a head injury, Robert. No matter how slight, I trust you have sought proper medical attention. You were always so careless with such things.

I am so glad that the parcels reached you. How wonderful to think of that. It doesn't seem possible. I have visions of a postman walking through the fields to you with his sack over his shoulder, whistling a tune, as though it were here in the village. You must think me so silly. From what you say it couldn't be more different from the peace of Tilnhurst.

I want to tell you, Robert, that I too am finding it difficult to express what I feel, but want you to know that your letter has touched me deeply. I understand only too well that it is not easy to put such things on to paper, but I can truly say that your efforts to do so have made me very proud of you. The proudest I have been of you in a very long time.

I hope you will continue to think about the way you have behaved in the past and about how you might change yourself for the better. Believe me, I know from my own experience that it is never too late to change, for the better or for the worse. The choice of path is ours.

Remember that it is said that there is always some good which comes from evil. Perhaps the good which will come out of this terrible war will be a power for change. You speak of the unimportance of the individual, the need to work with our fellow men if we are to survive. I pray that others will feel the same and help make the world a better place for us all, when, please God, they return. Change requires a great deal of bravery. I believe you have that special courage, Robert, if only you learn how to use it to good effect.

I will soon be sending letters to both of my sons in foreign lands. Paul's regiment sails for France next week.

You would be so amused to see him, Robert. Always the peacock, he has had so many uniforms made his trunk is positively bursting. I believe he is going to dazzle the enemy with his beauty, rather than go into battle with them. He becomes very angry when I mention it as he considers himself quite the grown-up nowadays.

Julia will be going to Ireland to stay with her mother for a while. Perhaps you might write to her, my dear. I am sure she would like to hear from you.

I have been thinking of ways to write the next part of this letter. I have thrown a lot of spoilt pages into that crackling log fire by which you imagine me to be sitting. I hope that I have succeeded in expressing it clearly this time. You ask me to forgive you for all the things you have done in the past. But, my darling, how can I? I am in no position to do such a thing, but I can offer you my love and some advice. Look deeply into your heart, Robert, and see if you are ready for forgiveness. Know if those you hurt would be convinced that you are genuine in your regret, and be certain you are not responding in fear, reacting to the horrors that you have seen in that dreadful place. And forgiveness for what? you must ask, and of whom.

I hope I do not depress you, Robert. I genuinely wish you every happiness and love for this new year, but I want you to find out about yourself and your dreams before you decide what you really want from life. I pray that you stay safe to return to me, so we can grow to know each other as friends.

One day we will share our hopes; let us keep them safe for the future. It is there waiting for us.

With love, Robert,
from Mother

Dear Mum and Ted,

Here I am in France. That surprised you, didn't it? They didn't send us to Belgium after all. Funny old place it is. But I haven't had a lot of chance to see much *of it. Most of the time I'm in this bloody trench. It's more like a river than a trench. I hope our Ted don't believe all that stuff in the papers. It gives me and me mates the right hump. A load of old cobblers most of it. You think yourself lucky you're still too young to join up, Ted. Tell you what, Mum, the rats here are bigger than in Burton Street and that's saying something. And the nits and bugs are horrible. Everyone's got them even the posh blokes. You should hear them. They don't half talk funny. Can't understand them half the time, but they still have a lark with us. We go into the town sometimes. The French girls are a bit of all right and they like us Tommies. And the food ain't bad and there's plenty of it. I reckon I'll come home fatter than when I left. You won't recognise me.*

Anyway, Mum and Ted, that's all for now. Write to me soon and tell me how Dad, Charlie and Jess are getting on. Do you know where they sent Dad's ship yet? Thanks for the things you sent but don't go wasting your money on me. I'm doing all right.

Love from Sammy

Ted folded the letter and handed it to his mother across the table.

'Yer sure that's all it said?' demanded Rose, looking uncomprehendingly at the scribbled words, then flashing a warning glare at her son. 'Yer didn't leave nothin' out, did yer? 'E ain't 'urt or nothin'?'

'That's all there was, Mum. Promise,' said Ted. 'An' I dunno what yer lookin' so miserable about. Sounds all right to me. Plenty o' grub, an' all them foreign gels.'

'That's enough o' that talk,' said Rose. 'Now go an' chop that bit a firewood for me. Go on.'

'Mum,' he moaned.

'An' none of yer complaints, thanks very much. Do that choppin', then yer can 'ave yer tea before yer take a few bundles of sticks round to Miss Feldman's for me.'

Before Ted could object, Rose lifted her hand.

'Don't even say it, Ted. We've got enough on our plates without you showin' off.'

Ted dragged sulkily into the back yard and began half-heartedly splitting the offcuts he'd brought back on his hand-cart from the woodyard. All the time he swung the axe he complained loudly to himself about the injustice of it all, being treated like a kid but expected to work like a man. If he was a few years older, then they'd all see, he'd be away fighting like his brother.

'Stop yer noise, Ted,' shouted Rose over all the banging and crashing that Ted was deliberately making out in the yard. 'Or yer can get yerself up to bed with no tea.'

Rose smiled to herself as Ted's reply was muffled by the loud splintering of another half-plank. She couldn't hear him properly but she could guess what he was saying to himself.

'That smells 'andsome,' a voice called along the passage from the open street door.

''Allo, Joe,' said Rose, poking her head round the kitchen door. 'Come in. An' pull the door to be'ind yer. Young feller me lad out there left it wide open for a change.'

'Just on the latch?'

'Yeh, that'll be fine.'

Joe walked in and shivered. 'Cor! It might be May, but it's turned freezin' out there tonight. Like winter again.'

He took off his cap, then produced from under his jacket a parcel wrapped in newspaper which he put down on the kitchen table.

'What's all this?' said Rose when she turned round from seeing to the stew that was bubbling away in the pan.

'Bit a best end o' neck,' said Joe. 'To repay yer for what yer've been doin' for Mum.'

'Yer didn't 'ave to do that, Joe.'

'I know I didn't 'ave to. I wanted to. An' now I'm doin' the dock run as well as the markets, I can sometimes get me 'ands on a bit extra.' He winked at her. 'An' if anyone deserves it, Rose…'

'All right, that's enough. I only give 'er a bit o' dinner,' said Rose, wiping her hands on her apron and unwrapping the parcel. 'Aw, ta, Joe. This looks lovely.' She slipped the meat on to a white plate, then took it into the back yard. There she put in in the mesh-fronted meat safe on the shelf by the kitchen window.

She came back in and held up the teapot to Joe. He nodded in reply.

'There's a cup o' tea in 'ere, Ted,' Rose called out.

The chopping and banging stopped immediately, and Ted was at the table before Rose had even filled the cups. His face was red with exertion.

''Ello, Joe,' said Ted, flinching as he gulped the hot tea. 'I'll be over for a couple o' games o' cards later, when I've 'ad me tea.'

'Mum'd like that, Ted,' said Joe. 'I'll get in a drop of ale for us.'

Rose narrowed her eyes at her youngest child. 'I 'ope yer ain't been goin' over Mrs Fuller's just so's yer can fill yer gullet with beer, Ted Fairleigh.'

'No,' protested Ted sulkily.

Joey saved Ted from having to explain this revelation further. 'Rose, yer know I wouldn't dream of interferin', but I've gotta say this. Yer dunno what a weight it is off me mind, with you takin' Mum a bit o' grub over, an' young Ted 'ere amusin' 'er with a game a cards an' all 'is daft stories.' He cuffed Ted playfully round the head. 'I tell yer, it's worth a gallon of ale to see me Mum 'appy, believe me. The little devil deserves every drop.'

Ted beamed, enjoying the unfamiliar praise being lavished on him.

'That's nice of yer to say so, Joe. I'm glad Ted's an 'elp. 'E's been brought up to be a good kid,' she said, looking at her son suspiciously, 'but I don't want 'im takin' no liberties with yer.'

'Rose, listen, now I've gotta do all this extra work, I'd be worryin' about Mum somethin' rotten. Thinkin' about 'er bein' by 'erself while I'm out all hours. An' that's what'd 'appen if it wasn't for the two of you.'

'She won't be by 'erself while we're 'ere, Joe.'

'I know that, Rose. An' like I said, I'm right grateful to yer. It means I can do me bit for the war. I might not be fightin' but I'm still doin' me bit.'

'We 'eard from Sammy today,' said Ted. 'Didn't we, Mum? 'E's 'avin' a right ol' time over there. I can't wait till I'm old enough to join up.'

'Don't wish yer life away, son,' said Joey.

Rose rolled her eyes and tutted. 'Lives in a dream world this boy. Yer'd think 'e read a different letter to the one I 'eard. 'Aving a right ol' time? I dunno where 'e gets 'is barmy ideas.'

Ted finished his tea and stood up. 'I reckon I must be barmy,' he said grumpily. 'I've gotta finish choppin' all that wood out the back before I can even 'ave me grub.'

'Aw, yer so 'ard done by,' shouted Rose over the noise that was coming again from the yard.

''Eard anythin' from Bill?' asked Joey.

'Yeh,' sighed Rose. 'But 'e's more worried about us lot than 'imself. All 'e wants to know is what's 'appenin' with Jess, 'ow's Charlie, what's Sammy got to say for 'imself, 'ow am I, is Ted doin' 'is share? 'Ave I 'eard from this one an' that one?' Rose shook her head. 'I do what I can to reassure 'im, be cheerful in me letters, like, but it ain't easy.'

'Well I think 'e's a lucky feller to 'ave you worryin' about 'im, Rose.'

'Daft 'apporth,' she said. 'It's no different from you, Joe, always worryin' about yer mum. That's what life's all about, I suppose, makin' sure yer family's all right.'

''Oo'd 'ave thought all this would be 'appenin' to everyone though, eh, gel?' said Joey wearily. 'Not even two years since it started, an' this war's turned the 'ole world on its bloody 'ead.' He took his watch out of his waistcoat pocket and studied it briefly, then put his cap back on and stood up. 'Anyway, I'd better be gettin' back. I put a knuckle of bacon on; it'll boil dry if I don't look lively.'

Rose walked down the passage to see Joey out. As she pulled the street door open Florrie was standing next to the step, peering keenly into Rose's front window.

'Can I 'elp yer, Flo,' said Rose loudly.

'Er, yeh.' Florrie's eyebrows shot up and she smiled know-ingly to herself when she saw Joey standing behind Rose. She'd been right, there he was, bold as brass.

'Well?' said Rose folding her arms.

'Er, I come to borrow, erm…' She thought for a moment. 'A drop o' milk. That's it. But I can see yer busy,' she added slyly.

'Yeh, I am busy, as a matter of fact, Flo. That's why Joey's just leavin'.'

'Aw, yeh, that's right,' said Joe, glad for the chance to escape. 'I'll see Ted later on.'

'Where's yer jug then, Flo?' asked Rose, looking pointedly at her neighbour's empty hands. 'Give us it an' I'll go an' fetch yer some milk.'

'Yer know, I dunno *what* I'm doin' some days,' said Florrie, not very convincingly. 'I must 'ave left it on me table.'

'Yeh, yer must 'ave. Now if yer don't mind I've got Ted's tea to see to. Yer can come back later. With a jug. If yer really do want some milk, that is.'

With that, Rose closed the street door and went back into the kitchen. She had enough to think about without letting Florrie Baxter's poison get to her.

> *Dear Bill,*
>
> *Ted is writing this letter for me. I hope it gets to you soon and that you are well. I miss you, Bill, and wish you were here with me. I'd love to know where your ship is and what cargo you're carrying and everything, but I know you're not allowed to tell us. I'm right proud of you and what you're doing, and I should be used to you going away to sea after all these years, but I don't suppose I'll ever get used to it.*
>
> *Jess is still in service in the country. She is very well and happy. Sammy writes when he remembers. I think he's too busy chasing all the girls over in France. Charlie said in his last letter that he's written to you, so you know he's doing fine. Sounds like it was the right thing for him to do after all. So we had all that worry over him for nothing. Trust our Charlie.*
>
> *Ted has joined up. You wouldn't know him. He's shot up again in the last few months. As tall as you are*

now. He is going to the station in the morning. It's his
last night at home so we are going to The Star. We'll
have one for you, Bill. Don't worry yourself about us
we are all well. You just look after yourself and come
home safe to me. I miss you.

Love from Rose

PS You can still write to Mum because Miss
Feldman will read the, letters but don't write no
personal or lovey-dovey stuff.

Love Ted (Private Fairleigh)

Rose nodded her approval when Ted finished reading the letter to her.

'Now, Ted,' she said. 'I want yer to write one to our Jessie for me.'

For once Ted didn't moan about being given something to do. He had been so keen to get himself off to the war, but now the time had finally come to leave his mum he wasn't so sure that he wanted to go after all.

'Righto,' he said.

Dear Jess,

Ted is writing this letter for me. We are both well.
I'm getting decent money now working in the factory
making uniforms. Piece rates it is. It's a lot more than
I ever earned scrubbing all them steps out in the cold.
I ain't felt so well in years and I don't hardly cough at
all now I'm in the warm. I've sent you some money to
get yourself something. Make sure you do.

Ted's joined up. Can you believe it? He's leaving
in the morning so I'll have plenty of time on me hands
and still be able to do for old Miss Feldman. I wouldn't
want to leave her in the lurch.

I have a surprise to tell you. She's going to take over from Ted teaching me to read and write. That surprised you didn't it, Jess? The poor old girl's been really suffering lately. Don't even come from Germany but cos of the way she talks foreign they're all saying her and her brother are spies. They was glad of him when they was pawning their stuff with him. It's all different now, and he's had to close up the shop. They kept breaking all the poor old devil's windows.

We won't be seeing your dad for a while. He come home for two days and a night then he was off again to take more supplies to somewhere or other. He wasn't allowed to say where, and he was right disappointed he missed you. But at least he knows you're settled. That pleased him.

'That's enough for the minute, Ted,' said Rose. 'Give us the paper 'ere.'

Rose smoothed the letter out on the table in front of her.

''Ere goes,' she said bravely.

She took up the pen and began to write in her shaky, ill-formed script, pausing only briefly to ask Ted how to spell the occasional word. The rest she had to leave to chance.

I'm writing this bit myself. Take no notice of the writing. When Dad was here on leave I told him where you was and all about everything. I couldn't stand him going away again and still not knowing about Sylvia and how happy you are and what a little love she is. He was well chuffed about being a granddad. You should have seen his face. I'm right glad he knows. He would have loved to have seen you both but you know how it is.

The boys still don't know. None of them do. They still think you went into service. That's best for now I reckon. I don't want them getting no ideas about going down there and sorting out you know who. I wouldn't put it past them. You know how mad they can go. We don't need that sort of trouble.

Rose finished writing her piece, then turned the paper over.

'There y'are, Ted. Yer can carry on writing on the back.'

'What's so secret, Mum?' he asked suspiciously. Always one to see himself at the centre of everyone's world, he grinned. 'I'll bet it was about me.'

'Typical,' said Rose. 'As a matter of fact it was about women's things, boy, if yer must know. Now shut up askin' questions an' get writin'. Yer ain't a corporal yet, yer know.'

'Corporal? Yer'd think I was a baby the way yer carry on.'

'Well yer are to me, yer great daft lump. Yer might be in the army, but yer still me little baby, ain't yer?' Rose pinched his cheek tenderly. 'Yer'll be shavin' next,' she teased.

Ted rolled his eyes and clicked his tongue impatiently, but he couldn't fool Rose. She knew that no matter what he said, how brave and grown-up he acted, inside he was still her little boy, and as scared as any other to be leaving for war. The relentless daily casualty lists printed in the newspapers and the stories being brought home by local lads on leave were enough to knock any glamorous ideas out of a young man's head, even Ted's.

Rose did her best to dismiss from her mind the visions of her family at war, the images that filled nearly every waking thought and even her dreams. She began dictating the rest of her letter.

I hardly suppose it matters to anyone nowadays what's happened, Jess, there's too many other things for people to worry about. My old mum, your nanna, used to say that it was them with nothing better to do what talked about other people. Well, girl, we've all got enough to think about nowadays and that's the truth. Write to me soon, Jess, and remember it's Miss Feldman what'll be reading it to me.

    Love from Mum and Ted

Leonore got out of bed as though she was still in a dream and went to sit by the window. She had had a chair placed close to every window in the house. She had it done after Robert had talked in his letter about imagining her sitting looking out at the view over the countryside. It had made her feel a little closer to him, being able to sit there. She usually looked forward so much to reading his letters, but today her hands trembled as she tried to open the envelope. She stared down at the letter in her lap as though it might explode. What did it mean? A letter from Belgium but not in Robert's writing. What terrible news did it contain? She didn't know if she could stand anything more happening to her family; she already felt as though her heart would break. She ripped at the flap with the paper knife. There, it was done, she had opened it. Mouthing a silent prayer that nothing had happened to her elder son, Leonore drew in a deep breath, unfolded the sheets of thin paper and began to read.

    Dear Mother,
        Yes, this is from me, Robert, but Nurse Allerton is writing it.

As she read the words again, to make sure that she wasn't mistaken, tears of relief ran down Leonore's cheeks: her elder child was safe. She wept softly, not bothering to check the tears, as she read the rest of the letter.

> *Don't panic. I'm not too bad, a bit shaken, that's all. I'm in a casualty clearing station. Please don't worry, we are well behind the lines and I am recovering swiftly. Especially with Nurse Allerton here. She said to say that she didn't want to write that, but I made her promise to write exactly what I say. It makes a change for the patients to have the chance to bully the nurses for once.*
>
> *In my letters I have tried to describe what it is like at the front, to explain about the volunteers. I thought I was getting used to it. But since I've been in here, I've had more time to talk to people. I know now that I will never get used to how some of them are forced to spend their lives. I can hardly believe what they tell me about how they live back home in England. Many of the men are from the same labouring families I once thought of as being little better than farm animals, there for me to use and discard as I felt inclined. I had honestly never realised, never bothered to think about how they lived. I never understood the struggle many of them had just to survive. They are so puny, Ma. Nurse Allerton says it's the poor diet and terrible housing they have. I wonder that some of them are considered well enough to be out here. I talked about it with some of the other officers. It left us wondering what the men are like whom the army reject as unfit.*

But I'd better get on with my news; if I don't, Nurse will be called away and you will be left with only half a letter.

I have now not only seen, but have experienced personally, the bravery of one of those working men. My life was saved by a private, in reality a boy, who in Kent I would have knocked down rather than go to the bother of reining in my horse. I had been left unconscious during a bombardment. I cannot recall what happened, but I understand that Private Andrew Johnson left the safety of his bunker and scrambled through coils of barbed wire, all whilst under enemy fire, with the single purpose of dragging me clear of the shelling.

Private Johnson got me to the dressing station, God alone knows how, where they sorted me out before I was sent here. I'd been knocked out cold and the gas had begun to get to me. I owe him my life. I would have caught it for sure if he hadn't risked his own life to help me. He came right through the gas to get to me. He laughed afterwards, can you imagine? He said it was nothing, that he had his mask on, and I should have been wearing mine, if I didn't mind him mentioning it. Me being an officer and all. What an amazing man.

The gas, Ma. We couldn't believe it the first time the brutes used it on us. It drifts across looking so harmless, in a silent blue-white cloud. You can tell when the men have been had by the stuff. They come running blindly towards you. Their faces grey, like death. They spew and cough. The choking makes their streaming eyes bulge out of their sockets. They clutch at their throats. And if they're really bad, they get confused and run the wrong way, and pandemonium breaks loose. They stumble into the trenches or fall on to the barbed wire and get stuck. Then they are shot. They look like so many crows hung out by the gamekeeper. Nurse Allerton was not keen to write that, but I want you to know what is really happening out here. The truth has always been important to you, as, I am glad to say, it now is to me.

The stories about the Canadians have amazed and impressed everyone. They won't give in to the gas. They soak their handkerchiefs or scarves in water, their own urine even, and cover their faces. They just keep on firing, holding their places. And the women here, they'd impress you, Ma. Women from all over have come out here to work as nurses and as ambulance drivers. They are wonderful. Nurse Allerton is pulling a face. In all this mayhem, they carry on like nothing's happening. Telling us to look tidy before the doctor's rounds, and telling us off for getting ash on the sheets. So bossy.

When I first got here I wasn't feeling too well, and one young nurse sat with me all night. Yes, it was Nurse Allerton. She's from Bradford. She used to work in the mills. Do you know she actually said if it wasn't for the pain and suffering of the soldiers she would be happier being in Flanders than she ever was in England; that, in some ways, her life is much better here. Imagine what she left behind to prefer all this. She said I was to explain that I haven't got that quite right, but you might know what she means, being a woman. I can't say that I do.

And the upper-class women, the 'toffs' as Nurse Allerton calls them, many of them say similar things.

The world's gone mad. How can they prefer it out here to being at home? But they're real heroines, Ma, potty or not. The men sing aabout them, 'It is the one red rose':

> *In the war's great curse*
> *Stood the Red Cross Nurse*
> *She's the rose in no man's land.*

If I stay out here much longer, I'll be writing poetry next. What would Father make of that? I wonder. I'm hoping to get back to the front soon. Not that I like the idea of battle but because I don't want to let the others down. Who knows, there might be a Private Andrew Johnson who needs my help. I know that some poor souls don't seem able to face going back there. They lie here, dazed and numbed, shaking with fear. But I don't think they're cowards. It's always there, even in their dreams. Nightmares, I should say. I know it is in mine.

How about your news, Ma? I long to hear about Worlington, but you never mention much about the estate. I dream of that as well. Being there in Kent. Has the war changed things much? The apple blossom will be out soon, and the swallows will be arriving. I wonder if they'll fly across here first? Tell me about it all when you write.

I sent a note to Julia. I hope she received it before she left for Ireland. Pass on my news to Paul and give my regards to Father.

Nurse Allerton is going to smuggle this into the bag to get it past the censors. A real little spy. I don't think there is anything these wonderful girls can't do if they set their minds to it.

> *With love,*
> *Robert*
> *PS If I were a swallow I would fly home to you at*
> *Worlington.*

Leonore dropped the sheets of paper into her lap.

The maid knocked and came into the bedroom, but Leonore didn't seem to hear her, she just stared at the letter.

'You've not touched your dinner, m'lady,' the young woman said, picking up the tray of food from the bedside table. 'Can I get you something else?'

Leonore looked up at the maid and frowned as though she didn't understand what she was saying to her.

'Do you want me to leave it?' the girl asked. Leonore shook her head in reply, and the maid took away the untouched food.

Leonore turned and looked at the view from the window. Robert was right, the trees were in blossom. But she didn't smile with pleasure to see the sun setting over the glorious English countryside as it spread out below her. In fact, she looked as though she would never smile again, as though her world had come to an end.

She walked mechanically over to her desk and lethargically picked up her pen.

> *My dear Robert,*
> *This is the most difficult letter I have ever written, and although I think you may already have heard by the time this reaches you, I have to tell you myself. Robert, Paul was killed in action in France. He will not be brought home for burial, but will be laid to rest there. It seems so wrong; he was so full of life, and now he is dead. There.*

I have written the words. He is dead. I used to think this war had at least some purpose; now I feel only bitterness.

I am sure that you also know, or will not be surprised to learn, that Julia will not be returning to England. She has decided to stay in Ireland with her family. Even with the trouble over the execution of the rebels she insists she won't leave there. Now Paul is no longer with us she says England holds no interest for her. I am sorry to be so blunt, Robert, but I think it is for the best for these things to be out in the open.

I cannot write any more tonight. I will leave this for now and finish writing to you tomorrow. Goodnight, my darling.

It is three days since I began to write this letter.

I have read and reread your letter many times and thank God that you were saved. Private Johnson will have a place in my prayers for ever, alongside those I offer up for Paul when I pray that he did not suffer.

Please give my sincere thanks to Nurse Allerton. She sounds a wonderful, brave girl. All those women you wrote of have my admiration. It makes me quite ashamed that I have not joined them. But I have been doing work of my own, Robert. Now, after all that has happened, I have decided that I must share a secret with you. I wish I had told Paul so that he would have known me better. Now it is too late. But at least I can tell you. Before the war I became involved with the suffragettes, taking part in many of the campaigns, and I am still deeply involved with my work at a centre for destitute women and girls from the London slums. Yes, Robert, me.

You will not be surprised to know that I have never shared this secret with your father. I was not involved with the militants, however, unlike Dolly Carstairs, who now seems to be using her energies to do war work. Dolly is working in France, one of those 'toff' nurses your young nurse from Bradford spoke to you about. I might not always agree with Dolly's politics, but she has always had the ability to make me laugh. Apparently she was patching up a young soldier recently and was sure she knew him, but couldn't quite place from where. It turned out he was a constable before the war and had arrested her for agitating at a suffrage meeting. She had objected strongly to his actions and had blacked his eye for his trouble. Good old Dolly. She'll keep order in those wards out there.

It feels so strange writing to you like this, Robert, but I would like you to understand me better. I became involved after I met some people who introduced me to Sylvia Pankhurst. (This is still a secret from your father, remember, Robert; I still have to live here with him.) My cousin Amelia and I – for she too is part of the conspiracy – do what we can to improve the lives of some of the women and children who live in the slums. They, like me in some ways, are unfortunate prisoners of their birthright. Having the vote would mean very little to most of the women I meet, I think. But I am very unsure at times what I should think. I wonder too if I am right when I think you will be able to understand more about me now, Robert. I wonder if you can appreciate that, like you, I had to learn about the evils of poverty. What good is life for a woman if she has no food for her children and yet another baby on *the way? Many of those brave men you write of must be married to women like the ones I meet.*

I really do hope that we are learning to understand more about one another and about ourselves now, Robert. I really do. I am certainly unsure whether I understand Sylvia Pankhurst's views on pacifism, however, even though she speaks so eloquently about the war and the exploitation of the poor for profit. I really can't make up my mind whether she's right or wrong. Particularly since Paul was taken from us. Perhaps that's one of the things we will discuss when you come home, Robert, when we discover what it is like to be friends. I so look forward to that time.

There is so much I want to tell you, my dear.

So many things I am keeping in my heart to share with you when you return to Worlington.

With my fondest regards to Nurse Allerton, and my heartfelt thanks.

And with my love to you always, Robert,
Mother

Leonore sealed and addressed the envelope. Then she went over to the window to sit and watch and wait.

–

Ted dipped the nib into the inkpot, and with his tongue firmly held between his teeth thought about what to write in his first letter home. He'd been in France for almost two days and it was all so exciting he didn't know what to put first. But he'd promised his mum he would write and let her know he was safe, so write he did.

Dear Mum and hello Miss Feldman,

I got to France safe and sound but I ain't seen our Sammy yet. It's a lot bigger out here than I thought it would be. The trenches ain't that bad. I don't know what our Sammy was going on about, wanted us to feel sorry for him, knowing him. The blokes have got some of the dug-outs all done up like little houses. Pictures and everything. When you think how some of them lived down The Buildings they must think they're in bloody palaces. Sorry, Mum, but all us soldiers swear. Worse than that and all. Should have heard them on the ships. You'd have gone potty. The officers moan a bit. They say it's all squalor and there are a lack of facilities. Or something like that, but it don't seem that bad to me so far. Mind you, Mum, they all say it's rotten when the mud and snow comes. But I don't think I'll be here to see the bad weather. It can't last much longer. They said it would be over in three years. But it'll definitely be over by this Christmas.

Here, how about this? Some of them what gets gassed have been sent to a big hospital in Kent near Tilnhurst. Used to be a loony bin they reckon. Blimey I never knew there was a bin there when we was down hopping. I'd have been right scared of the nutters if I'd have known. Still that old Kent air'll do them gassed blokes a bit of good. Like it did your chest eh, Mum? Do 'em even better if they could do a bit of hopping as well. We had some laughs down there didn't we. Remember when Home's Arthur nicked that pig?

Still had no word from Dad? Let's know when you hear some news. I bet he must have been to every country in the whole world by now. I might have some good news soon. Nothing definite, but they reckon you can get promoted ever so quick out here. Can you imagine, Corporal Fairleigh. Like I said, nothing definite yet but honest to God, Mum, they promote lots of blokes. Right young ones and all. If you don't get your head blown off first I reckon you could be a colonel after a few months. (Joke.)

Lots of love from your loving son Ted and give Miss Feldman a kiss for me. That'll surprise her.

Chapter 17

A Different World

'So I'll be leaving at the end of the month, Lady Worlington,' the maid said matter-of-factly. 'If that's all right with you.'

'I only wish you had spoken to me earlier, Daisy,' said Leonore, throwing up her hands in exasperation as she rose from her armchair by the window. 'I had no idea you were unhappy with us until Tyler came to me.'

'Yes, ma'am.' Daisy looked very bored. She examined her fingernails.

'When Tyler informed me you had employment elsewhere I was shocked to hear it,' said Leonore, walking over to the girl. She was standing close to the door which she had left wide open. 'I might have been able to help you, Daisy, had you discussed it with me first.'

'Oh no. It's nothing like that, m'lady,' Daisy said sullenly, shifting her weight from one foot to the other. 'I wasn't specially unhappy here. Wasn't specially happy either. I've never known no different really. Always worked here, haven't I?'

'You are not making this very easy for me, Daisy. Please, I want to know. Has somebody upset you? A man?'

'I know what you're talking about,' said the maid, smiling archly, brave in the knowledge that she would soon be leaving. 'It ain't nothing like that. Nobody's touched me or nothing.

Anyway there's hardly any boys left round here to try and "upset" me, like you say. They're all over in France.'

'That wasn't exactly what I meant, Daisy. But I still don't know why you want to leave Worlington.'

'I'm off to do war work, actually, m'lady,' she said.

'You, Daisy?'

'Yeh. Why not me?' she asked impudently, then thought better of her tone; she hadn't collected her wages yet. 'I'm going to be a factory girl,' she said more evenly. 'Doing the munitions at Woolwich. I'm going to stay with Milly.'

'Milly?'

'Yeh, Milly Garnett.'

'Mr Garnett's daughter?'

'Yeh. She's earning a fortune. Nearly thirty bob a week with overtime.'

Daisy's enthusiasm for the wonderful new life Milly had made for herself made her tongue run away with her.

'And when her work's finished she goes home to her own room and everything. In a lodging house in Bermondsey it is. She said it's hard graft but it was hard when she worked here. She loves it there.' Daisy lifted her chin and looked Leonore directly in the eye. 'It's a different world now. And I want to be a part of it.'

'But Milly's working for my cousin in Belgravia,' said Leonore, trying to work out what all this could mean.

'Not any more she ain't,' answered Daisy with a barely suppressed snigger.

-

Leonore walked through the orchard towards the Garnetts' cottage. 1917 was nearly over and still the war dragged on. There was not a family in the land which had not been touched by the death and destruction, who had not heard bad news from some unknown place in a foreign land. Daisy was right; it really was a different world. Everything she had been so sure of in the past had been turned upside down. Leonore hardly knew what to think about anything any more. But there was one thing about which she was always sure: as soon as Sylvia saw her grandmother, she would run to her and welcome her to the cottage with a happy laugh and a hug. Leonore thanked God that something still made sense. She thought more and more about how wonderful it would be if she could tell Robert he had a child, so that he and Jess could make a proper family for Sylvia. Perhaps after the war was over it would be possible. Perhaps.

'Sylvia, come and give Grandmama a kiss.' Leonore scooped up the giggling child and carried her into Mrs Garnett's kitchen. 'Good morning, Jessie. Is Mrs Garnett around?'

'No, yer've missed 'er,' said Jess, looking over her shoulder. She was standing at the tub washing Sylvia's clothes on the rubbing board. 'She went out really early with Mr Garnett. Into town.'

'Does she never say anything, Jess?' asked Leonore as she wound one of Sylvia's golden curls round her finger. 'Never ask any questions who the father is? About how all this could have happened? Why I take such an interest?'

'No, like I said, I reckon she just accepts yer doin' yer duty by me cos I worked 'ere. Never says a word about it.'

'She's an amazing woman.'

'Yeh, she's that all right. Been like a mum to me she 'as.'

'But you still miss Rose terribly?'

'Course I do,' said Jess, rubbing vigorously at the cuffs of Sylvia's blouse. 'It really 'urts me to think 'ow she's missin' the little 'un grow up. An' since she's been in the factory, we don't even see 'er at 'oppin' time. Just them odd days she's managed. Breaks me 'eart it does.'

Leonore sighed loudly. 'When I think about how all this happened, Jess, I really do feel so dreadfully guilty.'

'Yer mustn't get me wrong, Leonore. I'm 'appy 'ere, honest. An' it's lovely for Sylvia bein' in the country. An' it's 'ardly your fault. I wish I could go 'ome, that's all.'

Leonore decided it was time to say what had long been on her mind. 'I wanted to talk to you about that, Jess. About going home.'

Jess let the washing drop back in the tub, then turned and stared at her, suds dripping unheeded from her hands on to the clean floor. ''Ow d'yer mean?'

Leonore put Sylvia down on the rug to play with her building blocks and moved closer to Jessie.

'Jess, even though you have never been officially released from the asylum I don't see any real reason for you to continue hiding here. Not any more.'

'Yer mean I can go 'ome? To Poplar? When?'

'Don't get too excited, Jess. Listen. Let's sit down.'

Jess wiped her hands on her apron and she and Leonore sat opposite one another at the table.

Leonore kept her eyes on her hands; she patted her fingertips together nervously all the while she was speaking.

'If you had tried to leave here before, my husband would have been sure to have found out that you had been released. From the carriage driver, from the porter at the station, oh, in any one of a thousand ways. From any one of the many people whom he owns around here. And he would have sent you straight back to the asylum, or somewhere even worse, miles from here. I'm afraid there will always be people willing to sell information for money, Jess. And there will always be people willing to gossip simply for the pleasure of it. Especially in somewhere as small as Tilnhurst.'

'I know all that,' said Jess, lifting her daughter on to her lap and cuddling her protectively. 'So what's different now?'

'Since Paul was killed,' said Leonore and stopped. She looked around the little kitchen, focusing on the inconsequential details of the Garnetts' domestic life, struggling to maintain control of her churning thoughts and emotions. 'Since Paul died.'

'Yeh,' Jess coaxed her gently.

'Since that happened, his father has not been himself. He has lost interest in everything. Even his beloved horses. He lives in a daze, not caring or knowing about anything. He's no threat to you any longer, Jess.'

'I'm sorry to hear that. It must be 'ard for yer. But I still ain't gonna risk getting found out, Leonore.' Jess shook her head resolutely. 'No. I've got to say it. I ain't gonna risk yer son...' Jess paused, taking a deep breath, trying, like Leonore, to remain calm. 'I ain't gonna risk Robert finding out about me.'

Sylvia squirmed irritably, wanting to get back to her game. Jess lifted her off her lap and sat her back on the rug. She spoke softly, not wanting to upset her daughter by letting her hear the tension in her voice.

'I've changed, Leonore. I ain't the same little gel what let 'erself get shoved around an' lied to. I've grown up a lot in the last few years; I've 'ad to.'

'I know, Jess, but...'

'No, I'm sorry, Leonore, I'm gonna 'ave to stay. Yer tell me if yer can what's to stop yer son findin' out about us, an' stickin' me an' Sylvia back in that 'ole? Yer said yerself, people love runnin' and tellin' stories. I'd only 'ave to go near that village an' it'd be all round like wildfire. Everyone knew about 'is carryin' on. Someone'd be sure to tell on me. I'm sure yer precious Robert'd pay well for the information. Anythin' rather than 'avin' me cause 'im any embarrassment. An' I ain't gonna let 'em put me away again. I ain't. Yer came in there to see me, an' I'll always be grateful for that, but yer don't know what it was really like in there. No one 'oo ain't been locked up can know. I'd rather be dead than let 'em take me an' Sylvia back in that place. I mean it.'

'I'm sure you do, Jess, but please don't say things like that. You know how hard I tried to understand what it was like for you. And I would never let anyone take you back there. Ever. You must believe that.' Leonore rubbed her throbbing temples with her fingertips. 'Jess, I want you to know something of great importance. It is no longer possible for Robert to do that to you. Not now. It couldn't happen.'

A sudden feeling of sick panic swept over Jess. She closed her eyes. 'Yer don't mean 'e's copped it?'

'No, Jess, he's fine. Well, he has been injured again, but he'll recover. After he has had surgery, he's being sent back to England to recuperate.'

'So 'ow does that 'elp me an' Sylvia? Sounds worse to me. 'E'll be closer than 'e is now.' Jess frowned and looked round at her small, golden-haired child playing contentedly on the rug, chatting happily to the rag dolly Mrs Garnett had sewn for her.

'Jess, I can't explain it all to you. Not easily. But, like you, Robert has changed. He too has grown up. Being in Flanders has *changed* him. Seeing all the horror and pain. If he knew you have his child, he'd never do anything to harm you. Either of you. I know he wouldn't. In fact just the opposite, if you would allow him the opportunity.'

Jess bent down and picked her daughter up again. Sylvia wriggled, eager to get on with her game, but Jess wouldn't let her go, hugging her close. 'I'm sorry, Leonore, but that don't sound very likely to me. I don't mean to be 'urtful after all yer've done for us, but 'e's too much like 'is ol' man for me to be able to trust 'im.'

Leonore went to speak, but Jess carried on. She was determined to have her say.

'Sorry. I meant, like 'is old man *used* to be, when 'e stuck me away.' Jess looked from Leonore to Sylvia. 'No. There's no hope of me takin' no chances like that. For Sylvia's sake.'

'I've not explained myself properly, Jess. If only you'd listen.'

'I'm sorry, but if yer don't mind I've got to get on. Sylvia wants 'er breakfast an' I've got a lot to do before Mrs Garnett gets back.'

Leonore bit her lip anxiously. 'Don't be angry with me, Jess. I've said the wrong thing, I know that. But there's no harm done. I haven't told Robert about you and Sylvia. I promise he doesn't even know he has a child. You do believe me, don't you?'

'Yer've confused me, Leonore, I know that. I thought yer wanted to protect us. Now I dunno what to think. An' it's no good yer gettin' yerself all worked up about it, cos I won't ever trust 'im. No matter what yer say.'

'Jess, we haven't gone through all this together to stop being friends, have we? Please, forget it. Forget I ever mentioned it.'

'I've forgot it already.'

Jessie's words convinced neither of them.

–

Ten days after Christmas, Leonore travelled to Shropshire to see her son. The journey to the military hospital was long and difficult, but Leonore would gladly have made the trip many times over. She was so full of optimism for the future. It would take time, but Jess *would* be convinced that Robert had changed. She could not fail to be once she had seen him. Nothing would go wrong. Leonore hadn't realised it, but she had been planning for that very thing to happen in the future since the day she received Robert's first letter from the front. And now the future had almost arrived.

Leonore told the cabman to leave her at the entrance gates. The convalescent hospital had been set up in Myntton Park, a large Queen Anne house not unlike Worlington. As she walked along the imposing tree-lined drive, she was pleased with the thought that Robert must feel quite at home in such a setting. She passed men in wheelchairs, clad in dressing gowns and pyjamas, their legs covered with tartan rugs. Nurses who looked hardly strong enough to manoeuvre the big, high-backed wheelchairs pushed the patients deftly around the gardens, taking advantage of the unseasonably warm afternoon.

At first Leonore failed to recognise her son. The thin, slightly greying man had to wave and call to her several times before she realised he was addressing her. She dropped her parcels on the drive and ran across the lawn to greet her only remaining child.

'Careful, Mother,' he said, flinching from her embrace. 'I'm still a bit tender, you know.'

'Oh, I'm sorry, darling, did I hurt you?'

'You will do if you don't stop that snivelling. I told the chaps I had the best-looking mother in the place. Don't let your nose get all red and spoil it.'

'Oh, Robert.' Leonore buried her head in his shoulder, struggling to hold back her tears of joy and relief.

Leonore and Robert talked away the whole afternoon, Leonore pushing his chair around the grounds and meeting his fellow patients. She felt guilty about doing so, but still she offered up silent prayers of thanks when she saw so many of them with injuries far worse than Robert's. Mother and son laughed together and cried together, remembering some things and choosing to forget others.

'So how's Father doing?' asked Robert as they paused by an elegant stone fountain.

'It's been very difficult for him since we heard about Paul's death,' she answered faintly.

'Still drinking?'

'Yes.'

'Worse?'

Leonore sighed. 'These days it is very rare for your father still to be sensible by mid-morning, Robert. It is as though his life no longer has any meaning.'

'Not even the horses?'

'No.'

'Poor you.'

'This is silly,' said Leonore, doing her best to hold back her tears. 'I came to visit you, to uplift your spirits, and all I do is cry.'

'Well, watch this. This'll cheer us both up.' Robert grasped the arms of his chair, raised himself shakily to his feet and took a single, wobbly step towards the fountain.

'Darling, that's wonderful,' Leonore exclaimed joyfully, grabbing his arms to steady him.

'Careful, you'll tip me over. I haven't quite got the hang of this standing business yet. But I should be walking unaided in a couple of months. I might have a bit of a limp, but I think it'll look rather dashing. Quite distinguished, in fact. What do you think?'

Soon the rapidly fading afternoon light had driven them indoors where they joined the other patients and visitors taking tea in the palm-filled conservatory.

'I can't tell you how happy spending these few hours with you has made me, Robert. Just seeing you, and knowing you'll soon be well.'

'I'm glad, Mother. It can't be easy at home.'

'I thought we weren't going to talk about that. Listen,' she said, eyes suddenly bright, 'I've made a decision. To celebrate your homecoming I have decided to tell you a secret. Something I never believed I could have trusted you with knowing.'

'Not been arrested with those suffragette chums of yours, have you?'

'Don't tease, Robert, I'm being serious.'

At that moment a young woman in a brilliantly white starched uniform came striding into the conservatory. She lifted a heavy brass bell from a side table and rang it vigorously.

'Don't ring the bell yet, Nurse,' pleaded Robert. 'They've only just got here.'

The nurse smiled at him. 'Think you can get round all of us, don't you, Bobby? Think you can get us to break the rules just for you?' She flicked him playfully under the chin and turned to Leonore. 'Your son is *such* a flirt. All of us nurses have to watch him. Any opportunity, eh, Robert?'

Much to the amusement of the visitors, the other patients joined in the general frivolity directed towards Robert and his escapades, readily contributing their own rowdy innuendos concerning Robert's reputation with the nursing staff.

'Take no notice of them, Ma. They're jealous of my good looks, that's their trouble.' Robert guffawed loudly. 'And they've nothing better to do, any of them, than besmirch the name of an honourable man.'

Leonore managed to produce a thin smile. 'You seem very popular, Robert.'

'All helps to pass the time,' he said, winking broadly at the nurse.

She rang the bell again. 'Sorry, Bobby,' she said flirtatiously. 'Matron's orders. Now there's one lady you can't twist round your little finger.'

Leonore hurriedly gathered her things together and tried to put on her gloves. 'Blast these things,' she said as her nail caught in the lining.

'Calm down, Ma. What's wrong?'

'Nothing, Robert. I have to go, that's all. The cab will be waiting at the gates to take me to the station.'

'Can't stand saying goodbye, eh?'

'That's right,' she said, straining to produce another unconvincing smile.

'You're not getting away as easily as that,' said Robert accusingly.

'What are you talking about, Robert?' she asked, no longer able to hide the strain she was feeling.

'Before you go, Mother, I want to know this deep, dark secret you said you'd share with me.'

'I'm sorry, Robert. It'll have to wait,' said Leonore. 'My cab.'

–

During Robert's months of convalescence in the hospital, Leonore struggled with her conscience. Could she really trust her son with the knowledge that he had a child? On more than one occasion she had reached the point of telling him everything. At those times she not only felt he was ready to know, but he had every right to know that he had a daughter, that he had made such a wonderful contribution to the world in the form of little Sylvia. But each time something happened to persuade her otherwise, his manner or actions convincing her that he had not changed at all, that he was still a Worlington through and through.

For Robert, the whole thing became quite a game, guessing if today was the day when it would be revealed – whatever 'it' was.

On 9th July 1918, Leonore was forced into making a decision. Robert was declared fit enough to return to Worlington Hall, and she was going to collect him. To take him home.

–

'I feel like I've been released from prison,' said Robert as he climbed cautiously into the cab, gingerly testing the power of his legs to mount the step. 'My dash to freedom,' he said, the effort showing in his voice. 'I didn't think those brutes of nurses would ever let me go.'

'Don't be so stupid, Robert,' snapped Leonore tersely, as she settled herself next to him. 'You were not in the hospital against your will. And the nurses were hardly warders. Look at them all waving to you. They treated you royally. If you had been imprisoned, you would know it is an entirely different matter.'

'You're a trifle touchy, Ma,' said Robert, grinning happily and waving back to the nurses and patients who had lined up to see him on his way down the drive. 'The old suffragette hackles rising, are they? Thinking about your jailbird friends?'

'I am growing extremely weary of your suffragette jokes, Robert.' Leonore pressed herself back in her seat.

'Sorry. Point taken.' Robert flinched as the cab picked up speed.

'No, Robert, it is I who am sorry,' said Leonore, seeing her son's pain. 'I have a lot on my mind.' She sounded worn out.

'Father getting you down?'

'No.' Leonore looked out of the cab window towards the flower-sprinkled hedgerows but saw none of them. 'I was wondering about your behaviour with the nurses.'

'What?'

'It appeared to me you had gained yourself quite a reputation amongst the other patients.'

'Me?'

'Yes, Robert, you. A reputation for being, well, a man not unlike your father used to be. In fact, the way you yourself used to be. Before you went away, I mean.'

'You'll have to take things a bit slower, Ma. I'm not sure you're making any sense.'

'I shall say it more plainly, Robert. Do you still behave in the irresponsible manner which your father encouraged so outrageously?'

'Do spit it out, Ma.'

'With girls, I mean, Robert. With girls.'

Robert took his mother's anxious face gently in his hands. 'You are funny.'

'Robert. I asked you a question,' she said, pulling away from him. 'Please do me the courtesy of answering.'

'Very well.' Robert dropped his head back against the rough upholstery of the cab and closed his eyes. 'Making jokes, playing the fool, they're ways of coping out there. Everyone does it. If you don't keep things light-hearted you begin to see the reality of what's going on around you.'

He screwed his eyes tighter, trying in vain to shut out the memories.

'The death. The maiming. The filth of it all. And it's the same in the hospital. You make light of everything. Even having your legs amputated if it happens.'

'Oh, Robert.'

'It's not bravery, it's so you don't have to think. Or remember. Don't have to recognise that some of the poor buggers won't ever get out of that place. And when you lie there in your bed at night and the nurse switches off the lights you see it all so clearly. As though you were still out there. The flashes and explosions lighting up the night sky. And boys, not men most of them, but boys, being blown to pieces. Bits of them dangling on the barbed wire. Right in front of your eyes.' Robert clenched his jaw tight. 'And the stench of rotting flesh. And always the same picture in your mind of your friend's head coming away in your hands when you try to lift off his helmet so you can help him.'

'I don't know what to say.' Leonore's voice was hardly audible. 'I hadn't thought.'

'Thank God you don't have to think about such things.' Robert opened his eyes and looked out at the green countryside. 'Especially on a beautiful day like this.' He turned to face Leonore. 'There's no way to really deal with it, you see, so you lark around. Play tricks and laugh. It stops you having to think. The nurses too. They say we went out as boys and girls and came back, if we were lucky, as what? Grownups? I never knew that seeing your friend's head come away in your hands was part of growing up.'

'Oh, Robert.'

'I know, Ma,' he said, trying to comfort her. 'There's nothing anyone can say.'

'But there is, Robert. There's something I want to say to you. The secret.'

'That's more like it,' said Robert, pleased with the diversion. 'I could…' He swore under his breath, wincing as the cab bumped to a halt in the station forecourt, jarring his still painful legs. 'My bloody luck,' he complained good-naturedly, 'we're at the station. I suppose I've missed another chance to hear this damned secret.'

'Language, Robert. I'm still your mother, remember. But you're wrong, you will hear the secret. If we can get a carriage to ourselves, that is.'

'Righto,' said Robert enthusiastically. 'If that's all you want… Porter! Over here.'

–

'She was born on the sixth of June 1914, her name is Sylvia.'

Robert ignored the waves of pain which shot through his legs with every swaying movement of the train. After the death and destruction he had witnessed on the battlefields, the idea of having a child, a living, breathing child, was like a miracle.

'She was four last month, then. My daughter.' He was stunned by the wonder of it. Suddenly he spoke with panicked urgency as if it had occurred to him that life would always dash his hopes. 'I suppose she will forgive me.'

'Robert, Sylvia doesn't even know she has a father.'

'No, not Sylvia. Jessie Fairleigh. Jess. Will she let me, I don't know, make amends?'

'I hope so, Robert, I really do. For the three of you. And for me.'

–

Robert and Leonore were alone in the Chinese Room. Outside in the hall Tyler was busily fussing over taking Robert's things up to his room. Because of the war there were no footmen to carry out such menial tasks in the household, so Tyler added an importance to the most trivial of jobs in an effort to maintain his status. Sir George was safely settled in the library, having already started on his second decanter of port.

Robert stood in front of the fireplace, leaning on the mantelshelf, taking his weight on his forearms, his back to the room.

'It's strange,' he said, staring into the grate. 'It's as though I've never been away from here. I can almost hear the gramophone playing, and see Julia and Paul dancing in each other's arms. Poor Julia. I wonder if she'll ever be happy again.'

Leonore went to her son's side and touched him softly on the shoulder. 'Would you like me to speak to Jess?'

'Yes, oh yes.' He turned round to face her. 'Would you?'

'Of course.'

'Do you think it's too late to speak to her this evening?'

'I'll go now.'

–

Always discreet, Mr and Mrs Garnett took Sylvia out to their kitchen garden and attended to some suddenly urgent weeding, leaving Jess and Lady Worlington alone in the cottage.

'It ain't that I've got nothin' against you personally, Leonore,' said Jess stiffly. 'Yer know that. But yer shouldn't 'ave told 'im.'

'I know how you feel, Jess.'

'Yer should do. We've been through this time and time again over the last few months. Yer knew I 'adn't changed me mind, an' yer still told 'im.'

'But won't you at least see him now he's home, Jess? He so wants to make amends. To be able to help you in some way. To make life easier for you and Sylvia.'

'The men in yer family ain't been exactly honest with me, now 'ave they?' said Jess coldly. ''Ow do I know 'e don't wanna steal Sylvia off of me, an' stick me back in the bin again?'

'He wants you to forgive him, Jess. Not to harm you. Truly. He wants to make amends. *He* said that. I'm not making up any of this. He doesn't want to hurt you. He wants to help you.'

'No. I don't wanna 'ear any more, an' I don't wanna see 'im. I *won't* see 'im, Leonore. I mean it.'

'Listen to me,' said Leonore urgently. 'You don't have to agree to anything to do with Sylvia. Not yet. As much as Robert wants to see his daughter, I understand your worries. But at least let him see you, Jess. Let him talk to you, and show you that he is sincere. I'll bring him here to the cottage in the morning. I'll stay with you for the whole time. I'll speak to Mrs Garnett. She'll look after Sylvia, take her out for a walk or something. We'll be here alone and Sylvia will be safe. No one else will know. Please, Jess, then you can see for yourself. He'll only stay for as long as you want him to. Please hear what he has to say. Give him a chance, Jess, please. For me. See for yourself how he's changed.'

'Yer make it all seem so easy, the way yer talkin'.'

'Would it be so very hard, Jess? To let him have his say?'

'I'd better get the lamps lit,' said Jess. 'It'll be dark soon.'

As she watched Leonore walk back through the orchard path to the Hall, Jess resigned herself to what would happen. She knew she had no choice.

Chapter 18

Home with the Milk

Rose pulled her shawl down from the banister and draped it round her shoulders to cover her nightdress.

'All right, all right. 'Old on,' she snapped.

As she opened the street door, Rose's hand flew up to her mouth. 'Jess. Whatever's 'appened? What yer doin' 'ere?'

'I'll tell yer in a minute,' said Jess wearily. 'Ain't yer gonna let us in, Mum?'

'Aw, course. Course. Come in, quick, before Florrie sees yer.'

'Even she won't be nosin' this time of the mornin', will she?' said Jess, stepping inside.

'Don't yer be so sure. I think she stays up all night, that one, in case she misses somethin'.'

Rose poked her head outside and looked anxiously along the road towards the Baxters'. No sign of life. With a bit of luck they were all still asleep and wouldn't have seen anything. Rose shut the door tight.

'Sorry to get yer up so early, Mum.'

'It's all right, darlin'. I wasn't asleep.'

Jess followed her mother along the familiar passageway and into the kitchen of Number 8 Burton Street. She dropped exhausted on to one of the hard wooden chairs.

'Take Sylvia off us, will yer, Mum? She weighs a ton.'

'Don't wake 'er up. 'Old on a minute. I'll fetch a blanket from upstairs.'

While her mother was out of the room, Jess noticed the half-full cup of tea on the table. Rose had meant it; she hadn't been asleep.

'Right, let's sort this out.' Rose came into the kitchen with the blanket and a pillow from her bedroom. She bent down and made a makeshift bed on the kitchen floor by the range.

'There yer are, sweet'eart,' she said as she took her sleeping granddaughter from Jess. Sylvia moaned softly in her sleep. 'She's out like a light.'

'Poor little thing. We've been travellin' 'alf the night.'

Rose gently settled her granddaughter. 'She's such a little beauty,' she said.

'Takes after 'er gran'mother,' said Jess.

Rose looked down at the sleeping child. 'I'll pour yer a cup of tea an' yer can tell me all about it,' she said as she stood up, then turned and looked at her daughter. 'If yer want to, that is.'

'Course I want to, Mum,' said Jess. She waited a moment then said, 'Why couldn't yer sleep?'

Rose fussed around with the kettle and teacups. 'Eh?'

'Well, yer don't usually get up to 'ave a cuppa tea at 'alf past four in the mornin', do yer?'

'I was thirsty,' said Rose flatly.

Jess was too preoccupied with her own troubles to make anything more of it.

'I ain't got no sugar, Jess,' Rose said, tucking her long, thick hair behind her ears. 'Ain't been able to get none lately, but I've got condensed milk.'

'That's lovely, Mum.'

'There yer are.' Rose gave Jess her cup and sat down.

'This old table's 'eard a few tales over the years,' said Jess, stirring the thick, sweet milk into the tea.

'Yeh. If only it could talk, eh?' said Rose sadly. 'Think of all the memories it'd 'ave.'

They sat sipping their tea.

'All right if I stay for a few days, Mum?' said Jess quietly.

'Yer don't 'ave to ask, darlin'. This is yer 'ome.'

'Ta.'

'I'm so glad to see yer, Jessie,' said Rose, reaching her hand out across the table.

'Me an' all, Mum.' Jess stared into her cup.

''Ow d'yer get 'ere? No one saw yer, did they?'

'No. It was pitch-dark when I left. The guard let me get on the milk train at Tiln'urst. 'E wasn't goin' to but Sylvia started cryin' an' carryin' on. So 'e give in. Didn't even 'ave to pay nothin'.' Jess gave a weak little laugh. 'Good job an' all; I never 'ad no money on me. I left the cottage a bit quick, see.'

'Yer didn't 'ave a row with Susan or nothin', did yer?'

'No.' Jess shook her head.

'I'm glad. She's a good 'un.'

'I made sure I left Mrs Garnett a note to say thanks for everythin', but I 'ad to go away, like. She'll miss Sylvie. She treated us both like we was 'er own.'

Rose suddenly burst into tears.

'Blimey, Mum.' Jess took her mother's hand. 'I'm so full of me own troubles. What's up? What's the matter?'

'Yer'll 'ave to know some time,' sniffed Rose. 'It might as well be now. I was goin' to write to yer later anyway.'

Rose stood up and went over to the mantelpiece. She took an envelope from behind the clock, handed it to Jess and sat down again.

Before Jess could open it, Rose said softly, 'It's our Sammy.' The tears streamed unchecked down her cheeks.

'Oh, Mum, no.' Jess dropped the envelope on to the table as though it had burnt her fingers.

'"Missin' in action" it says. An' 'ow sorry they are. Not 'alf as sorry as me they ain't. What do they know?' she sobbed. 'They ain't 'is mother.'

'Mum, don't cry.' Jess closed her arms round Rose. She felt ashamed that she hadn't noticed before just how worn out her mother looked.

'Yesterday, it come. So that's me Sammy gone, as easy as that.' Rose's lip trembled. 'An' there's still no word about yer dad. Aw, Jess.' Her whole body shuddered. 'I can't stand it. I can't stand any of it no more.'

'We don't know for sure what's 'appened, Mum, do we? They might 'ave got captured or somethin'. That 'appens all the time.'

'I suppose so, but I've got this terrible feelin', Jess.'

'P'raps they've written to Ted or Charlie,' said Jess. 'Yer'll see, we'll 'ave a letter from one of 'em in a day or so, givin' us all the news. An' yer'll wonder what on earth yer was worryin' about.'

Sylvia whimpered and rolled over. Jess let go of her mother and knelt down next to her child, patting her back until she settled.

Rose rubbed the tears roughly from her face and looked down at her sleeping grandchild.

'I'm so glad yer 'ere with me, Jess. I can't tell yer 'ow glad, but yer mustn't get yerself in trouble comin' 'ere. I couldn't stand it if anythin' 'appened to you an' all.'

'Me problems don't seem very important now,' said Jess.

'Somethin' else's 'appened, ain't it?' said Rose, gripping the edge of the table. 'I'm right, ain't I? That's why yer've come 'ome.'

'Don't get worked up, Mum.' Jess sat back in her chair. 'Things 'ave changed down at Worlington, that's all.'

''Ow d'yer mean?'

'Leonore's old man's 'it the sherbert right bad. 'E don't know one day from the next. So 'e's no threat to me an' Sylvia any more. Well, so Leonore reckons.'

'Jess,' said Rose, squeezing her daughter's arm. 'That's 'ardly a problem, is it, love? Not for us any'ow. It's the best news I've 'eard since I dunno know when. But poor old Leonore, eh?'

'There's somethin' else, Mum.' Jess hugged herself. She felt suddenly chilled. 'Leonore's son.'

'Robert?'

Jess nodded. ''E's come 'ome from the army.'

'But what does that matter? Yer said 'e didn't know nothin'.'

''E didn't. Not until yesterday, that is. Leonore says 'e's come back a different bloke. The war's changed 'im, or somethin'. So she's gone an' told 'im all about us, me and Sylvie.'

''Ave yer seen 'im?'

'No, I ain't,' said Jess emphatically. 'Didn't get within a 'undred yards of 'im. It's all right for Leonore sayin' 'e's right sorry for what 'appened an' 'ow 'e wants to make it up to us. But... Aw, I dunno.'

Rose frowned. 'Yer don't trust 'im?'

'Too bloody right I don't.'

'Can't say as anyone'd blame yer.'

'Leonore thinks I just don't understand. She said once I saw 'im, an' 'ow different 'e was now, then I'd 'ave to give 'im a chance. An' it'd all be 'unky-dory.'

'But yer didn't wanna risk findin' out?'

'Right.'

'So yer did a runner.'

'Yeh. An' 'ere I am.' Jess yawned and blinked her aching eyes. 'Hidin' still. Well, not really 'idin'. It'll be obvious where I am. But I'm no 'arm to any of 'em 'ere, am I? Per'aps they'll just forget about me.'

'Look, Jess, there's no use yer worryin' yerself about it this time of the mornin', is there? Why don't yer get yer 'ead down for a few hours? You and little Sylvie come in me bed with me. Like yer used to.'

–

'Mummy. Mummy,' Sylvia wailed.

For a moment after she opened her eyes Jess couldn't think where she was.

'Mummy,' Sylvia persisted, 'I want wee-wees. Now.'

'All right, darlin',' Jess said, focusing on the familiar brass bedstead. 'Mummy'll take yer.'

Jess threw back the patched cotton sheet and stepped on to the bare floorboards of her parents' bedroom.

'Where are we, Mummy?' asked Sylvia in a timid little voice as they went carefully down the narrow wooden stairs.

'Nanna Fairleigh's.'

'I want to go home, Mummy.'

'Sssh. Yer'll wake Nanna.'

'I want Mrs Garnett.'

'Sssh, Sylvia, stop grizzlin'. Yer'll upset Nanna, I said. Now be a good girl. Come on, out 'ere.'

Jess unbolted the kitchen door and guided her daughter into the lavatory in the back yard.

'I don't like it here.'

Jess pulled Sylvia's knickers down and sat her on the wooden lavatory seat.

'Yer'll get used to it, baby.'

'I 'eard Sylvia cryin'. She all right?'

Jess turned round. Rose was standing behind her. 'She's mixed up, Mum. Dunno what's goin' on, she don't.'

'Like a lot of us since this stinkin' war,' said Rose bitterly. 'Look at 'er, poor little mite. It's a bit late for breakfast but I can do some toast and drippin'. Want some, Sylvia?'

Sylvia's hunger overcame her shyness. She nodded.

'It'll be on the table when yer ready, sweet'eart, an' Nanna's got a surprise for yer,' she said, walking back indoors.

'See? It's good 'ere,' said Jess, coaxing her with what she hoped was a convincing smile.

But Sylvia did not look convinced.

She *was* totally convinced, however, when her grandmother took her hand and led her to a chenille-covered shape in the corner of the kitchen. Sylvia clapped her hands with pleasure when she saw the tiny monkey blink its eyes as it became accustomed to the light.

'Mum, you've still got 'er. Look, Sylvia, it's Ginny. Look at 'er tiny little 'ands an' fingers.'

'Your Ginny's kept me company on many a long night, an' that's the truth. Knows all me secrets she does.'

'I don't suppose the canary's still about,' said Jess, pushing her finger through the bars. She stroked the little creature's head, as it held it first on one side then the other, enjoying the attention.

'No,' said Rose wistfully. 'Come down one mornin' an' the poor little thing was dead on the bottom of the cage. Died of fright I reckon. Yer should 'ave seen it that night. The aeroplanes dropped that many bombs. Never seen anythin' like it. It was like daylight with the flames an' everythin'. An' the noise.'

''Ow close was it?'

'It was close. The 'Arry in Brunswick Road copped it.'

'Aw, Mum.' Jess stood up and went to her mother's side.

Rose's eyes were fixed on the floor. 'It made it dirtier and foggier than ever for days on end, it did. But the night it 'appened...' She frowned, remembering. 'Yer should 'ave seen it, Jess. The 'ole sky looked like it was alight. The 'orses round the back of the dairy went ravin' mad. Kicked their way out of their stalls they did. Went gallopin' up the street. They was terrified. So yer can imagine what that poor little bird thought about it. Tell yer the truth, Jess, I was terrified an' all.'

'All by yerself. I should 'ave been 'ere with yer, Mum.'

'Leave off, Jess, yer 'ad me granddaughter to think about.'

'I like her, Nanna,' said Sylvia, and dragged her grandmother over to the monkey's cage.

'Shall we go for a walk now Sylvia's 'ad 'er bit of breakfast?' said Rose, untying her apron and hanging it on the hook behind the kitchen door. 'It's such a lovely day.'

'Good idea, Mum. An' we might as well get it over with. Let Florrie 'ave a good ol' nose, eh?'

Rose managed to laugh. 'We'll give 'er somethin' to talk about.'

-

The three generations of Fairleighs made a handsome sight walking along Burton Street towards the open space near the Mission hut. Sylvia walked along between her mother and grandmother, holding their hands. She had cheered up considerably and was becoming more and more fascinated by this new world so full of houses and people. Rose and Jess had so much to talk about, and it helped them both forget their fears about Bill and Ted for a while. Their faces were lively and animated with the simple pleasure of being together again.

'No, me cough ain't been too bad at all lately,' Rose said with a shrug. 'It's this new easy life I've got, see. Since I've been at the factory I don't 'ave to get up nearly so early. An' I don't 'ave to kneel on them cold steps with me 'ands in a freezin' cold bucket of water neither.'

'I remember when we was little an' yer did them cleanin' jobs, Mum. Yer was always out before we was even awake. It must 'ave been 'orrible on winter mornin's. Us kids never realised 'ow 'ard it was for yer.'

Rose sighed. 'I used to go to bed in me frock, yer know. It was too cold to get up and 'ave to get dressed. The water was frozen solid in the pipe anyway, so I couldn't 'ave 'ad a wash-down even if I'd wanted.' She laughed. 'The good ol' days, eh?'

'I'm glad yer kept doin' for ol' Miss Feldman though, Mum. Sounds like she's 'ad a right rough time.'

'They've said terrible things about that ol' lady, Jess. Yer'd think she started the bleed'n' war single-'anded to 'ear some of 'em round 'ere. I'll never 'ave nothin' bad said about 'er when I'm there though. She's been a friend to me. An' so 'as 'er brother. A lot of 'em round 'ere should remember 'ow 'e's 'elped 'em out in the past.'

'Well, at least yer 'appier now yer in the factory, Mum.'

'Yer ain't kiddin'. I ain't 'ad to borrow nothin' off Uncle since I've worked there. Enough money to live on, pay me bills an' still 'ave a bit left over. Mind yer, we was a bit worried when the army uniform work dropped off, but we're doin' the nurses' clothes now.'

''Ere we are, Sylvia,' said Jess, pointing across the road to the little hut. 'This is where I used to go an' dance with me friends. An' before that, Nanna used to bring me 'ere when I was a little gel to play on the grass.'

'A little girl like me, Mummy?'

'Yeh, darlin', just like you.'

They walked through the gate in the railings, still hand-in-hand, and found a spot under the single cherry tree where they could sit in the shade.

'Make Nanna a daisy chain like Mrs Garnett showed yer.'

Sylvia soon became totally absorbed in finding and threading daisy stems.

'It looks smaller, some'ow,' Jess said as she looked at the Mission hut. 'I used to love them dances.' She stretched her legs out, warming herself in the sun. 'Don't suppose no one's 'eard nothin' from Jack Barnes,' she added casually.

'No,' said Rose. That was one subject she definitely didn't want bringing up, but she'd spoken sharper than she'd intended, and immediately wished she hadn't. She didn't want anyone sharing her suspicions, least of all Jess: she had quite enough on her plate already.

'There's plenty o' work on the nurses' uniforms, see, Jess,' she said briskly. 'Cos there's plenty of call for nurses to wear 'em. An' not just for the soldiers either. There's this 'flu thing started round 'ere. It's killed 'undreds already. Yer 'ad it down in Kent yet?'

'Not this year we ain't, no,' said Jess. She didn't question her mother's refusal to discuss Jack; she just presumed that Rose didn't want her getting upset about him all over again.

'Seems a shame, yer know, one of the girls at work was tellin' me about 'er chap what got it. Killed 'im, it did. An' they'd just got 'emselves engaged. Don't seem right, do it?' Rose plucked at the blades of dusty grass. 'Them boys comin' 'ome from France. All sorts wrong with them. Trench fever,

334

gas, legs missin'. Then they go an' get 'flu an' that does for 'em. Don't seem right at all. I'm glad she's too little to understand all this sufferin'.'

The two women watched Sylvia playing contentedly in the bright summer sun.

'Yer reckon yer job in the factory'll still be safe even if the war really does end soon?'

'I 'ope so, Jess, cos if yer dad 'as gone I'll need the money all right.'

'Don't say that, Mum.'

Rose's eyes filled with tears. 'I think we've got to accept 'e 'as gone, Jess. Not a word after all these months. Every time the boy comes along on 'is bike, I 'old me breath, waitin' for 'im to knock on the door with the telegram.'

''E'll be all right, Mum. Yer wait an' see.'

'Please Gawd 'e is, but if he ain't, I wouldn't be able to manage on the pittance they give to the widows,' Rose said, gazing unseeingly at the ground. 'Couple of bob a week, that's all they get. I dunno. They wanted our husbands an' sons but they don't want to look after us when they've gone.'

This time it was Jess who tried to change the subject. ''Ow's the others down Burton Street doin', Mum? 'Ow's Mabel managin'?'

'She ain't too bad,' said Rose, wiping her cheeks with her sleeve. 'Got a nice little job in the 'ospital. It was sad though, 'er last kid, the middle one, died after Christmas, just a couple o' weeks after she lost her oldest. So she's got no 'usband an' no kids at all now. All alone she is, but it was a blessin' really. They was such pathetic little things. Always so sickly.'

'I'm sorry. Poor Mabel. Never 'ad much luck 'as she?'

'No, poor cow.'

'Been a lot lost round 'ere, Mum?'

'Everyone in Poplar seems to 'ave lost someone. But I reckon there's been a lot lost everywhere, Jess. Florrie's oldest boy copped it, yer know.'

'Arthur? Aw, Mum, that's terrible.'

'Yeh. When 'e went off in 'is uniform, the twins thought it was wonderful. Cheered 'im off, they did. Wavin' flags they'd made an' everythin'. Out there two weeks, 'e was. Didn't even 'ave a chance to post 'is first letter 'ome to 'is mum. The twins don't think it's so clever now. Thank Gawd they wasn't old enough or they'd 'ave gone an' signed up with Arthur.'

'Arthur, eh?' Jess clicked her tongue. 'I knew Florrie'd lost 'er 'usband but I never knew about 'er Arthur. Wally was a nice bloke, Mum, wasn't 'e? A real good 'un. Remember down 'oppin', when 'e left that money for Mabel an' the kids?'

'Yeh. 'E was a good 'un all right.'

'Don't seem possible they're all dead.'

'I didn't write to yer every time it 'appened to someone round 'ere, Jess, or the letters would 'ave been all that an' nothin' else. Yer 'ad enough to think about.'

'Yer always thinkin' about everyone else, Mum, I don't know 'ow yer do it. With all the aggravation yer've 'ad, yer still think about other people.'

'There's enough wickedness in this world without me addin' my two penn'orth.'

'I 'ope I can learn to be as good as you are, Mum.'

Rose stroked her daughter's cheek. 'Yer good enough, gel, believe me. Yer always 'ave been.'

Jess bowed her head. 'Yer make me feel ashamed when I think 'ow I lied to yer when we was down 'oppin'.'

'Yer was a kid, an' yer made a mistake. Yer didn't mean no 'arm. Yer got carried away. An' we've all been stupid at times, Jess. An' look at that little angel.' Rose nodded towards her granddaughter. 'We shouldn't forget to be grateful for what we've got in life.'

'Yer sound like Dad,' said Jess, her voice quavering.

'Yer couldn't pay yer ol' mum a better compliment, love.'

''Ow did Win take it when Arthur died?' asked Jess. 'They got right close once Florrie 'ad the twins.'

'I don't think Win even knows, Jess. When 'er dad died she went an' married some right no-good from Stepney Green. An' 'e upped an' run off with some bird from Aldgate. Left Winnie with no money an' two babies to feed. She wound up doin' a moonlight. Florrie did 'er pieces. It was 'er spoke to the landlord to get 'em the rooms in the first place, see. She 'ad to find the two-weeks' rent what Win owed.'

'Poor old Win,' said Jess, looking at her happy child playing with the flowers in the sunshine. 'Like yer said, we should remember to be grateful for what we've got. An' I am, Mum. I really am.'

'An' me, Jess. In the middle of all this stinkin' war I get to be a nan. Me little girl with a young 'un of 'er own. I wish yer dad could see 'er. 'E'd be so proud. But 'e knows all about 'er. I wrote regular and told 'im all the news.'

'I'm glad, Mum.'

'Here you are, Nanna.' Sylvia toddled over to where Rose and Jess were sitting on the grass. With a very serious expression she placed the completed chain over her grandmother's head and arranged it around her neck. 'You're pretty,' she said, cocking her head to one side to admire her work.

–

As they walked back to Burton Street Jess found it hard to believe that, with all the sadness and devastation, life went on as usual. An Indian toffee man, a fruit stall, a sea-food barrow,

337

a muffin man, and even an elderly hurdy-gurdy player all still plied their trade at the kerbside.

'Some things don't change, do they, Mum?'

'Yer right there,' said Rose. 'Just look 'oo's spotted us.'

Florrie Baxter came rushing out of her house towards them, her eyes fixed on Sylvia. 'I knew it,' she bawled at the top of her voice. 'It's Jessie Fairleigh. An' 'oo's this then?'

'This, Flo, is me granddaughter,' said Rose proudly. 'She made this necklace for me, didn't yer, sweet'eart?'

–

'Don't cry, Nanna.'

'What's goin' on?' Jessie yawned as she stumbled into the kitchen, still only half awake. She raked her fingers through her sleep-tousled hair which hung loose round her shoulders.

'Nanna's crying, Mummy,' fretted Sylvia. 'Look.'

'All right, darlin', yer go back up to bed an' play with yer dolly. There's a good gel. I'll stay with Nanna.'

'Is she all right, Mummy?'

'Yeh. She's got a bellyache, that's all. Remember, like yer 'ad when yer et all them apples?'

Sylvia nodded wisely. Her nanna crying now made sense in terms of her little world. She was relieved enough by the explanation to happily do as her mother told her.

Jess waited until the sound of her daughter climbing the stairs had stopped.

'Mum?' Jessie knelt down by her mother. 'Tell me, what's wrong?'

Rose held out the envelope she had been clutching. 'I 'eard the bike comin' along the road, Jess,' she said between great gulping sobs. 'An' I knew. I just knew.'

'Dad?'

Rose nodded and held up the telegram.

The two women wept as though they would never stop.

'I loved 'im so much, Jess.'

'I know, Mum. I know.'

Chapter 19

Celebrations

'Jess. Yer in there?'

'Yeh, come in, Lil. I'm gettin' Sylvia dressed in the kitchen.'

Lil sat herself down at the table. ''Ello, beautiful. Mummy making yer look nice for the party, is she?'

'Yes. And Nanna made me this dress.'

'Yer'll be the prettiest girl there,' said Lil. 'She's a real credit to yer, Jess. Talks lovely an' all.'

'She's me little country bumpkin, ain't yer, Sylvie?'

Sylvia giggled at her mother's teasing.

''Ow's it goin' out there?' asked Jess, brushing her daughter's hair round her fingers to form bouncing golden ringlets.

Lil puffed out her cheeks and shook her head. 'Yer don't wanna know,' she said. 'I 'ad to come in 'ere to get away from 'em for a while. I couldn't stand it no more. They all wanna be in charge. All tellin' each other what they should be doin'. But no one's doin' nothin', of course. They'll never get it ready by this afternoon.'

'Now, who's shoutin' loudest and doin' least of all?' mused Jess. 'Let me think.'

'Florrie Baxter,' Jess and Lil said in unison.

'Florrie Baxter,' echoed Sylvia, laughing with delight at the new game.

'You three ain't doin' too bad yerselves,' said Ted, scratching his bare chest and yawning as he walked into the kitchen. 'Woke me up with all yer noise.'

''Ello, Ted,' said Lil. ''Ow's the arm?'

'Still 'urts, but it's gettin' better, thanks, Lil.' Ted bent down to his niece. 'An' what's goin' on 'ere, Sylvie? Why are they dressin' me best gel up like a little princess?'

'I thought they shot yer in the arm, not in the 'ead,' said Lil. 'It's the street party, yer big nit.'

'Aw, yeh. I forgot,' he said, hooking his braces up over the shoulder without the sling. ''Oo's gonna make us a cuppa tea then?'

Lil let out a loud, disbelieving laugh. 'Huh! Make it yerself. Yer know I saw 'im down The Star last night, Jess. 'Ad one too many I reckon. Made 'is brain go soft.'

'Got it in one, Lil,' said Jess.

'Sod me, if a geezer ain't entitled to get pissed the day war ends,' said Ted, wide-eyed with hurt at their playful accusations. 'An' what the bleedin' 'ell am I doin' standin' around 'ere lettin' meself be nagged by women? I'm an 'ero, I am. An' I'm a bloody corporal an' all.'

'Still me little brother though, ain't yer? An' if yer want a cuppa, well, there's the kettle,' grinned Jess, flicking him round the ear.

'Don't hurt my Uncle Teddy,' wailed Sylvia, grabbing Ted protectively round the legs.

'That's right, angel, yer tell 'em. Come on,' he said, picking her up with his good arm. 'Yer come with Uncle Ted an' we'll go outside an' see what Nanna's got for us to do. I dunno, Sylv, surrounded by women, ain't I?'

Sylvia chuckled appreciatively at her uncle.

'Don't forget 'er coat, Ted,' called Jess after her departing brother.

'Yes, Sergeant Major, sir!' he called back, before skipping nimbly over the front step and slamming the street door.

''E's lookin' well, Jess,' said Lil, cutting herself a thick doorstep off the loaf and spreading it generously with marge.

''E is most of the time, Lil, but at night 'e 'as 'orrible dreams still.'

'An' I'll bet 'e's got an 'orrible 'angover this mornin',' said Lil, spraying crumbs as she spoke. 'I left The Star at gone two this mornin' an' they was still at it. 'E was dancin' with me little sister, if yer don't mind. An' me Mum was leadin' the singin', of course. Talk about a show-up. Yer should 'ave seen 'er.'

'She don't change, do she? Yer can always depend on Elsie for a laugh.'

'Yer wouldn't say that if yer 'ad to live with 'er. It's like Casey's Court down our 'ouse, with 'er an' the gels. If they ain't fightin' an' rowin' about somethin' or other, they're singin' an' laughin'.'

'Don't complain, Lil. I'd rather 'ear a bit o' life about the place. There ain't been a lot of laughin' in 'ere over the last few months, I can tell yer.'

'Sorry, Jess.'

'That's all right, Lil. I don't wanna moan, but it don't seem possible, that's all. I keep expectin' Dad an' Sammy to walk in through that door. Same as they always did.'

Lil stood up. 'Come on, gel,' she said decisively. 'Get yer coat an' 'at. We've got a party to go to.'

'Yer go on, Lil, I'll be out in a minute.' She shook her head. 'I promise. An' make sure 'e's put Sylvia's coat on, it's perishin' out there.'

Jess ushered Lil, still protesting, out of the kitchen. She listened for the front door to close then took an envelope from her skirt pocket. She opened it, read the contents, then tore it into shreds. It was another letter from Robert Worlington begging to see her and Sylvia. Leonore must have got the hint by now, thought Jess; she hadn't heard from her for weeks. But the regular pleas from Robert were beginning to worry her. She really hadn't expected him to be so persistent. She didn't want to leave Rose again, but she didn't have much choice. There was no sign of Robert stopping pestering her, and one day he might turn up out of the blue and steal Sylvia away from her. She had no choice; she would have to get away.

Jess sat down and wrote a letter, addressed the envelope and put it on the mantelshelf behind the clock. She would post it first thing in the morning. Her worries and plans would have to wait until she could buy a stamp, and anyway, today was a celebration. The war was over and Burton Street was going to say good riddance to it with a right old cockney knees-up.

–

The party began sedately enough with the neighbours eating and drinking large quantities of sandwiches and tea that had been set out on the tables draped with Union Jacks. They organised games for the children and stood around talking. But when the landlord from The Star beckoned the men over to help him, and crates of ale replaced the plates and teacups, the mood was soon a whole lot jollier.

After swallowing a few drinks, Elsie persuaded someone to drag the piano from her front parlour out into the street, the singing and dancing started, and the party really got under way. The residents of Burton Street were joined by neighbours from the surrounding area, as well as by unfamiliar, but equally welcome guests who had simply been passing by and had been caught up in the festivities. Burton Street was packed with joyful, dancing people.

Jess was partnering Lilly Dorkin in a fair stab at a foxtrot when someone tapped her on the shoulder and asked politely, 'Is this an excuse me? May I?'

Jess turned round smiling broadly and put out her arms to join her new partner. But when she saw who was asking her to dance she backed away.

'Don't be shy, Jess,' urged Lil, pushing her towards the handsome soldier. 'Just cos 'e's got an officer's uniform. 'E won't bleed'n' bite yer.'

The man took Jess in his arms and whirled her away.

'What yer doin' 'ere?' asked Jess, her face white with shock. 'Yer never said in yer letters yer was comin'.'

'I'm not stupid, Jess. You'd have run away from me again, wouldn't you? I didn't want to make that mistake twice.'

'Yer've got no right comin' 'ere.'

'I know how you feel, Jess, but I must speak to you. You wouldn't answer my letters.'

'Bloody right I wouldn't.'

'You must hear me out.'

'Aw, must I?' she asked sarcastically.

'Please. I don't intend to make a scene. I don't want to alarm Sylvia in any way.'

'She ain't 'ere,' said Jess, too quickly.

Robert looked at her, then gestured with his head. 'That's Sylvia, isn't it? The little girl sitting on the kerb, the one with the golden hair and the beautiful face. The one who looks exactly like her mother.'

Jess's eyes opened wide with alarm.

'When I saw her sitting there, the image of you, it was like a miracle. I spoke to her, told her I liked her dress, and she smiled. Oh, Jess, she's so beautiful.'

Jess backed away from him, staggering into the dancing couple behind. She pointed her finger close to his face. 'Yer keep away from 'er, do you 'ear me?'

'If you agree to hear me out.'

Jess didn't answer; she just let Robert take her by the arm and guide her, ashen-faced, through the crowd, away from the music and dancing.

'I'll give yer five minutes,' she said, 'an' don't yer dare make any trouble. Or I'll get me brother on to yer.'

Jess's drama had not gone unnoticed. ''Ere, Rose,' said Florrie excitedly. Despite her problems, she still found the time to be keenly interested in whatever happened in Burton Street and most of the surrounding neighbourhood. ''Oo's that your Jessie's goin' off with? Wasn't it that...'

'I'm sure I didn't see,' said Rose instantly and truthfully. 'I was 'avin' a dance with Joey, as I'm sure you noticed. An' anyway, it's no business of mine. She's 'avin' some fun, Florrie, that's all. The war's over an' it's a party, see? So why don't yer go an' enjoy yerself? An' leave me alone.'

She turned her back on the open-mouthed Florrie and spoke to Sylvia who was still sitting on the kerb next to her Unde Ted, dapping her hands to the music. 'Want a drink, darlin'?'

'Yes please, Nanna.'

'I'd 'ave thought yer'd 'ave taken more interest in what she did, after what 'appened,' said Florrie to Rose's back.

'Nanna'll get yer some milk, sweet'eart,' said Rose and, straightening up, turned to address Florrie. 'Listen to me, Florrie Baxter. If yer looked after yer own business as well as yer poke yer nose into everyone else's, then perhaps yer wouldn't 'ave lost track of Winnie the way yer did.'

'Well!' was all the red-faced Florrie could say.

'I may 'ave spoken out of turn, Florrie, an' if I did, I'm sorry,' said Rose plainly. 'But I've only spoke the truth. Now, if yer don't mind, I'd like to be left alone to get me granddaughter a drink.'

—

'I used to go dancin' in 'ere,' said Jess, looking at the shabby Mission hut where they'd stopped. 'Missed it for four weeks I did, so's I could go down 'opping. Seems like a lifetime ago.' She shook her head sadly. 'Everything's changed.'

'And so have I, Jess. I've changed.'

'I wasn't talkin' about you,' she said coldly, running her hand slowly along the splintered wooden door. 'I was thinkin' about 'ow things used to be round 'ere. When I was a kid.'

'I've not come to talk about the past, Jess.'

'Oh no?' she said sharply, spinning round to face him. 'So what 'ave yer come 'ere to talk about then? Takin' me daughter away from me?'

'Why would you think that?'

'Don't play games with me.'

'Jess, please. You've got me all wrong. I don't want to hurt you.'

'Aw no, course yer don't. An' yer can get yer 'ands off me an' all.'

Robert dropped his hands to his sides. 'I'm sorry.'

They stood there staring at each other. 'Well, what do yer want then?' Jess finally asked, unable to stand the silence any longer. 'To beg for me forgiveness like Leonore reckons yer do?'

'Partly, yes.'

'Well, it ain't that easy,' she said, poking him in the chest, emboldened by anger and fear. 'It wasn't you what got stuck in no asylum with a baby. It was me. Me and Sylvia.'

'I knew nothing about that, Jess, I swear I didn't.'

'Would it 'ave made any difference if yer 'ad've known? Would yer 'ave come rushin' to get me out of there? Swept me off me feet an' carried me away on yer big shiny 'orse? Well? Would yer?'

Robert bowed his head. 'Probably not.'

'Least yer honest,' said Jess, turning away from him. She wouldn't let him see the tears.

'Let me finish, Jess. I meant probably not then. But I've changed now. Now I'm different.'

'So yer keep sayin'.'

'I understand things in a way I never did before.'

'Oh yeh. What things are they then?'

'That I want to marry you. That's why I'm here.'

'What?' She faced him, unable to believe his audacity. 'Yer the one 'oo belongs in the loony bin, not me, mate.'

'Don't mock me, Jess. Please. Won't you even talk about it?'

'What's there to say? Yer stark ravin' barmy.'

'I've thought about this carefully, Jess,' he said reasonably. He began counting off the items on his fingers as though he was detailing a campaign. 'I can offer you a home. And security. It can't be easy for you being alone with Sylvia. I can give her her father.' He looked at her, eager for her response. It wasn't what he'd hoped for.

'Yer leave 'er out of this,' she snapped back. 'D'yer understand me?'

'How can I leave her out of this, Jess?' His voice became pleading. 'She's real. She exists. When I saw her I wanted to

347

go over and scoop her up in my arms. Knowing that I have a living, breathing child is one of the most wonderful things that could have happened to me. And one of the few decent things I've ever achieved in my life.'

Jess looked at him contemptuously. 'Yer ain't got a clue, 'ave yer?'

'I know that there are at least practical ways in which I can help. She has to be fed, needs clothes, schooling.'

'She's got all them, thanks.'

'But she needs a father,' he said simply.

'She's got on all right so far without one.'

He saw a hoped-for opening in her argument – and spoke rapidly, trying to convince her of the sense of what he was saying. 'But that was during the war, Jess. When you were hiding away. Things are not the same any more. It's going to get harder, not easier. Housing, work. They'll both be a problem. I can help you. You have to admit there are things you'll need. Think about it. I promise I'll be good to you both. You won't regret it, Jess.'

Jess's chest rose and fell as she struggled to control herself. 'Why don't yer leave me alone?' she demanded. Tears of anger and confusion were streaming down her face. 'Why don't yer just get out of 'ere, an' leave us both alone?'

'If that's what you want, Jess,' he said quietly, 'I'll go. But I'll be back tomorrow and the day after that, and the day after that. I don't intend losing you again, Jessie Fairleigh.'

'Say I'm not 'ere when yer get back?'

'Then I'll come and find you. Wherever you are.'

Jess looked at him hard, trying to understand why he was saying all these things. 'Yer mean it, don't yer?'

'I do, Jess. I really do.'

'I'm goin' back to the party. I ain't standin' 'ere talkin' to yer no more. Yer gettin' on me nerves.'

'Fine. You go back and I will too. And I'll come again tomorrow.'

''Ow can yer get back to Kent tonight? Yer still a bloody liar.'

'I'm staying in London with my mother's cousin.'

'Aw yeh. Yer always did know a soft touch. Yer with Amelia, I suppose. Gettin' round 'er with all yer lies.'

'You know Amelia?'

'Leonore told me about her.' She raised an eyebrow, challenging him to disagree with her. She didn't get the reaction she expected.

'There's so much I don't know about you, Jess. So much I want to know. So much I have to learn. I mean no harm to you or to Sylvia, I promise. All I want to do, Jess, is to make amends, and to try and make you happy.'

'I told yer. Don't touch me.'

'I'm sorry, I didn't mean to offend you. But, Jess.'

'Yeh?'

'I'll ask you again tomorrow, you know. If you'll marry me, I mean.'

'Yeh. I suppose yer will.'

-

Jess walked slowly back to the party. She could hear the singing and laughter from the end of the street. Everyone was so happy. Even the ones who had lost their sons, husbands or lovers were relieved, as relieved as everybody else that it was all over at last. The war to end all wars had finished. There might be hard times ahead, but at least the world was at peace. If only Jess could be too.

'An' where do yer think yer've been?' asked Lil, leering drunkenly at her friend. She had her arm round the shoulders of a young sailor who had got through almost as much beer as she had. ''E was a bit of all right, that officer an' all. Looked familiar.' She frowned into the middle distance, then shook her head. 'Nah, too posh for round 'ere.'

'Just a feller 'ome from the war,' said Jess lightly.

'Where is 'e then? Let's meet 'im.'

''E 'ad to go an' see 'is aunt.'

'Cor, yer was a bit slow there, gel. Probably 'ad a few quid, bloke like 'im. Still, ne'mind, Jess, plenty more fish in the sea.' Lil thumped the sailor hard across his back. 'That was a good 'un, more fish in the sea, an' yer a sailor! Come on, Jack Tar, let's 'ave a dance.' Lil and her partner twirled unsteadily away from Jess into the crowd of dancers.

'All right, Jess?'

Jess smiled at her little brother. ''Ello, Ted.'

'Want anythin'?'

'No, ta.'

Ted took a long draught from his glass. 'Look at our little Sylvie,' he said, brushing the foam off his lips with the back of his hand. 'She's 'aving an 'igh old time. Taken to all the kids like she was born round ere.'

'Yer've been good about all this, Ted.'

'Me? 'Ow d'yer mean?'

'Yer never judged me or nothin'. Just accepted I 'ad 'er, never asked no questions.'

'Why should I ask questions? Yer me sister an' she's me niece. What else is there to know?'

'Mum's done a proper job bringin' yer up, Ted, an' no mistake. Give us a kiss.'

''Ow about 'avin' a dance with yer little brother?'

'I don't feel much like dancin'.'

'Don't be like that, Jess. 'Ow often do we get to dance?'

'Come on then.'

Jess and Ted slipped into a gap on the improvised dance floor and moved off into a waltz, Ted's bad arm tucked safely between them.

'Yer ain't bad at this, Jessie,' said Ted. 'Blimey, nor are they. 'Ave a butcher's over there.'

Jess looked in the direction in which Ted had nodded. There in the middle of the dancers were Rose and Joey Fuller, whirling in an elegant, effortless waltz.

'I never knew she could dance like that, Jess.'

'Nor did I, Ted, but I reckon there's a lot of things we don't know about a lot of people.'

–

The dancing continued until the revellers were finally driven towards The Star by the descending November fog. Some of the younger ones, including Sylvia, didn't make it to the second stage of the celebrations in the pub; they had fallen asleep in someone's arms and were being carried back to their beds.

'D'yer want me to come back with yer?'

'No thanks, Lil,' said Jess. 'Yer go an' 'ave a good time. That sailor's still got his eye on yer.'

'D'yer think so?'

'Yeh. 'E looks nice an' all.'

'Ain't bad, is 'e? Do I look all right?' Lil smoothed her crumpled frock down over her ample middle.

'Yer look lovely, Lil. 'Ang on, let me put Sylvie indoors an' I'll pin yer 'air up again for yer.'

Jess came back out of Number 8 to find Rose talking to Lil on the doorstep. ''Ello, Mum, ain't yer goin' down The Star with the others?'

'No, gel, I was sayin' to Lil, I've danced me legs off tonight. Now all I want is a nice cup o' tea.'

'I'm gonna pin Lil's 'air up, then I'll be in. Do one for me, Mum.'

'Goodnight then, Lil, an' say 'ello to yer sailor boy for me,' said Rose, stepping inside the passage.

'Sod me,' said Lil, 'every bugger knows about me. I wouldn't mind, I've only just met 'im tonight.'

'It's the twinkle in yer eye what we all saw,' laughed Jess. 'Sit on the step an' I'll do yer 'air up for yer.'

''E said I looked like a mermaid with all me 'air 'angin' down,' she sighed. 'Good job I never 'ad it done short like all them other girls down the factory, eh?' She twisted round, making Jess drop the handful of hair she had just managed to coax into the pins. 'Yer know, I think I might 'ave a chance with this one, Jess.'

–

Rose was sitting in the kitchen with her legs stretched out towards the range. ''Ere yer are, Jess, sit down in the warm an' drink yer tea. What with all that dancin', I didn't realise it was so cold out.'

''Ave a good time?'

'Yeh, I did. Funny. When I got the letters about yer dad and about Sammy, God rest their souls, I didn't think I'd ever 'ave a good time again. Then Ted come 'ome safe. An' I 'ad yer an' the baby with me. An' knowin' Charlie's all right in Chicago… Well, life 'as to go on. Things 'ave to work out in the end, don't they? An' I really love 'aving Sylvia 'ere with me. Like yer dad

352

always said, we should be grateful for what we've got. There's plenty of 'em left with less round 'ere than I've got.'

'I wish you 'adn't said that, Mum.'

'What?'

'That yer like 'aving us 'ere.' She tapped her thumbnail nervously against her teeth. 'Mum, I might be goin' away again.'

'Jess,' Rose stared at her daughter, 'ain't yer 'appy 'ere, darlin'?'

'Course I am, Mum. I couldn't be 'appier. 'Cept if Dad and Sammy was still with us. But I've gotta go away. It's Robert.'

'Robert Worlington?'

Jess nodded.

''E knows yer 'ere?'

'Yeh.' Jessie bowed her head.

''As 'e done somethin' to yer?' Rose jumped up from her seat, ignoring the cup she sent crashing to the floor.

'Not exactly.'

'What's 'e done, Jessie?' Rose's voice was shaking. 'If 'e's so much as laid a finger on yer, I'll… So 'elp me.'

'No, Mum, nothin' like that.' Jess bent down and began picking up the smashed cup and saucer, mopping up the spilt tea with a rag. 'Sit down, Mum.'

Rose sat down and stared into the range.

''E wants to marry me,' said Jess calmly as she wrapped the broken china in a sheet of old newspaper.

'Do what?' Rose couldn't take it in. 'Yer gonna go off with 'im? With Robert Worlington?'

'No. No, I'm gettin' away from 'im.'

'Jess, what're yer talkin' about, gel?' Rose shook her head, disbelieving what she was hearing. 'Yer've got me in a right two and eight.'

''E's been writin' to me, Mum.'

Rose looked at her daughter, but didn't ask why she hadn't told her before.

''E sent me these letters. Loads of 'em.' Jess spoke slowly, avoiding looking directly at her mother. 'I know it wasn't right, keepin' it from yer, rushin' to the door every time I 'eard the postman coinin' along the street, but I didn't want yer to worry.' She swallowed hard as though it was an effort to speak. 'The letters all said 'ow 'e'd changed, an' 'ow 'e never realised before about what 'e'd done to me. Over an' over again. An' that 'e's a different man to the one 'oo went to Flanders an' the war an' that. An' Leonore wrote an' all. She said the same, an'… Aw, I dunno, Mum.' Jess opened the back door, put the newspaper parcel of broken china in the bin in the back yard, then rinsed her hands under the tap. 'Well, the upshot is,' said Jess, drying her hands on her skirt, ''e turned up 'ere tonight.'

'In Burton Street?' Rose thought she must be going mad.

'Yeh. We 'ad a talk. An' that's when 'e said 'e wants to marry me.'

'What did yer say to 'im?'

'I said I didn't think 'e was tellin' me the truth. That 'e was up to somethin' again. I don't remember it all. I was confused.'

'Yer sure 'e was lyin' to yer again?'

'I dunno, Mum. I don't know nothin' no more. 'E did seem different somehow. A bit. But 'ow do I know 'e don't wanna take Sylvia away from me?'

''E did ask yer to marry 'im, Jess. An' yer could do worse for yerself. Yer've gotta be realistic, gel. Yer twenty-two an' yer've got a kid to look after.'

'Mum!'

'Listen to me, Jess.' Rose slammed her hand down on the table. Jess flinched at the unaccustomed anger in her mother's voice.

'What? Just like that? Yer sayin' I should marry 'im?'

'I said listen to me. When yer was younger yer never seemed to 'ave no interest in fellers.'

''Cept Jack. An' look 'ow 'e let me down. Made a right idiot out of me.'

'I ain't talkin' about 'im, Jess. An' anyway, I think there's more to that than yer realise. Perhaps one day we'll be able to sort it all out.'

'What yer sayin'? About Jack Barnes?'

'Not now, Jess. I ain't talkin' about that now. Leave it. It's what's 'appenin' now that matters. Yer've gotta see, if yer don't get married life's gonna get 'ard. Even 'arder than if yer do get married. 'Arder than yer might realise while yer've still got me around.'

'That don't make no sense.' Whether it did or not, Jess didn't want it to. Her only thought was to get away from Robert Worlington.

'Listen to yer ol' mum. I've always wanted to know yer was settled with a feller so's I wouldn't 'ave to worry about yer if anything 'appened to me, like.' She looked down at her hands. 'Jess, I think yer should marry 'im.'

Jess jutted out her chin. She was trembling. She had never spoken to her mother like this before, but she had to say it. 'Aw, yeh. Tell me then, 'ow can I love a bloke what did that to me, eh? Left me like an ol' worn-out boot to be chucked on the rubbish 'eap.'

'I ain't talkin' about love,' said Rose evenly. 'I'm talkin' about survivin'. Life ain't easy. You of all people should 'ave learnt that by now.'

'So why should I marry 'im? 'Im of *all* bloody people.'

'I know yer upset, Jess. But don't yer get lippy with me, gel.'

Jess turned her back on Rose. 'Sorry, Mum,' she said stiffly.

'That's all right. But yer listen to me, an' yer listen good. Yer should marry Robert Worlington cos 'e can give yer, an' the baby, a name. Respectable like. An' cos 'e can give yer both a decent 'ome. An' cos 'e's the only one what's asked yer.'

Jess spun round to face her mother, but Rose raised her hands, calming Jess before she had the chance to erupt.

'There's plenty of Florries in this world 'oo can make things very 'ard for someone in yer position, Jess. An' I won't always be around to look out for yer.'

Jess swallowed hard. 'Don't keep sayin' things like that, Mum,' she said quietly.

'I told yer, Jess, I'm bein' realistic. I mean, think of it, the landlord's already askin' if we can take someone in. There's no 'omes for people now the war's over, an' soon there ain't gonna be many jobs from what I can see. Women are gettin' laid off from the factories round 'ere already. They've told Elsie she's gotta take a cut in 'er money if she wants to stay on. Yer've gotta give Sylvie the chance to 'ave somethin' better than all that.'

'I *wanna* bring her up proper, Mum, like yer brought us up. But I don't know if I could put up with what you an' Leonore 'ad to. Dad never 'ere, an' 'er old man always on the booze.'

'It don't 'ave to be like that, Jess.'

'Don't it? Just look down this street.'

'No, you look, Jess. Look at the future with no money an' no 'ome for yer baby.'

'I'm too tired to think straight. I'm goin' up.' Jess bent forward to kiss her mother.

'Yer was always stubborn, Jess, but I never thought yer was stupid.'

'Don't, Mum, please.' Jess took the letter from behind the clock on the mantelshelf and slipped it into her pocket.

'That one of the letters from Robert?'

'No. It's a letter I wrote to our Charlie. I'm gonna post it in the mornin'.'

—

Jess woke up early. She didn't want to disturb Sylvia or wake Rose before it was time for her to go to work, so she decided to get dressed and go outside for some fresh air. As soon as the post office was open she would get the stamps for her letter to Chicago.

She shivered as she stepped into the street.

'It's cold. You need a scarf on a morning like this. Here, take mine.'

'What're yer doin' 'ere?' she asked, shoving the offered scarf away.

'I told you I'd be back,' Robert said, shrugging.

'I didn't think yer meant this early.'

'I couldn't sleep.'

'Nor could I.' Jess fingered the letter in her coat pocket. 'I've got to go up the road.'

'I'll walk with you.'

'If yer like.'

'Have you thought about what I said, Jess?'

'All night.'

'Well? What have you decided?'

'I've decided I won't 'ave much chance livin' 'ere on me own with Sylvia.'

'You mean you'll marry me?' Robert took her by the shoulders and pulled her towards him. 'Jess, that's wonderful.'

'I never said that, an' I told yer before, keep yer 'ands off.'

Robert kept hold of her. 'So what exactly *are* you saying, Jess?'

'I'll 'ave more chance in Chicago, that's what. Me brother Charlie's always said I'll be welcome to stay with 'im. An' now 'e's opened 'is club at last, 'e'll be able to give me a job an' all.' She took a deep breath and lied. 'So I sent 'im a letter last week, tellin' 'im all about Sylvia an' sayin' I'm goin' over there. Soon as I can.'

'Is Rose going with you?'

'No, she's stayin' at 'ome with Ted. 'E won't wanna travel nowhere for a long time. Perhaps one day they'll go. I dunno. That's up to them.'

'You're going alone?'

'No.'

'You've got someone else, haven't you?' Robert gripped her arms even tighter. 'Who is it, Jess? Who are you going with? Tell me.'

'I'm going with me daughter, if yer must know.' Jess pulled away from him and walked off, rubbing her arms. 'Yer bloody 'urt me.'

'Our daughter, Jess. Our daughter,' he called after her. Robert watched her as she went along the street towards the market. 'I won't let you leave me, Jess.'

Jess kept walking, biting her lip to stop herself from screaming with the pain, hurt and confusion of it all. If he had known that the letter was still in her pocket he would have stopped her. She couldn't let him do that. This was her only chance. She had to be strong.

Chapter 20

A New Life

Robert Worlington became a familiar figure in Burton Street as he kept his vigil outside Number 8 waiting to speak to Jess. On the way to buy his newspaper, Ted would wish him a resigned 'Good mornin'', and even offer his condolences for what he considered to be his sister's stupid behaviour.

'Yer know I'd marry yer meself if yer'd 'ave me, Robert,' he'd said one night in The Star. 'Yer a decent bloke, I reckon. Yer never bother Sylvia or me mum. I like that. An' yer never lose yer temper with our Jess. An' that takes some doin'. 'Specially when she's behavin' so pig-headed. 'Ave another drink, mate.'

Florrie Baxter had been there that night in The Star, craning her neck and straining her ears to glean what she could from their conversation; she'd been spending every spare moment doing her best to discover the identity of Jess's mysterious suitor. She had various theories, but anyone who had any information was not sharing it with her. One morning she had a lucky break while she was sweeping the pavement outside her front door – while she was 'on nose-ointment patrol' as Elsie always called Florrie's half-hearted outdoor cleaning efforts.

'Can I 'elp yer?' she called across to the expensively dressed woman on the other side of the street.

The woman never had the chance to reply. Before she had opened her mouth, Florrie dropped her broom to the ground and was halfway across the street.

''Ang on, I remember yer. Yer visited Rose that time, didn't yer. When 'er Jess was away.'

Realising it was Mrs Baxter, Leonore hurried on, doing her best to avoid another encounter with the garrulous woman. But Florrie would not be put off so easily.

'I've got it!' she yelled triumphantly. 'I know 'oo you are now. Gaw blimey, 'oo'd 'ave thought it? Yer only Lady Worlington, ain't yer? An' yer said yer was the charity lady.' Florrie narrowed her eyes suspiciously. ''Ere. What's goin' on?'

Robert could not have made a worse-timed entrance into Burton Street if he had tried. 'Sorry, Mother,' he called, sprinting towards Leonore. 'I didn't expect you for another hour.' He took her by the shoulders and kissed her fondly on the cheek. 'I'm so pleased you've come.'

'Mother! So that's 'oo 'e is. Yer bloody son!'

Florrie's mouth was so wide open that her chin was almost touching her chest by the time Rose had opened her street door to let Leonore and Robert inside. The door was then closed firmly in Florrie's face.

'What a bloody turn-out. Elsie! Elsie! Quick. Yer'll never guess what's 'appened,' she hollered as she ran along the terrace to the Dorkins' house.

–

'Won't yer sit down.' Rose pointed to the two over-stuffed armchairs that stood on either side of the fireplace in the front parlour. 'It's a bit cold in 'ere. We don't use this room much no more.'

'The days are getting warmer though,' said Leonore politely.

'Yeh, they are,' said Rose. 'I'll get Jessie to fetch a couple of chairs from out the back, then we can talk.'

'It would be fine in the kitchen if you'd rather,' said Leonore.

'No. We're better in 'ere. Ted's givin' Sylvia 'er breakfast in there. I don't think she should 'ear none of this.'

'Oh, of course,' agreed Leonore. 'How is she, Rose?'

'She's a fine girl, Leonore,' she said looking at Robert. 'Like 'er mother.' Then she left the room to fetch Jess and the chairs.

'I'm really glad you came, Ma.'

'You only had to ask me, Robert. You know that.'

'I know, but thank you anyway. You see, Jessie trusts you. Perhaps you can make her see sense. Make her change her mind.'

'Robert, I'm not here to interfere in your lives. I'm here because I care what happens to you all. And because I'm Sylvia's grandmother. What actually happens is not up to me.'

The door opened and Jess came in carrying the kitchen chairs. Robert rushed to her side and tried to take them from her.

'I can manage,' she said, snatching them back from him. ''Ere, sit down, Mum.'

'Ta, Jess. Right. So what's all this in aid of then?'

'Mrs Fairleigh,' said Robert, 'I want to persuade Jess to marry me.'

'Yer ain't going over all that again are yer?' said Jess wearily.

Robert ignored her interruption and concentrated on speaking to Rose. 'Even if she doesn't love me, I want to make up for what has happened. I can make life easier for her. And for Sylvia.'

Jess rolled her eyes and tutted impatiently.

'It won't be easy without a husband. And,' he looked at Jess, 'perhaps she could grow to love me, or become fond of me at least.'

'Jess knows what I think,' said Rose.

'Yes?' said Robert expectantly.

'I'm sure yer already know an' all, Robert. Ted must 'ave told yer. I agree with yer, an' I'd feel more settled knowin' Jess an' 'er young 'un would be looked after.'

Robert looked triumphant, feeling he had won an important point, but his face fell as she continued.

'Even though I don't think much of 'ow yer carried on in the past. But the past is the past. It's the future what worries me now.'

'Mum.'

'I've told yer, Jess, yer've got to be realistic in this life.'

'Leonore?' pleaded Jess. 'Yer on me side, ain't yer?'

'I'm on no one's side, Jess. I only want what's best.'

'Yer right, Leonore,' said Rose, 'an' times are gettin' 'arder for us all round 'ere. I know what it's like to go without so me kids can eat.'

'An' I know what it's like to be poor an' all, Mum. I know what it's like to be dumped, don't I?' She looked pointedly at Robert. 'But I know 'ow to earn me own livin'. I've always worked, everyone knows that.'

'We are not saying you haven't, Jess,' said Leonore. 'But life for a woman alone with a child is so very hard. I've seen the heartache, believe me. Young girls worn out with the effort of it all.'

'Yer've told me about all that before,' said Jess dismissively. 'Don't yer think I've seen enough of it meself down these streets? The East End's full of it. Yer talk like yer discovered 'ardship single-'anded.'

Leonore looked shamefaced and felt foolish that she had dared to preach to Jess about poverty. Jess, who knew more about it than she ever would, no matter how many hours she worked in the Centre.

'Yer watch yer tongue, Jessie,' Rose said, horrified that her daughter would put on such a show to a guest.

'Sorry, Mum,' she said. 'An' don't look like that, Leonore. I ain't bein' ungrateful to yer. Honest. But I ain't stayin' round 'ere, am I? So there's nothin' for any of yers to worry about. It's all sorted out. Mum knows. I'm gonna start a new life in America. Me brother's only too pleased to 'ave 'is little sister an' 'er daughter join 'im over there.' She turned to Robert. 'Our Charlie's making a right success of 'imself with this club 'e's started.'

'Let me come with you, Jess,' said Robert, grasping at any opportunity. 'Please.'

'Why *should* I, eh?' she asked him. 'Blimey, yer've got some cheek. What 'ave yer ever done but use me? What right 'ave yer even got to ask?'

Robert dropped his head and buried his face in his hands. He began to cry.

'D'yer wanna see Sylvia?' said Rose to Leonore. 'She'll 'ave finished eatin' by now.'

'Yes,' said Leonore simply and followed Rose out of the room.

Jess sat listening to Robert weep. 'I dunno what to make of yer,' she said, 'honest I don't. What yer did to me, an' now yer sittin' 'ere cryin'. I won't marry yer yer know, Robert. Whatever yer say or do.'

'I know,' he sobbed. 'And I don't want to hurt you again. I only want to be with you and my child.'

'Yer could come with me, yer know,' she said evenly.

Robert sat up, blinking away the tears still running down his cheeks. 'To America, with you and Sylvia?'

'Yeh. I've been thinkin' about it a lot since I got Charlie's letter.'

'I don't understand, Jess. You just said I had no right even to ask to go with you.'

'Well, way I figure it, yer Sylvia's dad when all's said an' done. An' no matter what I think, nothin' will change that. I loved my ol' dad, see, an' perhaps one day she'll love you. That's up to 'er. But I reckon she should 'ave the chance to decide for 'erself.'

'Do you mean it, Jess?'

'Yeh, I mean it. You can come with me, but don't get no ideas.' She looked at him steadily. 'No ideas about, yer know, living with me or nothing. We'll just 'ave to see 'ow it goes on that side of things. Me and Sylvie'll be stayin' with Charlie at 'is place, an' 'e'll find a room for yer with one of the fellers from the club till yer sorted out. All right?'

'Whatever you say, Jess. So long as I can be with you.'

'An' I want yer to get it straight, I'm goin' to America to make a new life. I won't accept yer pity an' I don't want no 'andouts neither. Charlie's givin' me a job. I won't be needin' none o' your money.'

'I have no money, Jess.'

'Are yer startin' again with yer lies? That was the reason yer all said I should marry yer. "Security" for me an' Sylvia.'

'Jess, don't get angry again. Please. I'm not lying. I have no Worlington money, I mean.' Jess went to speak, but Robert carried on. 'Please listen. When my brother was killed my father went rapidly downhill, rejecting everyone and everything, including me. What with his state of health, and the war, the estate suffered badly, even though Mother did her

364

best. But she has appointed a manager to help her now, and they'll need whatever money there is to sort the place out. She is determined to get Worlington back in order: to grow food and provide jobs.'

'I wouldn't put anythin' past your mother,' said Jess, her voice showing her affection for Leonore.

'But I don't need money to prove I'm worthy of you and Sylvia. I'll work. I'll help make a new life for both of you.'

'Worlington's got no 'old at all over yer no more then?' asked Jess.

'No, no hold. Except my mother being there, of course.'

'An' Julia what's 'er name don't want yer to stay there?'

'I have neither seen nor heard from Julia since I went to Belgium. She's living back in Ireland now with her family.' He stood up, daring to move closer.

'Jess, if that's what's been worrying you.'

'No. I only wanted to know we could start out on equal terms. Nothin' from our pasts to 'aunt us. I've 'ad enough lies an' 'idin' to last me a lifetime. I don't want it no more. For me or for Sylvie.' Jess stood up. 'I'll tell the others to come back in, shall I?'

A few moments later Rose and Leonore came back into the room, followed by Ted, Jess and Sylvia.

'Well?' said Rose.

Jess looked at her little daughter. It was as though she was seeing her properly for the first time; she was so much like Robert. She knelt down and took the child's hand in hers. 'Sylvia,' she said gently, brushing the thick golden curls from her daughter's forehead, 'this is yer daddy.'

'Gawd blimey O'Riley!' said Ted. 'I ain't never known a day like this.'

Sylvia hid behind Jess and clung to her skirts. 'Hello,' she whispered, peering round at the big man who had knelt down beside her and her mother.

'Hello, Sylvia,' he said.

—

'Please take it, Jess, I really want yer to. Take it for Sylvia, if yer won't 'ave it for yerself.'

'No, Mum, you keep it. If Charlie left the money with yer, 'e must 'ave meant yer to 'ave it.'

''E said it was for emergencies, Jess. I never even thought of touchin' it before, but this is different. Yer gonna be gettin' on that boat in the mornin', goin' all them thousands of miles away from me. Say yer need 'elp an' I ain't there for yer. Go on. Please, Jess, take it.'

'Yer know I'll be all right, Charlie'll look after me.'

'I know 'e will, but I wanna do somethin' for yer, an' I feel this is a way of…'

'Yer've done more than enough for me, Mum,' said Jess smiling tenderly at her. 'An' I can be just as stubborn as you can.'

'That's bloody true,' piped up Ted.

'Language,' said Rose. 'An' don't interfere when I'm talking to yer sister.'

'Sorry for breathin', I'm sure,' said Ted.

'An' less of yer lip.'

'Aw, I'm goin' out.' He bent down to his little niece. 'Shall Uncle Ted see if 'e can get yer a little present to take on the boat with yer?'

Sylvia nodded happily.

'No toffee,' said Jess.

'An' they don't sell toys in The Star,' said Rose.

366

'Bloody women,' murmured Ted as he stomped out of the bedroom.

'What was that you said?'

'Nothin', Mum,' said Ted as he clumped noisily down the stairs, slamming the street door before Rose had the chance to tell him not to.

''E's done well, ain't 'e, Mum? Wouldn't think that arm 'ad been damaged at all the way 'e uses it now. 'E'll be back at work full-time soon.'

'There'll always be a place for 'im at the woodyard, they said. So let's 'ope. Still, we can worry about that another day. Let's get a move on 'ere or we'll never 'ave this packin' finished for the mornin'. That'd be 'andy, if yer missed the boat. Come on, pass us them skirts.'

Jess handed Rose a pile of neatly folded clothes, which she arranged carefully in the almost full steamer trunk.

'I'll bet Robert's already waitin' down the docks,' said Rose. 'Frightened 'e'll lose yer again. Right taken with yer, that bloke is. Yer a lucky gel, Jess. But for the life of me, I can't see why yer won't marry 'im.'

Jess ignored her mother's attempts to open up the argument they had been having for the last two months. 'Doin' this packin's like gettin' ready for 'opping, eh, Mum?'

''Ardly. We never 'ad none of this posh gear down there.'

Jess laughed. 'Yer right. Our Charlie's been really good to us. I'd never 'ave been able to afford all this stuff for Sylvie.'

'Well, it's only right,' said Rose. 'Us Fairleighs 'ave always stuck together. We've always 'elped our own. An' that's why I want yer to take the money 'e left with me.'

'Not again, Mum. No! I've got more than enough. Yer know 'e sent me fare an' everythin'. An' Robert's got 'is army money an' Leonore lent 'im that bit extra.' Jess broke into an

367

exasperated smile. 'Yer 'ave me goin' through all this nearly every day, don't yer? I'll say it one last time. We're fine. All right?'

'It never 'urts to 'ave a bit extra. A bit put by.'

'Mum. Don't.'

'You're wilful, Jessie Fairleigh.'

'Now I wonder where I got that from, eh, Mum?' said Jess, all wide-eyed innocence. 'An' yer know I mean to pay back everyone an' all, don't yer? So I don't need no more debts now, do I? Yer keep the money.' She handed Rose the final pile of Sylvia's clothes. 'Tell yer what, keep it for yer fares when yer bring Ted out to see us.'

'Is Nanna coming on the boat with us tomorrow?' said Sylvia, suddenly interested in the adults' conversation.

'Not tomorrow she's not, sweet'eart,' said Jess.

'But 'oo knows,' said Rose, closing the lid of the trunk, 'we just might come over to see yer one day. That'd surprise yer, Jess, wouldn't it?'

—

'Joey's 'ere, Jess,' Ted shouted up the stairs. 'Jess, I said Joey's 'ere, cloth-ears.'

'I 'eard yer the first time,' Jess called down to her brother. ''Ang on a minute, will yer.'

'I can't believe this mornin's come already,' said Rose, biting her lip.

'An' Robert's 'ere now an' all,' hollered Ted.

'I ain't surprised he's turned up.'

'Nor am I, Mum,' said Jess, smiling.

'I knew 'e wouldn't be able to wait down at the docks for yer.'

'Come on, Sylvie,' Ted called from the passage. 'Yer come down at least.'

Sylvia picked up her dolly from the landing where she'd been playing and slid down the stairs on her bottom.

'Give yer uncle a great big cuddle,' he said, catching her up in his arms. 'Awwww, I'm gonna miss yer, princess.'

Ted carried Sylvia outside into the bright morning air. Burton Street had done the Fairleighs proud; the houses were all decked with bunting, paper flowers and good luck messages wishing them well. The neighbours stood at a respectful distance by their street doors, ready to wave and cheer their best. Nobody wanted to miss the opportunity for a knees-up, and a farewell party was as good a reason as any, even if the guest of honour would be steaming away on an ocean liner.

Jess flew down the stairs and made a dash for the street door, her hands held up in front of her, just in time to stop Robert from coming into the passage.

'Careful, Robert,' she shouted, her voice breaking with emotion. 'Don't tread on the step, Mum's just cleaned it. An' she's right proud of 'er step. Cleanest step in Burton Street that is, ain't it, Mum?' she said, turning to face her mother.

Rose threw her arms round her daughter. 'Jessie.'

'I love yer so much, Mum.'

'An' I love yer too, darlin'.'

'I know, Mum. Listen,' sniffed Jess, 'I don't want yer to come to the docks with us. All right? Or Ted. I won't be able to stand it. Saying goodbye to yer both again.'

'All right, Jess.' Rose fussed lovingly with Jess's auburn hair, tucking a stray curl under the brim of her blue velvet hat. 'Joey'll see yer off for me, won't yer, Joe.'

'Course I will, Rose,' said Joey getting out of the cab of his van.

'Bit smarter than the old cart, eh, Joe?' said Ted, running his hand appreciatively over the shiny new coachwork.

'I dunno, Ted. I miss me ol' Daddler,' said Joey. 'Even more than I miss me old mum sometimes, God rest her.'

'You get in, Jess,' said Robert, 'and I'll sit Sylvia on your lap.'

'I'll write yer loads of letters, Mum.' Jess sniffed loudly as she slid along the seat. 'Pity Jack Barnes ain't around to deliver 'em to yer, eh?'

'Jack?' said Robert as he got in next to her. 'Someone I know?'

'No, no one. Just an ol' mate of mine.'

'I thought I remembered the name from somewhere.'

'No,' said Jess. 'Yer wouldn't know Jack Barnes.'

'Thanks for takin' 'em for me, Joe,' said Rose, touching him lightly on the shoulder.

'It's a pleasure, Rosie.'

Ted cranked the starting handle until the engine spluttered into life. The cheers went up the length of Burton Street as the van pulled away with all the children running along the road behind it, waving homemade flags and hankies, calling out their farewells and best wishes for the journey.

''Ow about a drink down The Star, eh, Mum?' said Ted, putting his arm round Rose's shoulder. 'A port and lemon. Let's join in the party to see 'em off. Come on.'

'Later on, boy. Yer go down there. I'll see yer later on.'

'Yer ain't gonna get all 'umpy are yer, Mum?'

'No, son. Go on, they're all callin' yer. I'm goin' to pop indoors for a bit, there's somethin' I've gotta see to first.'

–

Rose went inside Number 8 and put the kettle on. She made a cup of tea and sat for a long time, just thinking. Then she went upstairs into her bedroom and took a package from behind the chest of drawers. She sat on the bed and unwrapped the crumpled brown paper. Inside was the wad of money she'd wanted to give to Jess, a lock of golden hair and a stained piece of cloth that could once have been a yellow paisley scarf. She took out the cloth and the lock of hair, and put them in her apron pocket. Then carefully she refolded the paper round the money, and put it back in its hiding place.

Rose went downstairs into the kitchen and slipped the lock of golden hair into the corner of the framed photograph of Jess and Sylvia, the present that Jess had given her that morning before she left for her new life in America. She stood the picture back on the mantelshelf next to the clock, and smiled at it. Then she took a taper and lit it from the range. Shielding the flame with her hand Rose went out into the back yard. Taking the dirty yellow scrap from her pocket, Rose held it up and set light to its ragged corner.

'Rest in peace, Jack Barnes,' she said, watching the flames take hold. 'Rest in peace. Whatever our Charlie did, I know 'e never meant no 'arm to no one. An' now 'e's gonna look out for your Jessie. She's gonna be all right after all.'

'They got off all right, Rose.'

Surprised to hear Joey's voice, Rose turned and dropped the burning cloth to the ground. 'Do what?'

'They've gone. On the ship. Yer didn't mind me comin' in, did yer? The street door was open. I thought I'd come in to tell yer all about it.'

'Course I don't mind, Joe. I'll be in in a minute. I'm just seein' to somethin' out 'ere.' Her voice trailed into a whisper as the last fragment of cloth burnt away.

'Yer carry on, Rose. I ain't in no 'urry.'

'It's all right, I've finished now.' She moved the ashes around with the toe of her boot, studying the patterns they made. She paused, took a deep breath, then spoke. 'Fancy a cup o' tea, Joe?' she said, looking up at him with a bright smile.

Five minutes later Rose was pouring Joe his tea from the big brown earthenware teapot.

'I'll 'ave to get meself one of them fancy little china pots from down the market,' she said. 'I ain't 'ad much use for this great big ol' thing in donkey's years. I don't s'pose even our Ted'll be around much longer, either.'

'Why's that?' said Joey, blowing on the hot tea.

'Got 'is eye on one of Elsie's gels, if yer don't mind,' said Rose, laughing. 'Sybil. 'Er youngest.'

'They've got good 'earts, Rose, them Dorkins.'

'Yeh. 'E could do a lot worse for 'imself. But I reckon I'll 'ave to get used to bein' on me own again.'

'Yer'll never be on yer own while I'm around,' said Joey shyly. 'Yer know that, Rose, don't yer?'

'Yeh, I reckon I do, Joe.' She smiled across at him, at his kind, open face.

''Ow about if we pop over The Star later on?' he said. 'Let me treat yer to a drink.'

'Why not?' she said. 'I'd like that, Joe. Ta.'

'Might as well give Florrie somethin' to talk about, eh, Rose?'